Going Through Ghosts

WEST WORD FICTION

MARY SOJOURNER

Going Through Ghosts

{ *a novel* }

UNIVERSITY OF NEVADA PRESS
RENO AND LAS VEGAS

WEST WORD FICTION

University of Nevada Press, Reno, Nevada 89557 USA

Copyright © 2010 by Mary Sojourner

Manufactured in the United States of America

Design by Kathleen Szawiola

Library of Congress Cataloging-in-Publication Data

Sojourner, Mary.

Going through ghosts / Mary Sojourner.

p.   cm. — (West word fiction)

ISBN 978-0-87417-809-8 (pbk. : alk. paper)

1. Casinos—Nevada—Fiction. 2. Indians of North America—
Religion—Fiction. 3. Mojave Desert—Fiction. I. Title.

PS3569.O45G665   2010

813'.54—dc22   2009036619

The paper used in this book is a recycled stock made from 30 percent post-
consumer waste materials, certified by FSC, and meets the requirements of
American National Standard for Information Sciences—Permanence of Paper
for Printed Library Materials, ANSI/NISO Z39.48-1992 (R2002).
Binding materials were selected for strength and durability.

Quotation from *The Tibetan Book of the Dead* on page 137–38 from *The Tibetan
Book of the Dead,* translated with commentary by Francesca Freemantle and
Chogym Trungpa (London: Shambala Pocket Library, 1992), p. 212.

FIRST PRINTING

19   18   17   16   15   14   13   12   11   10

5   4   3   2   1

for those of us who bet it All
on the turn of the River

Going through a ghost it gets cold.
You get scared, it picks up something like
A knife or sword, it tries to stab you—
But sometimes it tells you a story.

—Hopi children with Rolly Kent,
Talk About the World: Spoken Poems

Going Through Ghosts

1   The odds were even that so-called civilization might end January 1, Y2K. It didn't. But five months later Jesus won the World Series of Poker at Binion's in downtown Las Vegas, Nevada. With two nines. Figure those odds.

Maggie Foltz heard about Jesus's miracle just before dawn from a perky grandma playing Double Diamond nickel slots near the Crystal Casino's front doors. "Well, it wasn't really Jesus," the woman said. "It was that guy looks like Jesus, the guy with the long brown hair and beard, Ferguson. I think his name is Ferguson. He couldn't really be Jesus because you don't ever see Jesus wearing dark glasses and a cowboy hat with a rattlesnake band. Plus I don't think they had dark glasses in those days, but with Jerusalem being desert and all, they probably did have snakes."

"It's a weird world," Maggie said. She'd keep it simple. This was her tenth lonesome old lady of an already long morning and she didn't like how they reminded her of her probable future.

The old gal held up her hand. "Don't say anything more, honey. I'm at the part of my system where I play Max Bet. I gotta hold my breath for luck." She inhaled, dropped five nickels in, slowly pulled the handle, and closed her eyes.

Bar, Triple Bar, and the glittering turquoise Double Diamond fell on the payline. Seventy-five nickels jingled into the payout tray. The old lady exhaled. "Hot damn," she said, and dropped a handful of coins on Maggie's drink tray. "See, Jesus hasn't got all the luck. Fetch me a strawberry daiquiri. The doc says I gotta have fruit in the morning to keep me regular."

"I'm on it." Maggie heard a buzz and saw the three turquoise diamonds lined up in a row. Jackpot. One hundred twenty-five bucks.

"Damn," the old gal said, "make that a strawberry daiquiri *and* a melon colada and whatever you want for yourself. You're my good-luck charm."

Maggie laughed. "I'm glad to hear that. I thought I'd flat run out of that commodity."

SARAH MARTIN lurched awake. She opened her eyes long enough to note the red brocade wallpaper and a dusty chandelier. She remembered getting off the Greyhound bus during that trench of the soul between midnight and dawn. She'd gone into a little casino. There'd been a graveyard shift restroom attendant, a chunky Indian girl with teased hair, who had said, "Welcome to the Aphrodite Room, whatever an Aphrodite is," and let Sarah crash on a foldout cot.

The same girl sat at the makeup table hunched over a magazine. "Hey sister," she said, "you gotta get up."

Sarah raised her head. "Thanks, girlfriend." She rummaged in her jacket pocket and found a tiny perfume bottle and a dollar bill. She didn't seem to have anything else but what was on her back. She was not surprised. Only hungover. Not from booze. From worse.

On a gray Seattle morning three days before, it had made sense to get rid of almost everything. Start clean. Make herself have to concentrate on survival. She put the buck in the tip jar.

The girl smiled. "You from around here?"

"No," Sarah said. "I'm from Bone Lake."

"What tribe is that up there?"

"My aunt is Willow."

The girl opened a diet cola and handed it to Sarah. "I never heard of the Willow tribe." She had good manners. She didn't ask any snoopy questions. She just left Sarah room to say what she wanted.

"We're little bitty," Sarah said. "Three hundred people, maybe less. No casino. No nothing."

"We're River people down here," the girl said. "Got a couple casinos. Me and my mom are still waiting for our share of the big money."

They laughed. Same old same old everywhere.

"Well, you take care," the girl said. "My name's Philecitta. I'll be back tomorrow about three. Myrna should be here in a minute. She's an old white lady, but she's nice." The girl tucked the dollar back in Sarah's hand.

"Hey," Sarah said.

The girl closed Sarah's fingers around the bill. "What goes around comes around. I'm gonna play my tips and win 'cause of you."

"Wait," Sarah said. "I'm not in Vegas, right?"

"Creosote, Nevada," the girl said. "Catch you later."

Sarah rinsed her mouth, ran her fingers through her hair, dabbed a little perfume between her breasts, took a deep breath, and stepped out into the casino.

RUNNER—baptized Jesse Corbeaux—loved gambling in the morning. The place was always quiet. Julio, the 7–3 bartender, reliably sent over a shot of Kahlua with Jesse's coffee. It was like family from dawn till the first busload out of California pulled in—which it had, causing Old Ray, the one croupier, to line up the dice even more perfectly and straighten his vest.

Runner watched Old Ray tug at the worn satin and wince. Runner noticed the new waitress had gray-green eyes. His observations were connected. Ray'd been nagging him about his terminal singleness. "Single guys die young," he'd said. Jesse was forty-eight, which he figured only a geezer like Ray would find young.

Mojave Kate dealt Runner's card, then hers. He checked his, than put up insurance. Kate grinned. She'd followed his look from Ray to the new girl.

"Nice," she said. "I mean the new kid—though she's not really new. Sheree just rewarded her with regular days 'cause Maggie served six months of cruel and unusual punishment on swing shift."

"Maggie," Runner said. "I wouldn't say she's a kid. But, then again, neither are we." Kate dealt herself an ace. "Hey!" she said. "God paying you back for that remark."

Maggie headed for the bar. Julio sang out, "Ohhhhh, Maggie May . . ." She smiled brightly. For starters it was important to remember that the bartender can be a cocktail chick's best friend. For finishers, most guy bartenders needed to think they were real wits. Besides, she'd put Maggie May on her ID badge on purpose. Guy guys could make that same tired joke, which then allowed them to think they had a deeply personal connection with her, which *could* result in a fat tip.

Julio was working on her drinks when Maggie smelled perfume—elegant perfume, with a smoky undertone like adobo. Julio looked up.

"Now *that*," he said, "might be a little different."

A young long-haired woman walked toward the craps table, leaned back against the wall, and watched Old Ray. Maggie wondered what the big attraction was. The scene wasn't exactly riveting: 8:00 a.m. Wheelie-Dealie Wednesday at the Crystal Casino, and Old Ray giving out genuine Royal Flush clocks to lucky blue hairs.

Maggie wondered if she'd seen the woman before, wondered if she was a working girl. You didn't get a lot of them in the Crystal. It was a locals' casino and the local gents didn't dare pay for loving because the old lady was probably sitting two machines down helping feed their Social Security checks into the bank accounts of the rich and absent.

There had been a couple ho's who didn't last long. Pella. This chick looked like Pella—that caramel skin, that long gleaming hair, that gift of seeming like a perfumed curl of smoke. And she was dressed like Pella—smudged makeup, black hair trailing from that sex-cat-from-your-best-wet-dream do. She'd pinned a coral brooch on her old velvet vest between her round breasts. She was maybe Indian, Chicana, Filipina—those eyes, those cheekbones, Maggie couldn't tell, though the profile was pure Mayan.

Ray carefully explained the rules for dice. The old folks leaned forward to read the numbers. At that moment, the girl dipped her fingers into the pay-phone coin return. Sheree, the slot manager, looked up from her ham 'n' eggs special at the snack counter and took off mean and fast toward the girl. Maggie waved at the girl, jutted her chin toward Sheree. The girl gave her a flat look from her flat black eyes, walked calmly to the front door, and pushed it open. Zircon light ricocheted off the black mirrors. Maggie blinked. "Miss," she heard a voice both husky and polite.

A guy at the five-dollar blackjack table called for a drink. He didn't do it cute. A real gift on a long Wednesday morning. He was short, wiry, maybe forty-five, maybe older. He had black curly hair streaked with gray, and a stack of green chips big enough to make him young and tall.

Maggie dropped off the old gal's liquid breakfast and walked to his side. "Sir?"

"I saw you warn that girl. It was honorable. You deserve a medal."

"What're you drinking?" She was all business, no small feat in shorts slit to the DMZ. She told herself she had to stop thinking like that. No DMZ. No medals. No more Crazy Veterans from a war almost nobody remembered. "Sir?" she said patiently, "your drink?"

"Humble pie," he said. "You can run it through the blender."

For a second, she almost liked him. It was shit odds that a customer would ever apologize to a worker.

"Milk and Kahlua," he said, "and a cup of coffee on the side."

RUNNER watched the waitress stride toward the bar. Strike out. He felt like a real asshole, but that seemed to be normal these days. Not much was working: the blackjack, the dope—fine as the new breeds of cannabis could be; the perfect job that gave him the perfect income—and a 1968 Airstream on five acres of perfect solitude.

"Kate," he said.

The dealer's slim fingers paused mid-deal, graceful as a Balinese dancer's. "What, Runner?"

"Seriously. Getting old? You ever think about it?"

Kate grinned and went back to shuffling. "Not if I can help it."

MAGGIE walked past a couple galpals at Wild Cherry Nickels. Short gray hair, matching sweatsuits with rhinestone poodles, spotless white aerobic shoes. "Not me," she thought. "Please, not me ever." She shut up her mind. It was better to work without thinking.

It'd been nine months, maybe ten, since she took the job. You lost track of time in a place covered walls to ceiling with black mirrors. Day dawned and died, nights could be four, fourteen, forty hours long. The Crystal wasn't a big razzle-dazzle house. There was no gourmet pizza room or underpaid overtalented acts from the outskirts of Vegas. The roulette table didn't open till noon, later if old Ray hadn't gotten what he called his "Loseitall" pills quite right.

The Crystal was no Range Rover pit stop. It was where you parked your 1983 epoxyed Malibu for a month for the illusion of free.

The place had once been Papa Pete's, the tiniest pissant casino in Creosote, a pissant gambling town in the Nouveau West's most gloriously pissant state. In the days of what some people thought was a harmonic convergence, Pete's daughter had hooked up with a fake Sioux Californicater named Medicine Beau, whose ancestors told him Pete could double his profits by plugging into the wannabe Indian New Age crowd. Pete bought a brand-new sign in the shape of a giant purple crystal and hired Medicine Beau to paint totems above the dollar slots.

Unfortunately, the New Age went, if not moribund, to ambulating on a walker, like most of the Crystal's customers—the lame, the halt, and the local. When Pete had asked his daughter why the magic didn't seem to be working, she said, "The Divine Ones do not move on mortal time."

Nor did Julio. Maggie waited for him to make a fresh pot of coffee. She was grateful for the break, for time to think about mortal time, upon which she was assuredly not—mundane overdrive was more like it, fueled by caffeine and nickel slots. Plus she'd probably lived the good half of her life, which she'd found makes you want to multitask as fast as you could.

She'd been brain-talking with herself a lot lately, starting to think about crap she didn't want to face, beginning with the eternal weekend a year ago when she wanted to die for thirty-six consecutive hours and couldn't stop shaking long enough to do the deed—courtesy a one-night stand whose name she couldn't remember and the resulting bruises nobody else could see.

And there was the forbidden topic of how she was sliding steadily toward fifty-five. You didn't admit that in her line of work, or maybe anywhere. There was her love life, which was nonexistent, and her only kid probably repeating his old man's mistakes—that man, Dwight (aka Dark Cloud) Campbell, a beer-bellied trailer salesman now dead. It occurred to her to breathe.

SARAH saw a dozen big casinos lined up along the shore, their jewel lights gone drab in the morning sun. A neon arch spelled out RIVERSTROLL in fuchsia and gold. She walked under the arch and looked north. It seemed a hundred years since she had left Seattle, a thousand since she had last seen Black Peak sharp against the brilliant sky east of Bone Lake.

She would call her aunt and cousin in a few days. There was nobody else she wanted to talk with up there, except Will Lucas, and the last she'd heard he was somewhere in LA working construction—plus if he was in his right mind, he wouldn't give her the time of day.

A fake paddle-wheel boat lay fifty feet below. A scrawny black-and-grime cat ambled out from under the deck and checked Sarah out. "Not this morning," Sarah said. Four kittens bounced out of the shadows. Sarah reached in her pocket. The dollar was there. She could see a snack bar just inside the casino door. "Back in a second," she said.

The casino had that sweet morning quiet you can sometimes find in places which are normally tornadoes of human hunger and noise. Sarah bought a carton of milk and snitched a couple dozen creamers. The cat came to the door and waited. Sarah ripped open the milk, took a sip, and dumped in the creamers. She set it on the paddle-wheeler gangplank. The cat ambled up, stuck her head in the milk, and began to purr.

"See," Sarah said. "You can trust me. There's the big difference between Yakima and me, at least after the lust wore off."

The cat looked up. "Yakima," Sarah said, "is a guy, not a city."

She thought about that Apple's perfectly crafted e-mails and presents, the time he'd walked coolly into the lobby of a fake-classy hotel—a tall, wide-shouldered, snake-hipped Indian man with a ponytail and Lucchese boots—plucked a bouquet of pale gold lilies out of a vase on the reception desk, slipped a twenty into the doorman's hand, and knelt in front of her, the flowers offered up.

She'd dried the lilies. And, in the last five weeks, when he'd become a skin sack of amused cruelty in the shape of her lover, she'd taken the ferry to Whidbey Island, hitchhiked its length, and tossed the petals from the bridge over Deception Pass. "Minnie," she had whispered to the knife-wind, "I wish I'd listened to you." There had been no reply. Her old teacher, Minnie Siyala, had not answered. Sarah had then known she would have to figure her mistake out on her own. That was the true gift of a merciless teacher.

Now she, Sarah, a woman with an MA in political science—author of the thesis, "Contemporary Native American Women's Role in the Work for Indigenous Lands"—and a woman with the fervent prayer that Yakima hadn't infected her with anything fatal, was here. Empty. Everything stripped away—

except the need for a place to sleep, food, and the welcome concentration it would require to earn those.

She figured she'd take two jobs and work her ass off at what she wouldn't give a damn about so hard she'd fall in bed at night and know nothing till dawn. She wondered if you had to know somebody to get hired. The casinos around Seattle had been webs of family relations and who-fucked-who. "Well," she thought, "I've got no family here. I'll never let a man touch me again. There better be some sisters in this town."

Morning moved fast in Creosote. Heat began to cook up from the asphalt sidewalk. Sarah was thirsty and she wanted a cigarette. She looked back at the little casino. The big purple crystal on top glowed cool. She headed back toward where she could at least get a drink of water, and maybe bum a smoke.

RUNNER watched the waitress set down his do-it-yourself Caucasian and walk away toward the cocktail light flashing over a nearby dollar video poker. He eavesdropped. A pink-haired lady wanted club soda. Three of them. With big twists. Lime, not lemon. She wore four rings on each hand and ran her fingers over a six-inch-high stack of plastic racks full of dollar tokens.

"Your pleasure," the redhead said, her voice reflecting her delight in humping drinks.

"You betcha," the player nodded and tapped the Max Bet button. By the time the redhead came back, three racks were empty. Pink-hair lined up her sodas neatly and opened her purse. "Change my luck, darlin'," she said, and dropped a handful of tokens on the tip tray. Green Eyes glanced Runner's way. They grinned. They had been witness to a miracle.

He realized he'd begun thinking of her as Green Eyes. He realized there might be a glint of something new in his world.

MAGGIE looked away from the wiry player. The black-haired girl sailed back into the casino and ducked into the Aphrodite Room. Maggie followed. There was something about the dancer set of the woman's shoulders, the way she moved as though she belonged in every cubic inch of space she occupied. There had to be a story there.

The Aphrodite Room door stuck as usual. Maggie pushed her way in. The maybe-hooker, maybe Indian, maybe Chicana, maybe Filipina leaned against the sink. Myrna, the seventy-year-old Aphrodite day attendant, was talking earnestly about one of her dozen parakeets—the sickly one and how his little head got droopier and droopier. The maybe-hooker tried to look interested.

"Yeah," she said. "Uh huh. You bet." Her voice was soft. Maggie figured she might be Hopi. Their voices could be all whispery, which makes everything they tell you, even if it's nothing but an order for Miller Lite, sound like magic.

"Hey," the woman said, "it's hard loving *anything*."

Myrna nodded sadly.

The woman looked at Maggie. "I owe you one."

"In here," Maggie said, "we inmates take care of each other. But why'd you come back? My satanic boss will bust you in a heartbeat."

"I can take care of myself."

"In here," Maggie grinned, "we inmates take care of each other. But I repeat myself. "

"I'm sorry," the woman said. "I'm used to taking care of myself, but things have been weird. Weird week. Weird month. Weird year."

Maggie could hear DC. *Weird world, Maggie,* he would say, *this whole fuckin' country's flat-out dinky dau.* Two days off the plane from Southeast Asia he told her that, and for twenty years—betrayal, divorce, and all—he'd phoned her now and then, usually right before dawn, to say, "You're the only round-eye lady I've ever known that really gets it."

She'd say her part. "Right, DC, and you're there with somebody who doesn't get it, in your big bed where she just got it, and I'm here alone so please good-bye."

"No big thing," he'd say. "Don't mean nothin.' I don't blame me and I don't blame you."

"Thank you so much," and Maggie would hang up till next time. Till six months ago, there was no next time. Courtesy, Agent Orange. Courtesy, Copenhagen chew. Courtesy, old reliable Mr. Death, the one consequence Dwight *Dark Cloud* Campbell couldn't outrun.

"You still with us, Maggie May?" the new gal said.

Maggie realized she'd taken a little bitterness break. "I'm Maggie—Foltz, not May. That name's for tips."

"Yeah," the woman said, "done that. I'm Sarah Martin. I used to waitress in my aunt's place up north." She tilted her head. Indian, Maggie thought. Doing that chin-jutting thing because it's bad luck to point your fingers.

Maggie knew an "up north." It was a red-brown, barren, and beautiful place where you didn't get mad and you didn't say bad things and rain was holy. "I was up north," she said, "lived in Winslow for a while."

Sarah wasn't sure what up north Maggie was talking about, but she was grateful to be talking, grateful to be in the company of a woman who seemed to have a clue about how clueless a woman could be.

Maggie didn't tell her that living in Winslow hadn't exactly been living. Living in Winslow had been a job at Burger King and friends who were her seventeen-year-old coworkers and the BIA flunky that sold them dope. Living in Winslow had been getting busted for possession; doing thirty days in treatment and a year voluntary counseling—when that ounce that wasn't even hers had zero to do with what had been killing her.

Sarah looked at Maggie hard. Maggie remembered how those up-north Indians watched the white folks—the Lycraed half-naked Eurotrash, the gray dreadlocked wannabes wearing medicine bags. *Why are you here?* those looks said. *Soon you'll get bored and go away, and we'll still be here.*

"What?" Maggie said. "Why are you looking at me like that?" She remembered Pella, how she could go from normal to I'm-gonna-kill-your-puta-ass, gringa, in a flick of her ¾-inch Mylar eyelashes.

"Whoa," Sarah said. "I didn't mean to stare." She looked away. "I'm a little desperate here."

Myrna nodded. "You need a job?"

"I do, and I have a master's degree in political science. Plus I can make fry bread." She looked them both hard in the eyes. Say something. Go ahead, say something. "Well, inmates, got any ideas? And has anybody got a cigarette? Please!"

The door banged open. A six-foot-tall mahogany-skinned woman swooped past them to the sink. She scooped up cold water and splashed her face.

"I don't give a diddle," she said. "Not one deediddledee. Beltran can put his you-know-what in every ho he wants. But, this one, this white-girl wannabe, she calls herself Chi Chi. Is that the most pathetic thing you girls ever heard?"

Maggie grinned at Sarah. "You speak Spanish?" Sarah shook her head. "*Chi chi,*" Maggie said, "means tits.

"This is Bonnie Madrid. She's evening-shift cocktails. Beltran is, as it were, the cock."

Myrna held out a pack of cigarettes and sighed. "We were just talking about the heartbreak of love. A prick, a parakeet, they're all the same."

MYRNA had enough juice to get Sarah hired in the snack bar for minimum and all the deep-fried starch she could eat. The snack bar's official name was Food for the Soul. If your soul needed Tater Tots and popcorn shrimp, you were "saved." Leola, Food for the Soul's manager, loved Sarah's fry bread. In two weeks she promoted her to sous chef.

"*Sous,*" Sarah said, "means "under" in French. And under is definitely where I am."

You couldn't blame Leola. Indian fry bread was a gold mine. It was not much more than flour and grease, the tourons loved it, and, if you've got the knack, no big deal to make. Sarah hated every minute of the making. She told Maggie how much she hated it every time they plunked their tired butts down at side-by-side nickel slots and lost what was left of the day.

"That Leola's phony," Sarah said. "She's all sweetie-sweet up in my face, and do I get the days off I need? No!"

Maggie punched Max Bet, forty-five nickels, a real commitment for a Chump Change Queen. "You've been here two weeks. That's not quite seniority." Sarah looked over. Her eyes were slits. Maggie thought of something that could strike fast and hit deep.

"Two weeks is a long time," Sarah said quietly, and fed nine nickels slowly into Haywire. "Back in that kitchen, two weeks is a damn long time."

"I'm sorry," Maggie said. Sarah nodded.

Casino work was like being in the middle of any potential disaster. You could hardly know a person and still feel close to them. Maggie didn't know how old Sarah was, if she had a man or kids somewhere, how she got to Creosote, and why she ran from wherever she had been. Still, they traded off bitching and listening. They told stories nobody else could figure out. They shared a deep contempt for the academic experience and a more generalized wariness about men. And, they passed over a handful of nickels in the player's belief that giving a sucker money will change your luck.

They both had favorites among the locals, the regulars who lived across the river on a half acre of sand and scraggle they'd picked up for $299 down, $299 per month for the rest of their lives, before the shit-built red-roof housing development boom. There was an old couple, Pokey and Hal, who rolled in once a month on Social Security day, lost a chunk of it, ate three $1.99 sausage and egg specials in eighteen hours, and headed out the door, not with slumped shoulders and that "Why me?" look, but with a "See ya next month!"

Runner, the wiry guy, had his dream about ten miles from town. He'd told Maggie about the place—his piece of mind, he called it. He spelled it out for Maggie. P-I-E-C-E. And he said he didn't mean anything crude by that—peace of mind on a piece of earth. "Yeah," Maggie said, "you bet."

"Springtime," he said, "the prickly pear grow cherry-red flowers, and in the August rains you can smell how old the earth is." He'd hauled out a trailer and fixed it up and he sure would like her to see the place sometime, maybe come for dinner. Peace of mind on a piece of earth. Maggie figured it wouldn't be the first time some shaky midlife loner had confused "mind" with "ass."

"Sarah," Maggie said, to stop herself from thinking about him. "Why did you come back that day?"

"Nowhere else to go," Sarah said, dumped a handful of nickels in Maggie's winnings cup, and proceeded to lose for twenty-three consecutive plays.

2   Runner woke fast out of a dream. It was nothing new. He left the stuffy trailer for the ramada and wiggled his tripwire self into a soft hollow in the sand. It continued to startle him that such a hard land could be so tender. He thought of where he was born, remembered the mist-shrouded peaks, the duff-cushioned forest floor, the young cinder cones worn down by monsoons. Soft summer twilights, soft winter dawns. And still, that place had broken him.

He turned on his side. A half-awake dream carried him back: *He crouches at the base of the buffalo. Monsoon thunder rumbles to the south, bounces off the mountains to the north. There are lightning bolts thick as the old pines around him. He thinks of making love with a woman. Sharp and hot. Making love with a woman brilliant as this crazy light.*

Somebody's painted the buffalo white. It could be a ghost shimmering in the wet air. But this buffalo is bronze, his tasseled cock painted pink every year right after high school graduation when all that young blood is running hot and crazy. Runner's not sure how long the buffalo's been here, but he knows that back around 1967, he and his friends painted that cock the midnight before they headed out to Camp Lejeune; and a few months later, he'd found himself peering through razor-sharp elephant grass at another buffalo in a warmer rain, and heard what he thought was thunder and it wasn't.

Runner drifted awake and remembered when he had returned home three tours later. He'd gone up to the park and stared at the buffalo, which had been painted black except for the iridescent green peace sign on its butt, and he had said to himself and the buffalo that he would remember everything. He would trip enough and smoke enough and fucking well fuck enough to illuminate every dinky dau brain cell he had left. And, as he moved out into the dark monsoon air, he had given himself a new name. Runner.

GRAVEYARD, which Maggie was working as a favor for Sheree, only out of her lifetime guilt about everything, was the worst. Runner was nowhere in sight. Sarah had been scheduled for mornings. The bartender Tom was a guy who had to tell you every second about his tragic childhood that caused him to become a control freak, which he was except when he was mixing her order, resulting in Bloody Marys minus vodka and wine coolers minus cool.

Maggie could hardly wait to go home. She'd rented a mini-apartment with a back balcony big enough for a chair and TV tray. The kitchen was perfect for a small gerbil family. If you turned around too fast in the living-dining-bed-room you could redecorate in five seconds flat. The fridge was mostly freezer. It was assumed that one entertained frequently and required not much more than ice. Even with the swamp cooler going full tilt the place was an oven—but, it was hers, hers alone.

Riverview Heights was about fifty feet above the backside of the Creosote Winners' Mall and a half mile from the Colorado River. Directly below Maggie's back porch was the Riverview Heights World-Famous Heart-Shaped Pool, terminally afflicted with algae and screaming kids. No problem, as long as she could look out over the tops of the dying palms and see the Colorado at dawn and dusk, when it shimmered like pewter and the casinos could have been carved from ruby or emerald or cubic zirconia.

Tom cleared his throat. "I'm sorry, you know how I am. I forgot that last drink—what was it?"

"A draft beer," Maggie said.

He nodded. "Maybe you should speak a little louder from now on."

"How's this numbnuts? Maggie yelled.

"I didn't expect that," Tom said. "I thought what with you being an older woman and all, you might be a kinder person than some."

SARAH let herself into the trailer. It was past midnight. She'd tried to walk off back-to-back shifts—as if you could outrun sixteen hours of making fry bread and listening to Leola tell her how lucky she was to be an Indian in modern times. One more week and she'd have bus fare to Bone Lake, *if* she felt ready to go home. She knew she could call her auntie for a loan, or maybe even that cranky old healer, Minnie Siyala, but she understood that she had jammed herself into her mess and she was going to have to get herself out. She remembered Minnie Siyala calling her Mulehead Girl. "Damn for real," she muttered.

She'd stomped back and forth on the Riverstroll five times. Old couples wandered. Gaunt men with piss-hole eyes leaned on the railing over the water, any interest they might have had in a good-looking woman leached away by bet after losing bet. It was the safest place for a woman to walk by herself, especially a woman who knew tweakers ran the Creosote night.

Sarah had emptied a bag of breakfast scraps on the beach for the black-and-white mom cat and her babies. She had never really liked cats till she landed in Creosote. But this cat family was made up of such stubborn hustlers she had to love them.

She dropped the greasy bag in the trash and poured a glass of water. Sarah heard her roommate, Tina Rae, moving around in the back. It was only when Sarah realized that Tina's old Celica was not in its parking spot that she dropped the glass and bolted for the front door.

MAGGIE woke to copper light slanting through the broken blinds. She loved the day being gone, the brutal glare of the Mojave sun finally surrendered.

She was hauling herself upright when the doorbell rang. "Fuck," she muttered. *Another* born-again salesman. She checked the peephole. The wiry guy waited—with a Don's Deliteful Donut bag in his hands. Maggie threw open the door.

"Is there coffee?" she said.

"Why, it's you, Runner," he said. "So glad you could drop by."

"I need chemicals. Besides, how'd you find me?"

"I bribed Sheree for the address. Fifty-dollar gift certificate at the tanning place." Runner opened the top of the bag. "And I took the liberty of choosing our breakfast. Don's cake donuts, six of 'em. And, four twelve-ounce coffees. And cream."

"Hey," Maggie said, "did you ever think how weird it is that there are six tanning salons in greater Creosote . . . I mean, what was it today, a hundred and five—and it's May."

Runner handed her a coffee. "Somehow, I figured you'd like the cake donuts without glaze. No girlie frills. Looks like I'm right, what with you being a woman who operates logically before caffeine."

"Logic?" Maggie said. "What have I done to deserve this?"

Runner looked at her sleepy face. The sun was dropping behind him, and in its long low light he could see the gray in her auburn hair, the lines around those big gray-green eyes. He figured she wouldn't believe him if he told her that's why he was waiting at her door. With coffee and plain old cake donuts fifteen minutes out of the fryer—and a longing for conversation that wouldn't require translation, as was necessary with his last mistake, i.e.: *Arthur Lee was a god. The Righteous Brothers were, indeed, righteous. Raymond Chandler should have won the Pulitzer. We didn't win the Vietnam War. Which was in Vietnam, a little country shaped like a shrimp in Asia. You know? Across the ocean?*

"Should I just hand this over like I was the delivery boy?" he said. "Maybe I jumped the gun?"

It occurred to Maggie that "jump the gun" could mean "trouble sooner or later." She put on her glasses. It was the first time she'd seen him in daylight. She tried to check him out without checking him out. She saw a wary sharpness in his dark eyes and that his curly black hair had just been washed, and she knew he definitely was going to be trouble. Sooner.

"Well?" he grinned.

Maggie waved him in. They went out to the balcony. Runner picked up her second chair and set it on the other side of the TV tray.

"May I?" he said, and sat down. Maggie leaned against the wall. The sun began to set, the river going bronze.

"From here," he said, "you'd never know that river is dying."

"From here," Maggie said, "maybe we could just enjoy the view." The topic of the river was one of the few things besides tanking slot credits, the irresistible pull of gravity on a well-endowed woman, and Tom the whining bartender that could really piss her off.

Runner set the bag on the table. "Help yourself, Ms. May."

Maggie pulled out a donut. "Tell you what," she said, "you tell me your real name, I'll tell you mine."

Runner opened his coffee, dumped in creamer, stirred it for about a minute. He took out a donut, unfolded a napkin on the TV tray and set the donut square in the middle, the coffee off to the side, moved the coffee into alignment. He thought about how busy a person could get when they wanted something a lot—and to get it, they might have to give up more than they've given in a long time.

"Nice feng shui," Maggie said and grinned.

"My name's Jesse," he said. "Jesse Corbeaux."

Maggie studied his pale skin, the almost black eyes and battered hands. "Cajun?" she said and sat down. "A Cajun crow?"

He laughed. "Mongrel. A little French, a lot Hungarian—my grandfather called himself a son of the road."

"That's why you're Runner?"

"More or less."

Maggie knew to leave the "more or less" alone. "Pleased to meet you, Jesse Corbeaux." She shook his hand. He held on. She thought about pulling back and didn't.

You had to move quick in a casino town. People were in and out faster than a bad fuck. December through February, the snowbirds pulled their rigs into the casino parking lots, spread out the fake turf, strung a few Xmas lights along the roll-out awning, held up a beer, and hollered "Party time!" You'd yell "Be right there," pull out your pictures if you had them, eyeball theirs, the kids, the grandkids, the boat, the place back home. Maybe there'd be microwaved supper, maybe real stories, but you knew in a couple weeks or months—depending on how their luck ran—they'd be gone.

And that was just the guests, as Sheree reminded her constantly to call them. Employees, whose official status did not rule out being guests, were random as grackles.

"You know," Maggie said and stopped. She wasn't sure she wanted that train of thought out in the open. Then her mouth ran the show. "Did you notice how nobody's around here for long?"

"There's Old Ray," Jesse said. "He bartended at Binion's for twenty years before the casinos went up here, been at the Crystal ever since."

"OK," Maggie said, "and there *are* the perennials, the old gals with the poodle in the Bounder and the industrial-strength bras and cast-iron designer jeans." She realized this was his Test. She wondered if he knew it.

"I love them," Jesse said. "They don't believe for a second they've been retired. All they know is the old man finally died or took off with a trophy babe, and they got the ranch."

"Yeah?"

"Watch 'em," he said. "They snuggle up to video poker like they're gonna get it off. And any lucky cowpoke in range."

A+. Maggie was exactly five major holidays short of fifty-five and still didn't know what she'd be when she grew up. He was giving her career goals.

"Want a beer?" she asked.

"No," he said. "No beer. Just one request. Call Sheree and see if you can get tomorrow off. I want you to see my place."

Maggie stared at him. "Beer's easier. You know Sheree."

Jesse held up his hand. "Nope. I'm heading out on the road in a couple weeks, don't know for how long. I'd like you to come out before the place is a full-time furnace."

Heading out on the road. Maggie thought, Runner. "Hey," she said, "what do you want me to call you? Jesse or Runner."

"Jesse," he said.

"I'm not Maggie May," she said. "Well, I'm not now." She dropped her eyes. "Seeing as how you've been holding my hand for five minutes, I'm Maggie Foltz," she said, "and I'm fifty-four years old."

"I'm forty-eight," he said, and watched her pick up the phone.

THIS IS NOT FAIR, Sarah thought. Not now. Not when a week from now I'd have enough money for the bus to Bone Lake. This is too soon. I have too much left to do.

MIDMORNING, after a night split 99.9/.01 between talk and one kiss, and a few hours of sleep in his own bed, Jessie picked Maggie up in his impeccably clean and ancient truck. "Eighty-three Ford," he said. "It's got everything a man needs to live."

"Why?"

"You never know," he said. "Shit happens. No more questions. Just sit back and relax."

Maggie looked down at her hands. *Relax. As if.* Her palms were sweating. She missed her beautiful battered 1988 banker's gray Firebird, her guaranteed access to outer and inner space.

Jesse pushed a tape into the deck. "Check this out," he said quietly. "Dave Alvin. A minor god." The music was molasses—dark and anything but sweet. Maggie was glad for it. She could be silent and therein disappear.

She knew the rabbit trick of being still and invisible when you wanted to not be somewhere. She'd agreed to come. She'd bullshit Sheree. Still, she couldn't get the night before out of her mind, how he'd asked if he could kiss her and the kiss had been sans tongue, and only one kiss, so that she wanted more, all of which made her want to be sitting on her balcony staring out over algae and dead palms, with nothing for company but her pure lonesomes.

"I want it personal," he had said. "That's all I ask. Whatever happens."

She'd wanted to tell him she'd *been* personal with Dwight. They'd been sweet, honest, and hot; then he'd gone away and when he'd come back he was DC, and Dwight was gone; and she was the only one being personal—for ten years, until he discovered that the woman he'd been *really* looking for was, in fact, not her. And then she'd done it not personal with any guy who stood still long enough for her to unbuckle his belt.

Maggie watched Jesse's hands on the steering wheel. "Guys' hands on a steering wheel are the sexiest thing in the world," Sheree said. Maggie didn't want that to be true in Jesse's case, but it was. He turned off the highway onto a dirt road. A cloud of dust rose behind them and blurred the way back. Maggie guessed if she got out now she could make it on foot back to Creosote. But, she'd have to say something, something that would sound crazy to a man who seemed anything but crazy.

There had been one redeeming quality to Dead DC. He'd understood how being safe in someone's pocket can make certain people antsy. Hanging upside down in concertina wire above an advancing trickle of burning gasoline; and a Vietnamese Montagnard village he had to leave behind when that was the last thing he wanted to do taught him that. And gave him his Green Beret name: Dark Cloud.

Maggie wondered if Jesse had served over there. She wondered that about every guy his age. It made a difference. The ones who did, who were in country, not just REMF's, they knew. About sweetness, about clarity, about the ultimate buzz, about how somebody you had just split a joint with could die in your arms, how the next time it could be you looking down at the hole in your chest. "Those guys would just look amazed," DC had said. "Like, 'Who me? Naw, not me.'"

It wasn't just the older vets. She'd seen that thousand-yard stare in the eyes of some of the young guys who'd been in Desert Storm. The guys who had stayed here she didn't much respect—unless they had survived some personal meltdown that had been closer to a near-death experience than a valuable life lesson, or somehow understood the only honorable hunt is armed human for armed human. The uninitiated always had the idea you could keep something forever. Maggie could usually read it right away, but with Jesse there was no telling.

SARAH couldn't believe how long it took. For hours, there was only the hooded man's careful observation of her trussed-up body. Then there was more. Soon she was past feeling anything. Except how long a second could be, or a minute, or the infinite then/now/will be of an hour.

JESSE turned onto a rocky two-track. There were low ragged mountains and miles of cactus, creosote, and light. If you didn't know what those miles held, you could have believed desert meant Big Nothing. Cactus meant saguaro, a gawky giant of a plant waving the filthy skyline of a bloated desert city good-bye.

On the far western border of Arizona, there was diamond cholla, shimmering at twilight like a phantom. There was blue yucca, its flowers ivory flames becoming embers in the long, slow sunsets. There were gray-green bursts of Mojave yucca and wine-red barrel cactus starred with fat blossoms. And there were Joshua trees, black and twisted against the night sky.

Maggie's heart grew tighter by the mile. She touched Jesse's arm and was startled by how warm it was, till she realized her fingers were icy.

"Whoa!" he said. "What's up?"

"Time. I think I want to go home. I think I made a mistake."

Jesse looked at her profile. She was not smiling. "It's simple," she said. "We turn around. I pay for half the gas. You drop me off. I have a quiet day at home, which I need due to how much I love my job, to which I have to go back. Tomorrow. At 7:00 a.m. You know."

"Hang on," Jesse pulled over and climbed out. Maggie closed her eyes. She listened to the truck engine laboring. Something cold and wet touched her wrist.

"Lemonade," he said. "Ice. Go ahead, drink. It'll help."

They sat in silence. Jesse could wait. He had the advantage. It was his truck. Maggie started to cry, those slow dumb tears that just run down your face. She watched the ice in the plastic cup catch light, bounce reflection off the dashboard. You could disappear watching something like that. "I don't cry," she said.

"I see that," Jesse said. "Look, I know we're going kind of fast."

"Maybe you ought to call me Maggie May and take me home."

"I know we've hardly talked," he said. "But, I don't know—these days, our age, it's not like we got forever."

"What age is our age?" she said.

"Not having forever. Not having for-fucking-ever."

"Yeah," she said. "There it is."

"There it is," he said quietly. "Come on. We'll get you settled in the ramada, get you more lemonade, tortilla chips and my home-brewed salsa, put your salts and fluids back in balance. Then we'll just sit and watch the light change."

He had her. Back home after DC was long gone, she'd allowed twilight to be her last resort. She and her kid, Deac, would move the rocking chairs to the porch, light a candle, and watch the northern summer evening go pink, silver green, then black.

They'd track the tiny pale moths fading in and out of the dark. One night they'd watched a moth drop into their candle and flare up. It had burned for hours, a wick of crumpled wings.

Jesse pulled off the two-track onto a patch of hardpan and parked. He dug in the sand just in front of the truck, tucked something away in his pack, and opened her door. They were parked next to a squatty travel trailer half-hidden in a thicket of ocotillo, datura vines, and dried cornstalks. The place looked like it was springing alive from the shadowed sand.

"Home," Jesse said. "My first real home."

Sarah.

JESSE settled Maggie into the ramada. "I built it with ocotillo," he said. "Look up there." The corner stalks were leafing out. "Even after they've been cut, you stick them in the sand and they flower."

He'd woven bandanas into an airy rooftop and tucked juniper in the gaps. The ramada smelled of living desert and the wildcat piss scent of the juniper. Maggie settled into a camp lounger and closed her eyes again. It was not like her. When you couldn't see, you couldn't keep track.

Jesse's voice was soft. "When it rains," he said, "the cloth holds the rain, so you can sit here a long time before it gets hot again. Rain runs down from the gutters into the horse trough in the corner. You could take a bath there."

"I could?" She opened one eye. The horse trough was indeed big enough for a woman to immerse herself full-length—and who knew who else.

"I meant 'you' like in general," he grinned, "and that shack just beyond the big Joshua, it's got a moon carved in the door. That's Moon Manor."

Maggie appreciated his delicacy. A guy regarding her as a platonic pal would have just told her where the shitter was.

He went into the trailer. Maggie wanted to ask him if he ever saw the movie *Alice Doesn't Live Here Anymore,* how the hero ended up taking the brave waitress and her kid off to a ranch and rabbits and hand-cranked ice cream.

She wanted to tell him she learned a long time ago a movie is a hoax. Instead, she relaxed into the lounger and watched the dust specks glittering in the blades of sun.

Jesse brought her a refilled glass and chips.

"I like it here," Maggie said. "I love the word *ramada.*"

"I sometimes wonder," Jesse said, "if the desert taught nomads how to make ramadas. There would always be more building materials. They knew they could leave them without a thought."

"Runner," she said. "You're talking like a runner."

"Jesse," he said. "My name is Jesse. And this ramada isn't a symbol; it's just a sweet place to unwind." He kissed the top of her head and went back into the trailer, where he started banging pans around.

Maggie felt like a cautious but almost happy zombie. With DC and too many others, she'd always been the drink-bearer, the kisser, the pots and pans banger. She thought she might be learning how some takers felt. Suspicious. Even unworthy.

She could see how takers might get lulled into a wary peacefulness, might be afraid to do something to break the spell and, so, do nothing. She saw how it might have been for DC when he came home and she'd been bound to make it perfect—perfect backrubs and perfect head, perfect advice and perfect excuses, and as her best shot, Daniel David, the perfect kid. She remembered DC slumped on the couch, how he could look for hours at nothing; for days, say nothing; for weeks and months and years, touch nothing and let nothing touch him.

She considered going into the trailer, tapping Jesse on the shoulder and saying: "How about the too-many-to-count one-night stands? Hey, Jesse, how about amnesia for a few hundred names? Still want to cook me a meal?"

She pulled herself out of the lounger, walked in through the trailer door, tapped Jesse on the shoulder, and said, "When do we eat? I'm starving."

Sarah.

JESSE and Maggie ate his mesquite-grilled ginger chicken and a salad loaded with avocado and blue cheese, pungent with olives he'd scavenged and preserved. Desert was raspberries and perfect quiet.

He brought her coffee. "None for you?" she asked.

"Not my plant in the evening," he said. He pulled out a little brass pipe. "Here's my vegetable."

"For you," she said. "Dope doesn't like me."

She watched him bend over the pipe as though it was a sacrament. He toked hard, closed his eyes. The smoke drifted around them, skunky, familiar. "Yes," Jesse sighed, and tapped the pipe out on the sand.

THE WESTERN HORIZON was pink when Jesse made their bed on the ground.

"Join me?" he said softly.

Maggie touched his face. "In for a penny," she said just as softly, "in for a pound."

They slept covered with a thin flannel sheet, and they did not have sex. Maggie watched the stars circle slowly. She woke to find Jesse's arm warm across her. She slept and woke again to stars and his embrace. Nothing more. Again and again. Stars and embrace and nothing more. She felt old and undesirable and relentlessly, stupidly horny. But when he pressed tight against her back, it was as though liquid stars trickled down her spine, and she could breathe easy.

She woke at last to dawn shining on the western mountains, and Jesse's kiss gentle on her cold face.

"It's all new to me too," he whispered. Then, his hands were on her like a blessing, and when he moved into her—slow and gentle because it had been a long time without for both of them—his body was so familiar to her, his rhythm so tender, she was closing sweetly wet around him before she had time to be afraid.

He kissed her, smiled against her lips. "I knew it," he said.

She looked up. "It's you."

Sarah. It was the voice of that old healer, Minnie Siyala.

"It's too late," Sarah said.

No, girl. It's about time. Sarah, you listen to me.

"I don't have a choice. As if I ever did."

Stop your rudeness. I have to tell you something.

"What." Sarah was not really Sarah anymore, but she answered as Sarah would. What. Flat. Just polite enough to be rude.

It is not time for you to cross over.

"Where am I? Where is my body?"

You are in between. Your body is back there. It is too broken for you to use.

"Then how can I cross over?"

You still ask too many questions. We will find the way.

"I don't want to. Maybe I can go back. There is too much there I want, too much I didn't finish. Or even start."

Too late.

"What about Will Lucas? What about when I get the bus fare to Bone Lake and I can go back and tell my aunt about Yakima and the money? I have to do that. I promised."

Sarah.

"You never liked me, old woman."

I love you.

"What kind of love takes a girl and puts her in a whiteman school away from her family, puts her where no one speaks her language, puts her where when she speaks her language the white people make her stand in a corner and reach for the stars for an hour, till her shoulders hurt so much she forgets how to talk in any language?"

Girl.

"I am not a girl. I am a woman."

If that's so, then you know it's not time for you to cross over. And you can't stay here. I won't allow that.

"Here. Where is here?"

In between. It is not Willow way here. It is from another place, a place where a person killed as you were is trapped forever in between. I have heard that these people are called hungry ghosts.

"I am not a hungry ghost. Whatever that is. I will not be one, not ever."

Good. Then you will let me teach you how to cross over. You will let me show you how to find the living one who can help you. And you will sass me only part of the time.

3   Maggie came home to a sweltering apartment. She cranked up the swamp cooler and checked the answering machine. "Sheree. You're scheduled before, during, and after Memorial Day. Two shifts back-to-back. Say thank you." There were six or seven hang-ups, one of them her son, Deac's caller ID. There was no Jesse.

Maggie dialed Sarah's number. Time for girl talk. There was no answer. She called the Crystal. Leola told her nobody'd seen hide nor hair of Sarah, who'd been scheduled to work morning shift. "I figured the two of you had the same bug, thick as you are."

Maggie wrote Deac a letter and told him he didn't have to play tricks. Then it occurred to her that the wife had made the call. She'd been trying to make peace since landing in the middle of the mess Deac called the "family from Uranus." Maggie shredded the letter. No matter what she wrote, it'd piss him off.

Everything about her pissed him off. Her one kid, Daniel David Campbell—Deacon because he'd been preaching about the unfairness of life since he could talk. The counselor at the last women's shelter had pointed out Deac had just cause. The woman had been unprofessionally meddlesome, genuinely kind, and had somehow gotten Deac to write Maggie.

"YOU as mother," he'd printed carefully, "was better than a poke in the eye with a sharp stick. P.S. At least Dad was nothing!"

Maggie called Sheree back and told her Memorial Day was just swell. She thought about calling Deac, maybe taking a run out to Jesse's, and decided to keep it simple and see if Sarah was at home.

MINNIE was abruptly gone. Sarah was in between. It wasn't what she'd been told. Not by Minnie; not by the old woman's nemesis, the priest Father John; not by Dr. Eric We-Are-All-One Clark, Sarah's former comparative religions prof. No valley lush with game and berries; no gigantic knee of God she was supposed to sit next to; no diving joyfully toward an innocent dove, her soul contained in a red-tailed hawk.

There *was* a phone booth in which a yellow light glowed behind cracked windows. Sarah stepped in and dialed Maggie's number. The machine greeted her. Sarah left her message and hung up. The phone booth fell away from her as though it had been nothing but shadow. She thought of Minnie's ceremonial blanket, that old dark red Hudson Bay and how when Minnie let it fall from her shoulders, you knew it was Holy Time. Holy Time. Whatever *that* was.

"Thanks so much, God. Thanks, Spirits. Thanks, BuddhaAllahJesus-Whatever. Thanks for nothing. I wish I'd paid a little more attention." Cold green light flowed around the toes of her sneakers. "OK," she said. "I wish even more I'd never left Bone Lake."

MAGGIE drove through the neon blizzard to the edge of Creosote. Sarah had found a sagging yellow trailer in a Creosote trailer park. There was the standard dry patio fountain, clanking swamp coolers, a busted pop machine, and signs everywhere telling you what you must *not* do.

A keno girl from one of the big casinos roomed with Sarah. Tina Rae worked days, Sarah worked mostly graveyard, so it suited them both. Maggie'd met the girl. She'd wandered out of the bathroom once, her makeup half on, and Maggie had seen the girl was like that, half-pretty, half-plain, half here now, half in a fuzzy future she'd confessed to Sarah. "I think if you're nice," Tina Rae would say, "if you show these guys you're not like the other girls, you can find a nice one and have something decent."

Some nights she didn't come home. "I'm careful," Tina Rae said. "You have to be these days. But, you have to give them some loving. Give it to them and still be nice. They don't realize a modern girl can be like that."

Tina's old blue Celica was gone. Maggie knocked. A stained glass unicorn sparkled in the kitchen window. There was a whiff of something fat and sweet, as though somebody'd been cooking breakfast at dinnertime. Maggie knocked again, and felt a shiver up her spine.

She turned and saw a little boy watching her, his eyes red-rimmed, the lashes crusty.

"Is the Indian lady home?" she asked. The boy fled. Maggie wrote a note to Sarah and taped it to the aluminum door.

BACK HOME time went funny, as it does if you're waiting to hear from the clinic about something to do with being female and heedless, or from the sensitive married guy who'd promised to call after the talk with the Wife. Maggie walked the length of her living room a couple hundred times and called the police.

The cops went to the trailer. The younger cop found Maggie's note. She and her partner broke the flimsy lock, walked in to find the dried-out sausages, the crumbling Pop-Tart, Kool-Aid scum in the bottom of a glass, and Sarah propped up in the tiny bathroom.

Her face was dappled with neat bite marks, her eye sockets empty, her nipples chewed off, her sex so charred you could only guess she'd been a woman. There was an incision over her heart as though the killer was going to cut it out and had stopped.

The young cop saw the victim's hands were clenched so tight her nails held them shut. When the medical examiner would finally pry them open, he would find a pencil stub in Sarah's right palm. Later the cops tossed the trailer, front to back, ceiling to floor, but they never found what she might have written.

The young cop didn't tell Maggie any of this at first. Her voice was gentle. "Your friend," she said. "She appears to have been murdered. I'm sorry."

Maggie held her breath. It changed nothing. "Thank you," she said. "I mean, oh my god. No. That's crazy."

"I'm sorry," the cop said again, and Maggie believed her. So she asked the cop to tell her the details. It was the clinical iciness of "incision" that triggered Maggie's tears.

SARAH watched the fox fire ripple around her feet. It occurred to her that the light was waiting for her. That seemed like a totally insane idea, and then she remembered the bighorn trail up Duckwater Mountain. It switchbacked, as though the bighorn knew going straight up would kick rock loose. Mostly the tribe were the only people who knew about it. Now and then, some kid would try his dirt bike on it and get thrown on the first sharp turn. Always. Like a trail could have a mind of its own.

She took one step forward. The light went with her, not enough to see by, more than enough to make her curious. "I should be scared," she said. "I'm dead. I've never been dead before. And I'm not scared. Maybe I'm crazy. I might as well follow." She stepped forward and kicked something soft. The light pooled around it. Her grandmother's shawl lay on the ground.

The embroidery was still bright against the dark blue cloth. The red bear. The white heron. The yellow you're-not-old-enough-Sarah-to-know-what-it-is. "Now I'll never know," she said. Her voice was a child's. She brought the shawl to her face and breathed deep. "I will never know."

MAGGIE drove out to Jesse's. When she told him about Sarah, he was quiet. It was the perfect nothing for him to do.

"I'm cold," she said and went into his arms. He took her to the ramada, laid them both down in the warm sand, and held her as though he could take her shuddering into his flesh. "Be warm," he said. "Just be warm."

She closed her eyes. As she drifted in and out of sleep, it seemed that she and Jesse drifted in and out of each other. She thought Jesse was the scared one, and she the one who could let pain move through, who breathed into it, the yellow stink of burned flesh, the charred hair and bone, the place where nothing would live ever again. She turned her face to Jesse's chest and heard his heart. Her throat locked up around knowing how often she had moved through so much alone.

She saw Sarah standing next to them, whole and grumpy. "Jesse. She's here."

He murmured into her hair, "That can happen. You're safe. Let her be."

If she looked at Sarah too closely, the image began to fade. Jesse slept quietly next to her. She leaned up on one arm and watched Jesse's chest rise and fall. She matched her breath to his. A soft breeze came up. The ramada scarves fluttered like wings against the pale dark.

Near sunrise the cries of Inca doves drifted blue and clear. Maggie found herself huddled in DC's hooch with Sarah, Jesse, DC, and Deac. They were wrapped in mildewed blankets. Wet light the color of lichen seeped in through the roof. They ate slimy meat with their bare fingers. It hurt to swallow and to breathe. She opened her mouth to speak and smoke poured out.

SARAH raised her face from the shawl. "Minnie Siyala," she yelled, "where are you now? I need you."

There was no answer. Sarah unfolded the shawl and draped it around her shoulders. The light around her feet pulsed. *Whoa,* she thought, *Party Time.*

She couldn't believe she giggled. She stepped forward, the trail opening out ahead of her. She smelled leaf mold. Green shadow contained her. Tree roots thick as snakes twisted across the path. It seemed as though she was being watched.

"So what," she said. What else could happen? She kept walking. The air was warm, then hot. She remembered the women's sweat cave up in the hills above Bone Lake. But this air was different, not sharp with sage, not filled with soft voices.

The path curved. She couldn't see ahead. As she moved up into the curve, she felt a sudden ache in what must have still been her heart. It was the bruise of homesickness. Of the loss of a place, not because you cannot go back, but because the place was gone.

She pulled the shawl tighter. She knew, as though she walked a loop in time, that the source of the bruise was bone-deep and it lay ahead at the far curve of the trail. She reached the place and saw only jungle and the path winding into deep shadows. What once had seemed to crouch there was gone. She knew that for centuries, the village children had seen a big ape in the rock, squatting on its haunches as they did. There was nothing left. Even the evidence of the boulder's annihilation was overgrown with vines.

Sarah stepped forward. When she came to the place where the great stone ape had once rested, she dropped to her knees. "Minnie, come back. How can a person not know where she is and yet remember the place?"

JESSE brought coffee to the ramada. They were quiet in the juniper dawn. He handed her a plate of warm corn tortillas, and when she couldn't eat, brought water. "I wonder," she said, "if I will ever wake up from this."

"This?"

"Sarah. You."

Jesse looked at her eyes. He remembered that look, as though the person is watching something a thousand galaxies away. He started to tell her about the real reason for the name Runner, and then she shook her head and said, "Time to be Maggie May. I gotta pay for my day off."

He waited. She touched his face. "Thanks, I owe you."

"I'm happy," he said, "to hold your markers."

THE APARTMENT WAS QUIET. The answering machine light glowed steady. Maggie carried a load of wash to the laundry and was granted the miracle of an empty machine. She dumped in her clothes and waited. She could hear kids playing in the pool. She wondered what they were doing home and realized school was over. She liked having ordinary thoughts and wished she had a cigarette, just one or maybe fifty. What was left? No smokes. No booze. Jesse refusing to be anything but a sweetheart.

The timer went off. She tossed the clothes in the dryer and walked slowly back to her place to fill hours till it was time to go to work. She was grateful for the refrigerator she hadn't cleaned since she had moved to Creosote.

JESSE watched the dust plume rise from the Firebird. He carried their coffee cups into the trailer. The quiet seemed, for the first time, a little too quiet.

He was glad for work that would carry him a few days. He was walking into dangerous ground. He knew the signs, though he hadn't felt them since high school—and those two-centuries-long two years in the village northwest of Da Nang.

At first, you thought you'd be fine, a guy on his own, a guy who has walked it alone for long enough that he knew he could move solo the rest of his life. Then you went into the body of a woman and she was not just any woman. You found she had occupied your mind, your heart, maybe even your DNA, so thoughts were feelings were longings; and your perfectly good life was suddenly flat without her. Her eyes. Her voice. Her touch.

He shook his head. "In for a penny, in for a pound," he whispered to the quiet trailer and hauled his pack down from its hook. "Time to go to work." He took out a heavy knotted bandana, carried it to the ramada, and unfolded it on the sand.

There was a fist-sized lump of red and black obsidian, a broken deer antler, a striking platform. He considered the job ahead. The man who ordered the knife was thirty-eight. He lived in Chicago with his wife and child. He had explained *his* work to Jesse, "10 percent of my work has purpose; 90 percent is the daily re-creation of a disguise for the purpose."

"I've never killed anything," he had said, "but I honor the warrior within me."

Jesse understood the longing. He saw how the young men of his country were without a war, except for the aerial crack-rush hyped as Desert Storm.

And still, so many modern guys were hard—no, brittle. Afraid. Busy. So busy.

"Five thousand dollars," the man had said. "I know you can make me the perfect knife."

Jesse studied the obsidian, held it for a long time, felt for the point of fracture. You could hone obsidian to an edge sharper than surgical steel. When he finally bound the blade into the bone handle, he would have given his full attention to every moment of the making. Before he tied the final knot, he would spit on the sinew. The man would never know.

That man and his kind seemed to know so little. They didn't know that no matter how much they heli-skiied and X-climbed and day-traded as though they were riding the hottest impossible ho who would leave them skeletal and longing, they were still soft. They were going-gray boys who didn't know that no matter how little fat they ate or how many reps they did, they were still going to die.

Jesse set the chipping tool against the obsidian and struck. Too hard. The stone fractured. He gathered the ruined stone in his hand, watched light shimmer along the elliptical break. He ran his thumb over the fracture line, drew blood.

He marked his forehead with his blood, and remembered the perfect bullet hole in his friend Nguyen's forehead, the lump of human shit resting on his black hair, the dark stub between his lips that you thought at first was an American cigar stub and wasn't.

He remembered the words in the Civil War book he'd only now been able to bring himself to read: "a common type of debris removed from the flesh of wounded men by surgeons in the gunpowder age was broken bone and teeth from neighbors in the ranks." He thought of the expression he heard so many people use, "Don't go there." And, he knew, licking the blood off his thumb, that he had no choice.

There was a reason, a gray-green-eyed reason whose gaze was steady, whose touch was sweet, who was unwittingly knapping him as if he were obsidian.

MAGGIE drove into work. She watched the sun burn down behind the Blackstone Range, the desert glowing milky blue. She kept feeling as though somebody was watching her in the rearview mirror. When she looked up the reflection was filled with nothing but long shadows and highway.

She made the turn onto Casino Drive. Cars and neon jittered around her. She wondered how the Crystal would be. Maybe somebody would have draped the slots and the tables in black, maybe loaded the jukebox with money, played Sarah's tunes—Chrissie Hynde and Mötley Crüe and some Red rights band out of Flagstaff called Blackfire. Maggie thought it would suit Sarah's sense of justice if the snack bar gave out fry bread for free.

She parked and walked in through the smoky doors. The place was jumping. Carlo was playing his Sinatra medley, and the only empty seat at Food for the Soul was at the far end, right between Sarah's former roommate Tina Rae and two cops. Tina waved. The cops nodded and beckoned her over. Maggie went.

Tina touched her arm gently. "I'm sorry, Maggie," she said. "I heard yesterday. It's everywhere, all the girls know." She shivered. "I can't even think about it—'cause when I think about it I think that if I hadn't of been moving, I would of been there. I could of helped, you know?"

"Or got killed."

"Sarah didn't tell you about my moving, I guess?" Tina Rae said brightly, as though Maggie hadn't said those last words.

"Somebody nice?"

"Hopefully. But with this, you know, this kind of thing, it makes you stop and wonder." She gathered up her cigarettes and tucked them in her beaded purse.

"If I can do anything," she said, "you can reach me at the Moonglow. Lucky, lucky, lucky—I won't be there much longer, but you can never tell."

She left a buck tip for her coffee and stood. The older cop glanced over. Tina was dressed for work, her legs going on forever, slender as a pre-teen's. She was a Moonmaiden, one of the women who brought you your keno slip, who carried away your money and rarely brought it back. She tugged down the sides of her silvery high-cut leotard. The cop sighed and looked away.

"These outfits are terrible," Tina Rae whispered. "Hopefully," she crossed her fingers, "I won't have to wear them much longer."

"Good luck."

"Maggie May," Tina Rae said, "Sarah really liked you. She didn't show that much, but I could tell."

"Thanks. I liked her, too." Sorrow knotted Maggie's throat. "I hope you find what you're looking for, girlfriend, I truly do." Tina Rae kissed her cheek and wobbled away on her backless five-inch heels. The older cop sighed again. Maggie stuck out her hand. "I'm Maggie Foltz. Sarah's friend."

"I thought that girl called you Maggie May," the younger cop said politely. She was L. SHANNON, unless her name tag lied.

"That's my cocktailing name, Officer Shannon."

L. Shannon smiled, a real smile. "Can I call you Maggie, Ms. Foltz?" she asked. Before Maggie could answer, she said, "I'm more known by Lucy. You know, like Peanuts. The guys think I'm bossy."

Maggie started to tell Lucy she had never met a cop with a nickname before, then realized she didn't want a cop to wonder why she would have been meeting cops. "You can call me Maggie."

"We've got a few questions, just anything you might remember about your friend."

Maggie thought fast about what she'd tell her and what she wouldn't. Sarah had been private, but sometimes she'd tossed out dribs and drabs of the old stories her grandma had told her, a secret winter dance she sort of knew about, how there were wizards up home, not cute Disney types, but energy-sucking men and women who loved power more than anything. "They hate the light," Sarah had said. "That's why they're out there in those little slits in the rock that go back and back forever. They can be in the shadows in bars, in some people's eyes. We call them Empty Skins."

She'd let that stuff slip out and a bitter reference to some guy up in Seattle, then she'd go back to being Sarah Whatever. Maggie was the same. She'd never told Sarah how her mother's people once decorated their barns with hex signs and knew how to make a mirror that would show a girl her true love. She'd been waiting till they knew each other better.

Leola bustled over and gave Maggie the sad eye. "Ain't it a shame about our Sarah?"

"It is."

"I tried to warn her," Leola sighed, "but, she had that willful way about her." She played with her grandkid medallion necklace. Twenty of them, eighteen boys and two girls. God help us all.

Lucy perked up. "What was that you tried to warn her about?" The older cop stirred his coffee and tried to look nonchalant. Creosote city police tended to take a few psych courses at the community college and become experts in human motivation.

"Her uppity ways," Leola said. "She was always thinking she was above other folks." She leaned forward. "You know how *they* can get."

The older cop nodded. L. Shannon frowned. You could get Internal Affairs on your ass for racial profiling. She opened a plastic card case and gave Leola her card. Leola tucked the card in her apron pocket and wandered back to nag Ramon the fry cook.

"Ms. Foltz," Lucy said. "Your friend, Sarah? When did you last see her?"

She watched Maggie. The older cop glanced at the fry cook. Maggie saw Ramon take a shaky breath and knew what to do. She could move them all out of there, maybe save Ramon's perfect undocumented butt.

"I'm still pretty rattled," Maggie said quietly. "And I'm due on shift in an hour. Could we go somewhere else? There are too many memories here."

She looked right into Lucy's cool blue eyes. With all those Communication courses under the cop's belt, it was bound to get her.

"I hear you," Lucy said. "How about Denny's?"

THE COPS showed Maggie a photo of dead Sarah. After that, there was no possibility of eating. The face and body in the picture were not Sarah; they were no more than a cicada shell some vicious tweaker had tortured apart and burned. The cops set Sarah's employee ID on the placemat, and that wasn't her either. The blue-black hair was the same, the round cheeks, the Mayan nose. But she was no more in that picture then she'd been in the photo of her corpse. Maggie wondered how Sarah had stepped out as the shutter opened.

"That's her," Maggie said. "More or less."

Lucy shook her head. "Yeah, I know what you mean." She and Maggie asked each other a few more useless questions. The older cop finished off Maggie's tuna melt and they all said good-bye. Lucy turned back to her. "Hey," she said, "thanks for your help. I like to think it helped you too? To share? You know?" She gave Maggie her card. "Remember," she said. "My name's Lucy. You call if you need to talk."

Maggie nodded. "You bet."

WORK WENT GLACIAL. Sheree was alarmingly subdued, the rest of them on automatic. Old Ray stepped in on blackjack and spaced out twice at his station. AKA, who wouldn't wear a name tag and got away with it because he was the best dealer in the house, told Ray's blackjack clientele to lay off counting, to please play fair. "Old Ray can't see and he's half-deaf. Go easy on him."

The regulars stopped counting and dropped big tips. Players liked to think the dealers were co-conspirators. In some ways, they were. Maggie had seen Toupee Mel and Rikki, the Filipina, teach a new puppy how to play, seen them refuse to deal to an Alzheimered blue hair, seen them grin when one of the regulars was on a roll.

When you were a sucker yourself and couldn't forget it, that knowledge softened your edge. It made you merciless on the oblivious assholes, the chic pastel couples who won and never tipped, the loud jolly dicks whose eyes were shards, who lost and reported you to the pit boss for a bad attitude.

Maggie zombied through the shift. She had one eye out for Jesse, but he was no show. She would have called him, a violation of her proven theory that men need to be the predators, but there was no phone out there in the cacti, so she pooled in her tips and settled down at her favorite nine-line nickel slot to play the tension out. It had a drag queen Cleopatra with a deep alluring voice and too much eye shadow, and bonus pyramids that shot light out their tops. Sheree sat down next to Maggie. "Know why I'm such a living dead?" she said. "I am *shit*-scared."

"Me, too." Maggie slid a ten into the slot. Both of them watched for the ejaculating pyramids, which gave you fifteen free spins at three times the normal win. Maggie wasn't hoping for much, just watching the patterns, trying to soothe her whimpering brain. She hated computers—that's part of why she waitressed. But slot machines were different. They murmured, "OK, yeah . . . now . . . a fresh start . . . this one might be different . . . try again . . . this time . . . a fresh start . . . this time . . ."

Forty bucks and no bonus later, Sheree yawned. "By the way, there's a package for you in the office."

Maggie played out her last ten and picked up the package on her way home. It was soft and smelled of river.

THE APARTMENT WAS COOL. She held the package on her lap while she played back her phone messages. There was one from Jesse, no big deal, just "Good-night Ms. Sweetgirl and see you in a couple days." There were two disconnects.

And then: Sarah's voice. "Maggie, where am I? Call me back. No. You can't even if you knew where I am—there's no number on this phone."

4   Maggie's pulse hammered in her ears. She rewound the machine. It spit out the same message. "I know what to do," she said firmly to the phone machine, walked into the kitchen, grabbed the Tanqueray hidden in the back of the fridge, and took a big swallow. Molten emerald and glacier ice. How could a paradox that elegant be bad for you.

When she rehit the message button, Sarah was still there. Maggie slammed another swallow of gin. "Well, I don't know, Sarah," she said. "I don't have a clue where you are."

She hit the button. Sarah's voice wobbled. "And, maybe I don't care," Maggie said. "You had to go get yourself killed. Just when I was thinking we were going to be friends, like I haven't had one in ten years, but of course you didn't know that because we weren't going to get too deep." The gin was working its don't-give-a-fuck miracle.

Maggie poured herself another straight shot. With the aqua glow in the windows and the green phone machine light flickering, she could have been underwater. "I am a lovely human being," she said. "Sarah gets tortured to death and I am mad because she's gone. Tough. That's how it is."

MINNIE SIYALA patted the space next to Sarah as though the darkness was her old threadbare couch. "You sit here, girl. It's time for you to learn a few things."

Sarah sat down next to the old healer. It was easy: you just bent your knees, pretended there was a faded cushion under you, and relaxed. Minnie looked the same: long gray hair dyed flat black, fuzzy bedroom slippers, a plaid apron over the sparkly sweatshirt and pants she got as casino comps from the Rainbow in Wendover.

"See how easy it is?" Minnie laughed. She didn't have the predictable cackle of a ninety-three-year-old. Her laugh was rich and velvety. There were rumors in the tribe that the young men she brought in as apprentices kept her hormones in balance.

"I'm gonna talk Willow to you," Minnie said. "Even though you were too uppity to learn it when you were a girl, you'll understand me. The stuff I have to tell you I can't say in White."

Sarah waited.

"First," Minnie said. The words rolled from her mouth like that sound you hear when you are floating on your back in a river and the current under you is moving the pebbles along the bottom. Sarah thought of the snowmelt stream down off Black Peak, how it would ease across the playa until it disappeared, how she and Will Lucas would lie on their backs where the water poured out of Gray Horse Canyon and pretend they were being carried along, out, out, farther out into the April sun and down, down into the earth.

"Stop thinking of that boy," Minnie said. "You are not listening. Same old same old with you, Sarah Martin."

Sarah looked at Minnie. "I'm sorry, Grandmother. It's strange here, as though you think something and then you are there in the place you're thinking of. I wanted to be there, not here."

"For the newcomer it is strange," Minnie said. "For the impatient girl who hasn't learned what she needs to know." She was quiet.

"First," she said.

Sarah waited.

"First, you will learn to wait." Minnie laughed. "Second, you will learn to gather all your gsi'ki together very tight. Very clean edges. Very solid in their centers. So they can connect. When you do that, the person Over There will be able to see you, hear you. It will be as though you are alive."

"Third, you will learn to dissolve your gsi'ki so nobody can see you. You will be like you are now."

Sarah looked down at her hands folded in her lap. She understood that *gsi'ki* was "molecules" in English, something both the same and very different in Willow. "You mean invisible? I can see myself now."

Minnie touched her arm. "Here it is different," she said. "Over There is where few remember how to see."

Sarah started to ask Minnie what she was talking about, but Minnie ignored her.

"Fourth, you will learn to dissolve and gather your gsi'ki in such a way that you can take a different shape. This is not for evil purposes, not like those who change to play tricks or worse. If there is any badness in your intention, you will be helpless."

Sarah thought how formal Willow sounded to her, how scientific and moral.

"Fifth, you will learn when to gather your gsi'ki and when to dissolve. You will learn when to be something different than you are."

Minnie fell silent. When she spoke again, it was in English. "Do you have questions for me? Only a few. I have just a little time left before I must go back Over There. It is harder to do this when you're ninety-three."

Sarah felt cold. She would be alone again. Maybe forever. "Why should I learn these things?" she asked.

"You are going back Over There," Minnie said. "You have lost something and you have to hunt for it."

Minnie laughed then. "I forgot to tell you. When you are invisible, anything you hold will be invisible. Otherwise people would see one of your damn cigarettes hanging in the air."

MAGGIE had moved through pass out, wake up, drag yourself to bed, wake up, and listen to your heart ricochet off your ribs and pass out again, when suddenly she came to. White light glittered in the crack under the bedroom door. She threw her arm over her eyes and touched something soft. Brown paper, red string, and "Maggie" scrawled in red marker. She tugged at the wrapping.

An indigo shawl spilled out. It had frayed bare in places, but the animals woven into the blue were bright. She traced them with her finger—birds, fish, a sharp-toothed thing that might be a dragon or bear. The other creatures' great oval eyes seemed to be sighting along Orion, or seeing, as cats do, those places humans rarely visit.

Maggie remembered her coworkers at the Winslow Burger King. They had once hauled her out to the local park. In the midst of December starlight and broken beer bottle glitter, they introduced her to the only sufficiently gentle dope she'd ever smoked. They had laid her down on Fat Boy's jacket, covered her with a musty sleeping bag, and told her to look up. She had listened to them giggle, sing a slow chant that could have been the chorus of "Mr. Brownstone," and after a while she had seen things in the stars and the space between them that made her terrified and happy.

"That's why I smoke this shit," Carlena had said. "See those things that make you scared, make you feel good too. That's what makes me a headbanger."

Maggie jammed the shawl under the pillow. "Sarah," she whispered, "where the hell are you?" A word came to her, a word her Pennsylvania Dutch aunt had once taught her: *Zwischenraum* . . . the space between things, and she knew that was exactly where the hell Sarah was.

The worst aspect of a hangover had always been the potential for infinite terror. There were only two cures, one immediate and temporary, the other delayed and supposedly thorough. You could take a drink. Bingo, no problem. Or, you could not take a drink, and face more problems than even you thought you had.

Maggie was not ready for the latter. She mixed gin and OJ, settled back, and trusted in that which restored electrolytes. The pool below her balcony had filled with kids. It was the weekend, when families straggled in to visit Gramps or Grandma, or a distant cousin they didn't see but once a year when they came to the wicked west to party and live for free in somebody's already too small place.

Or the kids arrived alone, stepping off the bus from Phoenix, visiting the parent that hadn't quite made it through the custody nuking. The kids tended to be scrawny or puffy, as though they were raised on Hamburger Helper minus the burger. The girls' eyes were too old, the boys' too frantic. They were at each other, not like animals, because even puppies or kittens all eventually pass out in a warm heap. These kids never stopped moving.

Two going-on teenage girls prowled the edges of the pool. They started to play like kittens and caught themselves, sucking in their flat bellies, sticking out their not-quite-breasts. The girls made Maggie think of Sarah, her barely there breasts and the brooch that glowed between them. Maggie remembered the delicate shift of Sarah's hips when she spotted some long tall Blood stepping slow and gorgeous through the Crystal door. She could see crow light flicker off Sarah's hair. Maggie wanted to yell down to the two girls something wise about being careful what you fish for, but she didn't. Why terrify kids who were probably already scared numb?

She finished off her medicine and considered going to work early—look for Jesse, and if she couldn't find him, somebody close enough. She considered fixing another Orange Blossom and waiting for the phone to ring. When she further considered how it would be to be half-loaded, wearing a nightie that said *I may be a loser, but I ain't no quitter,* and hear a dead woman's voice on the line, Maggie figured Jesse or somebody close would be the wiser option. Must, she thought, have coffee.

She walked carefully into the kitchen, an elegant lurch she had perfected in the last years of raising Deacon by herself. *See. Mom's not drunk. Nope. And, here's your nice warm Chef Boyardee. And, oh yes, a guy I met last night is coming over later.*

She followed leftover coffee with a mouthwash chaser, pulled on a knee-length T-shirt, put in her silver dice earrings, and closed the front door on everything. She was halfway to the Crystal when she remembered she had left the shawl crumpled under the pillow.

JESSE had saved the last of his hashish for a weekend exactly like the one that was stretching out in front of him. He filled the pipe and lit it with a Zippo replica his last girlfriend had brought him back from Hawaii. There was the scent of pine, then the smoke hit the back of his throat like welcome cautery. He sucked it in.

The knife blade was at the delicate last stage. At this point, each strike on the stone could be the one that destroyed it. There was a thin line of red obsidian in the black, not a flaw but a part of the stone. It tied in somehow with something Jesse'd been thinking—about Darwin Yazzie, about the way a man's action can be the flaw and the beauty *in* a matrix. He'd been thinking about night under triple canopy. About a young man's blood.

Jesse flicked the Zippo and held the flame in front of his eyes. Fire was a door. The old Bru had told him that. "You think what you Americans do destroys the Communists with your sky-fire. They know that fire is a door.

Souls go out. Full of sky. It is when you kill with a knife in a certain way that the soul begins to wander and starve."

Jesse wondered, as he always did, if he should have stayed there, should have married Yuan, helped her old man do what he could no longer do. At least he might have learned how to live with what he had learned. At least he would have never met Red Lindall, never would have taken part in what finished off his hope for twenty years.

He shivered. Dope was a persistent guide. He did not want to go where he was headed. Wyoming. Lindall widening the opening to the coyote den, uncapping the gas can and pouring. Jesse could still see the vapor rising, wavering in the sunlight as though one of the headaches was coming on. He had had to remind himself to breathe. Aviation fuel. That fucking smell.

He had talked himself through it: "I'm having a flashback. That's all it is."

They had moved away from the hole. Lindall tossed his lit cigarette into the dark opening. The air shuddered. The dark imploded. Flames blew out from the tunnel. Lindall lit another cigarette. The radio in the work truck went static. Fire crackled in the earth.

I need this job, Jesse had told himself.

Then Lindall had poked a straightened-out coat hanger into the hole and fished out the first charred pup. The little mouth was open wide as it could go and the tiny paws were splayed wide. Jesse had backed away. Lindall looked over at him. Jesse shook his head. "I gotta go," he said, and took off running.

Jesse opened the trailer door, made himself stare at the black mountains and shimmering creosote till his eyes ached, and he knew he was both years and a heartbeat from that coyote den. He closed his eyes and watched hashish flowers blossom on the inside of his lids.

He longed for Maggie. It made him feel weak. Still, he wanted to tell her why they called him Runner. He wanted her to know everything. He wanted her to know about the certainty of suffering and, how once you knew that, you have maybe a shot, if only a tiny shot, at love. "I am *fucked up,*" he said and drew another toke deep into his body.

SARAH studied Minnie's face. "What I lost? Are you talking about Will Lucas?" She wanted that to be the case. Will—not Yakima. But the way Minnie's rules could twist you around to face what you didn't want to see, it just might be that prick. "Or what happened in Seattle? Or what I need to ask my aunt? What are you talking about?"

Minnie smiled. "I am talking about naat'hai." *Naat'hai,* a word that meant "beautiful flying"—the same word in English was "death."

"You remember," Minnie said, "—*if* you were listening when I was telling you kids stories—what happens to a soul that cannot go on."

"We wander," Sarah said. "Forever. In gray. Alone. Always hungry, always eating and always hungry. See, I was listening."

"Do not say *we,* you must not call yourself one of those things. *Here*—and when you go Over There—your words and thoughts are very powerful. Don't say *we* when you speak of those hungry things."

Sarah could feel the pull of Over There. She wanted nothing more than to go back. To Will Lucas. To tell someone what happened in Seattle. To sit next to Maggie playing nickels on those damn machines. To her family. To Bone Lake. "How long will I have Over There?"

"It is different for each soul," Minnie said. "You will know you have to hurry when the gsi'ki begin to lose their hold on each other and you can't gather them back."

Sarah looked at the old woman. She wanted to give her a gift for the lessons she wasn't sure she wanted. She looked for the shawl. It had disappeared. Minnie shook her head. "No, child, you and your friend will need it. Besides, you will see me again. There is a new apprentice—you remember that Black Lake boy. I am not ready to cross over yet."

Her laughter rang out like light. It wrapped Sarah as dawn might, held her long enough for her to be able to smile, and was gone.

5   Orlen Jackson caught himself sliding off a hard plastic chair. He smelled weird green air, not woodsy green, but sick green. He was in the fuckin' va clinic. You could tell by the green air. Always made him think of body bags, and old people, like that place where his Ma had to be right before she'd died. He'd leave that place and no matter how many times he ran his clothes through the Laundromat, he smelled that green smell.

He fetched himself a cup of weak coffee from the big pot. The clock on the wall was busted, but he figured it must be about noon. They had the blinds down, but the light that cut through the broken slats was glare. If he had it right, he'd been sitting in that chair four hours. For five minutes of the VA doc's time.

Orlen knew what the young guy was going to tell him. Porferieea cute-an-ee-a . . . that's as close as he could get to what the kid said last time. "Dioxin." Orlen knew that one, he'd read it in the papers. "Cowbird," the doc had said. "Your liver's fucked. Let's clean up those blisters, and I told you before, you need to find another job. All that axle grease and oil isn't making this better—and cut out the drinking!"

Orlen knew that one, too—heard it a thousand times. It made him want to drink. He finished the lousy coffee, crumpled the cup, and tossed it in the wastebasket. The lady at the front desk didn't even notice him leave. He stepped out into bright mountain air, hitched down to Whisky Row, worked his way, a bar at a time, down Montezuma Street, out Gurley, and then it was night and he was walking and hitching.

He woke for the second time in less than a day not quite knowing where he was. He remembered lying down somewhere for a while, looking up at stars, thinking how the sky looks different in different places but the glory of it stays the same, thinking about what can come down out of all that beauty and the shit that did. This wake-up he realized he was lying under somebody's god-damn fifth wheel in a parking lot in the middle of hot-as-hell, and he wanted to tell somebody: *You think those fuckin' blisters hurt all by their lonesome, you add in a hangover and you'd know why I drink.*

Orlen edged out from under the trailer. He didn't know whether he was glad or sad to see the big purple crystal on top of the dinky casino about fifty feet away. He remembered the last time. Or maybe the time before. Then he remembered he was a Missouri boy and it was a new day.

SOMEBODY had dumped a box of French fries in the Crystal parking lot. Scavenger birds with boat tails, iridescent wings, and bright eyes bounced happily through them. Maggie sidestepped the mess and went into the razzle-dazzle gloom.

Nobody'd seen Jesse. "He's like that," AKA had told her more than once.

"He disappears, then bam, he's back." He'd wondered about that, AKA had told her, but, as we well knew, it didn't pay to wonder too much about anything.

"Can I cut you in?" AKA said, "seeing as how you ain't on till seven." Maggie pulled up a stool and slid her twenty across the felt. Things were nicely warm for a while, up ten, down five, then up thirty steady. There was a friendly half-circle of players, mostly regulars out of Kingman or Bullhead. Maggie played prudently, a keep-it-simple, sweetheart count AKA had taught her.

AKA went off his shift. Larry stepped in without a word. The regulars liked that. They didn't need to be chatted up. Larry's silence let them believe for a few hands that they were as hip as they had once believed themselves to be.

An hour later, Maggie was up eighty bucks. She looked down at her modest winnings and up to the lounge, where there were two distinct possibilities for trouble, and one lanky snake-eyed most probable.

"You in?" Larry said.

"Later." She tipped him out. His face didn't change expression.

Maggie steered herself away from the possibility of the bar. Never cruise on an empty stomach—and sat down at Food for the Soul. Sue, Leola's best friend, set Maggie's lunch in front of her without asking. The workers got the Special for the Day. Didn't matter if they liked it; if they wanted to eat for free, they ate the dread employee special. Friday it was ribs. They were slathered with industrial-strength bottled sauce and accompanied by genuine Texas cowboy beans, which, like their namesakes, were remarkable in having no taste. Maggie sighed and dug in.

Leola caught the sigh and smiled her dead-frog smile. "We do like to put out a nice plate. Not like those so-called gourmet buffets. You won't find any cheap shortcuts here."

"Sorry," Maggie said. "I feel like shit."

Leola's smile cracked for as long as it took her to figure out something new might have happened on Planet Sarcasm. "Maggie, are you OK?"

"Scuse me," a voice said cheerfully, "can I snatch you guyses Tabasco sauce?"

Leola reached the sauce across Maggie's shoulder to the voice.

"Thank you, ladies."

Leola frowned. She was not partial to Red-skins, Nee-groes, Mexkins,

Eyetalians, or A-rab ragheads. And, above and beyond all these goddamn foreigners, she deeply hated Hipp-eye types. This Hipp-eye type held out his hand. "I'm Orlen Jackson, otherwise known as Cowbird. Pleased to meet you ladies."

Leola flapped a napkin at him. "You wash up," she said. "Look at you."

"If you don't mind, ma'am," Cowbird said. "I just cleaned up in the men's room." Sue patted Leola on the shoulder and took Cowbird's order for hot water. When she brought it, he shook in the Tabasco. "I need me a pick-me-up."

Maggie grinned. She knew the feeling. "I'll get you the all-day Breakfast Special if you'll tell me why your name is Cowbird."

"You know them birds scarf up the leftovers in the parking lot? Cowbirds is them. Plus me. Cowbird, as in A. I got no regular home. B. Somebody else raised my kids and I don't mind. C. In the right light, I look good. And D. I get by."

"Oh my gawd," the little old man next to Cowbird said. "Microbes. Everywhere." He fluttered his hands over his plate. Age had shriveled him so he was half-swallowed in a red sweatshirt with the vicious Raiders guy on it.

It worried Maggie that none of this seemed strange; in fact, if she had to put a word on it, "comfort" came to mind. "One Breakfast Special," she yelled to Leola.

SARAH sat in the shadow of the fake palms below Maggie's place. She was getting used to being invisible, though she still flinched every time one of the kids ran through her. She was surprised to feel hungry, surprised to find a purse on the deck next to her leg.

"We'll give you what you need," Minnie had said. "Within reason."

There was five bucks in the purse. "Within reason," Sarah said. "You got that right." She walked into the ladies' room. The place was empty. She locked herself in a stall and began to gather her gsi'ki. She wondered if she remembered it right. There was no real feeling, just what would have been shivers in her former body.

Kids' voices burst into the room. "Mindy," a little girl said, "don't go in that one. There's a lady in there. You can see her sneakers."

I did it, Sarah thought. She rested her face on the cool metal door. I can feel, she thought. She pushed open the door. Three little girls washed their hands at the sink. The oldest saw Sarah in the mirror. "Hi," she said, "we're visiting our mom. Our dad is in Riverside. I'm not supposed to talk to strangers."

"You don't have to worry," Sarah said gently. "I live here."

JESSE duct-taped black cloth over the windows of the trailer. As he worked, he remembered his mother talking about the older war, about how his grandfather had sat in the straight-backed chair in the hallway, an empty rifle held in his lap. By that time, the old man had forgotten any English he had learned. He would whisper in Hungarian, words Jesse's mother didn't know.

"I felt so stupid," she had said. "My father spoke five languages, my mother six. I was a stupid American, stupid about everything but hiding behind blackout curtains, stupid about teaching you kids what was important."

Jesse's father had worked the three jobs that had killed him. His mother's spells had led her to the expensive men in white coats, the men who told his father she needed shock treatments, the men whose useless knowledge cost thousands of dollars, and his mother's life. "We don't know what happened. With shock treatments there are always risks."

Jesse taped the last strip of cloth over the window in the trailer door. Now there was no way to know whether it was morning or night. Now he could get on with it, let it take as long as it took. He sat on the couch when all he wanted to do was to throw open the door, climb in the truck, head into Creosote, and find somebody, anybody, who wanted to talk. He would listen. Through the gravel radio playing in his head, he would listen.

"Jesus," he thought, "I am a joke. Another fucked-up loser grunt stuck in a time that was more real than anything since."

He wished what he knew was coming was over. And, he knew the only way to reach the end was to let it begin. He lit the candle on the table next to him, opened the book, and read the words he knew by heart: . . . He couldn't forget them. There had been a river, the Dak Bla. American planes had sprayed defoliant on its banks. Later, the corpses of fish had clogged the water. Thread of blood came from their mouths. They were poison red around the gills. "When we cut into them," an old villager seemed to whisper in Jesse's mind, "they flared strangley, like matches."

He closed the book. When he held his hands around the candle flame, he saw his bones inside his radiant flesh. He was careful not to burn himself. This was not about some religious idea of expiation.

This was harder.

BONNIE MADRID stubbed her smoke out in the planter and went back into the Riverbelle ladies' room to repair the damage to her mascara caused by what Caroline had told her about Beltran and that baby bitch wannabe named Chi Chi.

In the ten minutes she'd been gone, somebody had scratched *Adi is a ho* on the door of the handicapped stall. Bonnie sighed and looked in the mirror. Her mascara was gone, but the pink in her eyes had faded. She freshened up her makeup and went out to fill in a form for Lou, the security guard, so he could fill out a form for Ronnie, nobody was quite sure what he was, so he could fill out a form for Rico, who was the emperor of the physical plant and who'd gotten the corpogods to pass a rule that *all* employees had to be on the alert for damage to the physical plant.

Lou was behind the security podium watching the keno runners' butts. As soon as he spotted Bonnie, he picked up a pen and made like he was actually working.

"Bad news, Lou," she said. "I gotta fill out a vandalism report."

Lou frowned. This meant he would have to bend over and look for the forms, which was *really* bad news since he weighed three hundred plus pounds.

"You sure?"

"I'm sure," Bonnie said. "Somebody scratched 'Adi is a ho' on the handicapped door."

"For chrissake," he said. "Rico had the boys paint that room a month ago."

"You're so welcome," Bonnie said under her breath. She stretched the report out as long as she could, smoked another cigarette, listened to Lou grouse about the suits that ran the show. "Yeah, give me the days with The Boys. They had class. They knew when to trust a guy and when to fuck him up."

"Unless you were a chick," Bonnie said. "All they got was fucked up. You can take those days."

"Hey," Lou said, "I'm sorry I'm such a whiner. It's been a shitty morning. Cops all over the place 'cause of that Indian chick that got killed. Those guys act like they're the only ones with any brains. You know what I mean?"

"I sure do," Bonnie said.

"Thanks, sister."

"No problem," she said. "If you see Beltran, tell him I'm on till eleven."

"Bonnie?" Lou said. "You mean the guy, still that guy, oh fuck, never mind . . ."

"You got it," Bonnie said.

MAGGIE finished her BBQ, tipped Sue out, and decided to walk down by the river. You could get to the river two ways: walk the main drag to the bridge while suicidal drunks and blue hairs on heart medication played bumper cars around you, or go out the Crystal back door to the gravel bank fifty feet above the water. You walked across broken glass and half-chewed grackle feathers, past sleeping drunks who looked like piles of junk and bloated bodies that turned out to be garbage bags.

The river at full noon was flat as a roadkill snake. Maggie held down the barbed wire that kept nobody from the Palm Springs Development Company's private chunk of riv, climbed over, and picked her way down the slope. She crouched at shoreline. Pebbles shone under the water. Maggie scooped up a palmful, silver-rose blood-rock veined with turquoise; dull gray holding the whorl of an ancient shell.

She raised her eyes to the blue blade of sky. Later, swallows would hunt in and out of its fading light. They would dip and skitter, sunset glowing on their underbellies like pearl, twilight turning them to shadows. She'd once seen a kid jump off the bridge in the first moment of dark. He was a black arrow against the molten pour of headlights. The birds parted for him, swirled back, and he was gone.

"Hey miss," a man yelped. The Cowbird skidded down the slope. "Hope I'm not intruding."

"No way."

"That's kind of you," he said. He hunkered down at the water's edge. "You work here?"

"I waitress at the Crystal. If you need a job, I could talk to somebody."

"See," Cowbird said, "I'd like that, but I'm on kind of R'N'R. A doc told me I've gotta make some changes."

"Welcome to the club," Maggie said.

Cowbird laughed. "Back home, we would of said, 'Sometimes you're the hammer, sometimes you're the thumb.'"

Maggie handed him two green chips, enough for a couple weeks' food. "They give it to me, I give it to you," she said. "I just would of given it back to them sooner than later."

"You needn't to do that," he said. "I can take care of myself."

"I know that," Maggie said. "You're the Cowbird."

He ducked his head. "Thank you, miss. I mean it."

"I gotta get back," Maggie said. They climbed the slope. She gained ten yards, felt the sun's weight like a shot of Thorazine, and slowed down. By the time she caught her breath and reached the asphalt, Cowbird was gone.

SARAH stood in front of Maggie's door. She'd been wondering if it would be a worse jolt for Maggie to answer a knock and find her there, or to have a few omens before the big surprise. She'd decided on omens.

Minnie had taught her how to dissolve gsi'ki just long enough to move through solid objects. Sarah checked out the balcony that ran the length of the second floor. There was nobody around. She followed Minnie's instructions and found herself standing in Maggie's tiny front hallway. She gathered back her gsi'ki, set the groceries on the kitchen counter, and wished Minnie were with her, wished she could see the old woman's mica eyes, hear that twilight laugh, have Minnie say, "You are not crazy, girl. This is real."

She pulled out a package of Pop-Tarts and dropped a couple in the toaster. They would be the first thing she had eaten since before her death. She wondered what they'd taste like. They were apple-cinnamon. The scent began to rise from the toaster, and she realized she was hungry, not starved hungry, just hungry.

ZACH MARTINEZ was half Anglo, which meant when he was in Albuquerque for the Dad half of his life, he had no friends. The white kids wouldn't hang with a smart chunky Mexican, and the homeys took one look at his pale blue eyes and wrote him off as a pinche gringo.

His second favorite moment in life was when the doors closed on the Vegas-bound Greyhound bus in Albuquerque and he looked out to see his dad, Dr. Carlos Martinez, and his stepmom, Mrs. Dr. Vicki Jennings-Martinez, waving good-bye.

His total favorite moment was when the bus doors opened onto the parking lot of the Riverbelle Casino in Creosote and he stepped out into the perfect neon air for the Mom half of his life. That moment had come.

It was midnight. He could smell river and he knew exactly who he was. Zach made himself walk slowly down to the riverbank. He was alone on the dark beach. The water was black and shiny. More than anything he wanted to run into the Belle and find his mom. Instead, he lifted his Guadalupe necklace off, the one his mother had given him even though she was born again and not too sure about the Virgin Mary. Pink and green neon sparkled over the Virgin. He dipped it into the water. "Thank you, Our Lady," he said. "Muchas gracias, Nostra Señora."

Then, even more slowly, he climbed the steps to the Riverstroll. It was the next part of the ritual. He was a kid, but he'd learned that if you hold off joy, it makes it even better. He stopped to say hello to the fat koi fish shining in the moat around the Riverbelle. "I'll be back," he said, "after Mom and me have breakfast. I'm getting an extra waffle for you guys."

Then, he was at the smoked-glass back doors of the Riverbelle. He could see the faint glow of slot neon. He set down his duffel bag and leaned his skateboard against his leg. He almost wanted to cry. He pushed open the doors. It was the first hit of cold smoky air against his face that brought his tears. He was home.

Frank, the lanky security guard who Zach's mom said reminded her of a heron, was up behind the podium. He saw Zach and said in a bored voice, "Sorry kid, you gotta get off the floor."

"It's me," Zach said. "Caroline's kid."

"Holy shit," Frank said, "I didn't recognize you. I thought you was some goofy punk. How you got your hair and all."

"Thanks," Zach said.

Frank laughed. "I'll call your mom. She's just about off her shift."

COWBIRD used the green chips the only reasonable way a sensible man would. He cashed them in and headed for the 3/6 Texas Hold'em table. The regulars were there: Crick, the middle-aged limey who dressed like he was Shaft; Monica, who always talked about being affluent and in some club for smart people; and that prick, Beltran. There were a few newbies, a bluehair couple in matching wind suits, and a Negro gal.

The Negro gal was a big woman. And most unusual looking. Cowbird watched as she gathered her cards in with the tips of her long fingernails. Her nail polish was the exact red of Gallo burgundy. She had rouge on her cheeks and forehead. There was a gold screw in her right earlobe.

He picked up his cards. Diamond Queen, Heart Queen, all the rest shit. The Negro gal scooted the ashtray next to her. She lit a cigarette that smelled like cloves. Cowbird wondered why he was noticing so much about her. He had nothing against colored people, but it had been twenty years since he'd been with a woman he hadn't paid. He guessed from her perfume and the six gold bangles on each wrist that she might be a working girl who was definitely out of his reach.

"Excuse me," she said, "would you mind not staring at me?" Beltran nodded. He had his cold-ass "mi vaqueros will be waiting for you outside" expression on his face.

Cowbird looked down at his cards. "I'm sorry, ma'am," he said. "I was just, I don't know, I was just wondering where you got them clove cigarettes. I ain't smelled them since 1969."

She held out the pack. "Go ahead. Try one. You don't inhale with these, but they kinda help with the jitters."

Cowbird took a cigarette. He was in the shit now. He hadn't smoked in years and he didn't want to start. "I'll save it for after I haul in the pot," he said.

The woman laughed. "You gonna have to catch up with me and Beltran, cracker."

The dealer glared. "No racial talk here," he said. "You know the rules."

"Wasn't no racial talk," the woman said. "Just calling a Ritz a Ritz."

MAGGIE'S shift slid by—not a good night, not bad. She pulled out of the parking lot and considered stopping for an answering machine tape at the all-night Maverick on the AZ side. She kept driving. Sarah could stay put. Jesse-Runner could find her at the usual place. It was time for the poor and hungover woman's tranquilizer: crackers and warm milk.

The apartment was almost cool. She buttered some crackers, nuked a mug of milk, and found a burned Pop-Tart in the toaster. It was weird. Maggie was pretty sure she hadn't bought or seen one of the things since Deac had left. She wondered if she'd had a blackout, started to yank the Pop-Tart out, and didn't want to touch it. She automatically checked the incoming call light on the tapeless answering machine. It was flashing. "Oh no you don't," she said firmly. "I'm not coming over there."

A thin glow came from her bedroom and was gone. Maggie checked the room. Everything was the same, one-twentieth the inventory of the Creosote Bookmobile scattered around the bed, dresser cluttered with pebbles, earrings, shells, a bottle of almond oil in case she got lucky, a Virgen de Guadalupe candle in case the nuns had been right, and her only bona fide souvenir, a tin Mexican candleholder, holding two badger skulls and the tattered wings of a luna moth. Same old same old. Except the shawl was stretched neatly across the bed.

Maggie set her crackers and milk carefully on the nightstand. She was scared to touch the shawl, but nowhere to run, baby. She picked it up and began wrapping herself in it, running her hand over birds, fish, and star-beings. Blue light crackled under her fingers. Just static. She slid carefully into bed, leaned back against the pillows, and ate her crackers, every crumb, and washed them down with milk, every drop. When the phone rang, she sat it out.

She licked the salt and milk from her lips. Nothing could happen to a person who had carefully chewed a few 99-Cent Store crackers, and had had nothing to drink for sixteen hours and twelve minutes but milk. The phone rang and stopped. The bedroom door moved.

OK, Maggie thought. I give up. If I make it to morning, I'll drive immediately to the generic twelve-step meeting in the baccarat room at the Moonglow Casino, sit down with the other lost souls, and say, "Hi, I'm Maggie. I'm a nutcase."

"I wish it were that simple," Sarah's voice said. "Believe me, it's not."

Maggie pulled the shawl tight around her and smelled cedar. Sarah stepped into the light.

"Sarah," Maggie said. Sarah nodded. She wore her second-best dress-up outfit, skin-tight black Wranglers and a French-cut indigo tee with *Girlfriend* picked out in rhinestones. There wasn't a mark on her. Her dark eyes were harsh. "You should have said something to those little girls by the pool," she said. "How it can get dangerous for a girl."

"Oh shit," Maggie said, "have I hit bottom?"

"No such luck." Sarah leaned against the wall. "But *they* might." She lit a cigarette. "You didn't return my message."

"You didn't leave a number." Maggie closed her eyes. When she opened them, Sarah was still there. "Plus, why are you acting so tough?"

Sarah smiled. "I'm practicing," she said. "I don't feel very tough."

"Do you disappear with the sun or anything like that?" Maggie said. She realized she was so happy to see Sarah she wasn't afraid of what must be a psychotic episode.

"No way. None of that stuff is true. No vampires, no werewolves. Just people's sorrows, people's vengeance hanging around." Sarah held her hand up to the mirror. "Look, I have a reflection. But there are Empty Skins, Maggie. There are hungry ghosts. There is, most definitely, evil."

Maggie smoothed the shawl, as though she could put things to order. This was not the Sarah she played slots with, the woman who'd lose, grin, and say, "Hey, I'm a real Indian. We are a simple but spiritual people."

Sarah wished things could go back to what they were. She realized she understood what Maggie was thinking, and that trying to talk with a live person could get a little cluttered. She decided to really keep it simple. Because she missed how it was, because she didn't like being in the same room with her friend and missing her.

"When you were playing blackjack today," Sarah said, "there were three of those Empty Skins at the bar, not together, they're never really together, but there were three of 'em."

Maggie remembered the two possibles and the snake-eyed probable. "No," she whispered. "I don't believe in that shit."

Sarah remembered when she would have once said the same thing. "Well," she said. "It takes a while." She tucked the shawl around Maggie's shoulders. "This, I've had it since I was little. When I was scared I used to hold it close to my eyes and those things that you can't tell what they are would seem like dragons to me and I'd feel a little safer."

Maggie stared at her. "Sarah, you mean *you* don't know what they are?"

"I'm afraid so," Sarah said. "Listen, I have to go for a little bit. I'll be back."

"Wait."

"One more thing. That shawl is for your eyes only."

"Wait. Are you really coming back?"

Sarah was gone. Morning burned through the window.

"Did it hurt?" Maggie said. "Did you pass out before it hurt? I've got to know."

Sarah paused in the foyer. She didn't want to remember. She wouldn't. She knew Maggie could not see her. She knew Maggie knew she was there. She stepped forward and opened the door.

"OK," Maggie said. "It's your call."

6   Jesse drove into Creosote just as the sun floated down behind the glittering bulk of Traintown. Things seemed to be coming apart. He knew he ought to just, as they say, sit on his hands, but a week alone behind the blackout cloth hadn't worked its usual hard alchemy. He'd thought about calling Maggie, but he knew the wreck he might make of what seemed to be their maybe one shot at love. He'd called his ex-wife Cheyenne, and she'd reminded him of the last time they tried again, and why she was now happily married to a very boring guy in Dayton, Ohio.

You wanted to change your luck, you did things different. So, he took himself into the Crystal not in the morning, but in the blue twilight. He didn't rush things. He ate a prime rib special, got a couple straight tequilas under his belt, and sat down at Rikki's table. She was a tiny Filipina, her hands wide and strong. "I'm not from that hole Manila," she had once told a customer. "I'm from Mindanao. I'm a country girl and we don't take bad manners from nobody. When you do good, you say thank you. Like we do. In Tagalog. 'Salaamat.'"

"Hey, Jesse mon," Rikki said. Her boyfriend was Jamaican. "How's da presshuh?"

Jesse shook his head. "Deal me an escape valve, I'll be OK."

Rikki dealt. Queen of diamonds, ace of spades for him. Six of diamonds, ten of clubs for her. Jesse waited. Rikki dealt her third card. Six of hearts. Bust. Jesse scooped up his chips and tossed her a big red.

Roselle sat down at the end of the table. "Honey," she said for the hundredth time in Jesse's memory, "get ready. 'Cause I ain't no cliché. Never was. Never will be." She ran her long fingers over the eagle tattoo across the tops of her wrinkled breasts. "This is not some wannabe yuppie Harley bird. This is the real deal."

Rikki dealt. She had a six. Jesse checked his first card. Sweet sweet Jack o' Diamonds. Second card a nine of clubs. Roselle looked at her card and grinned. "More please." Rikki flipped over a six. Roselle pressed her hand to the eagle. "More." Rikki kept going: four. Jesse grinned at Roselle. She had her eyes closed.

"Please please please," Roselle said.

Rikki turned over her second card: five. Third card: two. Fourth card: nine. Roselle opened her eyes, checked out Rikki's bust hand, looked down between her breasts at the eagle head, and said, "Thank you, baby."

She turned a brilliant smile on Jesse. A side-tooth was missing, her lipstick chewed off. "See," she said, "a genuine Indian princess drew the tattoo for me. She said eagles bring luck. I sent you some."

Jesse nodded. "I reckon you did."

Rikki turned over his cards.

"Salaamat," Jesse said, and tipped in American.

Roselle blushed. "You can touch the eagle if you want. You're a gentleman, not like some."

Jesse traced the arc of the eagle's primaries. "Beautiful. Absolutely the real deal."

Roselle gathered up her chips and headed for the cashier.

Rikki pulled in the cards. "She was once so beautiful," she said quietly.

Jesse stacked his bet. "You can see that."

Rikki began the deal. Even though there were a handful of players at the table, they were tourists, so it was like Jesse and Rikki were alone. They knew it. The tourons didn't.

A dozen deals went down. Jesse was on automatic. Not thinking. Aware of everything. He knew what all real players know. A good hand falls down like the Virgin descending on Guadalupe. A blessing now in place. Ace of clubs.

Jack of clubs. The dealer goes bust and you raked in two hundred bucks just like that. A miracle. A fucking shower of coins. A woman could drop into your life the same way.

"Jesse," Rikki said. "Ground Control to Jesse. You in?"

He nodded. The waitress stopped by. He ordered another tequila. He could tell this was going to be a long lucky lonesome night.

He hung in till midnight, then walked away up fourteen hundred bucks. Two months' expenses. He stepped out of the casino into bath-warm air and the sound of jackhammers over by Traintown. He was startled at just how lonely he felt—for Maggie's trip-wire brain, for how they could be together and not talk. He found Roselle in the front seat of her old Lincoln, curled in on herself, the doors unlocked. He let himself in and held her while she slept.

He was mostly awake, and when he did sleep he dreamed of Dook'o'ooslííd. That mountain had brought him home to Flagstaff, brought him back more or less alive, brought him home carrying the weight of the absolute absence of Darwin Yazzie, his best high school friend, the guy he'd mixed blood with, cut wrist pressed to cut wrist, just before they left for Nam. "Now you're part 'Skin," Darwin had laughed. "Can't get killed if you're a 'Skin."

And Jesse had been left to wonder if his blood, as white blood always did, had thinned Darwin's, had tampered with the protection Darwin's Grandpa had woven, so the jungle that spared Jesse still held Darwin's vaporized bones.

Jesse rested his face on Roselle's warm back. He felt his failure to prevent Darwin's death pressing on his shoulders like stone wings.

SARAH sat on the edge of the Riverbelle's boat ramp. The carp drifted below her. They were the one animal she wouldn't feed. They had scared her the first time she saw them, their big black bodies, their huge mouths gaping open, bright pink, looking like a wound or some weird doorway to a place you didn't ever want to go.

Like Yakima. That Apple activist, Yakima—red on the outside, rotten white at the core. Shit, she was thinking about Yakima. She thought about Yakima all the time. She didn't want to think about Yakima all the time. She didn't want to think about Yakima at all. She decided she would ask Minnie what to do, how to get rid of a ghost of a living man who'd been, in his words, joined with her at the level of DNA, and who had altered so completely that he might as well have been dead.

"Get out," she muttered. "Get out of my mind."

Minnie hobbled down the boat ramp. "Hey," she said. "You got something you need mended?"

"Oh no, not me. Shoot, Minnie, if you know what's broken, why don't you just mend it. I know, I know, I'm supposed to ask, otherwise the teacher can't teach, blah blah."

"Uh uh, girl," Minnie said, "that's some of the mumbo jumbo that professor told you. Willow way doesn't have rules like that. Besides, I got somebody for you to meet. He says he's a Hopi guy, but he could be any tribe. Watch out for him. Indian guys are always telling stories, thinking they can talk their way into you know what."

Sarah looked up. The man came past Minnie. From what she could see, he made the carp look good. Then he turned his head the other way and it was all she could do to not jump up and run into his arms. "Will Lucas," she said. "How did you get here?"

Minnie laughed. "See, he got you. He ain't Will."

The man held out his hand. Sarah understood she was to rise to her feet. She took his hand and he pulled her up to face him. When he spoke, his voice was wind moving through her hair.

"I'm the first but I'm also the last. You know I am near when you gaze across the dark that lies under the moon that cannot be seen, and far away you see small fires moving and you don't know what they are. I dance. I consume.

"I emerged from this river. I hail a cab in Vegas, pass out in the gutter in Reno. I am the breath gurgling in the open chest wound and I breathe in the dying child's mouth and give it life. I am lightning sprung from the rocks near Ash Springs, rocketing across the sky to a heart in the red dirt highlands. I am the hidden shrapnel that journeys across an ocean in a boy's flesh, is still for twenty years, then moves into the inner river of blood and washes up in a grown man's heart.

"At first when you see my face, you turn away. Burned flesh, black holes where my eye once was, my nose part gone, my mouth a cave, big enough to hold you and all you dream of. You look again. You cannot help yourself."

Sarah made herself look into the crater that had been an eye. The man turned. She gazed into the familiar warmth of Will Lucas's brown eye.

"I am beautiful. I am young, my hair long and black. In the flickering shadows you think you see a blackbird. I have painted my face with hematite and hung turquoise around my neck. Take a bead."

She held out her hand. Something cool and round lay in her palm. She saw nothing but sun on her skin.

"There. By all that I love, by gossip and betrayal, by compassion and desire, by juniper and sandalwood, iron and quartz, by rabbit and boar, by the Mother River that winds and roars through Mother Canyon to Mother Sea and breaks on the Asian beaches where so many of your men have come to me, I bring you home.

"Do what you will. I have made you mine."

Sarah looked down. She held a pebble of turquoise so dark it was nearly black. Her hands tingled. She threw the bead into the water. The carp gathered and the bead was gone.

The man laughed and was gone. Minnie was gone, leaving only the last of her laughter and her voice. "See. I told you how those Hopi guys are. Fancy talkers."

THE TEXAS HOLD'EM PLAYERS were thinning out. Crick muttered something about having to make an important business call and headed for the pay phones. Beltran busted early and left. The Negro gal hauled in five pots in a row. Cowbird was near broke. He gathered in what was left. Twenty bucks.

The gal looked up. "You leaving?"

"I got no choice," he said cheerfully. "Plus it's 11:03, so that steak'n'eggs special is on in the Blue Velvet Room."

Bonnie Madrid considered her stacks of chips, considered the stubby guy in the pearl-snapped Western shirt, considered his grin. She saw that his belly was clearly the graveyard for more than a few steak'n'eggs specials, and he'd just made a useless effort to slick back his hair. It was kind of cute that he wore what the hippie kids used to call "granny glasses." They were duct-taped, and the gray eyes behind them were friendly. "Tell you what, baby," Bonnie said, "how about if I come along?"

Cowbird's mouth went dry. Twenty bucks minus two $1.99 steak'n'egg

specials, beverage not included, wouldn't leave him enough for a hand job.
"I," he said, "I beg your pardon . . ."

The gal laughed. "No, not like that darlin.' I'm too wired to go to sleep and I don't want to eat alone." She held out her hand. "I'm Bonnie Madrid."

Cowbird tucked the twenty in his breast pocket. He was suddenly very happy he'd put on his last clean shirt. He took Bonnie Madrid's hand in his. "I'm Orlen," he said. "Jackson. Some folks call me Cowbird."

"Now," Bonnie said, "that has got to be a story. I'm starved. You can tell me all about it while we eat."

She stood. Cowbird wondered how she could be starving. There was a lot of Bonnie Madrid rising from the chair. Fine big chest, fine big butt, fine big legs. He asked the dealer for change, tipped him a five. Bonnie Madrid slipped her arm through his, and Cowbird said, "I'd like to buy you breakfast, ma'am."

Bonnie smiled down at him. "I'd be honored, sir."

ZACH sat on his duffel bag at the foot of the security podium. There was not much in the bag but his clothes, his CD player, and a few CDs. He'd left his laptop in Albuquerque, since his mom had told him there was a surprise, which he bet was a new computer since her old one had died of menopause. He wondered how a mom who was an Arkansas born-again Christian could be truly funny, and then he remembered that his dad, who was big on *the only intelligent concept of god, small g, Zach, is a mystery,* had never said a funny thing in his life.

"Hey," his mom said, and she was standing there with her arms wide open and he was in them, A-frame hug, and away before he started to cry again.

"You," she said. "Look at you."

Frank cleared his throat. "Caroline, you know I've gotta get him off the floor."

"No big thing," she said. "I want us where Bonnie can see him though. She was socked in at the 3/6 table a few minutes ago, but she's not there now."

"Go sit on the stairs," Frank said, "that way the kid's not on the casino floor, which as you know, is strictly illegal." He winked at Zach. Caroline picked up Zach's duffel bag despite him trying to wrestle it away from her, and they climbed to the fourteenth step of the double-wide red and gold staircase that swooped down to the casino floor.

It was the perfect seat. Nobody went up and down the steps at 3:00 a.m. All the old ladies and geezers took the elevator, or if they were feeling frisky, the escalator, on which, Zach's mom says, you can breathe and see what's going on; plus you don't have to figure how high you'd have to jump if the thing crashed.

"Aunt Bonnie still honing her skills?" Zach asked.

His mom shook her head. "Must be. I just hope that Beltran isn't at the table. God help her." Her voice trailed off. "You know what, honey? It's none of my business, that's what." She pulled her beat-up Bible out of her purse and opened it on her lap.

Zach nodded. Aunt Bonnie, who wasn't really his aunt, what with being in her words, "a true and glorious African-American Queen," was the most fun of any grown-up he'd ever known. Even though she was strict about how kids should be raised and would not curse in his presence, though she didn't care what he said, as long as it wasn't the N-word, or gangsta garbage.

Zach looked down at the casino floor. It was like a kaleidoscope made of rubies and emeralds and diamonds, old women and punks, foreigners, guys who looked like they didn't know it wasn't 1975—and girls. He studied the babe waitresses wearing few clothes and pretended to look at the bible his mom had in her lap. This was his real Christmas. Oh yes, Feliz Navidad, amigo.

JESSE was awake most of the night, a little crazy by dawn. He was seeing the casino lights as flares, heard the traffic as the whine of a huge animal. Roselle moved away from him. He watched a delicate green dawn flow up from the Cerbat Range. He eased his arm out from under her and slipped a Franklin in her pocket. He wanted coffee bad enough—and fast enough—to go to Food for the Soul. He hoped it would either wash Darwin from his mind, or bring him up sharp enough to know what the fuck came next.

7 Maggie woke to the phone. Noon light slanted across her thighs like a hot hand. She jump-started to catch the phone, stopped, and wrapped the shawl around her. She wanted something around her strong as the look she'd seen on dead Sarah's face.

She caught the phone on the sixth ring. Jesse ran his gypsy pitch. He had new desert for her and some surprises in store. Maggie didn't understand the knot that tightened in her gut. She hoped it was an artifact. She put it off to not enough sleep and the shock of seeing a dead friend in her bedroom and talking with her more or less as though they'd parted the day before after a few hours losing nickels.

"In an hour?" Jesse said.

"Make it two." She wanted him to walk through the door that instant, but she had to have a little routine time as her own. And, she knew the number one rule of guys: the guy is the hunter, the chick is the prey. Better to be the flame than the moth.

She set coffee dripping, scrambled an egg, then took everything to the balcony and set her plate next to a black glass ashtray. The tail end of one of Jesse's roaches was stuck in the ashes. It was good stuff, no seeds. She loved the smell—forest floor after rain, wet dog fur, and something like the smell that comes up off high school lovers when all they can do is neck.

She tried to think about the night before and couldn't. If it wasn't real, she was crazy. If it was real, there were no words for how her life had changed. She wanted a drink—nothing spectacular, maybe just a beer, maybe just a nice warm mug of Thorazine. She wanted to play Cleopatra till her eyeballs spun.

She sat tight. A gal with her kind of memories was not great company. But for the next hour and fifty-three minutes till the doorbell rang, that was what she had.

"I can't believe it's morning," Bonnie Madrid said. Cowbird couldn't believe she'd just ordered another Blue Velvet Fresh-Made Strawberry Creme Waffle. He had never seen a woman eat the way this woman ate.

"I've got an idea," she said. "Finish that story about the topless chick, I'll eat my waffle, and then we can head out to my place."

Cowbird checked his pocket; he had six dollars and seventy-five cents after the second waffle was paid for. Bonnie slapped his wrist. "Get over that, Ritz. This is about being friends."

Cowbird didn't know if he was glad or sad about that news, so he just went back to his story. "So, this fat suit and his flunkies sit down at this little table at the edge of the stage. Minette's dancing. She is coked out of what teeny little brain she's got.

"The suit puts a fifty between his teeth and leans forward. Minette yells, 'I'm yours, big darlin,' and jumps off the stage. She lands ass-first on the table, the table goes over, the chairs go flying.

"When the air clears, the boss is lying on his back with Minette on his chest. She's laughing so hard her makeup's running down her face. Because the boss's toupee is lying a foot away looking like a rat-ugly dead cat."

"You know," Bonnie said, "I might of known that sister."

CAROLINE set the laptop on the table next to Zach's bed and slid in the CD. She waited till the words appeared: "Jay Adams: The Original Virus." Zach opened one eye. Caroline turned up the volume and sat at the foot of the bed.

Zach reached over and clicked on Bio. "Jay Adams," he whispered. "Jay Adams. Oh my god, Mom, this is unbelievable. Thank you. You are an honorary dude!

"Mom, this guy nailed it. He says that Jay couldn't be put into any category. He says that Jay was a total wizard—like he should of got a patent for what he did.

"He says Jaw as a *virus*! Like Jay was the microbe that spread to all of us. This guy's an old guy and he gets it, how a kid could just be so weird and true and for real.

"But this is the best part: he says that when he watched him skate—how lucky can a dude get?—Jay did something new every time. Like he destroyed the old and made what never was. There's this expression, 'Skate and destroy.' He says Jay was the complete king of that."

"The original virus," Zach whispered. "Skate and destroy."

"First," Caroline said, "you eat breakfast."

JESSE was a shadow in the doorway. "Hey, it's me," he said. "We're going bird-watching."

"Right," Maggie said.

"Really." He picked up the cooler and carried it to the truck. He'd set a tub of ice and water on the floor for her. "You know how you greenhorns are. You still got the north in your blood." She climbed in, kicked off her flip-flops, stuck her bare feet in up to the ankles, and settled back. He was steady at the wheel, packing and lighting his hash pipe without missing a trick or drawing heat. She watched with absolute pleasure his small beat-up hands on the steering wheel and how the muscles in his arms bunched and relaxed.

They crossed the bridge to Bullhead. Jesse wove in and out of the terminal Bullhead traffic, deft as a hawk on a thermal. Maggie felt her blood cool, the knot in her gut loosen. She was about to tell Jesse about Sarah when she saw the couple walking along the edge of the asphalt, the cloud-dark bruises on the woman's upper arm, the skinny baby in the guy's arms.

Jesse was oblivious. He slid Santana into the player. The *Supernatural* album. "Put Your Lights On." The guitars began, one a pulse, the second a wail. They carried you steady, they floated you up. Maggie closed her eyes.

Jesse took a long hit off the pipe. He loved seeing how peaceful she seemed. He wished they could just keep on driving. Time would hold still. They'd find a place, north maybe, around Jackpot, or farther, eastern Oregon, obsidian world. He'd feel exactly the way he did that moment, and with that thought he felt the change begin.

He tried to fight it. Maggie's face suddenly seemed not relaxed, but sneaky, as though she was faking the calm. He tried to concentrate on the road. Suddenly, the strip malls lining the highway were pure glare. His eyes ached. He thought of what happened to Sarah, he couldn't stop thinking of what happened to Sarah, and he thought of lesser cruelties, of the self-inflicted sucker punch of doing exactly what you know will result in your solitude. Guaranteed.

MAGGIE jolted awake. They rolled past pale olive eucalyptus and feathery tamarisk. Her mouth was dry. She wanted to tell Jesse about Sarah's visit. She said, "Jesse, there's this weird . . ." He frowned. His jaw muscles twitched, he leaned forward to stretch something out of his neck and shoulders. She'd seen that move before. She knew she somehow weighed on him. She tried to think what *she'd* done to be so heavy.

"Shit," he murmured. "Don't take that personally. I just need to be quiet for a little while." Maggie remembered DC, how a low front would move in from some ridgeline in him and he'd be gone, how at first she'd ask questions, then be quiet, making herself as small as possible. She thought about what AKA said his kung fu teacher told him about stepping aside.

{ 63 }

"You OK with that?" Jesse asked like he didn't really want to know. Maggie kung fued. "Just fine."

"Just fine," he laughed. "Right. You got that woman thing in your voice." He wanted to bite back the words but something had kicked in. He heard Cheyenne, "I hope you can change that mean motherfucker in you. You're the only one who can."

Maggie started to watch.

Jesse was dead quiet till they lurched to a stop at a chain-link gate. "Can you get the brake?" he said. His parking brake had been dead for years. Maggie pulled her wet foot out of the water and set it on the brake. He climbed out and shoved a rock under the front wheel just as her foot slipped.

"The fuck!" he said. "Pay attention." Maggie gave him a thumbs-up. She watched him fish around in the back for his binocs. Beside the fact that she was doing research in preparation for who knows what, she loved watching him move. Even angry. She liked the sunlight catching gun-metal blue in his black curls. Her kung fu slipped.

"Hey Jesse," she said, "are *you* OK?" He stopped fussing with the toolbox and smiled. She relaxed.

"No big thing," he said. "Feeling a little crowded, maybe like you want something I won't be able to give."

"Huh?" She caught her breath and saw Jesse's red-rimmed eyes, his flat smile, as though she looked through warped glass.

"Maggie?" Jesse said. "Maggie." He started to put his hand on her shoulder. Without moving her body, she kung fued away. He dropped his hand.

"Fuck," he said, "don't go chick on me."

"Oh no," she said. "Not me. What's bothering me? My friend was murdered. Nothing you can fix."

He put his arm around her. She leaned into him. Jesse thought he could let the moment just be. The fear seeped in again. He started too busily massaging her shoulders. Maggie pretended to like it. She pretended to relax. Through the rest of that long hot afternoon, she pretended to listen, to point her binocs in the direction he waved, note flight patterns, how sunset glinted copper and green off wings. But really, she kept studying him for clues. And she knew he was watching her for mistakes. She made nine. She knew because she counted them, each one a pinch in her gut.

Just before twilight, Jesse said, "Let's find a camp. I hate setting up in the dark." He took her hand. "And, baby, don't take this personally, but on the way back to the truck, could you walk a little more quietly? No offense, but there might be night herons here. They spook real easy. That's all."

"No problem," Maggie said, and proceeded to be a shadow.

Jesse drove forever trying to find the perfect place. By the time they found it, the perfect place was new moon dark. He dragged mesquite from the edge of a wash and made a fire. They hauled the mattress out of the back of the truck. Maggie made up the bed with the sheets and pillows he'd tucked neatly under the mattress. Jesse was an Eagle Scout when it came to camping. "I could drive this truck beyond where the dirt roads end, and more than survive for six months. Someday, maybe we'll go together."

She remembered when he'd said it. He'd had one leg thrown over hers, his face against her cheek, so the words were as much a vibration as a sound. She wondered where that guy had gone.

Maggie was setting up a place to eat, and Jesse was frying peppers when she realized they hadn't said a word to each other since the don't-be-a-klutz alert. She was new to his camping style anyhow. She was used to Sergeant Dark Cloud's listen-up, told-you-once, now-do-it-NFG technique.

Or her own. Travel alone, keep it simple. Maggie wanted to do just that, get out onto her own private parameter. She wanted away from the new lost Jesse crouched in the firelight. She opened the spaghetti and, uneasy as she was, dumped it on the sand.

Jesse startled. He wished she hadn't done that, wished he could hold back the words that jumped from his mouth. "What's with you? Swear to god, you've got the feng shui of the Sargasso Sea. The last thing we want is fire ants all over the camp."

"Sorry." The word was out before Maggie could stop it.

Jesse picked up the millimeter of joint sitting on the top of his soda can and swallowed it. It suddenly seemed reasonable to him that Maggie was like every other woman he'd ever known, desperate for attention, a sweet piece on her way to being a leech. He turned and stared at her. "Do you screw up just to get attention?"

Maggie looked up, past his eyes hidden behind the flames mirrored in his glasses, up past the twisted mesquite branches behind him, toward the highway lights slipping by. A woman, even a big on-her-way-to-old woman, didn't hitchhike in this part of the world. She looked hard at the black bulk of the hills and stars beginning to scatter to the south, as though the looking could take her away. She wanted to be home in her haunted cube, feeling the shawl velvety in her hands, waiting for a ghost to pay a call. "Jesse, if I wanted a shrink, I'd hire one."

He looked surprised.

"I've known myself longer than you have," she said, picked up the spaghetti, brushed it off, and set it on a rock. "There. No big deal." She walked to the edge of the wash, sat down, and buried her icy fingers in the sand's lingering heat. She felt for pebbles, tried to forget there were scorpions, and breathed in the clean evening air.

"Sarah," she whispered, "where are you when I need you?"

SARAH was painting her toenails. Hot Damn Ruby. She glanced at Minnie Siyala, who sat in the patio chair next to her. "You can't go to her," Minnie said. "I haven't taught you how to yet."

"What if he's one of *them*?" Sarah said.

Minnie shook her head. "Even if he is, she has to wake herself up. How is she going to do that if you go over there and fix things?"

"You could fix it," Sarah said.

Minnie laughed. "Uh uh. I'm not a fixer. I'm a mender. I only go in when nothing else works. Fixers are like white people doctors—they add stuff, cut out stuff, give people those pills that make their brains work harder. A mender takes time. A mender helps the broken one find the threads that are pulled out of the weaving. A mender waits till the person weaves them back in. What was unwoven is never all the way mended. You can always tell there was a break."

"I could wish her something though," Sarah says. "I learned about how thoughts have power in that religion class."

"Girl," Minnie said, "you sound like one of those rich woo woo ladies."

MUSIC drifted on the warm air. Jesse was playing Otis Rush's "Mean Old World," a dry drunk blues they'd loved to make love to. Though Maggie was thinking past tense, she was not surprised to feel grateful to hear his step, feel him crouching behind her, and know he was aroused. He cupped her breasts in his hands.

"Hey," he said. "Hey, girl." He touched her cheek, gently turned his face toward his. He didn't kiss her. He just traced her lips with his tongue. "Sometimes," he whispered against her mouth, "sometimes, I don't know. Sometimes I'm just a mean motherfucker."

And, as his tongue teased its way into her mouth, Maggie wondered if maybe he was right—about her clumsiness, about her making mistakes, about her wanting too much. Jesse eased her back on the sand. She moved up against him, let him move into her. For the first time she couldn't come. For the first time, she pretended.

Jesse pressed his face to hers. He felt their tears on her skin and wished he could turn back time. She sighed, a long gentle sigh. "You scared me," she whispered.

He felt her warmth, how she did nothing but breathe with him. She was more than he knew he had wanted around him. He stroked her hair.

"Sometimes," Jesse said. "Sometimes I *am* a mean motherfucker. Can you accept that, just, I don't know, let it be?"

Maggie was quiet.

He buried his face in her neck. "You've got to, please, you've got to not let me push you away."

MAGGIE woke to the soft dark before first light. Jesse was turned away from her. He reached behind his back and pulled her close. His eyes moved under his lids.

The thin green light went tourmaline, then rose quartz. She remembered waking once in the night and seeing what might have been a swarm of comets moving across the low mountains. Jesse sighed, turned, and she felt him hard against her hip.

"Too early," he said, "too sleepy." He was more awake than he let her know. He couldn't remember much of the day before. It seemed wise to hold off the questions he was afraid they might both ask. He turned his face west and watched the morning light move up the rocks and into the spidery creosote.

Maggie wondered what he was dreaming. She looked east, wished she could let what was once her life be eaten by the light. Just as the sun burned up from the dark mountains, she closed her eyes and saw a scarlet cloud drift across her eyelids.

JESSE gathered a circle of rocks. He turned each one in his hand, holding it to the light, tasting it, rubbing it on his skin. Maggie crouched behind him and held his body tight to hers. She traced the scar that ran across his right shoulder and branched down his back.

"No questions," he said.

"Let's name this place," Maggie said. She rubbed his bunched shoulders, felt tension smooth out under her fingers. "We stake a claim."

He gently took hold of her thigh. "All of It. Let's just call it All of It."

"Oh no," she laughed. "Then when we're not here, what will we have."

"Itsa then," he said. "Like 'Itsa bird, itsa plane . . .'"

He stood, kissed her on the forehead, and handed her a tiny jasper pebble. He held an obsidian chip in his hand. "We put these in the root circle. Then we have a way to come back."

Maggie wondered if she'd imagined the day before.

SARAH capped the nail polish. "See," she said, "he never told her anything real. That was how it was with Yakima. Lies. Lies not with words, but lies with what the guy doesn't say."

"I told you," Minnie said, "those Hopi guys'll tell you anything. So will an Apple. So will a white guy. That's why I like my apprentices young. I can teach 'em how hard truth is, harder than their dicks, and a lot more dangerous."

"Dangerous to who?"

Minnie laughed. "Not to the mending, that's for sure."

8   It was still cool enough in early morning to sit on the balcony. Sarah touched up her toenails with Maggie's polish. Maggie was slouched and bitching, a condition she was beginning to find herself in more often than she liked. "I thought Jesse was different," she said, "but it's getting weird. It started on that camping trip. He gets critical, or I can tell he's holding back

being critical, and you know how you can know when the guy doesn't want to talk about something which you don't know what it is, which I hate because at first we could say anything with each other. One minute he's the guy I always believed might be out there; the next he's a chunk of dry ice."

"I believe we've already gone over this," Sarah said. "He's a guy."

"Yeah but," Maggie said. "This is different. One second, Sweet Jesse, next second, somebody else there, like that old movie, *Invasion of the Body Snatchers*. Like a guy, but more."

"As I have been known to say," Sarah said, "he's a guy."

"And, no matter which Jesse he is, *I've* started waiting. For the phone. For the sound of his truck. I hate this!"

"You're a chick. He's a guy and you're a chick."

"I'm five decades old. I can't be a chick."

"A chick is forever a chick." Sarah bent over her pedicure. "Don't you think this polish goes perfectly with my skin?"

"How do you do that?" Maggie asked. "Keep it all simple but spiritual— and still use up the last of my Hot Damn Ruby polish?"

"I can't tell. It's one of the Lesser Mysteries. Like college and the government."

"Don't change the subject," Maggie said. "Will Minnie or the Big Whatever ground you if you help me out here?"

"You are so pushy," Sarah laughed. "Didn't those headbangers teach you anything at that burger stand in Winslow?" She capped the polish. "You still want to try to figure out Jesse?"

"Sarah," Maggie said, "maybe what it is with guys is they want us when they don't have us, and when they got us, they want something else. It's a kind of brain damage."

"Yeah," Sarah yawned elaborately, "that's probably it. Of course, I wasn't like that, not me. I didn't walk away from Will Lucas when he wanted to give me everything he had. And, you wouldn't catch me with my hand in Yakima's jeans while he had his hand in the Save Our Indigenous Lands and People Emergency Fund. Uh uh."

What Sarah didn't say, what she wanted to forget forever—except that if she did, then it would be as if she and Will had never been—is how grief for their lost love would tear its way up out of her, thoughtless and unbearable. And how, when it came to Yakima, there was only the feeling that she was sand-papering her brain with memories.

Maggie went into the kitchen and came back with a pint of Hard Core Chocolate ice cream and two spoons. Thunderstorms hovered over the western mountains. Sarah sat on the iron railing.

"Suppose you got hit by lightning," Maggie said. "Would you feel it?"

"Less than you would." Sarah looked down at the scarlet polish shining on her dark toes. "Now I think this is a little gaudy. My aunt always said we Indian women have to be careful to not be gaudy. Especially when we have master's degrees."

"I'm the only one who can see you and I think you look just fine. Though what are you going to do when that shirt and jeans wear out?"

"I sure hope," Sarah said, "I'm all the way dead long before these clothes wear out. This halfway is no way at all.

"The trouble is, it's my fault I'm halfway. I was even before I got killed. I wouldn't walk the path those old Indians tried to teach me. I wouldn't walk the 'for your own good' the BIA school tried to push me on. The nobody's-the-boss-of-me path I took led me straight into the hands of that thing."

She folded her arms over her chest. "I did, you know. I walked right into him and I made the big mistake: I took him for a fool."

She'd told Maggie before, how he had wound piano wire around her neck and blindfolded her. And it didn't really matter who he was, because she wasn't tracking the killer, or even a way to undo what had been done. She was tracking a way to go on home. And she didn't really know what that meant. They were Minnie's words: *You got to find your way back to your people. All your people.*

"He was smart. He thought he knew me," Sarah said. Her voice was flat. "I'm sorry. I have to tell it again.

"You know, all of it—the saw blade, the ice pick, the fire—that wasn't the worst. A person can go up out of their body when it gets unbearable. The most awful thing was that *I* kissed him. He said something about women using him. 'You know how that can be, Sarah, you learned that in the mountains,' he said. 'If you just kiss me, we'll be OK and I'll let you go.'

"I nodded my head. He kissed me. He spit down my throat. You can't imagine." She turned away. "He said he wanted to teach me something. For my own good. He said he'd just wanted me to know how he felt, how all the men in my life must have felt. And, then he started in."

"He thought he knew you," Maggie said for the first time. "And, he did know something. About the mountains. He wasn't a total stranger."

"None of them are."

"Jesse." Maggie remembered how during their first few times together, she would look at him and think, I know you, stranger.

Sarah heard the unspoken question and remembered Minnie's words: "She has to wake up. How is she going to do that if you go over there and fix things?"

Sarah closed her eyes. "You know—making love was my greatest joy. It was the only time my brain shut up." She smiled. "Which, sure as shit can make it hard to think."

Maggie remembered how it was at first with Jesse, how she'd thought, *I haven't forgotten this, I didn't go dead with DC and the too many others.* She realized the innocence with Jesse was not more than a few months ago, and it seemed forever gone.

IT WAS A SHAKY DAY. There was movement on the periphery of Jesse's vision. Coffee tasted funny. He couldn't get Maggie out of his mind—or all the way in. Even Estrellas Road seemed different. He'd driven here a hundred times, for the same reason he was driving here today—Ray needing a ride to work because Ray was getting shakier with every dawn.

Jesse slid onto the gravel two-track that led to Ray and Helen's trailer. Light glared off a busted bottle. As the sun-spot faded, he saw a black figure at the side of the road. Ray stepped toward him and disappeared.

"What the fuck?" Nine in the morning and the sun rode Golden Valley like a dirt-bike punk. Behind Jesse, the highway was a quicksilver mirage. Maybe he had imagined Ray.

Something glittered in the barrow ditch. Jesse pulled over. He thought he'd glimpsed a silver dollar. Couldn't be. You never saw money on the ground, not seventeen miles from the casinos. The coin moved. There was a moan and Jesse saw the silver disk was a watch face.

Jesse climbed out and looked down at Old Ray, who could have been a mummy looking up at him with an expression more malicious than you might expect from a mummy whose right leg was bent at an impossible angle.

"Help," Ray whispered.

There were, impossibly, clouds coming in hard and fast as fighter jets. Jesse was drenched, the highway a river. Brown water boiled up in the ditch, a smell, rot and mildew and orchids, a brown corpse rolling and bobbing.

He heard Ray. "For cryin' out loud, do something."

Jesse shivered, the flashback faded. He eased down into the ditch and took hold of Ray's wrist.

"I like ya," Ray rasped, "but I'm not holding hands."

"I'm checking for shock," Jesse said. "You're OK I'm going up to the trailer and call an ambulance."

"*No!*" Ray twisted out of Jesse's grip. "No ambulance. No hospital. No fuckin' docs." He looked hard into Jesse's eyes. "And no leaving me."

"Fuck, Ray Cooper, are you nuts? Your leg's broken. You've got a bad ticker. And, you're older than God."

"Get me outta here, Jesse. Just get me outta here."

Ray sunk his fingers into Jesse's shoulder and tried to pull himself up. "God-dag-dickshit-damn it to hell." He settled back.

Jesse rechecked his pulse. A little fast but steady.

"You'd think," Ray whispered, "God'd have something better to do than fuck up an old fart who hasn't had a drink in fifteen years, eight months, and twenty-six days. And hasn't got one now. This isn't how the deal is supposed to go down."

Jesse looked into Ray's iceberg eyes. He saw that there would, by God, be no, by God, compromise. "Listen, kid," Ray said, "we can do it."

Jesse slid his arm under Ray's shoulder. A tear fell on the sand. Sparkled and was gone. *Lang Vei. Tet. That Bru village he saw vaporized in an instant of the worst brilliant beauty you can imagine.* Thirty-plus fucking years ago. Yesterday.

"Thanks, kid," Ray said.

Jesse got him to his feet. "You OK?"

"Kid, I don't think I can talk and stay alive at the same time, so I'm not sayin' nothing till we're up there."

Jesse grabbed the base of the road sign and started to pull on Ray's dead weight. "Oh boy," Ray said.

"Shut up," Jesse muttered, eased Ray's shoulders up over the edge, dropped down next to him, and pushed. Ray passed out. Jesse rolled him all the way out. Weird luck, pal, he thought, and checked Ray's pulse. Steady. Weird great good luck.

There was a boom to the west. Real clouds—fast and hard as arty. Jesse sucked in dry air. Wished it were dope.

"Jesse," Ray whispered. "Jesse, you havin' one of those backflashes?"

Jesse ran his hand over his eyes. All he was looking at was monsoon over Spirit Mountain in a sky of molten chrome.

JESSE and Ray picked up Helen at the trailer. "What the hell do you think you're doing?" she said as she smoothed Ray's bald spot. "Let me tell you, when we get back from the doc, you've got some explaining to do."

Ray sighed. "I love you too, old woman."

The doc in the Bullhead Emergency Department was more stubborn than Ray. "You're gonna be our guest for a while, maybe a couple days," he said. "We've got to set that leg and make sure your heart and blood pressure behave." He ordered morphine. Within five minutes, Ray did nothing but grin and agree with everything anybody said.

Helen left to get Chinese takeout. "You're not eating that hospital slop," she said. Ray fidgeted with the IV, kicked the covers away from his feet, and mumbled at Jesse. "For chrissake, I'm OK. Go on. Get out of here. Go do what ya gotta do."

Jesse saluted. Ray knew. Stoned out of his gourd, trapped the last place he wanted to be, one leg strung up to a pole, Ray knew the all of it.

"I'll keep an eye on Helen," Jesse said. "And, I'll do what I gotta do."

ZACH googled: "skate, Creosote, Nevada." In less than a minute, he found the site he needed: Skate to Annihilate: Creosote. There were two chat rooms. He hovered around the first, in which JasonX asked repeatedly, "Is anyone sponsored?" and Fleeb messaged "YOU I'LL KILL JUST FOR ANNOYING ME! fleeb has returned!"

Zach knew that despite Grasshopper's words, "Always Alone, Never By

Myself, But Always Alone," this was a loser gang. He punched in a fake name, asked, "Do any of you guys actually skate?" and switched to the second chat.

Spooky wrote in plain English. He told Catclaw there was a plan for midnight. Catclaw messaged, "I'm in. See you there." Zach scrolled down through a series of vague commitments from other skaters, trying to figure where the plan was going to happen. No luck. Finally, he gave up, signed into the site as Jayghost, and jumped into the wordstream.

He watched the words roll past him. Then, Spooky: "Jayghost, Who r u?"

"New kid in town." Zach waited a second.

"No IM?" Spooky asked.

"Jayghost don't need no stinkin' IM," Zach wrote.

"LOL," Spooky responded.

"Yo Mama," Catclaw wrote. "Yo mama."

"What you say . . ." Zach typed.

"Hey, you losers," Spooky wrote, "this is 2000, not 1978."

Zach typed in "BFN," signed out, and checked his e-mail. Shegirlollie15@yahoo.com. He opened the message. "CatTown 10 p.m. Bring kibble. The Spook."

"In. BFN," Zach fired back.

CatTown. It had to be the Riverstroll behind the Tidewater. There was a series of ramps, stairs, and a long curve between the back door of the TW and the Crystal. There were curbs so you could ollie to grind, and once, just once, he had skated a bench and landed perfect. Plus there were cat moms and kittens living under the ramp.

Plus Spooky was a chick. Even though she was a year older. Plus, it was the beginning of summer, the fuckin' beginning of summer.

IT COULD HAVE BEEN a lifetime since since steak'n'eggs 'n'strawberry waffles. Cowbird was amazed to find himself sitting in the breakfast nook of Bonnie Madrid's travel trailer, happily drained of most of his bodily juices despite her request that they refrain from ordinary conjugal relations. He sipped a mint julep and watched her flip pancakes. "Cowbird," she said, "I haven't had that good a time in a long time. Even without you know what."

"Me neither." Cowbird thought how much he admired delicacy in a lady.

"One thing I really like," she said, "is stories—and you got more stories than any white man I ever met."

"I sure am white," he said.

"Cracker," she said.

"Country," he said. And then she was slapping pancakes down on his plate and he didn't give a hoot who was cracker and who was what she called African American. This woman was the best cook he'd ever known.

Bonnie's phone rang. Cowbird wondered if he should step outside. She grabbed it and wandered out to the patio. It must have been one of those cell phone things, like you always saw the pimps and business suits whip out. He concentrated on what seemed to be the genuine homemade Missouri-hog sausage on his plate. Bonnie's voice was low. He hoped she wasn't talking to that dick, Beltran.

"Yes," she said. "No." Her eyes were huge. "I'm on my way," she said. "Yes. Tell her I've got some roots, we'll boil them up. They'll help."

She hung up, dropped to her knees on the floor, and rested her forehead against Cowbird's leg. "Oh no," she said.

Cowbird couldn't believe what he said next, without thinking, just spitting it out, like a desperate teenager, "Is it Beltran?"

"What?" Bonnie looked up. "How do you know about Beltran?"

"Everybody knows about Beltran," he said. "It's not like I'm jealous or anything. I know better than to fence in a woman fine as yourself."

"No," Bonnie said. "It is not about Beltran, which, if it was, wouldn't be any of your business, which you seem to know, which just saved your white ass."

"Cracker," he said.

"Country," she said, and then she wrapped her arms around his legs, hung on tight, and sobbed. He patted her back. Finally, she looked up at him. "Leola, that busybody old bat at the Crystal snack bar—she was killed."

SARAH stayed on the balcony while Maggie went inside to dry off. Sarah practiced organizing her gsi'ki as fat raindrops, then as the almost-mist her Navajo cousin called female rain.

The phone rang. "Maggie?" someone said, the voice whiskey-rasped.

"It is." Maggie heard slots in the background.

"Maggie, it's Sue." Maggie came close to praying. Every now and then one of the snack bar waitresses would forget or flat refuse to show up and Sue would enlist anybody unlucky enough to be at home when she called. "What?" Maggie said.

"Don't get upset," Sue started to cry. "Leola's dead. That bossy old coot is dead."

THIS TIME Maggie knew there'd be no black crape, just the same three light bulbs out over the craps table, the keno board flashing like a hangover. She and Sheree huddled near the smoke-blue windows at the back.

"She was lying in the middle of her bed," Sheree said. She chain-lit a cigarette. "Fuck, I'm smoking again. There wasn't a mark on her except where her heart was gone. 'The guy must of been a surgeon,' that fat cop said. "It was an absolutely clean cut. Her necklace wasn't even out of place."

"How's Sue?"

"She keeps telling everybody to buck up, then she sneaks off into the john and Myrna can hearing her crying her guts out.

AKA walked toward them. "I could definitely use a cigarette," he said. He hadn't smoked for three months. Abstinence and fad diets moved through casino workers like epidemics. He took a drag off Sheree's smoke. "The cops hauled Cowbird off, just wanted to ask him a few questions."

"Come *on*," Maggie said. "He's a real threat to society."

"He was a grunt near Kontum, got sprayed with Agent Orange. 'These guys are coo coo,' the old cop said. Sue told the cop to get fucked, said *she'd* been over there too and Cowbird was nothing but a harmless nut. They wanted the fry cook. I told them we hadn't seen him since May Day."

"We haven't? You mean the pretty one?"

AKA nodded. Factoring turnover in Creosote was a branch of quantum math.

"We need a house meeting," AKA said grimly. House meetings were on your own time. They were terminally boring, and if you didn't show you'd find yourself working all the shifts you hated and odd little mistakes in your paycheck, requiring appeals to be filed and endless confusion to begin. This was the first time in the Crystal's history that an employee had requested a house meeting.

"Sunday, 1:00 p.m.," Sheree said. "But, don't blame me."

SARAH went invisible. She slipped through Maggie's front door. The light was fading. She walked down Red Butte Road, crossed the main drag, and melted through the fence to the river. Minnie waited. The old woman sat at shoreline, her scarecrow feet in the silver water.

"You didn't tell me there would be more killing," Sarah said. "I don't mean to be rude, but you should have told me."

Minnie smiled. Her eyes were sad. "You are getting some respect, girl. Thank you."

Sarah nodded.

"I didn't know there would be another death," Minnie said. "Things are slipping. Bad stuff everywhere." She patted the sand next to her. Sarah sat. Minnie said a word Sarah had never heard before, not in English, not in Willow. "It's *that* time," Minnie said. "The time the old old ones warned us about."

Sarah tried to say the word. Her throat locked up. "What does it mean?"

"Like cancer," Minnie said.

"Like when Mr. Jim died," Sarah said. She knew she needed to be careful about what she said. Willow were not like Navajo; they didn't believe the spirits of the dead could hurt you. Still, when she thought of Mr. Jim's death, she felt so much horror it could poison the air around them.

"He was so ashamed," Minnie said. "To lie in his own mess. To try to call the nursing home people when his throat was filled with so many sores he couldn't speak and he was too weak to reach the buzzer."

"There is worse than death," Sarah said quietly.

"There is much that's worse than death," Minnie said. "There is something you need to know. Not Willow. About a way that is different from ours. A young woman traded me for this story. She had skin like ours, eyes like ours, but she was not Willow. She was asking for money outside the Hotel Montella.

"This is what she told me." Minnie's voice changed. It became higher, harsher—she stumbled over some of the words.

{ 77 }

Each syllable in our language can be sounded six different ways. The word "ma" can be pronounced to mean phantom, but, mother, rice seedling, tomb, or horse. It is how you make your voice go. Up. Down. Short. Long. Like a wave.

Our mother was planting rice seedlings when they came through.

We were poor. My father gone, only my sister, my two young brothers, and me. We had no way to pay for a ceremony, for a tomb, but even if we did, they killed our mother in such a way that she could not be buried, she could not go to heaven.

And then they killed my sister. Same same, in that way that is so terrible we do not speak of it. Now, so many years later, so many miles away, I remember our stories, and when a double rainbow appears and stretches down to the dark and wild Grass River, I know those two hungry souls are near. "Ma," I say, "ma, ma, ma, ma, ma."

Minnie stared out across the water. "She said their rivers were like oceans. She said she would die if she didn't go back."

Sarah reached for Minnie's hand. The old woman took hers. "You know," Minnie said, "our Willow men are sometimes soldiers. I don't know why. We are people of peace. Like the Hopi. Maybe wars now are more than just wars between tribes or countries."

She fell silent. Sarah wondered what she meant. She knew if it was right for her to know, Minnie would have told her.

"I was killed like that girl's people were killed," Sarah said. "Why?"

Minnie drew her feet from the water, dried them with the sleeve of her jacket, and scuffed on her slippers. "I don't see that answer," she said. "I think you are the only one who can see that answer.

"I have to go back. That Black Lake boy is going to show me a movie tonight on his mother's television. It is called *The Matrix*. He says it is about gsi'ki. Did you ever hear of it?"

Sarah laughed. "I watched it when I was a teenager. It is about gsi'ki. Back then, I thought it was about how a girl could save a boy with love."

9   Jesse pulled up to the ramada and parked in the shade. "Go do what you gotta do." Ray's voice stayed with him. It wouldn't take long to begin to finish what he had to do. He'd be back on the road in an hour,

at the Crystal by two. Maggie didn't go on till three, and her rule was never play slots before you go to work, so he had time to leave the drawings for her. And then he'd drive north and let himself be pulled forward by what was missing.

The trailer was cool and dark. He lit the kerosene lantern on the kitchen table, put on his headlamp, and went into the closet. The drawings were in an old ammo can. He carried them to the kitchen table and spread them out. *May 1969. June 1969. September 1969. September 1969. December 1969. December 1970.*

They'd been drawn with map pencils, the reds, greens, and blues faded by three decades. The figures seemed to move in the flickering lantern light.

He knew Maggie knew a little about what had been. But when she saw these, she might be able to understand. Then maybe someday down the road, someday after he did what he had to do, maybe they could talk about it. Maybe he could tell the whole story. Not just what happened over there, but how the doors in his mind would slam down and he'd become someone he did not want to be.

He gathered up the drawings. He imagined a few of the things he might say. "I couldn't save my best friend. I ran from the woman I loved. I am the father of a child of dust. Sometimes I freeze out whatever touches me."

Ah fuck, he thought, what melodrama, what lousy reality. He picked up a pen and began to write. He'd get his road stuff together later. That would be the easy part.

Jesse packed jasper, obsidian, and chert. He wrapped each chunk of stone in scraps of worn-out flannel shirts. He put them in an ammo can, set the striking platform and antler chipping tool on top, and closed the lid.

It was critical to have work that was portable. He'd known that when he was twenty. A week back from Laos, watching some TV president tell America there was no American presence in Laos, his mother setting a plate of chocolate chip cookies in front of him, his father popping another beer, his own personal weed-whacked brain converting the TV screen to mosaic, Jesse knew he had to go.

A week away from his folks' living room, he'd been up to his elbows in carburetor and carbon when the boss slammed his hand on the Chevy's roof. Bam. "Incoming," the guy yelled. And it was time to go.

A year later, a drunk Indian kid at his door. Jesse's hand became a blade. There were no charges. Self-defense. But Jesse knew he'd broken his vow. And consequently it was time to go. It was time to find work that was portable. And theoretically harmless.

Flintknapping. Custom knives. Collector items for guys whose battlefields were offices. Work that was portable and, given the nature of its owners, thoroughly harmless. What could be better?

Eddie Toogood had said everything that needed to be said about work in '69. Shotgun artillery busted the night and things they didn't want to think about dropped out of the triple canopy on their naked shoulders, and Toogood said: "You always workin' for the man, bro. Don't matter what you do, you be some rich-ass doctor, some little street ho, you always workin' for the man."

Now, ten thousand miles and thirty-plus years from that night—and farther still, not by time or distance, but by god farther from his final killing, Jesse packed the bone handles in buckskin. How had he come so far? How had he come no distance at all?

He finished packing, checked the trailer, set the old Montagnard knife blade up across the track into his place and covered it with sand. For twenty-five years it had kept strangers away. He had no doubt it always would.

At the highway, he turned toward Creosote. As the sun arced toward the Old Woman Mountains, he drove into the shadows, straight down between day and night.

MAGGIE missed the house meeting. In fact, she missed the entire day, week, and month. When she let herself in the apartment, Sarah was hunkered in the dark in front of the phone machine. She had the shawl draped across her lap.

"Sarah?" She didn't turn around. "What's wrong?"

"Come over here," Sarah said. "Sit next to me." Minnie's voice echoed in her mind. *Come over here. Sit next to me.*

The apartment was oddly cold. Maggie flicked on the kitchen light as though that would help and crouched on the floor next to Sarah.

"What is it?"

"It's time for us to leave. Now. Sheree found a Polaroid of you. The eyes were burned out."

"That's lovely," Maggie said. "That fucker is really subtle." She stood and looked wildly around the room. "Goddamn it, Sarah, we've gotta didi." It was Dead DC's word, fixed in his brain in Vietnam; surfacing when the going got tough and the tough got drinking.

"Didi?"

"Get out. Now."

Sarah nodded. "It'll get you next, and if you die, I can't. I'll help you pack." She unfolded the shawl. "Put the important stuff in here for, for if we need to pray."

"The moth candle," Maggie said, and remembered the final didi years— when DC turned vicious and she needed to get her and Deac out fast and how she'd tell herself out loud what she needed to pack. They'd dump as much as they could into plastic trash bags and she'd try not to think about where and when she and the kid would unpack.

"Guadalupe, the moth candle, my tapes, clothes, what's left of my nail polish, the black ashtray Jesse gave me." Maggie shrugged. "Jesse. Oh shit."

Sarah punched the rewind button on the phone machine.

"Maggie," Jesse said, "gotta take a little break. It's not anything about you. It's me. I'll be in touch. There's a package for you at the Crystal. Sweet dreams, sweet girl."

"Oh well," Maggie said. "Déjà vu." She locked the lurch in her gut away.

They gathered up her clothes, her music, the sequined flip-flops, and her hiking boots.

"Take your backpack," Sarah said. "We might have to ditch the car."

"What do you need?"

"Nothing. If I do, I'll borrow yours."

They dumped kitchen stuff in milk crates, dismantled the coffee pot and packed it in a shopping bag. Six bags of Tim Macy's Wiener Melange dark roast, a cowboy coffee pot.

Sarah disappeared. "Figures," Maggie said, "time to load the car and you go transparent."

There was no answer. Maggie took one last look around. The light on the answering machine glowed. She punched the button. "Sweet dreams, sweet girl."

She heaved the machine off the balcony.

They were almost at the bridge when Maggie remembered the rest of Jesse's message. "Jesse's package," she said.

"Forget it," Sarah said.

"Not a prayer." Maggie pulled a U-ey and headed back.

Five minutes later, Invisible Sarah set the envelope on her invisible lap. They pulled onto the main drag. Two in the morning and the traffic was bumper to bumper.

"I am going to miss this place," Maggie said. "I must be in need of professional mental health care."

"Me too," Sarah said. "But I can't stop thinking. Leola. The postcard with your eyes burned out."

"Ask the Big Know-It-Alls. I mean, what's the point of dying if you don't know more than you did when you were alive."

"It's not like dead in a casket," Sarah said. "It's confusing. Sometimes, it's like being ordinary alive. Other times, I see doors, caves, broken windows. I want to look in and I don't.

"Up home we have these spirits called Smoke Dancers," Sarah said. "They come at a certain time to deal with naughty kids. They scared my cousin so bad she got sick. Things like that could be on the other sides of the openings, like our religion prof told us about Tibetan Buddhism: You die. Then you have to go through this cosmic obstacle course. Bardos. He called them *bardos*."

She reemerged all the way. Maggie drove to the shoreline. Downriver, Creosote was a neon bruise.

"This is too close to town to camp," Sarah said.

"We're not camping," Maggie said. "I just want to pick up some river stones, a little water." She parked near a patch of tamarisk. "First, I've got to do this." She unpinned her name tag from her blouse and carried it to the river. "Good-bye, Maggie May. You were a good waitress." A spark curved out over the water. There was a tiny splash.

Sarah carried the shawl bundle and an empty water bottle to a huge cottonwood stump at the water's edge. The animals on the shawl glowed softly in the starlight. Sarah leaned back against the cottonwood. Maggie sat by her. They looked out over the water, the river the silver-gray breast of some great bird.

"Maggie?" Sarah said. "Did you ever meet a guy around here named Willy Peter?"

Maggie remembered DC drunk and babbling, . . . *you gotta look out for white phosphorus, we called it Willy Peter. If it got on you, it burned clear down to the bone. The only thing you could do was cut it out of the guy's muscle.*

"It's not a guy," Maggie said. "It's an incendiary."

"That thing said, 'This is like Willy Peter,' right before he started in."

"They used it in Nam. It makes a fire you can't put out."

Sarah shivered. "No, he used lighter fluid. I could smell it." She paused. "My uncle was in Vietnam. He'd be around for a while, then he'd disappear, show up again six months later. He'd work, give my aunt a little money, then all of a sudden he'd be gone again. She said he went up to Wyoming, did Sun Dance stuff up there."

"Sundance?" Maggie said. "The resort? Why would a Hopi go to Sundance."

"Sun Dance is a ceremony," Sarah said. "And I'm not Hopi. I'm Willow. Up north, in Bone Lake." She looked away. "Open Jesse's package. I don't want us carrying it till I know what's in it."

"Maybe that's a private event."

Maggie saw the flash of Sarah's grin. "There are no more private events," Sarah said. "Not till I'm gone."

"I'll open it in the truck," Maggie said.

They left the doors open, the scent of river soft around them. Maggie opened the package. There was a sheaf of drawings, four pages of writing, and a folded note. Maggie held the note to the map light. "This is for my eyes only."

"What's the rest?" Sarah said.

Maggie fanned out the drawings.

"That war," Sarah said, "was over twenty-five years ago."

There were six pictures and a few words: *I made the drawings with map pencils a long time ago. That's why they're faded. I drew them when I was 19. I wrote the four pages last night.*

Nobody's seen any of this but you. Some day send the drawings back. I don't plan to leave Creosote, send them c/o Old Ray at the Crystal. I suspect he's eternal.

Lovely. *Some day send them back.* Which is what you do if you are not in contact.

She turned the page. Red pencil. A chopper hovered over a burning shack, smoke plumes rose from burning fields. There was more sky than anything, sky holding a chopper as if it was an angel.

The next was in blue, five Boonie rats, your standard dragging-the-dead-bro-out-of-the-elephant-grass.

Green: A chaplain holding a slack-jawed kid. The padre was looking up, the kid was looking nowhere. *You think he's looking up to God,* Jesse had written. *He's actually looking up at the medevac coming in too late.*

Maggie checked out the first page of writing: *You won't believe this. It doesn't matter. I tell you there is more to lightning than electricity. Sometimes a soul coming in strikes like that. Sometimes one leaving.*

"Sarah, listen to this." She read a few lines. "I don't know what he's talking about, but I'm not reading anymore till morning."

"And where," Sarah said, "exactly will that be?"

They stared at each other under the dash light's fox fire.

"You know the way to Jesse's?" Sarah said. "We could go there."

"Maybe. Turn your head and I'll read his note."

"Be that way."

Maggie read:

Lady, I wish I didn't have to write this. By now, you've looked at the drawings, maybe read the memory. I'm drawn to you. I dream of you. I don't say that lightly.

But always for me, something happens. You saw it. A few years back I dated a former Army nurse who'd been up in Pleiku. Now she works the burn unit most of the time and when she can't stand that, she shifts to DPS Air Rescue. We were wonderful for about a month. Then, something happened. We came apart. Suddenly. Thoroughly.

Later, she wrote, "Jesse, for those of us who were over there, love lives only in the short time."

Maggie, I have to stop for now. And know that whatever you need, whenever, I'll be there.

With love, Jesse.

"Well, fuck this." Maggie glared out the side window. She hated the way loss sharpened everything—the river, the stars, the lights of Creosote—into gorgeous brilliance. "Fuck *you*, Jesse." Then she was sobbing like she hadn't for years, her throat tight, her rib cage aching.

Maggie forgot she and Sarah were on the run. She was alone, thirteen, in northern December twilight, watching the shadows move across the snow, the horizon going pink, then gold, then the same color as the opal ring she wore, the ring she tugged off her finger and threw across the fence. She was thinking, *I won't ever love anybody again. Ever.*

"Jesse," Maggie thought, "I broke my rule." She remembered his near-miss smile, that great 1930's detective movie smile. "I won't forget you," she said. "God damn it. Punk. God damn it."

"You ok?" Sarah said.

"Just talking to myself."

"We're not camping at Jesse's, right?"

"Not tonight."

"Oh well," Sarah said, "a guy is a guy."

"Thanks for the pep talk," Maggie said. "Thanks for the heart-felt support." They drove away, south toward the desert in which Jesse and Maggie had once made camp a thousand years earlier.

THERE WAS HARDLY anybody on the Riverstroll, just a withered alkie asleep on a bench, a Mexican couple laughing their asses off, rainbow lights flashing in the plastic heels of the woman's shoes. Zach watched a plane take off from the Bullhead airport, its lights bouncing along, then gliding smooth as magic up into the sky.

He glanced up and down the Riverstroll. No Security in sight. His mom had told him the big shots in Vegas were downsizing all the workers. Bad news for her and her friends, good news for a kid hoping to cop a few rides on one of the sweetest illegal skate turfs in the West.

He looked back out over the water. Cat shadows moved along the shoreline. He thought about trying to sneak up on them, but he didn't want to miss the skaters. A fake riverboat was moored at the end of a long, perfect angle ramp. He heard the silvery jingle of slot machines through the open doors of the Belle and the Tidewater. And then he heard low laughter.

"JayG," a girl said, much closer than he would have expected.

"Whoa," he said, "you snuck up on me."

"Well, yeah," she said, "I'm Spooky."

A skinny boy stepped out in front of her. "Catclaw."

Two other kids, Zach couldn't tell if they were guys or chicks, stayed in the background.

"You bring the kibble?" Spooky said.

Zach pulled a bag of Pounce and a bag of M&Ms out of his baggies.

"You rule," Spooky said. "Let's go."

10 Light shifted behind Maggie's eyelids. She opened her eyes. A giant cottonwood grew out of a crack in a huge boulder, dawn shimmering in the silver-gold leaves. Maggie loved this part of the day, this crack between the worlds. She crawled out of the sleeping bag, started water boiling on the camp stove, leaned against the cottonwood, and took Jesse's pages from the envelope. She saw that he believed in things she had never considered. He believed in the presence of absolute good and evil. He believed they had launched a war that had raged since humans evolved, a war that continued whether soldiers fought or not.

The cottonwood leaves shuddered in a small breeze. Delicate gray birds darted in and out of the mesquite thorns. Maggie tucked the pages away. She wondered if she and Jesse would ever talk about what he had written, if she would ever look into his eyes and say, "I'm not afraid of you anymore. Not any part of you. I want you to tell me everything."

Sarah pushed open the Firebird door. "I'm back," she said. She hunkered down next to Maggie.

"Where were you?" Maggie said.

"Far away."

JESSE woke more or less upright in the front of his truck. He had to pee like a Russian racehorse. "What's that mean, Darwin?" he muttered. "You never told me what that meant."

He was talking to himself again. And talking to a guy who wasn't even bones anymore. The windows were fogged; a pearly light began to glow on the passenger side. Jesse opened the door, unfolded himself from behind the steering wheel and out.

He was smack in the middle of a dirt road heading north. The sage around him was coming into full green. He headed toward a bush to water it, and stepped off the road into deep sand. His leg twisted. The ache in his hip burned. "Shit, Ray, it must be catching."

Piss steam rose. There was the bronze scent of wet desert. "Jesus," he thought, "I wish I had a joint." He wondered why he was going for the pure, why he'd left an ounce of superfine skunk grass back in the trailer.

He limped to the bed of the truck, set up the one-burner stove, and got water boiling. He dumped Kahlua in the mug and decided it was a two-shot morning, one for the coffee, one straight down his throat. For the millionth time he wondered why he drank the stuff—it tasted like cough medicine and hit his gut like penance.

The water boiled. He spooned in coffee, turned off the heat, and waited. The horizon shifted. Fog rose and lingered. There was no water for a hundred miles, two hundred. The Schell Creek Range lifted straight up out of dry country. It must have been smoke.

He poured the second shot of Kahlua, filled the mug with coffee, and leaned against the truck. The smoky light warmed, glowed amber. Snakes of fire twisted up toward what was left of night. Jesse drained his cup. Smoke billowed in the West. Black. Oily.

The voice of the old Bru came back to him. *If you stay here, you will have to learn. There are spirits. There are rules. My daughter was born into them. You are less than a child in our world. You know nothing. Tell me: What lies in the West?*

Jesse had been quiet. The copper bracelets on his wrist had given him nothing but friendship. No wisdom. No magic. No protection.

You do not know, his beloved's father had said.

I will tell you: Death. Death lies in the West. That is the first lesson.

Jesse's heart jumped. Darwin, he thought. Darwin, I am going to find you. I'm going to bring you home.

Jesse closed his eyes, and when he opened them, he was running. He was running West.

ZACH and Spooky sat on the Stroll. Cat shadows prowled below them. You could see a ribbon of pale light just above the Black Mountains. "You know what sucks about Albuquerque?" Zach said.

Spooky poked him with her elbow. "Uh, your dad, his wife, the white-bread kids, the Mexican kids, the way the grown-ups think they are sooooo fucking cool."

"Oh yeah," he said, "that too."

He wondered if she thought he was a whiner.

"You think I'm a whiner?" he said.

"As if. And, here's what I hate about Creosote. Everything except the Stroll, my mom and stepdad, and my skaters."

"OK," he said. "What I hate most about Albuquerque is that everybody's all 'Oh! The Light! It is sooo mystical,' and nobody ever stops to just look at it. Like, see, how it was green over there above the mountains, and now you think it's dark again, but any second now, there's gonna be pink and yellow and everything. But, you gotta watch if you want to see it."

Spooky looked where he pointed. She turned toward him. "Why isn't Cat-claw more like you? He's all 'When are you going to let me touch your boobs? You know I love you.' A. I don't have hardly any boobs. B. He doesn't love me. Which are two other things I hate about Creosote."

Again, Zach thought, fuckin' again. A girl likes me as a brother, and *this* girl was the best ever.

MAGGIE drained her coffee. "I love this. We're running from a murderer, the most current love-of-my-life bailed, we have no money, and I love this. The cottonwood, the light, not knowing what the fuck we are doing."

"Me too," Sarah said. "Look at these." She dropped pebbles in Maggie's hand. Obsidian, jade-green chert, quartz, and mica.

"My cousin Lorinda makes jewelry out of river pebbles. She sets them in silver. We could take them up to her."

Sarah looked away. Maggie knew the look. It was the careful neutral a woman went into when she wanted something very much.

"We could do that. We could go up there."

"Yes," Sarah said. "I want to see Lorinda. I want to see my aunt. It's time for them to see me."

"I thought I was the only one who could see you." Maggie realized she had fully accepted the possibility of what is not possible.

"Lorinda and Aunt Hannah see things," Sarah said, "not like see-with-your-eyes, but she'll be able to see me. She won't be scared." She paused. "I was up there last night."

Maggie waited. Between the coffee singing sweetly in her blood, road-runner tracks in the pale sand, and knowing she might never again have to listen to a drunk guy in Ralph Lauren whine about blowing ten bucks in nickels, she was ready to consider anything.

"Minnie took me up there," Sarah said.

"Who's Minnie?"

Sarah grinned like a kid with a fabulous secret she can finally tell. "Minnie Siyala is an old old Willow lady. She used to try to teach me stuff. We kids were scared of her. But this time, I wasn't scared. We flew. Like a comet.

"It was so beautiful. Redstone, Blue Shadow Canyon, Lake Valley cotton-woods leafing out, Black Peak, white people call that one Wheeler Peak. And, Beartrack Mountain—that's where I was raised. At the foot of it, in my grand-ma's trailer."

Maggie couldn't begin to imagine what Sarah was telling her—not just because of the impossibility of people flying. She didn't know the places Sarah named as though she touched beads on a rosary. "Where are these places?"

"Up around Bone Lake."

Maggie knew Bone Lake. It was on I-50, the highway people call the "lone-liest road in America." "I thought Bone Lake was a ghost town."

"Not quite. When the mine died, things got shaky. But, my people are Wil-low. They find ways to make it. They're tough."

Maggie remembered a hard-eyed blackjack dealer from Bone Lake named Cora who'd lasted almost three weeks and broken a croupier's heart in record short time.

"I'm Bristlecone Clan," Sarah said. "Willow is a tiny tribe. Our home rez is near Bone Lake; and there's a tiny outpost near Page, Arizona, courtesy some lousy treaty.

"My mom was a drunk, left me with my aunt when I was a baby and disap-peared. I got kidnapped by the BIA like all the other Indian kids and hauled off to school. I kinda lost my Willow ways for a long time.

"Now I'm remembering. Not just stuff like the Sage Hen dances and love magic, but how it was when I'd come home on vacation. Red pop and TV, fry bread, and you put a pinch of food in a little bowl in the middle of the table to say thank you. That may not sound like much, but my Aunt Hannah makes anything she touches home."

Maggie stretched her hand out so it was in both shade and glare. Sarah did the same. "This is how we both live now," she said. "Half one place, half another. I wish I'd listened to Minnie when I was little."

"I'm not sure who I should have listened to," Maggie said.

"Minnie took me almost all the way home," Sarah said. "I could see the shape of Beartrack Mountain in the north. It made me homesick, but I wasn't quite ready to go all the way up. Some of my people are afraid of ghosts. Minnie said I was right not to go. She went on.

"I brought myself back. I finally got the nerve to go through one of those weird doors, and there was the road running south out of Bone Lake. I followed it."

"I'm getting lost," Maggie said. "I can't make sense of this."

"You don't have to," Sarah said. "I'll show you how it works. Look."

Maggie saw not Sarah, but a little girl crouching by the tree, giggling, one hand over her mouth, the other setting twig dolls in the sand.

"How did you do that?" Maggie said.

"It's just imagining," Sarah said. She smiled. "I just wanted you to know it is possible. Minnie said more."

Maggie nodded.

"Minnie said to tell you we have to go to Bone Lake together."

"Did Minnie indicate who is going to finance this trip?"

"She did. She said 'Maggie's got one credit card that isn't maxed out, a paycheck with all that Memorial Day overtime, and a good waitress can always get a job.' Then she was gone. I saw the sky start to get light, so I came home."

"I'm glad," Maggie said. "At least, I think I am."

IT'D BE HARD for the average person to imagine that sun blasting into your face like a steel mill, and asphalt so hot you can feel it through your boots, would be welcome to a man. But if you'd just survived two hours of questioning by an old cop and his partner who looked like a cute lesbo, you'd step cheerfully out of the air-conditioning of the Creosote Police Substation and raise your arms to the sky. You might even say, "Fuck me running, thank you, Big Whatever—for freedom."

Cowbird wished he believed in something to thank. If he did, he'd elaborate, "Thank you for how they didn't go further back in my sheet than a year ago. Thank you for the fact the lady cop looked me in the eye and shook her head and turned to the old cop and said, 'Nope.'" As it was, Orlen Jackson grinned, hitched a ride over to the Crystal, and when the new waitress brought him his first free beer, he tipped her five bucks.

MAGGIE AND SARAH waited to know what to do. There was no burning bush. No old lady dropped in. So they did nothing. Midmorning the Mojave went flat. The horizons could have been ten, twenty, a hundred miles away.

"What's salient here," Maggie said. The word was perfect, the floor of the wash salt-white, her lips sweat-salty, what they were doing essential as salt. "What's salient here is that we do this right."

Her thoughts rippled like the heat waves rising between them and the big cottonwood. She looked at the driftwood on the floor of the wash and saw bones, saw how noon after Mojave noon was taking them down to pure mineral.

"Sarah," she said, "we've got to get your bones."

"There aren't any. They burned me."

"What?"

"They cremated me," Sarah said calmly. "Police substation refrigeration capabilities aren't that great."

"Aren't they supposed to get permission or something?"

"Sometimes we Indians fall through the cracks. The cops have the ashes, my earrings, a couple other things."

"What things? The pencil?" Maggie asked.

"The pencil?"

"The pencil they found in your hand. What were you writing?"

Sarah laughed softly. "It was going to be a note to Tina Rae. It was to tell her what her half of the electric bill was and wish her luck."

"We'll get the ashes."

Sarah trailed sand through her fingers. "I don't know about that. Willow don't release our dead with fire. We take the body back into the mountains. Dead Willow are buzzard and coyote food."

"But the ashes . . . ," Maggie said. She remembered her dead mother's body on the undertaker's gurney, her body gnarled as juniper roots. She had kissed her mother's hands. She had murmured what passed for prayer: "Make music. Make what you love."

"The buzzards and coyotes can't eat ashes," Sarah said firmly. "But the earrings were my best pair. Remember? The little gold gun and the roadrunner. I wore them all the time. They were the only present Yakima ever gave me."

JESSE ran till he reached the base of the mountains. He leaned back against the cool stone and slid to the sand. Knowing the mountain continued down beneath the ground, five hundred feet, a thousand, filled him with as close as he ever got to peace. He watched the shadows shrink toward him.

The air grew warm. Jesse closed his eyes. The thread of his own blood drew him back, and back on Blood Trail. Darwin, Nguyen, the boy who turned away from the VC antiaircraft site and saw him. Smiled. Jesse's arm drawn back to throw the knife, throw the knife at the boy he had smoked with, the boy whose dark eyes had mirrored his own, tiny black mirrors, the fine fine opium drifting in their breath, their blood, their smiles.

"Too late now," he whispered. "Too weak." Time became a pothole. His life basalt. There was not enough regret to fill the hole. Not enough grief to erode the stone.

He thought of Maggie. Of the bad camp with Maggie. How the pot had snaked in his brain, its tongue flickering, licking away love, licking away the honest truth, no fangs, no poison, just a little tongue of smoke dissolving everything.

He took his tools out of his pack and bent to the work. This time the break would be clean. He'd knap a Clovis edge, delicate serrations; inscribe three footsteps on the handle, three the number of incompletion. He would tell the man who wanted to be a warrior that the knife was his boot camp.

JESSE packed at dusk. For an entire day, he'd seen no one, not even the drift of a faraway truck's dust plume. A twenty-seventh/twenty-eighth moon hung over his way back, glinted off the truck's windshield, guiding him east. The little crossroads at Redstone sparkled in the dark. He moved slow, more tired than he should have been.

Anger's hungry, he thought. I'm food. He moved down into a little wash, moonlight like blue phosphor, shadows alive. An owl called.

The knife blade was wrapped tight in buckskin, hanging from a leather thong over his heart. In all the years, he'd never made one for himself. He owned no weapons. Not since the last killing. He remembered the Indian kid's voice, drunk, guttural. "I'm going to kill you and everybody you love, bilagáana boy." Jesse lashing out, the kid sliding to the stoop, his blood smearing the screen, and how, in that moment, Jesse had sworn he saw Darwin Yazzie. A ghost of a ghost.

Jesse crouched in the bottom of the wash. "Woman," he said, "what have you opened up?" He unwrapped the blade. Moonlight shattered on its delicate edge. He moved the point through the packed sand. Slow. Careful. Three words. I. Don't. Know.

AUNT BONNIE, Zach's mom, and Sue from the snack bar were in the kitchen. They hadn't even noticed Zach when he came in. Sue had a pint of tequila; his aunt and mom were inhaling coffee and sweet potato pie. He hated to pass up the pie, but he could tell that what was going on was like a wake. And it was just for ladies.

He figured he'd log on for just a minute, check his e-mail just in case, then crash. There she was, Shegirlollie15@yahoo.com. "JGhost, so fun. Tonight. Same place. Just you and me. Ms. S. p.s. Don't get any bright ideas."

FIREBIRDS were light in the rear. Even with a cooler, kitchen box, two trash bags of clothes, four boxes of books, and a ghost sitting on the trunk, the car fishtailed and hung up. Maggie hit the gas, hoping to gun them out onto pavement. Years of driving drunk on Northeast ice had not prepared her for sand. She dug them in.

Sarah climbed out. Maggie followed. "I'm a genius at unsticking cars," Sarah said. "I remember my otherwise forgettable graduation night. Me and my best friend Denise split as soon as the ceremony was over, got us some wine and weed, drove her graduation present out into the badlands till we were up to the fenders in sand. We sat in the front of that red 1989 Chevy pickup and laughed so hard we couldn't move."

Maggie grinned. "And you the girl with four scholarships and all."

"Pick up as many big flat rocks as you can," Sarah said, "and a bunch of brush. So, there's bad bad Denise and me. We do the only thing you can under those circumstances—we get higher. Then we stagger around, find a bunch of dry wood, and make a fire. We start it with our diplomas, and when it really gets roaring, we throw our caps and gowns in.

"There were sparks shooting up into the sky, we were singin' Mötley Crüe, and we weren't ever going back—but we forgot those gowns are made of weird plastic. It was a beautiful bunch of flames, orange and blue and greenish, and the smoke was evil. Denise kept yelling, *Toxic waste, toxic waste, we're the queens of toxic waste.*

"We were gonna find Mötley Crüe and tell 'em to write a song about the queens of toxic waste, but we passed out in the truck and morning came and we had to hike back to town and get Denise's brother to stick rocks and brush under the tires and tow us out, and then she ended up getting married to her first husband, and I headed to college." She handed Maggie a pile of rocks. "Shoot, I used to love fire. No more."

It took an hour till the Bird's wheels were free. Maggie drove slow, taking it easy on the tires. The road curved away from the river marsh, tamarisk thinning to honey mesquite, cat's claw, and bright yellow brittlebush. They pulled into a dinky snowbird town—trailers, icicle lights strung along faded awnings, and hand-carved signs that said Bide-A-Wee and Dun Roamin.'

An old woman rode by on a grown-up's trike. She'd woven plastic flowers through the pastel baskets hanging from the handlebars. Her pink license plate said Grandma Knows Best. There was maybe twenty years between her and Maggie. No thanks, Maggie thought. I'd rather swallow a bunch of pills, wander back into one of these washes and be coyote brunch.

Sarah grabbed her arm. "Look at that sign. Old Route 66 to Oatman."

"Why Oatman?" Maggie said. "We've got no clearance and low tires. Something smart and deadly is probably trying to find us and we can be in Vegas in two hours by the main highway, where there are telephones, friendly cops, and cheap buffets."

"There are burros in Oatman," Sarah said. "Little wild burros that eat out of your hand."

Maggie looked at Sarah's profile and saw the little girl under the cotton-wood—and remembered another little girl, green-eyed, scowling, her brown hair tucked up in a felt cowboy hat. "We can go to Oatman."

"It's OK. We don't have to. I know it's dangerous. I know that."

"No. We'll go. When I was a kid I used to walk down the main street in our little town and sing my favorite cowboy song at the top of my lungs."

"What were you singing?"

"Well," Maggie said. She remembered waiting to tell live Sarah about her mother's people and hex signs and magic mirrors.

"Come on," Sarah said.

"'Ghost Riders in the Sky.'"

Sarah didn't laugh. She leaned back in her seat. "Minnie says gsi'ki are everywhere. All the time. Past, now, and future all at once."

"What are gsi'ki?"

"Close as you can come in English is subatomic particles."

"So, maybe I sang a song about you and me," Maggie said.

"Maybe," Sarah said. "What I know for sure is that something killed my subatomic ass."

Maggie pulled into the one gas station, reinflated the tires, and waited for invisible Sarah to go into the place and return. She left the passenger door open. Sarah waited to gather her gsi'ki until they were back on the road and held out two candy bars. "With almonds or without?" she said.

"With," Maggie said. "Could you teach me how to do gsi'ki?"

11   There were no wild burros in Oatman. There were only tame gordos snarfing chow the tourists bought from curbside machines for fifty cents a pop. Everything else living was either flint-eyed souvenir vendors or what Sarah called Scuppies, senior citizen yuppies. "Oh well," she said. "This is a great road. Let's take it, find a safe place to camp, and see what comes next."

"You really want to leave?"

"You bet. We couldn't get out of the car anyhow. We don't have our matching Kokopelli T-shirts."

Maggie was grateful. Let the sun and dry wind do their work on these charming ghost towns, let the rowhouses and company shacks weather down to mesquite fertilizer. When she remembered DC fondly, it was because he had once stood in a meticulously restored bar in meticulously restored Telluride, Colorado, surrounded by meticulously retro-hippie millionaires and quietly pissed in the meticulously scattered sawdust at his feet.

She and Sarah cruised up the winding two-lane, between black volcanic spires that looked like goddesses and gods in a Javanese shadow play. She remembered a glorious R & R in Thailand, her and Dark Cloud's shadows weaving together on the bedroom wall. She remembered how the flickering light could confuse you, make you think the shadow lovers were real.

Sarah hummed Mötley Crüe's "Home Sweet Home." "I still love those guys."

"I love this," Maggie said, and pulled onto a rocky point. Late afternoon light threw blue shadows over desert the sheen of pewter, over a tangle of tracks, solitary creosote, and raw red boulders. Maggie crouched on the basalt. It was perfectly still, heat waves rippling up from a distant ridgeline.

She heard a crunch on gravel. A beige van pulled up, two sea kayaks on top. A couple climbed out. "God," the woman said. "God, this is a moonscape."

"No," Maggie whispered. Not a moonscape. It was home. Harsh, scarred, and utterly unto itself. A dirty yellow cloud floated over the power plant to the west, Creosote metastasizing below it, where it was midnight in broad daylight, where a bunch of people she might never see again were dealing hands, frying bacon, making change, and earning in two days what this couple might spend on dinner.

She understood why tourists had to redefine the desert. You could *visit* a moonscape, be amused, uneasy, bored, afraid. You might think you owed the place nothing.

Beer bottle shards lay at Maggie's feet. Amber. Green. "Name this," she thought and pressed her finger on one. The pain cleared her anger.

A video camera whirred. "Let's go," the guy said. "We're due in Santa Barbara by ten."

Maggie shaded her eyes against a sun starting to go faint gold above the far mountains. She looked out over the old mining roads, dune buggy tracks, a lone dust devil swirling up from the desert floor carrying specks of mica, dried grass, mesquite pods, and Taco Bell boxes.

Piss on those people and their sensitive observations. Piss on their fake truck. Piss on everything except the big river, the rock under her feet, Creosote's beat-up glamour, Sarah, and maybe Jesse. She was writing his name in the sand and thinking about mailing his drawings to him when Sarah yelled. "We gotta go, if we're stopping at the Kingman post office before it closes."

"Are you poking around in my mind?" Maggie sighed. If she was, she was. Welcome to whatever she dredged up there.

"You know," Sarah said, "sometimes those gsi'ki just won't quit."

JESSE set up his stove. He boiled water, steamed cooked rice, and shook in Tabasco. He remembered the 'Yards gathered in a circle, shaking Tabasco on their cold rice in the triple canopy pitch-black. They'd overshot the rendezvous. There was nothing to do but wait till dawn, their great good pal melted in above the tree line.

Chuck's night contained them. Mildewed velvet. Too late for hot food. Too late for a smoke. The flick of a lighter could be just the signal Mr. Death was watching for. Jesse's belly had rumbled. The 'Yard to his left had giggled. Then farted. Silence. Another fart. Another. All the way around the circle. Jesse considered how it would be to die at the end of a 'Yard joke. And, when it was his turn, he clenched his butthole and let loose.

This rice was perfect, doubly hot. He felt a true grin on his face. He brewed a cup of tea, took out the half-finished knife blade and held it to the moonlight. It shone faintly, five thousand bucks damn near in his pocket. For maybe two days' work. Two days' work for five months of freedom. A man could live alone on a thousand dollars a month easy. No rent. No house payment. Dried squash and corn from the garden. Gas for the truck. Kerosene for the lanterns. Insurance for the truck because it's easier to keep things legal. A few ounces of homegrown, maybe a pebble of hash, and more than a few prudently doled-out nights of two-buck blackjack. More than enough for the man who has everything, the man so full of the past there is no room for future.

It was a joke. A man too full for love, a woman the same. Dumb love found them. Jesse poured the dregs of his tea in the rice pot, scoured it with a hand-ful of twigs, and set it upside down in the sand to dry.

He would sleep here, work on the knife in the shade of the wash, then head up toward Pioche, stop at every cafe and bar on the way. He'd be cruising for stories; maybe some clue hidden in an old bro's endless reminiscence. It was lonely in eastern Nevada. People loved to talk. And, since they were mostly Mormons, all you had to do was listen.

NEXT AFTERNOON, he was on the road. Nobody was saying much—except about Jesse's immortal soul like they thought they owned it. He made no deals. Besides, he didn't know what he was looking for. All he knew was he was not finding it. Not in Redstone, not in East Paradise or Smithville, not in Beaver Dams or Enterprise.

Pioche had been infected with Moab charm. Gear shops with names like Cycle This! Bars with beer named cute. At least it was beer. He stopped for one, couldn't stand what passed for talk, slid the beer into his shirt, and went back out to the parking lot. I am on my way to being a miserable old fart, he thought. He wondered how the fuck Old Ray stayed as chipper as he did. He knew Ray would be only too happy to remind him. "Get yourself a good woman, boy."

Jesse climbed back in the truck. It was 110 degrees and all he really wanted to do was soak in the little hot springs he remembered from that long escape twenty years ago, on the straight-shot highways that took him away from Red Lindall and his offer of respectable slaughter. He remembered the sweet warm water running over emerald moss into a rock pool that the locals had built. He wanted to come up out of the spring like he'd found salvation more reliable than the ace and jack of spades. It was sixty miles out of the way, but his way hadn't exactly been mapped by AAA.

The blade and handle were finished. All that was left was the binding. He shifted his pack to the floor, one-handed the cooler to the passenger seat, took out an Old Mil, and slid it back and forth over his throat. His shirt was wet. The molten air pouring through the window evaporated his sweat, cooled him quick and natural. He never ran the air conditioner. It smelled like a morgue.

The road to Silverspur was almost empty. Even the assholes in their air-conditioned, computerized, pop-out dining room fifth-wheel rolling mansions were afraid of Lincoln County in late June. He saw a couple of primered pickup trucks, an aged biker, two Salt Lake City coeds—or maybe Vegas working girls—in a red convertible. They were worth a glance, nothing more.

"Maggie," he said to the wind. "Maggie, you've ruined me. I'm bored. For the first time in thirty years, I'm lonesome. Dope isn't working. Beer isn't working. The road isn't working. I want, shit, fuck it, you know what I want."

He remembered the grunts' mantra: *Hurry up and wait.* Five days of Big Nothing, then half an hour of blood, bone shards, and terror. And now, thirty miles out on a road with no mirages, he pulled into Mercury, a dead-quiet piss-stop, its sand and sky gleaming like its namesake. Jesse gassed up, couldn't find the clerk, left ten bucks on the counter.

There was a pay phone nailed on a stump. He pulled the truck into the one patch of shade and called Maggie. No answer. No answering machine. When he called the Crystal, Sheree told him she hadn't seen Maggie for two, maybe three days. She paused. "Listen, you better not be some closet serial killer Jesse, 'cause if you're the one that left the photo of Maggie with the eyes burned out in the men's john, your skinny ass is mine!"

He heard the fear under her words. He knew better than to mess with it. "Right," he said. "Sheree, you know me. You fuckin' know me." The fear that slammed him would have to wait.

"Call tomorrow," she said. "I'll let you know if I hear anything. Ray's still in the hospital. Helen called the kids. Come back soon from wherever it is you're at."

"Yeah," he said. "I'm gonna see if I can find Maggie."

"Good luck, boyfriend."

Jesse hung up. There was still no sign of life from the gas station. He grabbed some beef jerky and left another buck on the counter. The truck had cooled down enough to be a little less than unbearable. He popped an Old Mil, opened the jerky, and adjusted his salts and fluids. His brain picked up speed. He remembered Sarah was from Bone Lake, and Maggie was a woman who believed in the road as medicine. He understood, for the first time since he'd left Creosote, what he was hunting; and he remembered that Bone Lake was maybe sixty miles north of the hot springs. Cottonwood Springs. The name came back to him, and the soft green light that had shimmered there.

He drove ninety miles an hour. By the time both sides of an old Van Morrison album had played out, he was on the one-block Main Street, the big trees shattering the light, the shock of green busting up his panic. The long fence still ran along the east side of the road. This time there were signs blocking the main springs. "Future home of the luxury cottonwood hot springs and casino." Jesse grinned. The paint was fading. Bird shit lay chalky along the fence top. He imagined when the sign went up. Silicon Valley money, a van full of thirty-year-old guys in river shorts, sandals, and hundred-buck shades. Walking the property, scoping out the old ranch building.

The rusted-out pipes from the springs poked up at the edge of the fence. He saw the old buildings, adobe fragile as parchment, cracked windows, roofs peeling away. The signs had been graffitied. Not gang code, but local sentiments. *Die yuppie scum. You can't Californicate Cottonwood. Not here not ever.*

He saw the gas station up ahead and realized he was gulping air like a drowning man.

MAGGIE AND SARAH drove past the broken hoists and walled-up adits of the old Gold Road mine. Sun-bleached warnings, Danger! Peligro! floated like ghosts across the crumbling walls.

The new Gold Road mine lay in a valley below. There was a sign by the road: "All property on either side of the road for the next 1.2 miles is private. Trespassers will be arrested." Maggie looked at the miles of concertina wire and thought of Creosote and what was under the big casinos, at the base of the dams, Ransom, Hoover, Glen Canyon. She saw in the old walls how time and weather ate what humans made. She saw the promise of return.

"Hey," Sarah said. "There's a spring up there." A cottonwood arched over the road. The tree was luminous green against the dark rock. Maggie pulled over.

Sarah climbed out and walked around the curve of the cliff. Maggie followed. The mineral breath of earth took her by surprise. A cave no higher than her shoulders opened out. A pool shimmered at the front, then vanished into shadows.

Sarah pointed up.

A single acacia branch hung over the cliff face, mistletoe clinging to its leaves. A spider worked the intersections. Host and parasite, weaver and web were all pale gold. Sarah breathed on the acacia leaves. The spider darted to the edge of her web. Sarah smiled.

Maggie watched. She knew she was no longer thinking of Sarah as a ghost.

JESSE pulled into the Cottonwood We Got It convenience store, gas station, drive-in booze counter, and corn dog emporium. He found himself moving slowly toward the sweet cool dark in the store, slowly toward the green light under the cottonwoods, moving toward the next moment, and the next— toward his body slipping into the spring as though he was moving into Maggie.

He pushed open the We Got It door and stepped into the reek of hot oil and the clank of a dying swamp cooler. The clerk was a rosy-cheeked girl wearing a cross made of safety pins and blue beads. "No corn dogs," she said. "We're out. Ma's working on 'em."

"It's OK," Jesse said. "I just came in for ice and to ask you if a woman came through here in an old gray Firebird."

"Is a Firebird like a Ford?" the girl asked.

"More like a Pontiac."

"Like long in the back?"

"That's it."

"Is she, like, Mexican?"

"She's dark-skinned, but she's Anglo. Got red hair."

"Nope. Nobody like that."

He thanked her, bought a can of Spicy Hot V8, grabbed his ice, and headed for the door.

"Hey," the girl said, "you want to know something cool?"

"You bet."

"There's a real nice hot springs here. Pull out, go north about a hundred feet, take the dirt road to your right. Just follow it."

"Thanks," Jesse said.

She looked up at him. "We don't tell everybody. Don't you."

He followed her directions, though the way was as known to him as the scars on his body. He pulled up next to the oldest cottonwood and parked. He would hang around till six, have a few good hours of driving, a few good hours of softening light, then moonlit dark and the distant glitter of Bone Lake. Maybe Maggie. Maybe not. For sure, the Hotel Montella, honest blackjack, and a $5.99 plate of prime rib.

He sat on the fender, pulled off his jeans, considered taking off his shirt and didn't. Even though the air was 110 degrees and there was no reason for any-body but a blue-lonesome Boonie rat to want to slide into water a few degrees hotter, people could show up and he didn't want questions.

He stepped into jungle light. Emerald. Drenched. Somebody had taken a sledgehammer to the steps that once led into the pool, to the concrete wall that held the names of the Junior Job Corps kids and the words, "We built it so we could come."

He eased into the silken water. He felt his breath and bones release, the long muscles of his arms and legs going soft, the scars tightening, then seeming to melt away. He pulled off his shirt and draped it over the edge of the spring.

He slipped all the way under the water and opened his eyes. There was more green light. When he stood, water pearled on his skin. He stretched out his fingers. Light webs. Shining scars. He wondered if his mind was slipping. Seeing so close. Losing the big picture.

He imagined another man might cry. His tears didn't come. He envied that other man, most other men, in fact. It was the closest he would let himself come to sorrow. He dropped back into the water, leaned against the ruined wall. He slept, maybe for a few minutes, maybe an hour. There was a roar and Jesse bolted awake.

THE AIR INSIDE the Firebird was searing. Maggie and Sarah drank hot water from the bottle they'd stashed in the front seat. Maggie felt water trick-ling down, her throat opening. She remembered Jesse's lips on her arm, at the crook of her elbow. How later he had brought her a glass of water and she drank, the water a kiss, Jesse's next kiss as delicate. She had been afraid she would forget how his touch brought her into her body. Now she was afraid she wouldn't forget.

"Time to go," Sarah said. "Minnie says if you have something you need to do and you hold off doing it, you feed the—there isn't really a white word for it—the mess."

The road zigzagged down. Maggie pulled onto red cinders at the base of a long basalt rubble slope, and leaned back. "Mess or no mess, I've got to make coffee."

Sarah looked around. There was squatty juniper, tiny purple flowers, and fire rings full of scorched beer cans. "*This* is a party place," she said, and scrambled down to a basalt outcropping that seemed the edge of the earth.

Maggie joined her on the outcropping. Below was a cluster of shacks and trailers perched on the edge of a curving wash. She imagined living like that—sun-scarred travel trailer, no phone, no TV, no radio, trips into Kingman maybe six times a year whether you needed it or not. Waking into rose-gold dawn, the raw vegetable scent of juniper and mesquite pouring in through a cracked window. She was ready. All she needed was the mini-jackpot on Nevada Nickel Progressive.

Sarah sat next to her. They were quiet. Violet shadows crept across the broken rock. Lace agate lay at Maggie's feet, a swirl of translucent cream.

"That's Ed's Camp down there," Sarah said. "A desert rat told me about it. An old old lady is the caretaker. There are fire agates out in the washes."

"I wonder if the old lady would let a couple of fugitives crash in her camp?"

"Can't hurt to ask."

12 Jesse looked up over the edge of the spring. A gleaming King Cab Ford half-ton pulled in, rainbow Xmas lights jittering on the fenders. A seventies refrigerator-green Chevette parked next to the truck. The last in was a pin-striped Kawasaki chopper, fringed anywhere you could hang fringe, including the passenger's spectacular butt. Jesse heard the fat thump of *norteño* and a dozen kinds of laughter.

Jesse was trapped and company was coming. Lots of company. He remembered the opium den in Chu Lai, mama-sans and papa-sans, a thousand kids, pigs and a parrot, mama-san handing out the pipes while her baby tugged at the collar of her blouse. This time there was no perfumed fog veiling him from what would come next. Strangers. Noise. Chaos. So much movement there was no way he could keep track of who was where doing what.

A family, a fucking village, poured out of the Malibu and the truck, withered grandma to withered newborn. He pulled the shirt down over his shoulders. High heels clicked across the asphalt path to the spring. A woman sat on the edge and shrieked. She wore hot pants, gold high heels, and a fringed black leather halter barely doing its job.

She grinned at him, pulled off her shoes and shorts and stood in the water. Jesse couldn't tell if she was wearing a thong or a bikini. Her boyfriend thumped down next to his head. Jesse abandoned his research on the lady's underpinnings. The guy was five feet tall and five feet square. His right eye was gone. His mustache flowed down to his Adam's apple, which was working violently. "Yo," he said. "Par-tay!"

"You bet." Jesse looked anywhere but at the perfect ass moving slowly away from him and the fire hydrant—who was pulling off his biker boots and wiggling his bare toes in the air.

A half-dozen kids dive-bombed into the pool. Three teenage girls, luscious, more luscious, and most luscious, followed them. A wiry woman in denim tights handed a toddler down to Most Luscious. The girl danced the baby through the water.

Mariachi flooded Jesse's ears. The singer's voice rose, held one note for as long as it took Jesse to relax—which seemed like forever.

An old man in a straw cowboy hat led the rest of the men to the base of a far cottonwood. They settled into the shade, three hip-hop vatos with shaved heads and baggy pants, a middle-aged queen in a lime green tank top, two tired middle-aged guys who started passing a tequila bottle around. The old man took a long pull on the tequila and nodded at one of the vatos.

The kid slid off his jail scuffs and walked to the spring. Every step he gave Jesse a hard hard young young look. Most Luscious watched the boy. Her smile was huge. She held up the jet-eyed baby. Jesse looked away. He felt his scars tighten. The vato jumped into the pool and cradled the toddler to his chest. Most Luscious pointed to the baby's behind and pinched her nose. Papa laughed, carried the baby up to a picnic table, and cleaned him up.

Most Luscious beckoned to the boy-dad. She spoke in Spanish, "Elizar . . . ," then something fast and soft and irresistible. Elizar carried the baby back into the water. Jesse watched the girl turn away and look back over her wet shoulder. She stepped into the tiny rapid that led down out of the pool into the shallows. The vato carried the baby to her. She settled into the soft earth on the bank and put the baby to nurse.

A slim older woman nodded at Jesse. "Will you eat with us?" she asked.

"Gracias," he said. Having pretty much exhausted his Spanish, he just grinned. She laid pork chops, green chilies, and tortillas on the grill, put tamales to steam in a black pot. The hot-pants woman sat on the edge of the pool. She dried her feet and began to stroke polish on her toenails. "Mi hermana," she said, and waved the polish brush toward the nursing mother. "My sister. Her little boy. You are married? You have children?"

"No," Jesse said. "I am alone." He was lost in wet jade light, cook-fire smoke, air like water, water warm as blood. He was lost in memory.

LATER, after the cook had handed Jesse a plate of tacos, tamales, and chopped cilantro, and he had taken more than one pull off the fifth tequila bottle to go around, and a half dozen primo joints had circled around to everyone but the kids and the newborn (Grandma neatly pinching the roach and swallowing it); later, through that sweet vegetable haze of tequila and pot, Jesse saw the campfire flickering in the baby's dark eyes and knew what had to come next.

He made his good-bye. Abrazos and handshakes. "Mi mota, su mota," the viejo said, and pressed a fat joint into Jesse's palm. The cook gave him a bag of food. Most Luscious and her man had disappeared into the shadows beyond the cottonwoods. "Adios," they cried out as he climbed into his truck. "Buena suerte."

THE ROAD OUT of Cottonwood Springs to Bone Lake ran due north. There was an almost full moon. Jesse turned off the headlights. Though he had driven the road before, it seemed brand new, a highway of silver radiance and longing. He figured he'd go up to Bone Lake, get a good night's sleep, and head back where he belonged. He had a good two hours of driving ahead. He pulled a tape out of the glove compartment and slid it into the deck.

13 There was no Ed in Ed's Camp, no Alma. The Cactus Cafe's front door was broken, its glass woven tight with cobwebs; the windows of the other house had been painted dark green. Sarah tapped on the door of the house. There was silence.

Pebbles were scattered on a splintered wood table around a coffee can and a sign: Fire Agates — .25–5.00 Honor System Play Fair.

They took one apiece. Maggie left ten bucks. Sarah grinned, "You were raised Catholic, weren't you?" Maggie shrugged. "We're so broke it doesn't matter."

Sarah turned the little stone in her long fingers. The fire agate was the shape of a tiny gourd, smooth as if it had been polished, sunlight glowing in its honey-dark heart. She tied a shoelace around the stem and hung it from her neck.

Maggie's was a half-globe, mahogany and amber. She held it against her cheek.

"It's earth candy," Sarah said.

Maggie smiled. "I'm glad you're here." Which, she figured later, was probably what made Sarah disappear. You started to appreciate somebody, maybe even counted on their presence. You had some mutual jokes, some words and silences you didn't have to translate. You knew how they liked their coffee and wanted their burger. You started to appreciate that when you looked over, they were sitting there saying nothing—just being Sarah for instance. Right when you reached that part, you'd better get ready to be alone again.

MAGGIE dashed into the Kingman post office five minutes to closing. She bought a Priority mailer and three postcards. She wrote out the cards:

Deac, I'll call when I get settled.

Dear Bookmobile, my fourteen books, not yet overdue, are on, in, under, and around the bed in Apartment 4, Riverview Heights. Ask Eddie in the front office to let you in. Show them this note. Maggie Foltz.

And then, she resisted twenty different impulses and wrote only this: *Jesse, Ray will have your pictures.* She hesitated. *Maggie.*

She slid Jesse's package into the mailer and addressed it to Ray. She was unsettled to feel an ache between her ribs. As if she was mailing Jesse back to himself.

"Where you from?" the postmistress asked.

"Back East," Maggie said prudently, though it had been two decades since she and DC had become western nomads.

"I grew up near Gold Road," the postmistress said. "My daddy was a miner, and his daddy, and his daddy's daddy. I loved it. Vacations we ran those hills from dawn till dusk. Come September, we took the bus down here to school, pissing, moaning, and whining all the way."

"Do you know where Alma is?" Maggie asked.

"Oh, honey, you come through Ed's Camp, didn't you?" The woman looked away. "Alma. I am so sad to tell you she's in a nursing home here in town."

"I'm sorry," Maggie said. She imagined an old woman leaning against a window, breathing air-conditioned air, one hand pressed hard against the glass. "She has a beautiful name."

"It's a good old-fashioned name," the woman said firmly. "She was one of those strong ladies we used to get out here. She's ninety-eight and she ran that show till this year."

JESSE slid the tape into the player. It had been ten years since he listened to it. He half-hoped it had warped in the desert heat and would break. He hit Play. Time grabbed Jesse. The desert around him could have been ten thousand miles away.

The colonel spoke English. Jesse still didn't understand why the man had let him tape his words, much less even talked to him. It had been a slow night in the Tu Do street bar. The man had staggered in already drunk. Or maybe he'd just run out of whatever it took to carry horror another step.

I will tell you something. Perhaps it is a strange poem. I think that way, sometimes. As though the words are not mine. You know we believe those things, that the past can speak through a man.

Sometimes all you need is nakedness. You strip the misguided one and you remain clothed. Sometimes that will do the trick. If it doesn't, there are restraints, the naked body shackled, spread-eagled, the one who is teaching truth free to walk around the room, free to light a cigarette.

The cigarette. Sometimes that is all you need. Afterwards you look at the naked body and you can see the earth. You wonder if this is how the ancestors see us.

Looking down. Out beyond the Rabbit Moon. Earth as body, bomb craters as deep burns.

You see your country, and you unlock the shackles. Sometimes there are tears. You have long imagined that your country weeps. You hand the naked one his clothes. The burns will heal. The mistakes are gone. Your eyes meet, and in the silence you imagine you are brothers.

You light another cigarette. He flinches. You offer him the cigarette. He closes his eyes and draws in smoke. The guards take him out. You light another cigarette and you wonder how long it will be before your country lies unscarred along the great green ocean.

Do you understand, my friend? We are not monsters.

Jesse hit Stop. He looked at the silver desert. His country. Old mines. Cow-seared grass. Fluorescent plastic survey ribbons. Scars were scars. Monsters were everywhere.

"'BOUT TIME YOU GOT HERE," Zach's mom said. The restaurant was starting to fill up, the tour bus gang waving their comps at the hostess. Zach's mom slid French toast onto his plate. She handed him the can of whipped cream. "Have at it." He sprayed a mountain over the strawberries and finished it off with a two-inch swirl. Then he waited.

He suspected what was coming. His mom was unbelievably easy to read. She leaned on the chair next to him. Waitstaff was not allowed to sit with customers, even if the customer was employee-comped, even if the customer was a son.

"I was sitting behind the Riverview watching the cats," he said.

His mom was dead quiet.

"And watching the sun come up."

Nada.

"And feeding the fish."

His mom's silence could be like Darth Vader's.

"And talking with my friend, Spooky."

His mom looked down at her hands.

"Who skates?" Zach said. He heard his voice go up on the end like chicks' voices did.

"And is a girl. Like a sister? Just a friend, Mom? Just a freakin' friend."

"Good."

"Me and her, it's like a cool thing we do." He started to say, *like a ritual,* which he knew it was, but figured that would freak her out.

His mom gave him a quick hug and smiled at a fat biker who had gestured toward the whipped cream can. "Not quite done here, sir," she said and sprayed a blob on Zach's nose.

MAGGIE called the Crystal from a pay phone and asked for Ray. The girl said, "He's not here. AKA's covering for him." Maggie said AKA would do fine.

Forever later, Maggie heard his voice: "What can I do ya?"

"Hi, it's Maggie. Don't ask me where I am."

"Never would. What do you need?"

"Sarah's ashes, if you can get them. And I'm sending a package for Runner care of Ray."

"No problem on the latter, the former might be tricky," AKA said. "Shit, I gotta go."

"Wait," Maggie said. "The cops. Anything new?"

"Nothing. Haven't heard a word."

"Where's Ray?"

"Fell," AKA said. "Runner hauled him out of a barrow ditch. Ray's recuperating. Runner's running."

"What a surprise."

"God bless," AKA said. "You travel easy."

Maggie hung up and turned toward the Bird. There was no one in the passenger seat. No cigarette smoke. No nothing.

JESSE popped a beer and restarted the tape. The voice belonged to one of the older Bru. The man read a letter he had taken from a vc's body. He had told Jesse the words might have been a curse on the enemy; they might have been a lie:

What has been done to me has been done to others. Up here, in these mountains, a man does not go off to live in the forest alone. If he does, we know that something has entered him, eaten everything but bones and skin and occupied the shell.

I am such a man.

It is no less than I deserve. "Pan cuai" means to shoot. My cousin paid the sorcerer . . . he placed the can chai to his lips, this stone tube smooth as a rice kernel, and he blew into my body can trien, the bullet you cannot see. I was not there. I was some kilometers away, with my lover, my cousin's wife. We had finished our embrace and, suddenly, my heart was pierced.

"Can trien," I whispered and left her side.

From that moment on I heard the murmur of Tiang Ca Mui, the one who takes the soul. I followed the sound. I was eaten. I was occupied. My wife and children made sacrifices till nothing was left. Nothing.

Now, I live far from the village. I am eternal. All I know is hunger. You can see all of this in my eyes.

If you meet me, look away.

The tape crackled and went dead.

Jesse drained the beer and opened another. He watched the moon arc above the mountains. It was easy to imagine ghosts, easy to imagine the ghosts Yuan had said were starving, to imagine them chittering in the wet green air of what once was Bru country.

He had seen the hungry ghosts in his country. American phantoms: vets holed up in the little desert towns and brutal cities, guys who came out only at night, hunted for their too little and too late checks in the plastic bucket at the motel office, and started their sleepwalk off the main drag, heading for The Hoosegow or The Crow Bar, picking up speed around midnight, when they moved on to any bar not called a brewery—till the bartender shouted, "Last call for alcohol." Then, they stumbled back to fumble with the key to their door. They usually slept solo, with only the company of their memories; woke to wan coffee at the Circle ĸ and newspaper headlines like Thirty-Three Percent of Homeless Are Veterans.

He remembered nights when he first got not-quite-home to Flagstaff, walking downtown for hours till he could even *try* to sleep. He'd see those other spook-eyed guys till about two and then they'd disappear. What they really did in the long hours between last call and first had been a mystery to him. What he had known was that he was somehow lucky.

"HEY," Maggie whispered, "where are you?"

There was no gsi'ki shimmer. She bought a newspaper and waited. There was nothing in the *Mojave Miner* about Sarah's murder. The sun dropped fast through the last degree of its arc, going bittersweet, scarlet, and gone.

"Sarah," Maggie said, "we've got to get out of here. I'd like to camp before dark." It occurred to her it was a little strange to be sitting in a beat-up Firebird with Nevada plates talking to an empty passenger seat—and there were local cops who would be only too happy to agree with her. "OK, I'm driving out of town. You can find me, and if you don't, you can get your damn dead self home."

Maggie drove to a burger joint where she bought a Genuine Southwest Old Route 66 green chili cheeseburger, Genuine Southwest Old Route 66 fries, and a nonspecific coffee milkshake.

She checked the propane. Enough for coffee. She filled up two water jugs. She thought about driving straight to Vegas, but when she opened the map, the names in the country around her hijacked her plans: Grapevine Canyon, Spirit Mountain, Searchlight. She drove to a turnoff by the train tracks, ate her supper, and studied the road atlas.

If she let herself be seduced by the map, she, maybe they, would have to drive back over the bridge in Creosote. For once, she was grateful for bumper-to-bumper casino traffic in which you could be just one more car. There was a flyer in the folds of the atlas—a guide to the Joshua Tree Road to Nipton. Nipton, California, where more winning lottery tickets had been sold than anywhere in the world. Maggie looked out past the metallic glare of the security light to the darkness. "Come on back," she said. "We're going to change our luck in Nipton."

JESSE could have repeated what came next on the tape word for word. He pulled off on a ranch road and opened the truck doors so the speakers in the panels would move the voice out into the dark. No way he'd try to drive. If he was ever going to cry, this was going to do it.

Not some support group. Not some fucking therapist. "You might be right, Cheyenne, you might be wrong," he said to the memory of his last ex. "I might have a demon, but I sure as shit am not going to "get some professional help."

People like me, Jesse thought, don't get help from people they don't know.

{ 111 }

This is my help. Road and empty desert, and the words of an old Bru man disappearing into a big silence.

Jesse hit Play, cranked the volume, and sat on the sand. The voice began:

We used to live up there at the foot of that great mountain. I have seen the births and marriages of almost all who are now here. Look how few of the men are still alive. We could count them on your fingers and mine. Women—yes—widows and a few children. That's all. We have grown accustomed to death. The one which destroys the body does not frighten us . . .

But the death which destroys our memories, severs the links which give our life meaning and erases everything which is an extension of our bodies and souls: the mountain inhabited by a Yang, the river whose murmur I can still hear but which my eyes cannot see, the sacred grove against which no man would have dared to raise the iron head of his axe, the rock at the bend in the path, which speaks to us . . . everywhere there is silence, everything is empty today, everything is dead.

That kind of death frightens us. It kills more surely than the other. It has destroyed our soul.

"Xem," Jesse said. "My old friend. I'm lost." There were no tears, only Jesse's words, only the whisper of a man asking a dead man for help.

SARAH looked down at the Firebird. She glared at Minnie. "You should have waited. My friend is going to be worried. She's not used to this stuff. For that matter, neither am I."

"It's a new world," Minnie said. "You haven't got forever. You can be a big whiner or you can just pay attention." She gestured for Sarah to sit. There was a woven mat where a second ago there had been nothing. "Here," Minnie said. "You are here."

Candle stubs were jammed into a dirt wall. Sarah watched the old women feed her soup thick with heo rung and noodles. She swallowed and was silent. She was too young for words.

"Yoo tlaan," the old women said. "Little Bird, here is supper."

Sarah saw eyes black as fire rock, skin the color of monsoon rivers. She saw all this without naming.

Later, she couldn't know how much later, she would eat canned tomato soup. She would look into other obsidian eyes, into skin the color of blood rock, and she would remember "yoo tlaan." She would remember the smell of swamp, of gasoline, of kelp and ocean. She would hear a soft voice and know the words. The other time and stories would be gone.

"Sarah."

"Sarah," Minnie said, "where were you?"

"Underground," Sarah said. "Then not."

Minnie smiled. "You can go back to Maggie now."

"I'M BACK." Sarah shook the last French fries into her palm. "Let's go."

"You're gone for hours," Maggie said. "Then, you snitch the last of my French fries and give me orders. Where were you?"

"I'm not sure," Sarah said.

"Are you going to tell me?" Maggie heard herself. Sullen, an edge in it she remembered from the last years with Dark Cloud. "I hate it when you do that," she said. "Disappear. Bang. It's like a punch in the gut. It's like Jesse leaving his body, that mean motherfucker taking over." She began to cry. "Fuck it."

Sarah was quiet. She handed Maggie a napkin. She thought how good it would be if she could cry, but she was certain that if she did she would melt, too many gsi'ki washed away, nothing left of her to properly die. "I'm sorry," she said. "Sometimes, I don't have a choice."

Maggie wiped her eyes. "I'm OK now," she said. "This isn't like me."

"When you want to drive," Sarah said, "I know a camp. We'll go west." She didn't know where they were going. It didn't matter. All she had to do was give directions.

IF SOMEONE HAD HELD A GUN to Maggie's head and told her to return to their camp, she could never have found the way. They were off a dirt road, in soft air that smelled like life itself. Coyotes yipped somewhere in the east, the sand was hard-packed to satin, Joshua trees rose bony against Vegas's distant glow.

"This is it," Sarah said. She walked into the rattling bushes, bent, and handed Maggie a perfectly round dry gourd. "Old coyote gourd, you get some of those little stones the ants bring up when they make their cities. Cut a hole in the gourd and pour them in. You plug the hole and then you can paint the rattle with any picture you want. When you're done and you shake it the month of the Rabbit Moon, there's a rainy sound, shhhhh, shhhhh, so pretty. Soon the real rain comes down to be with its cousin."

Silver arced in the east, became a curved shard rising to huge and full.

"You can see it," Sarah said, "the rabbit up there. The Buddhists and the People don't see a man in the moon. They see a rabbit."

Silver washed over Sarah's face. Her dark eyes were mirrors.

"Where were you?" Maggie said.

Sarah poked around in the back of the Bird and brought out the bone and moth candleholder. "Light would be good." She lit the candle stub. "Minnie sent me somewhere," she said. "Two places actually. In the first there was a smell. Mildew, that nasty wet cloth smell. And chemicals. After the candle went out I couldn't see anything. I don't ever remember dark like that."

"Were you afraid?" Maggie said.

"No.

"How'd you come back?" Maggie asks. "Why?"

"They brought me. They want me here. You need me."

"I do."

They snuffed the candle. Instantly there was nothing—then everything. The moon was annihilated by a cloud. Star-fog drifted over an ocean of stars. Meteors arced over them—rose and silver and green, dark birds flying on wings of light.

Sarah was gone. Maggie rolled out her sleeping bag and kept watch.

SARAH was on her way. She flew through snow, except each flake was a star. The sun drifted alongside her. The moon was gone and full and gone again. Traveling like that, you lost count of how many times the moon emerged and vanished. In a breath, you arrived.

Rain slammed down. The light in the hut was watery—as though they lived deep in a river. They were all women. Everyone worked at something. Their voices clattered like parrots, the old old women who seemed carved from roots, the little girls, round and brown and lizard-eyed. Thunder rolled in the distance.

Sarah understood perfectly how to be here. She knew their chatter was a shield against the thunder. She knew the trail into the village had been bombed and she knew what was hidden under the fire pit and in the rice. The great stone monkey was gone. What was hidden under the fire pit and in the rice was means for vengeance.

Sarah watched a small woman fasten the ends of the loom around her waist and crouch. An old woman brushed a little girl's hair. When the thunder drew closer, the grandmother played a game of covering the child's ears with her hair. "Little Bird," she said, "you are in the waterweed. You must swim away."

Sarah knew the woman weaving was her mother. She wove a strap for her husband's gun. He was in the heart of the thunder. Many days away. Long ago, the old priest had knotted the fibers of her mother's and father's hearts in such a way her mother knew her husband still lived. Her shoulders moved with the weaving and they were his shoulders moving with the gun.

"Flower Three," Sarah's grandmother said. "Your daughter is hungry." Sarah's mother turned away from her weaving. Little Bird crawled toward her. Flower Three reached for the baby who was Sarah and tucked her under her blouse. A woven shawl held the baby close, her perfect mouth on the weaver's nipple. Flower Three's hands returned to the loom, her shoulders moving, her hands guiding the red line that was a little fish swimming through the cloth.

BONE LAKE was about as lively as Jesse's last sight of Old Ray—two cars parked along the main drag, the Hoosegow Club down to six slots, and an empty bar; the Oldtimers Club turned into a Laundromat. Jesse checked into the Hotel Montella. He slept hard, easy to do in a room with lace curtains, a fine old quilt, and nothing but midnight neon outside the window.

He ate breakfast in the coffee shop, perfect home fries, a splash of Kahlua in his coffee. The round cheery waitress told him her life story of abandonment and betrayal in the time it took to refill his cup three times. He leafed through a decade-old Vegas paper, stopped at a review of *Miss Saigon.* He wondered how Nam had become a hi-tech musical. How did you dance to the tune of "So scared shit is running down my leg . . ."?

The waitress moved toward him with another refill. Nothing could have been more ordinary. A middle-aged guy drinking coffee in an old casino in a dying town. And, he couldn't stop thinking weird thoughts, like: *The only thing he fears is what's unknown and undone.* Deep thinking for a guy one Kahlua and four cups of coffee to the wind.

"You ready for another, honey?" the waitress said. He nodded. "So, you'll find this hard to believe, but that was only my third husband, that one I told you about, and this one, the one-legged guy in the corner over there, is my sixth. You'd think practice'd make perfect."

"Hey," Jesse said, "we're all shaky."

"Bless you," she said. "You look hooked up pretty tight to me."

Metal pins and blind faith, he thought. "Thanks," he said.

14 Jesse drove straight to Ray and Helen's, knocked on the trailer door, and opened it to Helen already talking. "Ray's in that sonofabitch hellhole nursing home in Kingman. It was *not* my idea," she said. "It was the ungrateful kids. Little snots. Said I wasn't compos mentis enough to take care of my own husband." She waved Jesse in and slammed her coffee mug on the counter. "What could I do?"

"You could get me a cup of that coffee," Jesse said, "and maybe a little something to eat if it's not too much trouble and then you could tell me everything."

Two stuffed peppers, a pile of real mashed potatoes, a half pint of red-eye gravy, and one-fourth of a peach pie later, Helen poured his third cup of coffee.

"Ray's a lucky man," Jesse said. "We got to bring him home. He'll starve to death over there on Death Row."

Helen brought out a jar of homemade plum brandy and waved it over his coffee cup. "You bet," Jesse said, "then let's palaver."

They talked till near midnight. Helen made up the couch for him, and Jesse fell into the sweet sleep of the well-fed, slightly loaded, and all-the-way vengeful.

RAY opened one eye. "I'm freezing my ass off here," he said. Helen tossed a throw over his legs. Jesse put what was left of the plum brandy in Ray's right hand. Ray tilted the bottle to his lips and closed his eyes. "Oh well," he whispered before he took a sip, "there goes fifteen years, eleven months, and nine days of clean living."

"It's medicine," Helen said, "just for now."

"Medicine!" Ray said. "I need more than medicine. I need out."

Helen unpacked the thermos of real coffee. "We're going to spring you. Jesse called Lacey the Loser. It's all set."

Ray grinned. "I take it you didn't call the UK."

"Not hardly," Helen said. She saw Jesse's baffled look. "The Ungrateful Kids."

Jesse knew. He saw it all the time, the forty-somethings visiting the old folks in Party Town, at Xmas, Thanksgiving, Memorial Day for sure, when you can pack the kids off to the jet-ski concession, settle mom at the slots, pop at the blackjack table, and have a vacation with family—without family.

Ray dug into the tamales. Helen packed up his clothes. "We just walk you out," she said. "Lacey'll deal with the legal stuff later." Meaning Lacey would call in his markers with Judge Cathcart, aka The Catheter, in regard to The Catheter's working relationship with the redhead court recorder, Tammy "You betcha, sweetheart!" Ulrich.

Since Mohave Manor was criminally understaffed, nobody noticed Helen and Jesse helping Ray down the hall and out the door. Fourteen comatose bodies in wheelchairs were their only witnesses, and they did not budge, even when Helen opened the front door to an artillery crack of thunder and a downpour so solid the truck was nothing but an indigo blur.

Old Ray threw back his head and opened his mouth. "Do. Not. Ever," he whispered, "take me to the hospital again. Not. Ever."

Helen kissed his face. "I just got scared."

"Honey," Ray said, "next time haul me out to Secret Pass and put me out of my misery."

They made it to the truck just as the rain stopped and the Mohave sun resumed its fierce mercy.

SARAH watched Maggie sleep. She felt dawn drifting up behind her as though a wing brushed her back. The tops of the Shadow Mountains went pale gold. Maggie sighed. Her eyelids flickered. "Welcome back," she said. "Where were you?" They both knew that with those words, they had moved even further beyond pretending everything was the same old same old.

"I'm not sure," Sarah said. "There was green light. That river smell. Some women were weaving. Old ladies, pregnant girls. Not like Willow. With my people, the men weave."

"Did you weave?"

"I watched. But the loom was the same. You hook it up on one of the house beams, hold it in your lap. One of the women was making a strap. It was black with red and blue design, like geometry.

"I was a baby. It was my mother weaving the strap. There was thunder somewhere." Sarah didn't want to say more. It was too confusing. She thought that if they talked about it, about her being a baby in a place that wasn't Willow, about the thunder sounding like guns, she would know too much too fast. "We better get moving. I want to be in Bone Lake before dark."

They loaded the car and took off. Maggie watched for cues that might guide her return someday—the specific twist of a juniper trunk, a boulder glowing carnelian, how the sun rose to the left here, then, as the road switchbacked around a wash, to the right beyond a chalk-white mountain.

"Don't worry," Sarah said. "I'll draw you a map."

"I'm taking it in so some day I will be able to look back on us," Maggie said. "I remember the last night DC and I slept together. I saw his empty face and I knew that some moment I would remember that exact instant. This is that moment. And someday, I'll remember this."

Sarah fell quiet. Will I remember? Will there be memory? Will there be a Sarah? Was there ever really a Sarah? The dirt road twisted ahead, broken by time and weather, and she saw how even the stone was fractured by movement so slow it couldn't even be dreamed.

IT WAS A LITTLE WEIRD to go to sleep in the daytime. Zach felt like a lizard. He left Spooky's last message on the laptop screen before he closed the lid. "Kibble," she'd written, "do you think rituals are real? Can they help a person? Even if a person just makes them up?"

He'd wanted to message back right that second, but he thought about the tips for getting a girl to love you that he'd read on Yahoo. So, he had put the computer to sleep and hoped some awful magic wouldn't take her away before it was time to wake up.

He punched up the pillow and lay down. The River seemed different to him, more sad, more beautiful. He thought of Spooky's green-gold eyes, and it occurred to him he might be falling in love.

HELEN got Ray and Jesse squared away with brisket sandwiches and lemonade, and drove away to buy more groceries. "The woman's a squirrel," Ray said. He pulled open a cupboard. It was crammed with microwave popcorn packages. "She grew up during those Harlan County strikes. Her daddy was a miner. One summer they lived on eggs from their chickens, sack of store flour, and wild greens."

"Lucky for us," Jesse said. "I never ate better anywhere."

They took their food and lemonade to the stoop. The sun began to drop toward the Piutes. The smell of rain was gone. "This is Polaroid weather," Ray said. "Click, wait a minute, and you see something new."

He tapped the edge of his glass. Jesse fetched the pitcher from the trailer. "There's some booze in the cupboard over the stove," Ray said. "Help yourself. I'm back on the wagon."

"I could use it," Jesse said. "I got to ask you something personal." He brought out the vodka, poured a couple shots in his lemonade.

"You get my age," Ray said, "there ain't much left that's personal."

Jesse tilted the glass to his lips. It was as though he swallowed the dying sun. And still, words caught in his throat. "Did you serve?"

"Korea," Ray said. "Proud of it. And not."

Jesse was quiet.

"What the hell else could I be?" Ray said. "I was a kid. A dumb horny kid. Fighting a rich man's war like always happens. Following my pecker straight into trouble."

Jesse was thankful. He knew Ray was giving him what he needed. "No worse than Nam," he said.

"No better." Ray tapped his glass again. Jesse filled it with lemonade. "Jesus," Ray said, "a beer would taste good. If I'm gonna have to piss every ten minutes, it ought to be worth it." The phone rang.

Jesse took the call. It was Helen. She'd decided to hang out at the Riverbelle for a while, maybe take a comp room if Wild Cherry got cooking. Ray's pills were in the little plastic doohickey on the shelf above the sink. There was chorizo in the freezer. Jesse might want to get it out to defrost before they hit the hay.

"Helen's abandoned us," he told Ray. "But, there's chorizo."

Ray tapped Jesse's glass. "You got some catching up to do, and I'm not talking about spiked lemonade."

SARAH AND MAGGIE lost five bucks apiece in Searchlight, bought postcards and two lottery tickets in Nipton, passed up a riverboat casino moored in sand and creosote in Jean. And then, with a rush they should have been too jaded to feel, they were racing by the neon blowjob, suck-you-dry-honey-and-make-you-ask-for-more Vegas Strip. Maggie aimed them into the six-lane that led you out, past downtown, and extruded you onto I-15 hot-lining north.

"Piss," Maggie said. "The curse of menopause. I've got to piss."

"Do what you got to do," Sarah said. Maggie pulled a death wish U-turn, caught Charleston south, pulled into a gas'n'guzzle, and raced for the outside bathroom. The door was locked. Sarah watched her hesitate. She knew Maggie was considering ducking behind the building and squatting over the filthy cinders, but a motel faced the back wall, its residents leaning back in their plastic lawn chairs.

Maggie walked into the station with the dignity of a mature woman about to explode. The clerk nodded and pointed to the empty key hook. Maggie walked back to the bathroom door and leaned against the cement block wall. Sarah went invisible and joined her.

"I can't talk," Maggie muttered. "I can't do anything right now but not piss."

Three guys and a woman stumbled toward them. The first guy was a septuagenarian homey, his shorts hanging off his skinny butt. He was poking his fat pal's greasy chest and preaching, "You go wid a ho, you git what you pay fo." He stopped, stared at Maggie, and waited for her response.

Maggie nodded wisely. The four passed in a cloud of twelve-hour-old wine coolers, navigated the corner, and were gone.

Maggie and Sarah waited for centuries. The three guys and the woman came back. The old homey stopped dead in his tracks. "She ain't outta there yet?"

The door opened and a kitten-faced girl walked past them. Maggie bolted in and saw a plump kid in beige Calvin Klein knockoff shirt and unzipped pants flinch toward the sink. She saw him and the filthy room with perfect clarity and that something shimmered on the floor. She ducked out the door. The girl rounded the corner of the gas'n'go, waved a handful of bucks, and was gone. The kid scuttled out of the bathroom. The three guys, the woman, and Maggie nodded wisely.

Maggie shrugged. "I gotta pee."

"You're crazy," Sarah said. "You'll catch a fatal disease."

"You're young," Maggie said. "You don't know yet that a bursting bladder rules."

Sarah waited.

Maggie emerged. "That was close to the best thing I've ever felt. And, I think I have a new understanding of the real meaning of sex."

Maggie pulled up to the pump. "We've got one hundred and forty dollars, a five-buck Riverbelle chip, $111.44 left on my plastic, and a paycheck minus estimated tax on tips coming through, if Sheree remembers to mail it, which, being Sheree, she may do next year."

Sarah thought of the little ho. "Things could be worse."

BY THE TIME Jesse even started to begin to catch Ray up, he'd polished off the vodka and started in on some scary tequila Helen had stashed in the towel cupboard. "Old Popocatepetl," Ray said. "She buys direct from a janitor at the discount outlet." There was no worm and no label. "It'll do the job."

The moon was a spotlight. Jesse wondered if Ray ought to get to bed, if they both ought to go into the dark of the trailer. "No," Ray said, "the night is young," and Jesse realized he had spoken what he thought was only a flicker in his mind. "We got as long as we need." Ray's voice was quiet.

"Does Helen know?" Jesse asked. He hoped Ray's answer would let him off the hook.

"Know what?" Ray hunkered over, leaned his arms on his thighs, stared at the moon-silver patch of Helen's wild garden on either side of the path. Evening primrose, globe-mallow, datura unfolding like a cool ghost.

"Whatever you didn't want her to know."

"What would that be?"

"About the Korean girl," Jesse said, and found himself held fast by Ray's big hand around his ankle. He could have broken free. Ray was an old man, and Jesse was stronger than everything but what held him in place on the stoop of a beat-up Airstream, one step above an old man who did not turn to look at him, who did not let go.

"Yes," Ray said. "She knows about the girl—and the mistake."

"The mistake?"

"The mistake a kid makes when his best friend's brains are on his sleeve."

There it was.

Jesse saw it clear as the moon burning like dry ice. *Xi turned toward Jesse, dark hands on the antiaircraft gun. Smiling. How Jesse smiled back, turned away, and learned later that Xi's arty took out the chopper spooking toward the hot LZ, the chopper carrying wounded in from Laos where we weren't.*

"Opium," Jesse said. Ray waited. "I wish I had some now."

"Tried it once," Ray said. "Made me too fuzzy. But that gook beer . . ."

"I used to go to this place," Jesse said. "A mama-san ran it. She wasn't what people think. Just a woman whose old man was off somewhere with the VC, the ARVN—who knew? She had a lot of kids. Everybody worked except the baby."

"I met a guy. Xi. He was younger than me, fifteen, maybe sixteen. We smoked together, got talking like you do. He took me home to meet his family. They were country. Getting by. His sisters would come to the camp dump, take back everything, turn it into souvenirs—hash pipes, bows and arrows—and sell it back to us. They were proud. No fuckee-suckee business with us.

"Later, who knows how long, I'm on solo recon and there's a guy on an antiaircraft gun. He's not moving. There's a crack between the canes and bamboo. Just big enough for me to aim. I get ready, and he turns and sees me. It's Xi."

Ray was quiet. "You should be a shrink," Jesse said.

"I was a bartender," Ray said. "That's better, but the pay sucks. Have a little more Old Popocat."

"I smiled back and snuck away," Jesse said. "Later, I watched Xi's arty placement take out a medevac. Four of our guys and three Bru."

Jesse remembered the knife that fell out of the burning chopper, how it had glittered on the jungle floor, how he picked it up, knowing that as he did he severed himself from the possibility of expiation.

"There's more."

"You want to save it for morning?" Ray said. "Coffee? Get some chorizo in your belly?"

"No." Jesse held the tequila bottle to the moon. "Dead soldier here."

"Then, we're shit out of luck. You're gonna have to run on fumes."

"Xi's sister. She was smart and angry. I was a junkie. Pot, speed, opium, what have you. None of that kept us from falling in love. Or from what happened. I think I got her pregnant. Our team was yanked from in-country without warning. Stand-down time for America and me."

"What was her name?"

"Yuan. Her name was Yuan."

Ray hauled himself up from the stoop. "We'll catch a few hours sleep," he said. "Then I got a story of my own."

ZACH dreamed of Albuquerque. *His dad and his dad's wife took him to a Zuni dance. The Zuni kids slouched around in muscle shirts and buzz cuts. They didn't look at him once, but he knew they knew he wasn't one of them. He wasn't one of anybody.*

The lead dancer had bells on his ankles. He carried an ancient Walkman in his hand. He walked straight up to Zach and slipped the headphones over Zach's ears.

The Walkman lid was open. The tape was twisted. It snaked down to the plaza floor.

"You listen," the Zuni dancer said. "You listen, white boy."

There was nothing but the sound of a zillion wasps.

Zach woke. Big surprise, the phone was ringing. His dad had told him about symbols in dreams, had told him how to figure them out. "Fuck you," Zach muttered and grabbed the phone.

"Kibble, I gotta see you. Meet me at the cats." Spooky didn't give him time to answer. She hung up. He listened to the hollow where her voice wasn't. It was the kind of thing that made you think about how weird true love might be.

He checked the clock. It was three. His eyes felt like the dream dancer had thrown sand in them. He pulled on his shorts and headed for the john.

15

Sarah and Maggie were parked outside the Flamingo, a row of pink and black units on the main drag at the intersection of Walk/Don't Walk in Bone Lake, Nevada. There an '88 El Camino up on blocks in front of number 5. Number 3 had strung a washline from the door to a V-Dub van. You saw more than one open window with quarts of Old Milwaukee ranged along the ledge. It was a five-minute walk to downtown and just far enough from the mine train for the whistle to sound lonesome and sweetly blue.

"What do your cosmic supervisors think about this place?" Maggie asked.

"They are busy with an earthquake about to happen in the Middle East," Sarah said.

"Where else? Why not Vail? Palm Springs? They gotta sharpen their coordinates." Maggie took a deep breath of diesel exhaust and high country air. "This is it. Welcome home."

Maggie checked in. The landlady was huge, her rose-rinsed hair piled high. There was a parakeet sitting on her shoulder. "No drinking."

"No problem," Maggie smiled.

"No pothead boyfriends. Not one."

"No problem. Believe me."

"And, I'm absolutely strict on no hot plates."

"You bet," Maggie smiled. Her hostess hadn't said anything about ghosts or unfortunate personal histories.

She and Sarah let themselves into a pink cabin. They opened the curtains, pushed up the balky window, and let the late afternoon breeze blow through the place.

"How about?" Sarah said, "I get visible and we unload the car?"

"Our concierge was barely able to look up from the soaps to take my money. We'll be OK."

Sarah gathered up her gsi'ki and stepped outside. She already knew who lived here, drifting in, disappearing overnight. They were the lonely losers off the loneliest road in America. Desert-toast geezers on old bicycles, their rat-faced terrier riding in the milk crate duct-taped to the handlebars. Families, frantic kids, bruised skinny moms with melon bellies, dads who drank Bud around the first of the month, Old Mil in the middle, and generic at the end.

And, there were Indians. Not Native Americans. Indians. Drunk. Sober. Down to their last nickel. Cashy as white people. They slept in the car with the babies in the casino parking lot while the old man tried to win their past back. They went door to door in their dark suits with the Mormon message. They grabbed a bag of chips and a diet pop while they ran the Emergency Room Intake desk at 3:00 a.m.

Sarah hadn't said this to Maggie, but that was how it was—only Indians really knew about themselves. And, Indians could say anything they wanted about Indians. *We're noble. We're alkies. We're just like you. We're so far beyond what you think you know about us we can't even talk about it. We smoke pot. We can recite the AA Twelve Steps from memory. We like reggae better than our music which we have forgotten. Our old music beats in our blood. We can say anything. You can't say a thing. Even if you see it with your own eyes. Even if I tell you about it. Even if it's true.*

She scanned the Flamingo. There was always at least one Blood in a place like this, a man forty-five, fifty, who at first glance looked like a teenage kid. Usually, he didn't do much, maybe just sat on his four-by-four patio and watched tourist traffic on the highway, maybe paced the full length of the property from Office: Ring Bell, Don't Honk to the chicken-wire fence that separated the place from Ray's Radiator, a Great Place to Take a Leak. Maybe, and this was more rule than exception, he stayed inside and kept the blue television light burning from dawn to dawn.

Those men stuck their heads out their doors and blinked like owls in the high desert sunlight. They moved as though their bones were dime-store glass and flinched whenever the DPS chopper moved like a great, greedy dragonfly over the tourists' cars. One of those men could have been Sarah's uncle.

HELEN let herself in. Ray and Jesse were dishing up chorizo and eggs. Helen kissed Ray on the cheek. "Whew." She pulled a wad of Franklins out of her pocket. "I never even got to my hotel room. I bet my eyes look all squiggly like Coyote when he's falling off the cliff. Right?"

"You look fine," Ray said. "We had us a little party ourselves."

"Good for you," Helen said. "I got to tell you, it's just nuts how this gambling business goes." Ray rolled his eyes. She unclipped her slot card bungee cord from her fanny pack and looped it around the little gold plaster Buddha on the coffee table.

"Let's hear it," Ray said. Helen slid her feet out of her sneakers and wiggled her toes. "Jeez," she said, "it's a world of hurt when you're an old broad. You sit for six hours on those lumpy seats and next thing you know you can't feel your butt. So you stand up and your feet go, and then you can't remember why you stood up."

"Helen," Ray said, "what the hell were you going to tell us about something nutzy?"

"I'm getting to it." She counted out Franklins into a neat pile of Buddha's lap. "Twelve, thirteen, fourteen . . . that's my birthday you know, November 14, fifteen . . ."

"Sixteen, seventeen, eighteen, nineteen," Ray said, "which means you about break even for the spring."

"Don't be an old poop," she said, and slipped a bill into his pants pocket. "There, now are you glad to see me?"

Jesse wondered if he and Maggie were ever going to be this ludicrously in love, much less see each other again. He fervently hoped so.

"Well, boys," Helen said, "first off I couldn't get a hit on quarters to save my life. So I went and sat on the ShirleySal bench by the river and watched the catfish go after whatever the tourists threw them. That made me hungry, so I decided to go up to the buffet where they got that crab-leg deal. I had five minutes to kill, so I figured I'd try twenty bucks in that dollar jitterbug machine."

"And?" Ray was right there for her. You'd think he was one of those sensitive FemLib-trained guys.

"And, BAM! Free crab legs. Free play. Two thousand bucks right here on Buddha's tummy."

She looked over at Jesse. "You OK? You look like a bad case of Old Popocat."

"Ray made me do it."

"You eat some breakfast," Helen said.

Jesse picked up his fork. His head pounded and he thought he saw the eggs moving, but even if they were, he was trapped between Helen and Ray. "You go right at it," Ray said. "That grease is an antidote. If it don't kill you, it'll slide you right back on your feet."

Ray was right. By the time Jesse finished breakfast and slammed down four cups of Ray's industrial-strength coffee, he believed he might live just long enough to do what came next. Which was to follow Ray out into the shade under the awning and lower himself very carefully into a sagging camp chair.

Helen was watching a rerun of *The Honeymooners*. "I love that man," she said. "If he'd come my way, Ray would've been shit out of luck."

"There's more to life than soft shoe and a wise mouth," Ray hollered through the door. He settled into his chair. "I'll keep it short," he said. "I shot a kid. I left a baby with its mother. I don't know if it was a boy or girl. When we got back, it was weird, almost like we hadn't been there. There wasn't no talk of that PTSD. Doc gave me some sleeping pills. That was it."

They were quiet. Ray stared off toward the mountains. Finally he put his hand on Jesse's arm. "It's different now, boy. You got ways to find out things. See if that kid is still alive. They'll help you."

"They?"

"Army shrinks. There's groups go back to Nam. I heard Toupee Mel talking about it."

"For chrissakes," Jesse said, "I hate government. Clinics. Five million forms. I hate snot-nosed social workers who aren't real sure whether Nam is near Iraq or Cleveland. And worse than that, I hate career Boonie rats. Boo fuckin' hoo about when I was in-country." He shook his head. "Besides, you're OK and you didn't do anything?"

"I had Helen. And, you got a weird definition of OK."

Jesse was quiet.

"Who've you got?" Ray said. "That chopper nurse. The little Thai dancer at the Crazy Horse? Not Maggie, the way you're going."

"I don't need a woman. OK?"

"Listen, kid, I hear bullshit. Nobody don't need a good woman."

"I've got you," Jesse said. "That's good enough."

"God help you." Ray handed him the Old Popocat. Jesse grinned and waved the bottle away. "OK, I'll listen."

"I got an idea. You can skip the VA, maybe scout out the situation yourself. There was a line cook I knew when I was bartending at Binion's in Vegas. The guy was boat people. We got talking and he took me to a little 'Yard joint just off Charleston. Pho. Buffalo meat. You could go up there."

"I could."

"You will," Ray said. "It's not just for you. It'll maybe lighten my load a little. Plus they got a shelf of gook food. You can bring me a couple jars of kimchi."

"One more question," Jesse said.

Ray shook his head. "No, pal. Never found her again."

SPOOKY'D done something weird with her eyes.

"You look like a raccoon," Zach said.

"Shut up." She hunched over herself. "Fuck you. Nobody's the boss of my looks."

"Then, why'd you do that?"

"What?"

"Draw lines around your eyes like Kiss?"

"Because I wanted to."

Zach knew that somehow they were having a grown-up conversation between a dude and a woman.

"I hate my life," Spooky said.

Zach thought of Albuquerque and how he still hadn't been able to figure out how you hate perfectly nice people who make you feel suffocated and happen to be your parent and wannabe parent.

He kept quiet.

"It's not my mom," Spooky said. "Or even her boyfriends. They're all cool, not like, you know, grabby or anything."

Zach waited.

"It's Catclaw. Oh, Zach, did you ever love somebody who didn't love you, but you couldn't just walk away, and plus you never felt like this before, and there's nobody to talk to because nobody really likes you, and like that? And everything?"

Zach nodded. *Oh yeah, I didn't know any of that up until now.* "I'm a guy," he said.

"Oh right! Oh fucking right!" Spooky jumped up from the bench. "Fuck you," she hissed. "Fuck you and everybody else with appendages." She stomped away. And, stopped. Zach was laughing.

"Appendages?" Zach was on his feet, holding out one hand. "Appendages?"

Spooky looked down at her feet. "OK, dicks."

She walked back to the bench. "Well? Did you? Do you? You know, like all of that I said?"

"No," Zach said. "I haven't. I think Catclaw's an idiot."

SARAH brought the shawl bundle in from the car. She set it on the nightstand and called her aunt. They made the usual polite chitchat; then Aunt Hannah said, "There's a temporary job waiting for Maggie at Rita's cafe."

Sarah waited to ask her what she meant by "temporary."

"A month maybe. You know how our Redstone People are," her aunt said. "Rita hired this white girl who was always making those dream catchers and talking about how four is a holy number. So the fourth time the lady didn't show up for the breakfast shift, Rita called her and left a message on the machine."

"Yeah?"

"'That's the fourth time, honey, and we Redstone Indians got a saying: *Four strikes and you're out.*'

"Rita's cousin is coming up to Bone Lake to go to the community college and she'll need a job, but she won't be there till she finishes up her GED, so Rita needs somebody now."

Her aunt turned away from the phone. "Lorinda, you stop fussing with your makeup and go to work."

"Sarah," Hannah said. "Get settled and come up."

"Auntie," Sarah said, the words seeming to move from her lips without her thinking them, "has Will Lucas come home?"

"You come up. Minnie said she would meet you at the highway."

Sarah could see her aunt's smooth, round face, her dark eyes, how she was doing a million things while she talked, drinking an iced tea, setting bread dough to rise, watching Lorinda head toward the shop. Sarah knew when Hannah next saw her, she would smile her shy smile, the smile that warned a person not to be too emotional, because then Hannah would cry. And she knew her aunt wasn't going to cut her any slack on Will Lucas.

"I'll be up soon," Sarah said.

"Sarah," her aunt said. "I told Lorinda about you. She had to know. Bye bye."

Maggie came out of the bathroom. "Pure luxury," she said. "We even have free soap. Guess I have a job?"

"You do," Sarah said. "The Blue Bronco. Best home fries in Nevada. And, the miners tip big. But my aunt said it's only for a month."

"I'll take it," Maggie said.

"Just go over there tomorrow morning at six."

"Do you want to hit downtown?" Maggie said. "I'm gonna check out the Hotel Montella."

"They've got a deeply spiritual little slot machine with dolphins and silver moons," Sarah said. "But I'll pass. If I'm not here when you get back, don't worry."

JESSE stopped at Jackie Gaughan's Plaza Casino in Vegas for a dollar beer, fifty bucks worth of blackjack, an eighteen-hour reprieve from what he wasn't even sure he was going to do, and, maybe, the location of his moorings—more accurately, his internal coordinates. He knew where the pho shop was, off Charleston near the Pink Angel. That was the Pink Angel lingerie and leather store, not to be confused with the Blue Angel, which, according to Ray, was a rent-by-the-hour rockin' shop four blocks south.

He got comped a room at the Plaza. The place was jumping. A Filipino band had the crowd in the palms of its hands. Jesse settled down at five-dollar blackjack just as the lead singer said, "What you just heard was Jimbo singing Tagalog. It's our native tongue." The guy stuck out his tongue. The old folks howled. "In English," the lead said deadpan, "Carlos was singing, 'Without you, baby, I'm jackshit.'" The old folks pounded the tables.

Ching May from Thailand took Jesse's order. He bought in and was dealt a ten and a five. The dealer showed a king. "Sweet," Jesse muttered and signaled for a hit. Two. He sighed. Behind him, the Pinoy boy was singing a funereal version of the song from the *Lion King*. One of the other guys was growling. Ching May returned with his beer. He tipped her a five. Survivor guilt. The dealer hit fifteen, sixteen. Jesse felt a flicker of hope. The dealer slapped down her five. The band and the evening slogged on.

ZACH could tell his mom knew something was up. He was hopeless at keeping secrets. And, he knew she knew he knew she knew. She wouldn't ask him about it. She'd learned to wait him out. And talk about anything but the fact that he wouldn't look at her directly.

"Well," she said. "We won't be seeing much of Aunt Bonnie for a while."

Zach raised an eyebrow.

"She's in love big time."

"Not that creep again," Zach said. "He wears the most embarrassing boots I've ever seen."

"Not Beltran. It's this goofy old desert rat, Cowbird."

Zach truly admired the way his mom treated him like an adult. He piled scrambled eggs on his pancakes and poured Gunslinger hot sauce over everything.

"Is Beltran jealous?" He thought of Catclaw and how he wanted to commit a heinous act against him. Maybe accidentally snag the lug nut stuck in his left earlobe, or beat the shit out of him, which he had never done to anybody, and wasn't quite sure he knew how to do.

"Earth to Zach," his mom said. "Did you hear me?"

"Sorry, I was thinking about this ollie to grind I've almost got down."

"Beltran told AKA who told Rikki who told me, 'Beltran don't play that game with no pinche negra chingada puta.'"

It occurred to Zach that he wouldn't really have to know how to beat the shit out of Beltran; he could just step on the points of his fake vaquero boots, which with him being a large kid would immobilize the scumbag, whereupon he would punch Beltran in the nuts. "You gonna tell Aunt Bonnie what Beltran said?"

"I'm saving it," his mom said, "for the long run, for the day she's teetering on the edge of telling Jose Frio to kiss off."

"What I like about here," Zach said, "is that all you so-called adults are just as weird as me and my friends."

SARAH waited till Maggie's footsteps faded away. She spread the shawl out on the bed, studied the animals, the not-known things, remembered a slide show Professor WeAreAllOne had shown them, of bombed Cambodian temple carvings. The not-knowns were similar, seemingly broken, till she looked closer and saw what appeared to be damage was only a shift in the pattern. Where she expected to see a leg, a tail, there were streamers of tiny white dots, as though the not-knowns were on their way to being star dust.

She lay back on the shawl as though it could be a map, her spine a sensor.

She saw nothing, no coordinates, only the smoke-stained ceiling above her. Her thoughts drifted to Will Lucas, to the silver lightning bolt in his left ear, to his hand warm around hers as he had led her through Bone Lake's alleys, his body pressed the length of hers, how he lifted her up against the back wall of the Hoosegow and she had wrapped her legs around him.

She sighed and sat up. And was instantly through the locked door and flying, traveling ghost-way. The lights of Bone Lake sparkled below her. She knew Maggie was in the dying heart of their glow. Sarah wished her five silver dolphins with Max Bet, the bonus spinning through ten cycles, the credits shooting up like a reverse meteor.

She drifted over the dark highway, watched headlights sweep across the white line, picking out fool rabbits and moths. If you had been the driver below, had looked up and seen her, you would have believed you saw vapor.

That's what we believe. Willow souls are clouds. Late summer, they gather above the mountains and coming together, they weep. Late summer. Sarah wouldn't think of late summer. The night wind dried her tears and she drifted down.

She lay under a juniper just outside the village. There were no clouds, only stars. The Star Warrior was gone. For this season, he could be seen only in the far south. She wondered, as she had since she was little, if another girl was watching him. She wondered if another woman was wishing he would come to her bed. She thought of how her people had been brainwashed to love soldiers. Until they come home carrying foreign ghosts. She wondered what was happening to the ceremonies, especially the chant for a soldier gone to a place where he has seen unspeakable things. Her aunt believed love was the only ceremony necessary.

She slept. Ghost-sleep was raggedy. She moved in and out of stories the same way the living drift into dreams. There were so many ways to travel. And yet, Sarah was restless. Lonely. She missed Maggie. She was the first woman friend beside her aunt and cousins that Sarah had ever really had.

Sarah wished she could go to Maggie in this ghost-sleep, will her spirit to make its way to her in no longer than it takes a falling star to flare and be gone. Sarah turned away from the wish. She was going toward something solitary. Her loneliness took her hand and went with her.

IT WAS MIDNIGHT. Jesse stood in the window of his room on the twelfth floor of the Plaza. He was down four hundred bucks plus, distinctly not buzzed—even after six beers—and the chorus from the *Lion King* song was on loop delay in his head.

He looked down on the west end of Fremont. They'd caged what was the tiger heart of the bad and beautiful. The Four Queens. Lady Luck. Golden Gate. Binion's. He wondered if they still ran the World Series of Poker tournament there, then remembered Ray had said a guy named Jesus scored one point five mil with two nines. He thought how even the miracles were shaky in Vegas—like the jittering blue neon of the time-and-temperature clock ten stories below him; the relief on the slot players' faces by the dubious light of their machines; the improbably cheerful old broad working her walker down the long haul from nickel Super Sevens to the $5.99 buffet line. She was there as he thought of her. He knew it. She was always there—fat, skinny, bottle blonde, faded redhead, Mexican, Okie, Jap—and she hugged the machine before she dropped in her nickels.

Jesse considered returning to the tables for possible vengeance. He knew that was the thinking of a flabby college boy with a sloppy buzz and a limp dick. He pulled a chair over to the window and looked down on what-used-to-be Fremont. The lights never went out.

He thought of the long-legged women who moved like angels through the tourists, how only a fiercely lonely sucker could see their wings. "Ah shit," he said, and told himself the sting in his eyes was from eight hours of cigarette smoke.

"WAKE UP, GIRL." Minnie Siyala peered under the juniper branches. "I walked here all the way down the road from the village. I've got about another half mile left in my feet."

They climbed the dirt road to Hannah's. Her double-wide trailer was parked near the village water tower. "Some nights," Minnie said, "I fall asleep pretending the tower will burst and flood this place—on the other side, over where that old gossip Nanny Johnson lives."

First light frosted the tops of the mountains. In fifteen minutes, it would be dawn; in two hours, a furnace. Sarah had shifted a few gsi'ki and made herself visible, so if anyone saw her they would think two old women had hitched a ride from town and were slogging, maybe more than a little hungover, up the hill.

It was strange to Sarah how much freedom she had as a ghost. And, how little. She could give herself wrinkles, bigger tits, white skin, could be seen or not, and still she felt trapped in an earthly prison she loved: Black Mountain, cigarettes, the fry bread she could smell on the morning air, the possibility of Will Lucas's hands on her hips.

Sarah and Minnie looked through the trailer window. Hannah filled Mr. Coffee and flipped the switch. She was already dressed for work. The raw silk magenta skirt, the dark blue velvet top, and her silver wedding necklace. She wore no makeup. It turned off the tourists—though every other time she went out her face was gorgeous with exactly the right blusher, delicate shadow, lip gloss subtle as dawn.

The television was on. The television was always on. Sarah had never asked her about that, but she suspected it had something to do with the shape of her uncle's absence pressed into the old recliner. There were photos on the TV: Hannah's mother and father, her husband's parents. They were old pictures of young people, and newer pictures of people so old Sarah's cousin called them Willow jerky.

Sarah looked around. No one was watching; the curtains on the other trailers were drawn. One of the old women disappeared, and Sarah was back, a chubby girl in designer jeans, knocking on her aunt's trailer door.

"I'll see you later," Minnie whispered and shuffled down the side alley.

Sarah heard footsteps. You could hear everything in the tin shanties no matter how fancy they were, no matter what the salesman said about "better than a house." Hannah slid back the bolt and threw open the door. They were in each other's arms, apart, and back again so quickly Sarah didn't have time to see her aunt's face. Hannah was nothing but scent and warmth, cedar shampoo and coffee, and what had always been and would always be the pure scent of Hannah.

"Girl," she laughed, "my little girl." Her tears were cool on Sarah's skin. "Do you still love fry bread?"

JESSE woke thinking of vengeance and remembered one of Old Ray's favorite sayings: *There is no vengeance for the sucker.* Jesse repeated the words to himself, shaved and showered. He grabbed his wallet and a book. The elevator seemed to take forever. He realized he wanted to get on with it. And, he wanted to take his room for another night and disappear into young-titted lap dancers and scout for heroin and maybe the old bone-cold rush of checking out back alleys to see who he could whack the shit out of.

The elevator doors opened. A pair of honed guys with slick ponytails and one earring apiece boarded with him. They talked as though he wasn't there. The night before had been so cool, the dumb blondes, oops, that's redundant, the blow, oops, that's redundant.

The fucking elevator had mirrored walls so the only place Jesse could fix his gaze was on his boots. The elevator stopped again. Another ponytailed guy got on. Jesse looked up. The guy grinned at the two lame-asses. "Whoa," he said, "let your freak flag fly!" There was not one note of irony in his voice. "Hey," he said to Jesse, "lighten up, man." Jesse nodded. The guy took off his shades. He had the shifty eyes of a stoner or maybe a punk undercover cop.

A century later, the elevator doors opened out into the casino. Jesse skirted the blackjack tables and headed for coffee, sausage, and shit-on-a-shingle in the breakfast buffet. It was quiet. The waitress seemed to be on a mood-leveler that had rendered her incapable of moving. The busboy finally got him coffee. The kid was bird-bone skinny, his face pocked by old acne. He could have been Spec 4 Hagerty, but Hagerty—had he not stepped on the bouncing betty—would have been almost fifty.

"She's pregnant," the busboy said. "That's why she's like spacey."

"Thanks." Jesse imagined Maggie next to him, how she would nod, maybe ask the kid a question or two. "Thanks for covering for her," Jesse said. "Just keep the coffee coming and I might even fill out the evaluation card."

The kid grinned. "She's, well you see her. You see she's so pretty."

The waitress was dark-eyed and round as a mama quail. She dropped into a chair. The kid waved. She pulled herself to her feet. The kid held up the coffee pot and said, "No problemo." With a smile so full of gratitude Jesse decided he would hand her a ten before he left, the waitress sank back into the chair.

"See," the kid said. "See how she is? Beautiful. Some girls are just like that. You gotta take care of them. You gotta."

Jesse put down his cup. "You want to hear something strange?" he said.

The kid looked uneasy.

"I never took care of anybody," Jesse said. "Not ever."

The kid looked over at the waitress. "I'm sorry," he said. "You might be missing something."

SARAH told Hannah everything. As with all Willow stories, there were a dozen beginnings and no ending. Hannah heard the first part—how Sarah and Yakima were going to save the sacred land and what happened to *his* sorry ass—while they drank black coffee and ate yesterday's fry bread with honey out of the old plastic bear.

Sarah told the second part while they walked to her great-aunt's gift shop. Sarah kept her voice low. Hannah leaned toward her, a movement so subtle anyone watching would have seen a woman walking alone, perhaps tilting her face into the sun. What Sarah said—the terrible kiss, the fire, the way pain removed you from yourself—were words that could weigh heavy on the whole village, could blur the sun the way dirty smoke could hang over a city.

They opened the shop. "And now there's Maggie," Sarah said. "She's my friend." Her aunt opened the blinds, put cedar water to simmer on the hot plate, began the dusting she did every day. Sarah sat on the stool near the cash register. If she tried to help too soon, Hannah would tell her she made her nervous.

The shop was small, no more than two counters and three walls of shelves. The fourth wall was a window looking out on Beartrack Mountain. In winter, the sun broke over the mountain just as Hannah opened the door. This morning, the sun was already burning its path west, the desert and foothills nothing but glare. Hannah pulled sheer pink curtains over the window. The pale baskets on the opposite wall seemed to glow like coals.

She began sorting silver wire. Willow jewelers bought supplies from her. "There are plastic bags in the drawer under the register," Hannah said. She looped the wire into coils and taped them. Sarah opened the drawer. The bags were jammed in the back. When she pried them out, a piece of red velvet fell to the floor. It was a heart, a tiny gold safety pin stuck through the right lobe. "Ms. L." was written in sparkly letters.

Sarah tossed the bags to her aunt and held up the heart. "What's this?"

Hannah shook her head. "That's one of Lorinda's sweethearts."

"How many are there?" When Sarah had left three years ago, Lorinda had been a skinny gap-toothed kid who hated boys.

"Five," Hannah said. "Six? Is this Tuesday? Maybe eight? I'm afraid to keep count."

"Hey," Sarah said, "a hundred fifty years ago, she'd be on her second kid."

Hannah sighed. "Everything's different. Every day. Time running so fast. You've been gone three years and it seems like three hundred."

"Help me with these." She handed Sarah a dish of seed beads. Turquoise. Jet. Shell like particles of moonlight. Sarah ran her fingers through them. She remembered how some of the animals on the shawl seemed made from stars. And she heard Will's voice: "Sarah, you make me feel that way Jim Morrison wrote—you know, about things breaking up and dancing."

Gsi'ki.

Hannah looked at her. "Sarah, do you know why you're here?"

"Minnie told me a little . . . she said she doesn't know all of it."

"You are here for the Ka'gsi'ki."

All Willow girls were told about the women's Ka'gsi'ki. They dreamed of it. They imagined a cave, a riverbank, a hut built from curving reeds. There was no set time for initiation. Unlike the White Butterfly Dance and the Crying Circle, girls did not know when they would be called into the Ka'gsi'ki. All they knew was that whenever their mothers talked of the Ka'gsi'ki, their eyes grew soft and you could see the fine old women they would someday be.

Boot heels clicked up the sidewalk. Hannah and Sarah turned. A tall young woman flung open the door. "Cousin," she said. "You're here." She took Sarah into her arms and laughed.

Sarah looked up into Lorinda's young face. "You're beautiful," was all she could say.

"And," Lorinda said, "I'm smart."

16 Jesse finished his coffee and let the book fall open. It was his only way of asking that in which he did not believe for help: bibliomancy—the practice of seeking wisdom randomly in books.

"If you are going to be born as a *hungry ghost,* you will see *tree-stumps and black shapes sticking up, shallow caves and black patches.* If you go there, you will be born as a hungry ghost and experience all kinds of suffering through hunger and thirst. So do not go there at all, but think of resistance and persevere strongly."

Cheyenne's notes ran down the page. "Some hungry ghosts have changed their attitude while in the bardo state, and gone on to become, if not free, than freer. It's important to remember this.

"The guy who gave me this book said to contemplate the Great Symbol of emptiness if you can. He said, 'If you don't know how to do that, just watch what unfolds in your mind. And if that's impossible, try to stay unattached to what's happening. Cheyenne, pay attention. You can do this. Maybe.'"

"There it is," Jesse said. "Resistance, perseverance, and not giving a shit." He remembered when Cheyenne had given him the book as her good-bye gift. She said a Korean war vet had given it to her, and it was how she stayed a little sane in the burn ward. "It taught me to suck up the smell and say, 'Thank you.'"

JESSE wandered up and down Charleston most of the day, not because he couldn't find the pho place, but because he needed to stop for coffee, play a few bucks, hang out in the cool bar at the back of Willy's Wayside, sit in the Circle K parking lot and feel the sun turn the truck into a sauna. "Burn it out," he said, but then when he touched the incandescent steering wheel, he hated the pain. "Jesus," he said. "Jesus, the guy with two nines." And he knew one point five mil wouldn't begin to cauterize his wounds.

It was late afternoon by the time Jesse parked in front of the restaurant. You couldn't miss the place. P. H. O.* in bright red, *Papa-San's House of Oriental Cuisine, in acid blue.

The neighborhood was mean-ugly. He hoped no tweaker thought he was the Man. He didn't even know anymore just who the fuck the Man was—the shaved-head kid in the black Bronco, the flabby undercover cop in too much bling trying to look casual—all he knew was that it wasn't him.

In a Vegas twilight shape-shift, the street was suddenly gorgeous, neon Midas touch turning everything to rainbow prisms. Jesse locked the truck and walked toward the red bead curtain in the pho shop entrance. Just before he took a deep breath and walked through the soft brush of a hundred Saigon doorways, he looked down.

A drop of fresh blood gleamed on the sidewalk. It didn't make sense. He was kneeling on dirty concrete in what was left of hundred degree heat. The blood should have soaked in or dried black. He reached to touch it and heard a girl's voice. "Hey, you OK?"

SARAH slept on a cot in the trailer's hallway. She dreamed.

Willow stems soaked in a basket at the edge of the eddy. She crouched in soft mud. It had been a good summer for growing, a good summer for death. The willows were dark green, and when she split a stem with her fingernail, it smelled like something good to eat.

The sun had long dropped behind the Redwall. The river shone red, then gray like tears. Her littlest baby had died at dawn. Willow-thin, his bowels running clear as Matakat Creek. She began to fold the strip of willow. The baby did not have a name. But, he was a boy, so now his soul was hunting with the Star Warrior.

She hoped her boy and the star man caught something soon. She hoped her boy was not hungry. He would need what she was folding between her small fingers. A willow deer. To keep him company on his way. Until he came home again.

SARAH woke. Her aunt was in the kitchen, and she was singing one of the old songs, the one about the twins. Lorinda yelled. "Mo-om, can you keep it down. I'm trying to sleep." Sarah lay on the cot in the hallway, and it seemed to her that this place was heaven enough.

MAGGIE had abandoned the dolphins for Cleopatra a little after midnight. She listened to the drunks and amateurs shriek when they got a hit. Not her. She was a pro. When the three pyramids rolled into place and shot light out their tops, she just patted the side of the machine and murmured, "Good girl."

For once in her life, she was smart enough to leave while she was ahead— sixty bucks sitting right in her pocket. There was nobody on the streets, no sense of malice in the shadows. A scrawny ginger tomcat walked with quiet dignity out of a puddle of streetlight. She thought it might be sweet to settle in the place.

There was a note on the bed. "Gone to my aunt's. I'll call in a few weeks. Make big tips."

Maggie showered, felt cigarette smoke sluice off and down the drain. The water pounded on her back, and she thought of Jesse, curled behind her, his penis warm in her, his fists hammering gently on her shoulders, as he came, as she came. She missed him, she missed Sarah, and, for the first time in a long time, Maggie didn't want to be alone.

JESSE looked up. A dark-skinned gangsta girl stood next to him. She was no more than twelve, in a red sequinned tube top and blue athletic pants. She held out a glass of water. "This heat is terrible." She glanced down at the red dot on the sidewalk. "This retarded top," she said, "the sequins keep falling off."

"Thank you," Jesse said, and followed her through the beaded curtain into April 1966. There was a red lacquer bar with three bamboo stools. Joss sticks smoked behind a bowl of mangoes. There was an acid-turquoise lava lamp and a tiny withered woman opening a beer.

"Here," the girl said, "sit. My grandma will help you."

"Ray Kuzok sent me," Jesse said.

"I'll get my dad," the girl said, and went into the back.

Jesse studied the water, wondered what she might have put in it, caught himself. Crazy thinking. The only thing dangerous about the water was it might be Vegas tap water. He took a sip. Flat. Metallic. Particulate content unknown. Vegas H_2O.

Mama-san smiled a tight-lipped bar-girl smile, eerie in a tiny face brown and wrinkled as a walnut. Jesse ordered a beer. The girl came back and gave him a hand-lettered menu. "You want a table?" she asked. "You can eat at the bar if you want." There was a blue moon tattooed between her thumb and forefinger. She caught him looking, turned so he could see the octopus sprawling across her shoulder blade. "Cool, huh?"

Jesse nodded. Blue moon. Octopus. Code for what? "It's from the Little Mermaid," she said and put a plate of pepper-salt shrimp in front of him. "Try this. It's sooooo good."

He peeled the shrimp, put it in his mouth. "I'm Jennifer," she said. "The shrimp are excellent, right?"

"It is. They are." He couldn't figure out where to put the shell. Jennifer held out her hand.

"Don't get stressed," she said. "You guys are always like this at first. You'll be OK." She winked and went through the blue bead curtain into the kitchen.

Jesse worked his way through the shrimp. They were hot, salty, and sweet all at once. The old woman set another beer near the plate. She smiled again, and this time her face was softer. He saw her teeth had been blackened in the old way. "My son," she said. "This his place."

A small man came out of the kitchen. He moved with perfect economy. He wore leather sandals and his feet were wide, the toes splayed.

Breathe. Jesse heard Sarge Rounds. *Corbeaux, you gotta breathe. Come on, you dumb fuck, breathe!*

"Good evening," the man smiled. "Which table would you like?" There were four, one a long picnic table. There were bowls in the middle of each table—*nuoc mam,* a bowl of dried meat, soy sauce, and tiny chilies Jesse knew would stop your heart.

"A small one," Jesse said. The man seated him at a place between the bar and the window. Jennifer carried his plate over. Mama-san began counting up the day's take.

"Is it too late for me to eat?" Jesse said. "I can come back tomorrow." The man took back the menu. "Am I keeping you?" Jesse said. He hoped the man would tell him to go. He knew the man would be too polite to tell him the truth, but Jesse was American, so he looked up at the man and waited for an answer.

"No," the man said, "but perhaps you would prefer to eat with us?" He turned the window sign to CLOSED, drew the blinds, and motioned Jennifer toward the kitchen. "Tell your mother we have a guest."

Jesse nodded. *In for a penny, in for a pound.*

Voices rose in the kitchen. Not Vietnamese—the voices were harsher, higher-pitched. Mama-san brought the receipts to the end of the picnic table. "You," she said, "here," and patted the chair next to her. Jesse picked up his beer and sat down.

"We are not Vietnamese," the old woman said. Jennifer came out of the kitchen, a bowl in each hand, plates balanced on her forearms. She slid the food to the table, went back for more.

"Not like those in the low country," Mama-san said. "We are our own people."

The man and a slightly younger woman with a broad face brought out more food. There was no pho. But, there were four plates of meat and a platter of sliced omelets. Stuffed vegetables. Five little glass coffee pots, thick sweet milk in their bottoms. There was a covered brass bowl with metal straws sticking out.

"We are Bru," Mama-san said. "Different, not same-same like you maybe knew ARVN and lazy city people. This is my son. His wife. My granddaughter. More kids gone away in college. We are Bru. Now we pray. Yiang . . ."

Spirit. Jesse bowed his head, heard Sarge Rounds again: *Corbeaux, you got no choice. The fuckin' heat is on. Daisy cutters coming in. Time to fuckin' didi. Nowhere to fuckin' didi. Might as well go dinky dau.*

The man passed him the bowl with the straws. "My name is Phan Anrah. This is my wife, Marie. You have met Jennifer and my mother. My son, Christopher, is away at school in California."

"I'm Jesse Corbeaux," Jesse said. "Ray Kuzok sent me. He's a friend of that Cambodian bartender at Binion's." He bowed, then took a long pull on the straw. It was different, not as sour as the brew in the highlands, but still raw. He swallowed, said "sa-aun," and passed the bowl to the old woman. Jennifer served him meat. She giggled, "It's very American." Her father laughed. "Buffalo," he said, "with chilies and lemongrass."

"This is a feast," Jesse said.

Phan nodded. "Every day in *this* country we have a feast. You know." Jesse remembered a 'Yard diving out of the recon line; Jesse and his radioman dropping; the other 'Yards laughing as the guy rose up from the grass with a bird in his hands. That night there was rice, Tabasco, six 'Yards, two grunts, and slivers of an emaciated and unbelievably delicious bird.

"Ray sends us a man now and then," Phan said. "If he does, we know the man has something for us."

The brass bowl came back to Jesse. He drank.

"What we hope for," Phan said, "are stories. They are all that is left of our village. We were taken to Cam Lo."

"I was on the border," Jesse said. "Not in the camps."

"Still," Phan said, "when men like you tell us stories we find clues. That is how we found my mother."

Jesse looked at Jennifer. "My stories are not for children."

"She is strong," Phan said. "She understands. But she only knows America. Her brother the same."

Marie spooned stuffed eggplant onto Jesse's plate. "I met Phan here," she said.

Jesse knew what wasn't spoken. The first husband gone. The first wife missing. "My father was Korean," Marie said. Despite his best intentions, Jesse shivered. He remembered his lover's words: *Those ones, the ROK. I will kill myself if they try to take me.*

"My mother was Degar," Marie said. "Christian."

"Do you know what is happening over there now?" Phan said. "The American papers say nothing, so we read the news on the Internet." He handed Jesse a computer printout. "They are torturing my wife's people. See."

Jesse read. The government was clear-cutting ancient forests for coffee-growing and had brought in lowlanders to work the plantations. Every Montagnard village had been surrounded by tanks and ground troops. Planes flew overhead. The people had been commanded to remain inside the villages; no one was allowed to leave. The soldiers had beaten people. Food was running low.

"Jesus," Jesse said. "Dong moi b-n soan taa?"

"We don't know where my family is," Marie said.

"There it is, my friend," Phan said. "I learned to say that during your war."

Mama-san wrapped a sliver of betel nut in a leaf, sprinkled lime on it. She offered some to Jesse. He put it in his mouth and chewed. It went straight to his heart. He knew his lips would become the color of fresh blood. "Take him to the back," Mama-san said.

SPOOKY didn't show. Zach waited on what he was starting to think of as their bench, though it was in fact the ShirleySal bench, which might have made it a little unlucky since a bunch of ladies had dedicated it to their friends who had died instantly in a car crash on the way from Riverside, California, to the annual reunion of the Wheel of Fortune Gals at the Riverbelle.

He ran his fingers over the bronze plaque: "Shirley Marie Marcone

1935–1996; Roselle "Sal" Tucci, 1933–1996 Pals Forever." He wondered if some day there would be a SpookyZach bench on the Riverstroll. Their sign definitely would not say *Pals Forever*. It would talk about "real love," and he and Spooky would not have had to die for it to have been put there.

He went into the Belle to the pay phones. There was no answer at Spooky's mom's. Neither of them had cell phones, so all he could do was go back to their adopted bench and wait.

PHAN led Jesse down a narrow hallway. "My mother is a harsh judge of men," Phan said. "She has decided I can trust you."

The hall seemed too long for the building Jesse had entered centuries ago. Colored Christmas lights draped the door at the end. There was a table outside the door. It held a dish of water, a carving of a monkey, an alabaster plate, and a skein of woven fibers. Phan lit the skein, blew out the flame, and rested the smoking bundle on the plate. "Sweetgrass," he said. "One of our visitors, a man from your north, taught us this way to prepare." He washed his hands in the smoke and gestured for Jesse to do the same.

"You don't have to go further," Phan said.

"No," Jesse said. "I hope to begin to find my child."

Phan opened the door. "You go in."

Jesse stepped into absolute dark. A shimmering green rectangle shifted into a man's dark face. Jesse remembered Maggie's dream about the hooch and wondered if he was only dreaming—in the rice-lined tunnels near Cu Chi, the radio operator had turned toward him with that same soft gaze. And then Jesse knew he was looking into the ancient eyes of Bob Marley. He was looking at a screen saver on a small computer. By its light, he saw that rice bags lined every wall floor to ceiling. Phan was gone.

THE TEDIOUS NIGHTMARES were back. "I don't need this," Maggie whispered. She had no idea what she was talking to. The guy's face was fading above her. His eyes were dry ice. "Hey," he said, "you better face it. I'll fuck anybody. I can have one of our cosmic blastoffs and be hot for another woman in twenty minutes."

She opened her eyes. She went to the door, opened it, and looked out at a ribbon of cool green over the eastern mountains. "Never again," she said. "If I have to be horny the rest of my life, none of you, not one of you will ever touch me again." She knew exactly who she was talking to.

THE DOOR OPENED. "Sit down." Jennifer moved two chairs in front of the computer. Jesse sat. He had never used a computer. His work was in his touch; he could knap a blade with his eyes shut. "I don't know how to do this."

"It's easy." She moved her hand on the keyboard. Bob Marley morphed into a rectangle of what might be twilight. She moved her hand. Numbers and letters flashed across the bottom of the screen. In an instant, Jesse stared at a map of Vietnam—then, the Central Highlands, village names glowing bright blue. And the dates: 1965–68.

"This is the mouse," Jennifer said. "Put your hand on it." He felt cool plastic under his palm. "Feel the little movey things on the sides. Now, use the mouse to move the arrow to something you want and squish the left movey thing with your finger."

Jesse moved the mouse. The arrow flew to the top of the Highlands, then off into Laos. "Whoa," Jennifer laughed. "Slow down, dude."

He began again. Moved the mouse what seemed like millimeters, went slow, slower, felt the connection between his longing and his hand strengthen, the arrow come under his control, as though his hand and his intention moved everything forward into 2000. He stopped the arrow on Yuan's village. "Squish the movey thing," Jennifer said.

"Not yet."

He slid the arrow to Da Nang and pressed. A tourist brochure flashed in front of him. Dalat. More tourist hard sell. A quote from the *Lonely Planet Travel Survival Kit* for Vietnam: "Members of these 'hilltribes'—who still refer to themselves by the French word 'montagnards,' which means 'mountain dwellers'—can often be seen in the marketplaces wearing their traditional dress. Hilltribe women of this area carry their infants on their backs in a long piece of cloth worn over one shoulder and tied in the front."

Had she come into Dalat, carrying the baby close to her small breasts? Had the ARVN officers, unwinding in their villas after a hard day of talking strategy, seen her walk by? Had they longed for their own wives and children a war away in the south?

Lang Vei. Click. The screen flickered, shifted, and he stared at a death's head. The mouth was open, and inside the skull he saw what was left of the camp. Vines and flowers obliterating the rubble, the jungle taking back.

"This is an sf site," Jennifer said. "I'm not suppose to ask, but were you one of them?"

"Not really," Jesse said.

"Were you one of the guys that wasn't?"

"If I was," he let her see his smile, "I wasn't."

She put her hand over the screen and stood. "You got it. If you need me, our apartment's down the hall, on the right side. Just knock."

He was alone. He turned away from the computer and looked at the rice bags along the walls. Access to knowledge and rice—they were treasures beyond gold for a hill tribe.

He put his palm over the mouse and moved the arrow. To Lang Bu. Her home. And, clicked.

By war's end in 1975 around 85 percent of the Bru villages were either in ruins or abandoned. *Not one Bru, Pacoh, or Katu house was left standing.*

Of the estimated one million highlanders, between 200,000 and 220,000 had died. While many had died in acts of war, many died because the loss of their home killed them.

The door opened. "I came back," Jennifer said. "I was worried you'd get to the really bad part and run away."

"No," he said, "it's not something I can run away from."

Jennifer waited politely

"Could you bring your dad here?" Jesse asked. "I think I might need some help."

Jesse wanted to put his boot through the glowing screen. And still, he wondered if there were ways to go further on the thing, if there were skulls that led to other skulls. He could move the arrow from village to village so easily, not as he had once moved his body, the weight on his shoulders cutting to the bone.

Phan crouched next to him. "Lang Bu is gone," he said. "Most, maybe all of the villages west of the Co Roc Mountains were bombed to the ground. The people who fled into the mountains were killed."

Jesse moved the arrow from Bru village to village. Gone. Gone. Gone.

"What do I do now?" he asked. He couldn't remember saying those words before.

Phan put his arm around Jesse's shoulders. Jesse remembered the easy affection the Bru men showed each other, and the first time one of them had patted his back. The man had been ancient. They had just sucked down enough rice wine to turn the world emerald. "Nothing," Jesse said. "That's the answer, isn't it?"

"No," Phan said. "You can tell us your stories, and then, if you want, we can care for the spirits of your loved ones. They may be wandering. Your prayers can let them rest."

What about my spirit? Jesse didn't say the words. He knew no spirit house or offerings would help him. What he needed to do he could only do in the world of the living.

17 Jesse headed home on back roads. He'd always thought a truck on a dirt road was the perfect meditation cell. And a little too much rice beer could become the perfect teacher.

The Anrahs had sent him off with a plastic cooler of food and brew. He'd left behind two spirit houses. They'd told him it was better that way. They knew how to maintain the proper offerings. And since all Bru were family, it was as though two of their own were dead. "We don't really know if they are alive," Phan had said, "but it is better to pray for them as though they were gone. And, alive or dead, our wishes for them can only bring merit to their spirits." He had put an old copper bracelet on Jesse's wrist. "And ours."

Jesse had not told Phan about the two other copper bracelets he had worn. He drove the switchbacks up Spirit Mountain in last light.

He held his arm out the window and saw the bracelet catch sunset. Yuan's father had given him and Darwin Yazzie bracelets. And when he had come back into the world, he had gone up to the bronze buffalo and buried them deep beneath the statue's belly.

He reached the pass. He wondered where Maggie was, if Sarah's ashes had been claimed, if Old Ray was limping down the trailer steps to his evening vigil on the patio. He wanted to gun it down the winding road for home, but he had work to do. And, there was at least a quart of rice beer left.

He remembered two questions Cheyenne had left with him: "Where are your buddies? Who have you ever taken care of?"

There was Old Ray. That took care of both categories. Jesse shook his head. A piss-poor response. One old man. In twenty-nine years of being a man, he'd taken care of one old man—for maybe seven hours.

He thought of Darwin Yazzie. And how he had not taken care of him. And Xi, and Lou Santori, and the guys in the burning helicopter.

Jesse pulled onto the gravel near the wash that led to the little canyon. He climbed out of the truck and locked the door. Time was you hadn't had to do that. But the cooler was full of rice beer and buffalo and fish sauce and the most evil hot peppers he'd ever tasted.

He dropped down into the wash. Last light carried him forward. A silver thread wound out of the canyon opening. The rock face on either side of the opening glowed orange. The animals and spirals and mazes pecked there seemed etched with fresh ink. Jesse looked for the nova and the comet. They were gone.

His breath caught. The slab had broken free from the cliff. He climbed the slope to the fallen rock. It lay faceup, the nova and comet directly in front of him. He ran his fingers over the rock around them. He knew not to touch the petroglyphs. He knew what human touch could do.

Jesse wondered if Mojave Kate would know what this meant. Kate was a woman who walked two worlds. He thought of how she saved every tip she earned dealing so she could send her daughter to college. And, he remembered the time she took her break with him out by the river. She had pointed east to a place he could go. "Our men walk there," she had said, "after they have been to war. Ask James, the guy who heads up the Hard Count team. What happens there is one of those things only boys are taught."

Jesse couldn't believe the slab had fallen. There was no evidence the damage was human. And that scared him more than if it had been.

Jesse moved into the mouth of the little canyon and climbed to where the stream deepened. He followed it into a hollow in the rocks. There was a waterfall no wider than his hand and a pool maybe four feet across. He had just enough light to see. Delicate tracks led into the pool. He undressed and began to scoop water over his body.

When he was wet everywhere he stepped out of the hollow. A spot on the eastern horizon glowed scarlet. He watched as the light grew. He wondered if Creosote was burning, if some eco-outlaw had managed to blow up all the casinos at once. An arc of red rose out of the Black Mountains, and he remembered it was full moon.

"What the fuck am I doing?" he said. He was stunned to feel tears flooding his eyes. "Getting help," he whispered. "This is how some people get help. Wander around. Wait. Feel crazy. Wait. Half-ass give up. Wait. Till help comes, or it doesn't."

He pulled on his clothes, felt grains of sand against his skin and didn't brush them away. He started back down the wash. It was only as he saw his truck dark against the hillside, saw the windows holding moonlight and felt calmer, that he knew he had no idea what he'd do next—and that he would do it.

Something moved back and forth across the spot where the 'Yard knife was buried. At first, Jesse thought it was a moon-silvered coyote. And then he saw it was a white dog almost big enough to be a wolfhound, with the narrow hips and big chest of a husky.

He edged the truck forward. The dark-eyed mutt looked up at him. The end of its nose was blotched with scars and what seemed to be patches of dried froth. Its coat was scruffy, though there were no ribs showing through the thick fur. He couldn't drive in until he dug up the knife, which meant getting out of the truck and approaching the dog. He wondered about the patches of froth. The dog waited calmly. Jesse lifted the cooler lid. There was one beer left and six inches of ice melt. He opened the beer and set the cooler on the ground outside the driver's door.

Jesse popped the beer and took a long swallow. The dog stuck its head in the cooler and gulped ice melt. No hydrophobia, no rabies. Jesse climbed out. The dog considered him briefly. Jesse crouched, went eye level with it.

"Hey pup," he said. The dog raised its head from the cooler. Dirt on its muzzle had turned to mud. "You've been digging," Jesse said. He reached out slowly and scratched the dog behind the ears. It leaned into his hand. "Give me a second here and we'll get on home."

Jesse parked the truck. The dog waited outside. Jesse took hold of his scruff and edged him into the ramada. "Lie down," Jesse said, and the dog lowered himself gingerly to the packed dirt. "You're an old fellow."

Jesse knew he wasn't giving away the Anrahs' food to a strange dog. But there was the tri-tip he'd stashed in dry ice before he left. He put the meat on a pie plate and carried it to the ramada. The dog was asleep. Jesse set the plate by the dog's muzzle. "Hey," he said softly. The dog opened one eye and quicker than the other eye could open, Jesse's steak was gone.

Later, when the groceries were put away and he'd fired up the tiny pebble of hash left in his pipe, Jesse sat down next to the dog. He ran his fingers across the long spine, tugged dried grass out of the fur, and considered just how much he didn't need a dog.

"Old man," he said, "I guess I gotta start somewhere. It might as well be with you. Looks like your golden years are squared away." He paused. "Ralph Too," he said. "Hope you don't mind. That's what we're going to call you."

18 Maggie loved coming out of work midafternoon—especially on the last day of a temporary job. A month of it had been just enough. Even with customers like the guy who believed he was James Dean, and Harrison's Rockin' Roofin' Crew, who tipped like it was going to get them something.

Maggie headed down the dozen blocks to the motel. She had a wad of bills in her bag, a sack of leftover fried chicken and biscuits—most of the afternoon and all of the evening ahead of her.

The distant mountains seemed huge. Wisps of amethyst cloud wreathed their peaks. Scuppies wandered aimlessly, hoping Bone Lake might turn out to be Aspen. It wasn't—for which Maggie was only a little less grateful than for the fact she no longer had to take their orders, smile at them, make substitutions, smile at them, take back eggs too cold, too hot, too runny, too hard, too eggy; surf the hubbies' pitiful attempts at sexual charm, and find the tip calculated at exactly 10 percent.

She took a back alley toward the motel. There was nothing else moving except a gang of punk ravens and one black tomcat. The sun was warm on her head, the light soft, yellow crocuses glowed in the immaculate yards of the houses on the hillside.

The alley curved back to the highway. She felt as lucky as she had in a long time. She had a room, the Bird, a friend who weighed light on her heart, and an absent guy both mysterious and distant enough to long for. The afternoon freight rumbled by, the low beautiful haunt of its whistle wiping out time. She reconsidered checking out the slots at the Hotel Montella and opted for home.

FOUR WEEKS had gone by, braided from days that seemed to last forever and then were done. Sarah would wake to the pale sun in the notch on Beartrack Mountain, say "Thank you," take a breath, and suddenly it was time to watch the sun drop behind Duckwater Butte and say "Thank you" again.

That was the truth of the Ka'gsi'ki. It was right where a woman would expect it to be—in a beat-up double-wide a short walk from an Indian arts and craft shop, in work that didn't end when the sun went down. In a kitchen where two women ate breakfast and plotted.

Sarah poured herself coffee and squirted honey on fresh fry bread. "It would be good to meet your friend, Maggie," Hannah said, and handed Sarah the phone.

Maggie answered on the first ring. "My aunt wants you to come up," Sarah said. "Drive south to the Circle K. My cousin Jackson is clerking. He'll give you instructions. Here's my aunt's cell number. Call from there and let us know you're coming. Sometimes these roads can be tricky."

Sarah didn't tell Maggie *how* the roads could be tricky. She didn't tell her about what can hide in the glare. Drug dealers, the cops think. Laotian mob guys out of Vegas. Sadistic DEA. They were wrong.

"You're saving me," Maggie said, "from two days of filing blueprints. I owe you. See you soon."

"We'll have time to visit Minnie," Hannah said. "She wants to see you before your friend gets here."

IT WAS NEARLY NOON when Hannah's cell rang. Jackson's little girl, Sahmi, grabbed the phone. "It's the white lady."

"Shhhh," Hannah said. "That's not polite." She muffled the phone and shooed Sahmi toward Sarah. "Hey. This is Sarah's aunt." Then she nodded.

"Sarah's busy. You hurry up. I didn't cook all morning for nothing. Don't forget. Go right at the big water tank even though the main road goes left."

"Cooked all morning?" Sarah said. What they'd done all morning was find Minnie, wait till she finished up at Wal-Mart, and sit in the shade of her trailer awning while she told them too little about what might come next.

"Thank god for the microwave." Hannah started digging through the freezer.

MAGGIE found her way. It was easy as long as she didn't think too hard, which is precisely what Jackson had told her. She pulled up in front of a green trailer. A little girl flew out the door and fell on her knees. Maggie was startled to find herself wrapping her arms around the child. She hadn't held a kid since Deacon had been a toddler.

Sarah stood in the open doorway. "That's Sahmi," she said. "She's my niece." Sahmi took Maggie's hand and pulled her up the trailer steps.

Hannah stepped away from the kitchen counter and reached out her hand. Maggie remembered the kids in Winslow. "Shake soft," they had said. "That's what our grandmas and grandpas say. That way the other person knows you are not the enemy."

"Sit down." Hannah waved at the table. "I didn't cook all day for nothing."

They filled their plates. Hannah put pinches of nuked tuna casserole, fry bread, and fresh-roasted chilies in the little offering bowl. "Should I do that?" Maggie said.

"If you want to," Sarah said. "It's how we say thanks."

Maggie put food in the bowl. "You are a good girl," Sahmi said.

"I have a granddaughter," Maggie said. "She is smart like you." Sarah knew those words were a bigger offering than the pinches of food. She remembered Maggie talking about her grandmother instinct being even less evolved than her mothering.

Hannah asked the right questions. Maggie didn't ask any. Talk moved easily, talk of family and work and why it is that the world seems to have lost its ability to appreciate real women.

Sarah, Maggie, Hannah, and Sahmi cleared the table. Maggie stacked the dishes in the sink. Hannah turned to Maggie. "Here is the bad news," she said. "Now, we have to visit my mother, and eat again."

"Hang on," Maggie said. "No way."

"You have to," Hannah said. "This is what we do."

HANNAH'S MOTHER was a delicate woman with big dark eyes. Violet greeted them, hugged Sarah, and filled the kitchen table with hominy stew, home-baked rolls, Double Stuff Oreos, and diet soda. Maggie thought she might faint. Violet studied her. Maggie began to think her smile was a little sinister.

Sarah grinned. "Sometimes our white company explodes."

Maggie managed to live through Willow hospitality. "Now, we can trust you!" Violet said. "Come see the shop."

Violet unlocked the door and they went in. There were tiny turquoise badgers, black and beige pots with stone lizards curving out of them, Willow silver delicate as rain-etched riverbank. Sahmi slid a ring on each of Maggie's fingers.

The day eased forward, carried on a current of gossip and laughter, of silence and the stories women tell each other in the absence of men. Sarah wondered if she had ever loved her life more. She remembered what little Minnie had told her that morning about the road she and Maggie would take. How the shawl would become a map, Sarah's gsi'ki would become messengers, so she must not use them carelessly. Sarah did not bother to disappear when neighbors or customers came in through the door. They had no way to see her. Not anymore.

Jackson picked Sahmi up around 4:00. She snuggled into his broad chest. "You need anything?" Jackson said.

"A little privacy tonight," Hannah said. "The last bus is usually around five. I'll lock up after them. Maybe you and Kelvin could keep an eye on things."

Violet picked up her purse. "You can give me a ride home," she said to Jackson. "And, I got some things to tell you."

Jackson grinned at Maggie. "Here we go," he said. "I'm gonna learn more about how much I got to learn."

The customers kept showing up, the endlessly bargaining older white couples in Ralph Lauren nouveau Western; the women dripping with spiritual jewelry who talked about the ancient Willow prophecies. Hannah smiled politely and refused to bargain. "Willow prophecies?" she said. "I saw a book about that once."

And that was that.

The light outside Hannah's shop cooled to amber. Lorinda came in from school and flopped down on a chair. She wouldn't look at Maggie. Hannah glared at her. "AIM was twenty-five years ago, girl. You show some manners."

Lorinda extended her hand. Maggie touched her fingers. Hannah locked the door and perched on the stool by the cash register. "All you girls need to hear this," she said quietly.

Lorinda sighed

"You listen, girl," Hannah said. "You show some respect. Your cousin and her friend got a job to do."

Lorinda tugged her hair over one eye. "I'm listening!"

"This is how it is," Hannah said. "I was one month from my nineteenth birthday when Edward and I got married Willow way. He was twenty. A week later he shipped out for Vietnam. He was gone for two years."

Maggie shook her head. "Why did he re-up?"

"I don't know why he went back," Hannah said. "My husband never told me anything till a few years ago. He took photographs over there. He wasn't supposed to. We burned most of them last year when he was in that vets' ten-week rap group. He got drunk right in the middle of it. Remember?" She looked at Lorinda. Lorinda turned away.

"Your uncle," Hannah said to Sarah, "he went into Wendover and got crazy."

She walked over to the reed baskets and set them straight. "When he came back he was very quiet. He had some booze hidden and he drank it, and then he got his gun and he told me he was going to kill me and kill himself. Then he made me sit on the couch and he got out what was left of the pictures.

"There was a Polaroid of an old grandfather. 'That old man,' my husband said, 'when he first saw me, he pointed to his eyes and mine. He said, 'You same same like me.'

"There was a picture of Montagnard ladies coming down the hill to the GI's garbage dump. They had on little skirts and bare bosoms and they had baskets on their heads and they had like our corn baskets on their backs and they would come down and go through the GI's garbage and take everything they could back to the village. They would use what our soldiers threw out, and sometimes they would make things, like souvenirs, little arrows and such, and sell them back to the GIS.

"There was a little girl looked just like Sahmi. 'Her mother and father gave me a ceremony that made me their brother,' Edward said. 'That girl was my niece.'

" 'I killed their relatives,' he said. 'I ate with them and drank beer with them and they gave me ceremonies and bracelets and I killed them.'

"And he got up and ran back out into the night."

Maggie trailed her finger through a pile of silver bracelets. Lorinda opened a pop. Nobody looked at anybody.

"Did I ever tell you," Hannah said, "that white people used to think we were Mormon because Willow they thought was Reed, and there's all those Mormons named Reed?"

Sarah knew Hannah was trying to hold to good Willow manners, to balance sorrow with laughter.

"No," Hannah said, "that joke won't make this story go away. This story won't go away."

She was quiet. No one spoke.

"That Agent Orange, your uncle got hit with that too. And, Sarah, your McGill cousin Tessa, she's sick from it. There's a bad rash on her feet, her legs, it moves everywhere when it gets bad, makes blisters. We talked to the VA, they said her folks had to be married white, so there was nothing to do."

The walls of the trap that was the world Sarah loved drew closer. There were pictures on those walls she might never have imagined. "How come I never knew any of this?" she said.

Hannah reached over and touched one of the rings on Maggie's fingers. "That's pretty on you."

"How come you didn't tell me?" Sarah said.

Hannah looked her in the eye. "I was too ashamed."

19 Minnie visited Sarah that night. She wore her heavy red ceremonial blanket and sneakers with the toes cut out. "These bunions are about killing me. Rub my feet, girl."

Sarah took Minnie's foot in her hands. She pressed her thumbs into the sole. Minnie sighed.

"Sarah," she said, "I have something more for you. I brought your uncle. He's passed out behind the Rainbow in Wendover."

Sarah's uncle sat down next to Minnie. He was clear-eyed. "Hey, little girl," he said. "I haven't seen you in a long time." He reached out his hand and they shook Willow way. "That's good you're taking care of this mean old woman."

Sarah realized they were sitting on a sprung-out couch upholstered in fake velvet. There were hair oil stains on the back. She couldn't quite remember where she had seen it before, but it made her feel safe—its shabbiness, the places where old-timey men who carefully combed their hair had rested their heads.

Her uncle sat with his back straight. "I have something to tell you," he said.

"Here is how it is," he said. "Before the drinking began I had gone away from the village only two times. First time, this white man saw me playing in front of my mother's house and told her he could see I was a smart kid. I don't know why he would say that. Must have been a joke.

"He said he wanted to take me to where I could get a good education. A white man's education. My mother and grandmother decided I could go. So, one day, I went on the train all the way to New York City. I was ten.

"It was OK there. I went to school. This white man taught me about Jesus. He was pretty good to me. I had a lot to eat, good teachers, nice clothes, my own room. It was OK. But, sometimes, especially around the time of our ceremonies, I would miss what you see here.

"One day I was walking around the city and I found this big building and inside there was a painting all on one wall. It was an Indian guy running in the desert and it looked just like home. Same colors. Same blue sky. From then on, I went there every two, maybe three days. I would sit there, just sit there looking at the cottonwoods and the black mountains. I would pretend I was home.

"Second time I left my village, I went over to Vietnam. It's bright green there everywhere. There was nowhere to go that wasn't green. No wall with a picture of sand and sky and an Indian running. I could make pictures in my mind. But, the old ones had told me that's not such a good thing to do. So, after a while I stopped them.

"What makes me drink is the pictures in my mind. I can't stop them. The pictures are what make me drink. And, too much of the color green."

Sarah thought of how he would raise the wine bottle to his lips again and again, until there was nothing left but to try to find a way to get more. She thought of how the proper women and men in the village laughed at him, felt sorry for him, tried to get him to change.

She thought of the man Yakima, and how she had not been able to get enough of him. She remembered the day she came into the office and he was not in his office, not waiting half-naked in the huge black leather chair, not smiling as she came in the door, saying, "You know what I want. Give it to me." And how when she had searched for something that would tell her where he was, she had found the safe open and all the money they had just collected for the fishing rights lawsuit was gone. And how when she found the e-mails from so many women, all she could do was stare out the big windows and whisper, "Where are you? Don't leave me. How will I live?"

"Uncle," she said, "I understand."

But her uncle was gone. "You see," Minnie said. "It's not some white people vision quest, some all-of-a-sudden you got all the answers. We think it's funny those white people think they love the eagle so much. Any bird is sacred. Even those Jesusway people know that—how the gods watch the sparrows."

SARAH AND MAGGIE woke to the smell of coffee and bacon. "I wish I could stay," Maggie said. "But, I've got to earn some money."

"I'm going with you," Sarah said. "I have so much to tell you."

Maggie smiled. *Yes. Yes. I don't have to be alone, at least for a while.*

Lorinda drank a cup of black coffee and a diet pop. She shoved her eggs around on her plate and finally nibbled at her fry bread. "Can I talk to you a minute, Sarah?" Lorinda said. They went into the back room. When they came out, Lorinda was wearing Sarah's fire agate. Sarah had a black and red bead bracelet around her wrist. Lorinda sat next to Maggie and held out a second bracelet. It was identical to Sarah's. "For good luck," Lorinda said, and tied it around Maggie's wrist. "You don't have to say anything," she said. "Really."

Hannah packed stew and fry bread and chilies. Hannah and Lorinda held Sarah tight, then let her go. Maggie waited at the door. Hannah beckoned to her. "You are always welcome here," she said. "Remember that."

Hannah handed Maggie the food and a cloth bag, then pressed something into Sarah's hand. "For both of you," she said. "You know what to do." In that instant, Sarah knew how deep their troubles—and their work—lay.

She thought of Minnie's words. The old woman could say more in fewer words, and less in more words than the offspring of a Zen monk and a Jesus-way preacher. When Sarah had asked questions about what lay ahead, not in the future, but on the route Minnie had told her to let the shawl teach her, Minnie had said, "How would I know?"

SARAH AND MAGGIE unpacked the car. They set the gifts Hannah had given them on the dresser in the pattern Hannah had told them—sage pollen in the east, creosote in the south, cottonwood woman who is a man who is a warrior in the north. The west was to be left empty. It was a door.

"I want to check in with Ray," Maggie said. "Not from here. I'll be back in a few minutes."

"I'm going with you," Sarah said.

Maggie called from the phone booth in the Hotel Montella lobby. A couple bozos were having a roaring "You're beautiful, man" conversation at the dollar slots near the phone. "Where the hell are you?" Ray said.

"Raymond," Maggie said. "That's classified information."

"Sounds like home," Ray said. "It's OK, Maggie. Things have simmered down. We are having ourselves a little hassle getting the ashes. That can wait for you to come home. If you do, that is."

"How about Leola? Anything new?"

"Nothing much. And then, some punk drove his boat into his ex-girlfriend's new boyfriend's Jet Ski and the cops forgot about everything 'else."

"If you do get the ashes," Maggie said. "You can send anything to General Delivery in . . ."

Sarah touched Maggie's arm and shook her head no.

"Oh wait," Maggie said, "hold off on that."

"Jesse's doing fine," Old Ray said innocently.

"More than I need to know."

"Just thought I'd tell you. He helped me out when I busted my arm without my even asking."

Ray chuckled. "Gotta go, darlin.' The bus from Sun City just pulled in, God help me."

"Don't spend all those tips in one place."

"Wait, Maggie, I forgot—too much of that Loseitall—there's a letter here for you from somebody named Campbell."

"What?" Her heart lurched.

"A letter. Campbell. Fancy envelope and all supposed to look western, you know what I mean."

"Hold it for me. I'll call in a couple days. If you can, call back right away after I give you the number."

"Will do," he said. "Keep under the radar, young lady."

She hung up. "Too weird."

"I know." Sarah said. "I heard him. I was being gsi'ki girl."

"Look, I can't think about this right now. I'm going to play a few slots to unwind."

"I'll hang out with you," Sarah said.

By 1:00 a.m. Sarah realized Maggie was in for the long haul. She whispered "See you later" and started back for the motel. The neon of what once was bad bad Bone Lake faded out a block away from the Montella.

She saw men ahead, heard dumb laughter. Her first thought was: *run.* Her second: *I'm invisible.* She walked toward the guys. They were Willow men, she could tell by the way they spoke English, and they were mostly young, maybe hip-hoppers. Every third word was muthuhfuckuh.

She moved in closer. It was astonishing to be a woman and feel absolutely free from fear. She leaned against a wall and watched. They passed fat spliffs and screwtop port around the circle. She knew immediately who the tall one was. He said little. She could tell that he was stoned to the point of pure being.

"Will Lucas," a chubby kid said. "Muthuhfuckuh, I'm talking to you."

Will sucked in a hit. The burning joint illuminated his face, his gleaming eyes, the planes and shadows Sarah felt in her fingertips. He smiled. "I'm listening." He bowed his head. He had tied a green bandana around his long hair. Sarah saw the glint of silver in his left earlobe.

Memories took her as quick as Minnie Siyala could. Sarah was back seven years earlier, in the bar at the Montella. A twenty-year-old woman watching a sixteen-year-old boy who was already a man. He had turned his head. Sarah had seen the earring. It shone against his skin. She knew it was not the time to fall in love. She had bigger fish to fry, but there was the jukebox playing "Witchy Woman" and a 'Skin with lightning in his ear walking toward her, looking straight into her eyes.

"Didn't we go to school together?" he had said politely. "You're Sarah Martin. I'm Will Lucas. I was in fifth grade when you were a sophomore."

Later, when they were dancing belly to belly, he told her the story of the earring. "That woman held her hand over mine. I was dizzy. Agathla looked like it was moving from side to side. Thunder drummed out towards Cortez. She had picked me up hitching out of there. A white woman. Driving an old beat-up truck.

"She dropped the earring into my palm. 'Take it,' she said. 'Lightning equals rain. Lightning is ceremony whether we believe it or not.'

"Then she was walking back to her truck. Lightning blew up over Agathla. And there was a little streak of lightning in my palm. I crouched. There was busted bottles and cigarette butts everywhere. She climbed into her truck and drove away, drove awhile without turning on her lights. On that Death Highway.

"I somehow got the turquoise earring out of my ear and lost it down in the broken glass. I knew better than to try to put the lightning in or carry it in my hand.

"I put the earring in my mouth and started walking. 'Help me. Help me,' I was crying in my mind."

Sarah had tightened her arms around him. Willow people love lightning and they hate it. Sage burns like paper. Juniper explodes. And Willow women love impossible men for the same reasons. "When it rains," she had said to Will Lucas, "lightning dreams in my bones."

And then they had been in the back of his truck, and lightning had sung in every part of her.

"WILL LUCAS," Sarah said. "I'm home."

Will stepped forward. He threw back his head and laughed, a laugh of recognition, of joy and fear, the laugh of a man who has found the night trail up a twisting wash in which he was once nearly annihilated.

"Hey, bro," one of the guys said, "you passin' out. Hey, look at da crazy muthuh-fuckuh, he all the way fucked up."

Will turned and left the circle. He looked back over one shoulder. She knew that smile. It said, *Come here, girl. Come be with me.*

SARAH slipped in the motel door. She thought about a shower and laughed. Why wash away the scent of a man so loving and beloved? She set two coffees and a bag of donuts on the nightstand and watched Maggie wake.

Maggie blinked. "Girl, you look like a shadow, get away from that door. I don't need anything else creepy in my life."

Sarah fixed up Maggie's coffee.

"You're an angel," Maggie said.

"Not me." Sarah grinned.

"Look." She held out a bundle of purple and orange flowers. "It was on the stoop. It's globe mallow, from around here. He must have gone up into the mountains to pick the lupine first thing this morning while I was asleep."

"He?" Maggie said.

"Will Lucas."

The bouquet was tied with cotton string. A piñon jay feather and a note were tucked behind the string. Sarah unfolded the note. "Oh my." She handed Maggie the note: "You're finer than my cousin's '82 Firebird. I mean it."

"That boy," Sarah said. "He left us the coffee too." She handed Maggie the coffee, a triple, creamy and sweet with honey. Sarah opened the blinds. Maggie started to sip the coffee and stopped. A rattlesnake's diamond head perched on the sill.

Sarah slammed the window. The head dropped to the floor. "It's wood," she said. "I'll check it out."

She brought the body in. It was one of those articulated snakes you could buy in any Chinatown. There were words painted on the side: "Sarah, I will follow you wherever you go. Will."

Maggie shook her head. "No fair. You get flowers and a snake proposal. I get a letter from Dead DC."

Sarah put the snake on the altar, curved around the flowers, head touching tail. "For protection," she said. "A professor told us some people believe the universe is a huge snake biting its own tail. The venom is in the fangs. The antidote is in the tail."

"Yeah," Maggie said. "So. What matters. Do ghosts mess around?"

"Oh sister, that young man is sooooo much mess around."

Maggie swung her legs over the edge of the bed. "I'm jealous. And I hate to say it, but I want DC's letter. You said not to give Ray a forwarding address. Why?"

"You won't need a forwarding address," Sarah said. "We're going back."

"Now?"

"This evening when it's cooler."

"How do you know we're supposed to go back?"

"Minnie. She told me and Will. There's something undone in Creosote."

"We could fight from here."

"Maggie, believe me, I *want* to stay here. Lorinda, Will, there's everything for me here."

Maggie set her cup on the nightstand. The coffee was suddenly too rich, too sweet. Sarah began taking their treasures off the shawl. "My aunt gave me something else for us. It will help."

"I don't know," Maggie said. "I'm tired. DC and I were always on the run. All the time. Six months here. Six months there. Each time, he'd say, 'This is it. We're home now.' Six months later, 'This isn't working. We gotta didi.'

"I keep thinking about Jesse and his place. His so-called peace of mind. Where's mine? I thought we had a future here."

"I don't have a future anywhere, Maggie," Sarah said, "unless you help me." She turned Maggie's hand over, palm up. "My aunt gave me two of these," Sarah said. "They've been in our family for a long long time. She said to tell you it's for hunting." Sarah set a little twig deer in Maggie's hand. "This one is yours."

Maggie turned it in her fingers. "I thought we were the ones being hunted."

"Not anymore."

20 The sun headed down I-50. Maggie went for takeout. Sarah set the TV table on the stoop and opened a couple cans of iced tea. Shadows reached across the street and met. Sarah looked west. It was the direction of pursuit, the direction her people believed souls traveled going home. It was the direction they would go.

MAGGIE unpacked the food. "Will Lucas was there," she said. "The waitress called him that. 'Will Lucas,' she said, 'I thought you was in jail.'"

"It's an old joke," Sarah said. "He looks like a gangbanger, but he was Mr. A+ Honor Scholar. That's why he's so much trouble for a woman. Bad boy with a soft heart."

"And those eyes," Maggie said. "Ohmygod."

"Ugly as ever, huh?"

"Ohmygod."

"Still scrawny, huh?" Sarah said.

"Those shoulders ought to be illegal," Maggie said.

"They almost would be for you."

Maggie broke open a roll, wrapped it around a chunk of stew. "This is sooo good."

Sarah waited for her to tell more about Will. Part of why she loved Maggie was because she somehow had Willow gossip style—tease, wait, tease a little more, deliver. Maggie took a long leisurely pull on her tea and set her sandwich on her plate. "So?" she said. "Are you going to tell me more about what happened last night? Because I'm not saying more till you do. He looked pretty relaxed."

"Cosmic hormones, time travel. And, we've got our orders now." Sarah couldn't stop grinning.

"You're going to tell me. I know you are."

"Hannah says ladies don't talk about things like that."

"Excuse me," Maggie said. "We're not ladies."

They watched while Clara in 108 brought a tub of wash to her stoop, strung a line between her Dodge's roof rack and the light over the motel door. Sarah manifested great interest in the process.

Maggie nodded. "OK. I see how it is."

Sarah smiled sweetly. "Isn't this stew great?"

Maggie was quiet. Sarah figured they could have been in Hannah's trailer while the older ladies played poker and waited for Vi or Bethella or Hazel to casually say, "Oh, did you hear, oh never mind, my cousin told me this and you know what a terrible gossip she is." Gossip, Sarah thought, is the language of the Ka'gsi'ki.

JESSE woke before dawn to the sense there was someone at the front door. He pulled on his jeans and patted his side, as he always did, for the gun that hadn't been there for twenty years. He looked through the little window in the door. Only gray light and distant mountains lay outside. Something scratched gently on the metal.

"Ralph Too," he said. When he opened the door, the dog politely held up a paw. There were dozens of cactus spines in the paw leather. Jesse sighed and brought Ralph Too in.

IT WAS JUST BEFORE NOON by the time Jesse had pulled out most of the spines. It had taken patience. For both of them. Ralph T. lay on the rug. Every now and then, he took a shuddering breath. Jesse knew the wounds were going to have to be seen by a vet.

"Ralph Too," he said, "we're going in the truck."

Ralph's ears pricked up. Jesse saw what kind of beast he'd acquired. "Truck," he said again and Ralph creaked up to his feet. "Ralph Too," Jesse said, "let's hit the road—in the *truck*." Ralph limped wildly toward the door.

"REMEMBER," Spooky said, "that time I got hung up and didn't show for two hours and you thought I was just another asshole chick?" She bent over her board. Zach looked at her. He could have looked at her forever, not just her butt, which was sticking out due to her bending over the board, but at the way her eyes were fierce and her fingers were so sure and smart working with the jammed-up wheel.

"Yeah?" he said. "That was a zillion years ago."

"One month," she said. "That's all."

"So?"

"My mom says it takes a long time for women and men to really trust each other because we are practically different species."

Zach crouched down next to her. "I'm not a man. Plus, you're still a girl."

Spooky tightened the cotter pin. "Well then," she said, "let's skate."

MAGGIE and Sarah walked toward the small iridescence of downtown Bone Lake. "By the way," Maggie said, "I told Will what we're driving and our first turn off I-50. He grinned like a bull rider."

Sarah thought she should tell Maggie to be more careful, but she'd known Will Lucas since fifth grade. He *was* a bull rider.

They left Main Street, walked past a big box bottom-feeder, out to where town was not more than a glow. They took the old Flying M road west till they reached a stock tank. The sky had that watery shimmer before the first stars could be seen. Sarah trailed her fingers through the tank.

"Something's changing," she said, and held out her hand. Water beaded in the shape of her fingers. Skin, muscle, and bone were gone. "Time eats gsi'ki." She raised the outline of her hand toward the sky. It became a hand of stars and dark. "I think our time is running out to do what we have to do. If I don't find the way forward, I'll be trapped."

"What's next?"

"There's part of this I have to do without you," Sarah said. "We drive back till I know I move on alone. You go back to Creosote. I hope we will be together again before I . . ." She was surprised she couldn't finish the thought. Her final death held nothing awful. Still, she couldn't look at Maggie.

"Will Lucas knows all of it," she said. "He knows what happened. He'll be in Creosote when you get there." She started to say that Will was her bedrock, and she remembered the great stone ape blasted into dust. "He'll wait for me."

Maggie watched as Sarah shook the water from her hand. Sarah was a shadow, then back again.

"What about Jesse?" Sarah said.

"*What* about Jesse?"

Sarah remembered Willow good manners, how you didn't ask pushy questions because that is what white people did; and if you really understood what people were made of, you understood there would always be time for the stories to bring themselves out. Still, she saw what was in Maggie's eyes. "Do you miss him?"

"I don't want to." Maggie looked down. "I don't want to think too deep. Let's just do what we have to do."

Sarah knew better than to ask more. She knew what it took for a woman to contain what has to be carried. "I'm ready," she said. "Let's go."

JESSE pulled the truck into Helen and Ray's driveway. Ralph Too sat in the passenger seat. It was clear that he believed this would be just a quick stop on what was sure to be a long long ride in the *truck*.

Ray got out of his chair and peered at the truck. "Who's the babe with the big white ears?"

"Ralph Too is a guy," Jesse said. "An old guy like you."

"Hey," Ray said, "there may be snow on the roof . . ." He looked down at his lap. "Yeah, well, you know, those fuckin' Loseitall pills."

Jesse opened Ralph's door. It worried him that he thought of it as "Ralph's door."

"Come on," he said in the voice of a man who suspected a dog wasn't listening. Ralph Too wagged his tail. Ray said, "Looks like you got him trained up real good."

"He loves the," Jesse said, and then he was chagrined to find himself spelling, "T-R-U-C-K." He had never understood people who thought animals were people, and now he understood that wasn't what it was. It was that people *were* animals, and when you knew that you developed a loopy respect for creatures who wore fur or feathers or scales.

"I think I'm losing my mind," he said.

Ray laughed. "There's a bone from my breakfast pork chop. Let's see if that works for this good boy." He went into the trailer and came back with the bone. "Hey, fella," he said and set the bone at his feet. "Look at this beautiful *truck*!"

Ralph eased down off the seat and hobbled to the bone.

"What's wrong with you, buddy?" Ray said. "You're gimpy."

Ralph looked up politely.

"Go ahead," Ray said. Ralph picked up the bone, lay down, and the two men watched a dog whose brain was immediately blissed on bone.

"He got into a cactus," Jesse said, "and he's older than you are. I've got to find a vet."

"Cocker," Ray said. "He's the best animal man around."

"The carburetor guy?" Jesse said. "What do they call him—Clunker?"

"That's your man," Ray said. "I'll give him a call."

As Ray hauled himself up the steps, Jesse wondered why neither of them had mentioned his trip to Vegas—and he understood that when you've got a friendship that lasts longer than a tour of duty or a hand of Texas Hold'em, you've got time to talk about what matters.

COCKER hated houses. "No air in them," he said to Jesse. "A man's got to be able to breathe. And his dog too, if he's got a dog."

Cocker's dog was a Komodo dragon, a huge groggy lizard named ZZ that lived in the kitchen of the travel trailer that sat twenty steps northeast of Cocker's Carburetors, the only carb repair shop in 240 square miles of the eastern Mojave. The shop was a tin-roof shed surrounded by vehicle carcii.

"I planned the location of that trailer very carefully," Cocker said. "It's twenty steps exactly from the couch in back of the garage. During my first six months here I calculated over a hundred and fifty calibrations—while I lived in the garage and drank away my misery from a tragic love affair that I am still too pissed about to discuss."

Jesse and Ralph Too listened. Cocker was a big chunk o' fella. You sensed that when he talked, you listened. And when he said he was too pissed to discuss something, you'd better let it lie.

"Twenty-four steps taken by a big-foot drunk," Cocker said, "is the distance he can walk, if he is me, before he passes out. The extra four steps are the two up the trailer steps and the two that get you to the mattress on the floor."

Cocker handed Jesse an Old Mil. "You know, Jesse, you're a good man. You didn't call me Clunker." Jesse figured they were in for a long haul on Ralph's cure.

MAGGIE turned the key into the landlady and her parakeet. Sarah was already in the car. She pointed west. "Road trip."

21 Zach stayed on the kids' walkway at the edge of the casino floor. He didn't mind. He pretended it was the curl of a wave he would ride someday when he was old enough to live where he wanted, which would be Half Moon Bay, California, right near Maverick's Beach—with Spooky.

Frank was on security. He leaned on the podium, acting like he was alert. He wore his shades, which was against the regulations, but since he was the enforcer, who cared. Zach knew he was just checking out the new keno girl, Rocky, whom Frank was trying to convince he was a real cop. Rocky was a tiny chick as fierce as she was little, plus from Chicago, so Zach didn't have a lot of hope for Frank.

It was weird to him. A year ago, he hadn't even noticed how men and women were always noticing men and women. There was his mom still sad about his dad; and his dad, all calm and with useful thoughts about how she needed therapy to "get on with her life." But that had been pretty much it, except for sneaking into his dad's sociology journals to find the *Hustlers* buried in between June 1999 and July 1999.

Now, all he saw was women and men checking each other out. Now, there was Spooky. Or, more or less Spooky. Which was why Zach was cruising along the kids' walkway toward Lou, who might know where Aunt Bonnie was, whom Zach needed to talk to desperately.

"Hey," Frank yelled. "Kid. Your toe's on the casino floor. I can have you busted for that."

He stepped into the exact middle of the walkway and grinned up at Frank. "What can I do you, kid?" Frank took off his shades.

"Have you seen Aunt Bonnie? I kinda gotta talk to her."

"She's over on 3/6 poker," Frank said. "You want me to page her for you? Since if you tried to walk into the Poker Room, I'd have to bust you."

"That'd be good. I mean paging her so you don't have to bust me."

Frank looked hard at him. "You in trouble, or something? Some chick? Oh, jeez, Zach, watch out for the broads."

Frank paged Bonnie. Five minutes later, she strode toward them and swooped Zach up in a hug. "You saved my you-know-what, l'il bro," she said. "Where *have* you been? I haven't seen you hardly at all since you got here.

That's a month." She stopped. "Oh, baby, I'm sorry. I forgot that rule about not mentioning how much longer you're going to be here with your mom."

"It's OK," Zach said. "I was hoping we could go get a waffle, or something, and talk."

Bonnie hooked her arm through his and headed them toward the staircase. "Wait," Zach said, "my mom's on graveyard right now. This is more kind of private."

"Outside?" Bonnie said. "By the river?"

"That'd be perfect," Zach said, and he felt some stupid tears start up.

SARAH AND MAGGIE checked into an old motel in Tonopah. They woke late and made coffee in the little courtesy pot. "We're going to need about five pots of this," Maggie said. "How do most people get through the day on this kind of swill?"

Sarah looked at her. She saw the color of blood, muscle, and heart. She saw the color of stubbornness and crankiness and the way you feel sitting in an orange shag-carpeted motel room in Tonopah, Nevada, waiting for the phone to ring.

"I have a new talent," Sarah said, "kind of like seeing those auras the California ladies used to talk about."

"What color's mine?" Maggie said.

"Cheap carpet—no, uglier, the color of *why hasn't he called?* We gotta go. We were supposed to be out of here by ten."

"Five more minutes." Maggie stared at the phone.

Sarah thought of how many accumulated minutes, hours, and days she had once waited for Yakima and how all women, no matter their tribe, believe they can will a phone to ring. "You know that doesn't work."

"Hang on," Maggie said. "So I'm a chick; so I called to find out if Jesse's there; so Kate said if she saw him, she'd tell him and he hasn't called. That doesn't mean Jesse told her not to tell me he's there, right?" She shook her head. "Could Minnie help out here?"

"She wouldn't know how. She's never ever had a guy reject her."

The phone rang. Maggie grabbed it. "There's a message at the desk? You thought I was gone. Nope. Read me the message." She listened. "Yes. I know it's 11:58, I am out the door."

Maggie hung up. "Kate said no show. It doesn't really matter. I just wanted to have something to think about, maybe look forward to, after, you know, just in case you go on and I'm alone again."

In case. "We have awhile," Sarah said gently. "We have some things to undo." She thought Minnie must have been running her mouth. "Lots of things." She disappeared while Maggie finished loading the car.

The sun burned straight down. Maggie wrapped her shirttail around her fingers, opened both doors, and rolled down all the windows. "What a cheap shit I am. Did I blow $4.99 on the Tasmanian Devil windshield shade at the Circle K? Of course not."

Sarah settled into the passenger seat. "Let's hang around till twilight. We can play a few nickels. Eight hours isn't going to make a difference."

"We've got a couple hundred in cash." Maggie started the car. "You know what eight hours can do to that kind of nut."

"Guidance," Sarah said. "I figure we can't ignore guidance."

"Guidance?"

Maggie looked at her. "As in?"

"As in a car without air-conditioning determines the departure time of two women on the road in the Nevada desert," Sarah said.

RALPH TOO put his paw in Cocker's hand. "You're a sweet old boy, aren't you?" Cocker said. He took a magnifying glass off the tool table and peered at Ralph's footpad. "It's a good thing you brought him over. I think we ought to soak his paw for a while; then I'll get in there with the tweezers and pull what's left of those suckers out. From the shape, they're cholla. Probably hurt like hell at first, but there won't be any permanent damage."

He sent Jesse to the trailer for a pot of warm water. The Komodo dragon was asleep in a patch of sunlight. Jesse stepped carefully around him and filled one of the saucepans stacked neatly on a back burner of the immaculate stove. He wondered if Cocker had a woman.

When Jesse went back into the cool gloom of the garage, Cocker had rigged a light over a candy-flake bottle-green Camaro. He scattered powder in the water, stirred it with a lug wrench, and set the pot next to the Camaro. Ralph Too leaned against the Camaro's front tire and stepped into the warm water. Cocker handed Jesse another beer. "He's gonna be OK," he said. "That is, his paw is gonna be OK. But, I'm wondering what you're gonna do about the artheritis?"

"What can you do?" Jesse asked.

"I've got a liniment I make myself," Cocker said, "and some herbs I got from a flea market chick down in Quartzite. You boil up the herbs, let the water cool, and give him a teaspoon three times a day. You can't let the stuff sit overnight. You gotta give it to him fresh."

Ralph Too sniffed the water. Cocker jumped up. "Don't you drink that," he said. He went out the back door. When he came back, he had a bowl of water in one hand and two six-packs of Old Mil dangling from the other.

"We might as well settle in," Cocker said. "What the hell. That paw's got to soak a while, it's 110 outside, and you look like a man likes a good story."

"You read me right, Cocker," Jesse said.

Jesse popped his beer. He settled down next to Ralph Too and leaned against the Camaro. The metal was cool and the garage smelled like some of his better teenage memories.

"Well," Cocker sighed heavily, "this Chinese chick was playing next to me. We was in the fifth game of Texas Hold'em at the Waterbird, that Mojave casino on the river, you know, the one looks like it was made out of sugar cubes and fake turquoise. I glance down and this chick has put a picture of her naked self right between us. She was what you call one of those nude dancers."

He paused. Jesse smiled. He couldn't wait to hear what came next.

BONNIE AND ZACH sat on the ShirleySal bench. The river looked like molten steel. Zach remembered a video they'd watched in science class, how some guys who were shadows against hot outer space light had tilted a huge bucket and poured a stream of melted fire into a chute. "This was the old-fashioned way they made steel," the voice on the video said. "Now, machines do the work of man." Zach wished there was a machine to do what he knew he had to do.

"Zach," Bonnie said, "you've got something on your mind." She didn't say it as a question. She was treating him like a grown-up, which, he figured, he was heading too fast for being.

"I don't have a girlfriend," he said, "not like that, but I like a girl as a friend, well, actually, more, but it's really fucked, sorry, Aunt Bonnie, up."

"You mind if I smoke?" Bonnie said. Zach shook his head. He liked the smell of her little clove cigarettes. Sometimes in lame Albuquerque, his dad would take him and his stepmom to a coffee shop. If Zach got lucky, one of those hippie chicks who don't wear bras would light up a clove cigarette and he would close his eyes and pretend he was sitting on the ShirleySal bench next to Aunt Bonnie. Which, this time, he was.

"My friend is really smart," he said. "And, funny. And, messed up, I think. And, she is the best skateboarder next to Jay Adams you ever saw."

"I never saw Jay Adams, honey," Bonnie said. "They didn't do that kind of stuff where I grew up."

"My friend is the best kid I ever knew," Zach said. "But, I think if I leave in August, she's not going to have anybody like me, not that that's so great, but it's better than what she is going to have."

"Have mercy," Aunt Bonnie said. "We have a true believer here."

She thought of Cowbird. Then she thought of Beltran. "Does this girl like somebody who is going to lead her astray?"

Zach laughed. "Astray. Aunt Bonnie, nobody talks that way anymore."

"I do."

"There is somebody," Zach said. "More than one."

"Well," Bonnie said, "your mama sure did raise a fool."

Zach stared out at the water. He thought about Beltran, how the one time he saw the guy, he'd felt like he was looking at one of those tiny scorpions that could kill you with a sting.

"She's not like Beltran," he said, and wished he could swallow the words. Bonnie tilted her shades up on her forehead. "Child," she said. "Child." She looked Zach in the eyes. "Well, you can thank God for that."

Zach was quiet. The mama cat snuck out to the sand below them and grabbed a dead something.

"It's not just the girl, is it?" Bonnie said.

"No."

"What else?"

Zach pointed down at the skinny cat. "See her? She's happy here. She belongs here. Her babies are here." He put his hands over his face. *Fuck it. Fuck it.* "I don't want to go back to my dad's."

Bonnie waited. Heat flooded her from inside. *I'm getting old,* she thought and suddenly found herself longing for one of those paper fans her mama had waved to keep Bonnie cool at prayer meeting. She wished she could talk to her mama right that second. About how to help this beloved boy. About Cowbird and Beltran. About how it was to be a big beautiful African American woman getting old and feeling like a baby.

"I know," Bonnie said. "I know what you want. So does your mama." Zach leaned his head on her shoulder. She smelled of cloves and freshly ironed cotton.

"It's all right, baby," she said. "We don't have to fix everything right now."

TEAM MAGGIE 'N' SARAH lost, won, lost , won, won, won, and took off up one hundred and eighty-six bucks. It was a long sweet twilight, the earth spinning toward late summer. Maggie drove. Sarah fell asleep, into a dream as bright as waking.

She was in the little casino a few hours earlier, telling Maggie again she was afraid she was fading. She showed Maggie, let her see ghost-way, let her see Sarah's fingers turned to stubs. Maggie said Sarah's heart line was a thread. No one else saw any of it, not the chubby Chicana twins in the matching green velvet pantsuits taking turns working the Elvis machine; not the hound-faced guy in the United Mine Workers T-shirt on the other side. None of them moved when they hit jackpots. They were real pros.

Sarah woke. "So," Maggie said. "How long do you figure we have to do the job?"

"As long as you can see me," Sarah said.

A neon spaceship and the word *Carmen* glittered in the dark ahead. A mile later, Sarah and Maggie were there, parked in front of the UFO Cafe and Laundry.

An old man walked up to the Bird and leaned in close to her open window. "Welcome to Carmen, Nevada, sweetheart," he said. "I'm Dude Edmonds. I am the mayor of Carmen, the postman, and the entire chamber of commerce. If you got any questions, you'll find me at the UFO, which is run by my wife, Maybonne. We serve the best blackberry milkshake you ever drank."

Maggie shook his hand. "I was wondering . . . ," she started to say, when he kept going. "Now, ladies, just remember you can never tell who is real here and who is from Somewhere Else. We're on the extraterrestrial highway, you know. I've seen them UFOs myself, weird lights spinning just above my head, black shadows on a day with no clouds. 'Course, they didn't come down and get me or I wouldn't be here."

He paused. Maggie knew it was time to laugh.

He bowed. "And then," he said, "there's that Area 51. Do you gals listen to Art Bell? He's the smartest man in America."

Sarah almost wanted to go visible and tell him Art Bell didn't know a tenth of it. Maggie said they hadn't really checked out Art Bell, but she lived in Nevada so she believed in just about anything. "You won't believe how good those blackberry milkshakes are," Dude said. He waited till they climbed out and personally escorted them to the cafe.

Candles burned on two wooden tables in front of the windows. "I'll get milkshakes," Maggie said. "Meet you behind the buildings."

Sarah shifted gsi'ki and walked the two hundred feet of Main Street. She looked into the Laundromat window. The place was full of Indians, two guys asleep against the back wall, an old lady whose son was folding clothes on the rickety table, and kids running everywhere. Now and then the old lady looked up. When she did, the kids froze in place.

Sarah waited for Maggie to bring their milkshakes. People wandered by. An Indian boy with chrome-green hair. A white woman with a dried-out rooster head on a cord around her neck. Sarah walked through the alley to the back of the cafe, became a shadow, then herself. Maggie came around the corner.

"What next?" Maggie said.

"We watch a little," Sarah said. "Minnie told us kids we were never alone. There were always somethings she called the Interested Ones watching us. We'll be the interested ones till the milkshakes are gone."

She took a sip. It was possibly the best milkshake she'd ever had—tart and sweet. She thought of Will's lips on hers.

SLIM GIRL lay on the bench outside the coffee shop. She was tucked into her bedroll and four jackets, so she looked like a bundle of wash. Hippies came out of the coffee shop and sat next to her. Laughter tickled Slim Girl's throat, but she remembered how her grandma taught her. "You gotta be strong. You gotta know when to sit still and when to run, when to talk and when to shut your mouth. These people are gonna take you to a school far away and you gotta make it through."

A black man sat down next to the Slim Girl bundle. There were leaves in his curly hair and half a cigarette stuck behind his left ear. A name was embroidered across his breast pocket. LEONID. He set the cigarette between his cracked lips and waited.

"LE-O-NID," Slim Girl said inside her head. He had at least half a perfectly good cigarette, and she was dying for a smoke. But she didn't know what a Leonid was, maybe an alien.

The bench bounced. Two women sat almost next to her. One woman was white. The second woman seemed like she was made of glass. There were pink shadows inside of her. For an instant, Slim Girl was afraid, and then she remembered the doctor at the Indian Health Service telling her she was skitzo-frenik and skitzofreniks normally see things that weren't there. What was there was a cigarette in the glass woman's hand. Slim Girl unwrapped the blankets and sat up. "You got a smoke, sister?"

The glass woman handed her a glass cigarette, leaned over, and lit it from her own, and Slim Girl was surprised to find herself sucking in smoke as real as it could be.

22 Bonnie Madrid took her iced tea to the hammock in the ramada. She couldn't get Zach's words out of her mind: *She isn't like Beltran.* She wanted to feel all huffy about how smart-mouthed modern kids could be, but she knew Zach had been right to say them. Before Cowbird, she might have felt different.

It was strange it had been only a month or so since she and Cowbird had talked all night in the Ruby Room. She'd never felt close to a man, much less as close as she felt to Orlen Jackson. She preferred calling him Orlen, because the more stories he told and the better she knew him, she knew he only played at being a simple cracker.

He was away, gone looking for work. She was glad, and not. When Cowbird was around, she felt her pulse slow. The *ain't enuff* in her gut eased up. But, *without* Cowbird, she could think about Beltran.

Thinking about Beltran had been the finest drug she'd ever used. For five years, her thoughts of him had carried her through the surgery and the pills, through the ordinary dentist appointments and jammed-up grocery lines. It had nothing to do with feeling close, anymore than you could let yourself be close with a gorgeous coral snake.

She lay back in the hammock. For an instant, she thought she saw a flying ruby, then realized the hummingbirds were back. A second ruby strafed the first. The *whrrrr* was ferocious, the light shining off the bird's wings too beautiful not to look at, too brilliant to look at for long. Beltran.

She remembered their first meeting. She'd been working graveyard. A short wiry vaquero came in for the midnight special. He was pure Norteño, spotless white straw cowboy hat, butt-snug Levi's with a crease ironed down both legs, a black shirt embroidered with bird of paradise flowers, and pointy-toed cowboy boots. His gleaming black hair was just-right too long.

The hostess called, "One, nonsmoking." Bonnie pretended she hadn't heard her. She had learned to not look like you wanted what you wanted. She wanted the vaquero at her table. And, she knew, as he strolled toward her, she was going to get what she wanted, and she was about to live, as the old Chinese curse said, in interesting times.

He sat down. Bonnie waited a decent amount of time and walked over.

"Hell-o!" he said, in perfect unaccented English. "They have improved the decor up here."

Bonnie smiled. "Are you ready to order? Or do you need me to tell you the specials."

The vaquero stood. "Please," he said, "your voice is the voice of the only special I want to hear about. I am Eddie Beltran. My friends, and I pray we will be friends, call me Beltran."

Bonnie blushed. At first she thought it was the hormone treatments kicking in, and then Eddie Beltran took her hand and said, "It is not good manners to kiss the hand of a señorita, but I kiss your hand as a charm against your being a señora," and she knew the blush was anything but pharmaceutical.

"Who are you?" Bonnie said.

"I am a tropical bird," he said.

"What kind?" Bonnie said. The starting gates were open, the pistol shot rang in her blood, and she was going neck and neck with the cowboy. She looked away from his eyes. They glittered like the fake diamonds Lucille sold to the suckers who fell madly back in love after thirty years of a dead marriage because Fred got dealt the jack of spades for a royal flush on dollar video poker.

"I am a bird of paradise," Beltran had said, "and, I am going to take you to heaven."

Jive. Pathetic. Bonnie remembered the trashtalk of the city streets. She remembered gorgeous icy boys and girls throwin' down riffs that could have reduced this man to tears. And still, she had looked into Eddie Beltran's eyes and said, "Yes."

THE MOUNTAINS were a jagged indigo hoop around the desert. Rose sky burned scarlet, then ember. It occurred to Maggie that a straight highway across desolate land might be her favorite human creation. Cool air blew through the Bird's windows. She was driving a road she didn't know. She hoped it truly was a long way, long enough to give her breathing room before she opened Dark Cloud's letter, and, even more before she ran into Jesse while she hunted for a job.

She knew how it would be. Jesse would smile nicely. Her guts would jam up against her ribs. He would ask her how she was doing. She would not breathe, and somehow say, "Just fine. Job hunting. Know of anything?" He would shake his head. One of them would say, "Good to see you again. Really." The other would say, "Catch you later."

That would be that, except for the part where she would duck into the nearest ladies' room and lock herself in a stall for as long as it took her to come back from the dead, to come back from remembering the ten years between DC and Jesse, the guys who looked down at her and said, "Wow, when I first saw you, I didn't think you were going to be this good." And, as time marked her, "What I like about an older chick is they know what they're doing."

"Sarah," she said. "I've been thinking."

Sarah waited.

"Maybe almost fifty-five is a good time to retire."

"Oh please," Sarah said, "you've got seven years till Social Security and a whole future of poverty ahead of you."

"I mean no more men."

"You mean Jesse?"

"Jesse who?"

Maggie put her head down on the steering wheel. "Maggie," Sarah said, "time to pull over." Maggie looked up. "There's a dirt road on the right." Maggie swerved onto the gravel.

"Jesse's not the only guy," Sarah said. It sounded lame.

You will tell her . . . It could have been Minnie's voice in her mind. It could have been the whisper of the unseen ones who are interested, the ones who expect a human, even a ghost, to do *something*.

You will tell her not to die before her time.

Sarah put her arm around Maggie. She couldn't remember doing that with any woman but family, but she couldn't imagine how Maggie must feel—to think you have to be seen by people who don't see you. And then Sarah remembered the time her aunt had taken her to the fancy shoe store in Salt Lake City and the white girl at the counter had ignored them until her aunt had said calmly, "They're too busy in here to sell us shoes," and taken her out.

She remembered Will's hands on her back, circling slowly, the barest touch, moving around her sides, touching each rib as though it were fragile as lightning glass. She remembered how he watched her, and how she knew herself not in his eyes, but his touch.

"Maggie," Sarah said. "I don't think Jesse's gone."

Maggie sat up straight. "If he is, he is the last one, I promise you that."

"But even if he is," Sarah said, "you're not."

Maggie held her head high. "You know," she said, "if you always hold your head up like this, you don't get that turkey thing under your chin."

"No matter what you do," Sarah said, "you get that turkey thing and your arms go all flubbly, and if you're lucky you get old enough to have so many wrinkles you look like a dried apple. It happens to any woman who doesn't chop herself up with plastic surgery."

She heard Minnie clearly. *Girl, open your mind. You are in the Ka'gsi'ki right now. You are in the old stories. Here is what you both need.*

Minnie began to whisper in Willow, her words pouring into Sarah, a flash flood, an annihilation, and a blessing. Sarah knew what came next. "Start the car," she said. "We're getting out of here."

JESSE, COCKER, AND RALPH TOO had made it to the story about how Cocker had driven down from that ski resort in Flagstaff and ran over a frozen drunk in the road. "I thought it was a speed bump," he said. "Jeez, I couldn't believe my ears when my buddy yelled, 'Stop. You just might of killed a guy.' I hadn't. The old fella had been there long enough to freeze solid. Life can get kind of weird sometimes."

Ralph Too lifted his paw out of the water and shook it delicately. There were four beers left. Jesse shone the light on Ralph's paw, and Cocker went to work. By the time he was done, Jesse realized that he, Jesse, was impaired enough to be thinking of himself as *he, Jesse.* "I don't think Jesse ought to drive," he said. "At least not on the highway."

"You can crash in the backseat here," Cocker said. "ZZ don't like company unless it's girls. But, hey, it's the shank of the evening. How about I go get us some more beer."

Ralph Too bumped Cocker's shoulder. "He likes steak," Jesse said.

"Lucky pup," Cocker said. "So does ZZ."

THE MOON hung high in the east. White walls of an old adobe glowed ahead. "Stop here," Sarah said. Maggie turned off the highway, toward gleaming water and the black filagree of tree branches. "Where are we?" Maggie said.

"Willow Springs," Sarah said. "Our women have been coming here for as long as the Ka'gsi'ki has existed."

They climbed out of the Bird and walked to the fence around the pool. It looked recent, tight chicken wire and concertina coils. Sulfur vapor rose. Maggie wanted to sink into the pool and feel liquid mineral hold her.

"Damn," she said. "I wish there was a way in."

"There's a better place," Sarah said.

They followed a thread of water up into the dark hills. The stench of sulfur grew stronger, then was gone. Sarah led Maggie into the mouth of a little canyon. A waterfall no wider than Maggie's shoulders dropped to the wet sand and ran into a stone pool.

Sarah and Maggie undressed and slipped into the warm water. "I didn't know any of what I'm going to tell you before my aunt and Minnie began teaching me last month," Sarah said. "Some of it they told me four times, made me memorize it. 'You can't write it down,' they said, 'maybe parts, but not all. The story is the floor of the women's Ka'gsi'ki. Each time a woman tells it, the gsi'ki house is more solid.'"

Sarah leaned back in the water. "Before the white people came, there was always war between tribes. Red Canyon warriors against Twisting Trees, Mud Creek against Blue Mountain, all over the country, everywhere. For land. For women. For turquoise. Always for water.

"What was different from now was that no tribe killed its own people. Stories about that got passed on across the mountains, down from the Light Dancer people, in from the Big Water tribes. A Willow woman finally put it together: a warrior would not kill a warrior who carried his bloodlines.

"The Willow woman told her friends. They talked about what women do best. At first, they were afraid of what they knew. But when they remembered their own pleasure, they laughed.

"The Willow women became known as women who would take men from other tribes to their beds. Old women taught the girls every trick of pleasure. At first, the Willow men were angry. Then the Willow women had babies. Nobody knew for sure who the fathers were, but they knew the babies' blood could be from any tribe.

"Storytellers went from people to people. And, the men of other tribes stopped making war on the Willow people. The women were honored at home—and everywhere the story was told."

Maggie looked away from Sarah. "You're making that up," she said.

"No. It's true.

"When the white man came, they seemed at first to understand. A few fell in love, married Willow women. Others taught us their words: *puta, whore,* and they twisted one of ours: *squaw.* We died from their terrible diseases. When the Willow women began to hold back from the white men, the white men raped them. And then the white men killed."

"What the killer said to you about women using him," Maggie said. " 'You know how that can be, Sarah, you learned that up north,' maybe he was talking about that."

"Maybe about what I know," Sarah said, "or maybe about how I have no shame." She scooped up water and poured it over her head. Her skin gleamed. "I told you the story because my aunt wants us to go to the places the Willow women went for purification after the white men had finished with them. I thought it was just for me." She slid deeper into the water.

"It's for me too," Maggie said. Her voice was flat. "I was never raped. Agreed to all of it. A hundred different men, two hundred—I've lost count."

"It doesn't matter," Sarah said. She remembered the sad-eyed tribal cop who had met her and Denise in the Indian Health Service emergency room after the thing had happened to Denise, the thing Denise blamed herself for, the thing Denise never, ever—from that moment on—named. "Women get raped," he had said, "in all circumstances, no matter who they are."

Maggie was quiet. They rested in the pool as the moon slipped toward the mountains and was gone. Sarah watched the stars, they drifted in her gsi'ki; she was held by water black and glittering as sky. Maggie closed her eyes. The dark behind her lids was perfect. She thought of the welcome gift of not thinking. She could not remember ever feeling as peaceful.

Sarah sat up. "We need to sleep." She felt Minnie's hand smooth her hair. *Thank you, child,* Minnie whispered, *you are learning.*

Maggie opened her eyes. "I'd like to sit here alone a while. Maybe you could watch to make sure nobody comes."

Sarah couldn't remember ever, once she had left her aunt's, feeling safe in a wild place alone. "Of course," she said. Stars gleamed in the drops of water on her skin. Maggie thought of tears, of something so far gone there were no words for it.

"Thank you," Maggie said. "I need this. This water holding me."

"Water," Sarah said, "is medicine. And the river is one of the places our souls go when they are free."

Sarah walked down the trail. Maggie looked up into a velvet sky. She remembered being seventeen—riding in the backseat of a friend's convertible, the top folded back, her head resting on her lover's arm. The driver had sped over a roller-coaster road while aurora borealis rippled pink-red and green above their heads. The car had slowed; the driver had parked at the shore of a little lake and drawn his date into his arms. Her boyfriend had moved his lips over her naked throat, and she had believed she was the happiest she might ever be.

JESSE heard a whimper. His heart pounded. He had no idea where he was. The place reeked of aviation fuel. He was scared to click his lighter. Then a wet nose touched his hand and he knew he was safe. Ralph Too dropped his head into Jesse's hand. "It's OK, boy," Jesse said.

He couldn't sleep. He had the four-hour postdrunk wide-awake brain going a million miles an hour jimmy-jams. Darwin had taught him that diagnosis. Jesse pulled Ralph Too in next to him and decided to give Darwin's memory its due.

MAGGIE AND SARAH settled into the Firebird. Sarah unfolded the shawl across Maggie's lap. The big-eyed animals glowed in the dash light. Sarah traced a scarlet thread that ran through the shawl to its edge. "In the Ka'gsi'ki, this is a map," she said. She followed the scarlet thread out to the edge. "This line is a fish swimming away from a bear. It's what the Dine call a "spirit line." It leads the weaver's spirit out of the finished rug so she doesn't get trapped."

"Where's *your* spirit line?" The murmur of thunder echoed Maggie's whisper. Sarah smelled the shadow of rain. She touched the snake woven below the fish. "Maybe here, maybe this snake. Minnie says the snake gives names. Maybe I'm hunting my real name."

Maggie looked at her. "Why did the lady cop say your last name was 'Four'?"

"I don't know." Sarah wanted to tell Maggie figuring out wasn't going to get them where they were headed. They had to visit each place on the shawl-map. They couldn't *plan* a way to free her, to free a spirit growing stronger, in a body growing more fragile, a body more and more reluctant to be free. There was no plan. There was only the shawl. And moving forward.

"Girlfriend," Maggie said, "what I want more than anything right now is about three shots from Julio's gallon of Tanqueray, in a glass that is sitting between my slot machine and yours." She picked up a corner of the shawl. "We're in the friggin' Ka'gsi'ki right now, aren't we?" she said. "Right now."

"I'm afraid so," Sarah said, and was filled with a fierce joy.

"ok," Maggie said.

Sarah folded the shawl. "It was a good thing I knew how to make fry bread," she said, "and that Leola needed a sous chef."

23 Sarah watched through the night. Once she heard a car on the highway. She imagined desert without roads. Mountains without cell towers. Rivers without dams. She remembered that her people worked the roads and the dams, carried the latest cell phones as though they were coup.

Minnie did not show up. Sarah wished she could ask her how their people had been so thoroughly fucked. She thought of the early Willow women, how evil it must have been to find yourself under the violent body of a white man, being forced to give what you once had loved. She remembered her killer's kiss.

She thought of the offers that were so difficult to refuse, the offers that would put you under the white man quicker than rape. Big conferences at which an Indian woman with a master's degree is made to feel she is respected. Messing with some tribal chairman in his bad suit and turquoise bolo tie, even though your cousin was his wife. Because you were so lonely.

Sarah drifted into sleep. She surfed translucent worlds, found the ghosts of the place in which she slept, and woke before dawn, knowing what was about to happen to Willow Springs.

The chicken-wire fence was a black web against first light. Dawn melted in. Pale green. Sulfur. Rose.

Maggie sat up. "What is it? What's wrong?"

"Follow me."

They walked to the pool. There was a sign that said: "Lodges at the springs. A gated residential golf community in the heart of ancient beauty." There was a Scottsdale phone number and the name of the company: Your Greendreams, Inc. L.L.C.

"We could get ourselves over that concertina wire," Maggie said. "We could use my lipstick and at least leave a note."

"No." Sarah walked to the fence and pressed her face against the chicken wire. She wanted it to mark her, if only for a minute.

"Sarah," Maggie said, "they won't be able to pull this off. There's not enough water here." She read the rest of the sign: "Geothermal energy—not just for the Lodges—but for our neighbors. Solar power. Recycled gray water will irrigate the executive golf course. Your own five-acre homesite. Strict design code. Native wood and stone. Native petroglyphs within a five-minute hike. A waterfall. And, of course, the ancient springs. Call for details."

"I can't stay here another second," Sarah said.

Maggie twined her fingers through the wire. "I'm sorry," she said. She didn't know if she was talking to Sarah or the place.

MORNING was as bad as Jesse had hoped it wouldn't be. The hangover bit deep. He tried to relax and found his legs were shaking. He looked up. Ralph Too waited patiently.

"OK, old guy," Jesse said and scratched Ralph behind the ears. The dog sniffed at the patch of concrete on which a steak so long ago had rested and gave Jesse a deeply sorrowful look.

"We're out of here," Jesse said. He left twice what he would have paid a vet tucked under the last unopened beer and let Ralph and himself out.

He couldn't believe how hungry he was, a man whose mouth tasted like a dead bird had slept in it. He drove over the bridge just as first light glowed above the Cerbat Mountains. Ralph Too stuck his nose out the window and sniffed river. Jesse wondered how dogs rode in air-conditioned cars—it would be like living your life in a condom.

ZACH opened the blinds. It was the cool light just before dawn. He heard his mom in the kitchen. She'd be making warm milk, taking it to her bed on the fold-out couch in the living room. He felt the minutes going steadily, like waves breaking in sets. There was no way to hold them back. There was no way to speed them up. He could only feel them in his blood, maybe surf a few if he was brave.

His mom snored. He pulled on his shorts and sneakers, tiptoed past her into the kitchen, grabbed a quart of OJ from the fridge and his skateboard from the hall. The sun was still below the mountains. A breeze lifted his hair. He hunkered down on the trailer steps and wrote his mom a note. "Skating while it's cool. Home by nine."

The Riverstroll was quiet. It was time for the Loser Patrol. Desert rats with eyes like zombies. Couples slogging back and forth between the RiverBelle and the Tidewater, trying a few bucks in one place, tapping out, hitting the ATM in the other casino, trying a few bucks, tapping out, and finally slumping on a bench above the river.

Zach warmed up on the level walk between the Belle and the TW. He felt his brain relax, felt his body kick in. He pretended he was carried on a current in the river. All he had to do was breathe.

JESSE pulled into the covered garage at the Tidewater. Ralph Too sniffed the air, pulled his head back into the truck, and looked at Jesse. The dog's dark eyes were worried.

Jesse put his head down on the steering wheel. For the last ten minutes, he had been thinking about a tall Virgin Mary, then another, and another. He had imagined his brain cells soaking up the vitamin C. It had seemed possible that he could then live through the morning. It was clear he couldn't leave Ralph in the truck. In an hour, it would be over ninety degrees. Jesse was thankful he was too hungover to think of the future, a future in which Ralph Too was writ large.

"Ralph Too," he said. "Help me out here."

Ralph waited patiently. Jesse looped his belt through the dog's collar. "You are about to become a health professional canine," he said.

They climbed out of the truck and limped toward the elevator.

MAGGIE AND SARAH drove south. Sarah clicked on the radio. The news faded in and out. A cloud of dust from the Gobi Desert was drifting over Nevada. Sarah saw the hills ahead through a delicate haze, the far ranges smoke blue, the nearest indigo. A dust devil spiraled up into the silvery air. She saw the seam of red across the arsenic green cliffs. "There should be a ranch road soon to the left."

Maggie pulled off and stopped at the gate. Sarah climbed out, untwisted the wire, and swung the gate open, a dozen memories filling her. She and Hannah going off into the little canyons that wound back into Beartrack Mountain. Will Lucas and her hunting for a place to be alone. Her uncle taking her to a huge old sage bush hung with feathers, and telling her each feather was a person's prayer.

The Bird fishtailed over the sandy tracks, skimmed over center rocks, and caught sage under the back axle. They smelled it smoking. Maggie stopped. Sarah rubbed her hands in the smoke. "We use it to protect," she said. "Go ahead, you do it too. We're both going to need it."

The dirt at the base of the cliff was gouged deep where some ATV bogger had mired in spring mud. Bright-red and piss-yellow shotgun shells lay everywhere. A clutch of blue grouse feathers lay next to three pairs of talons.

Sarah looked up at the red vein snaking six feet up across the dark rock. "It is soft mineral," Hannah had told her. "You can scrape it away and mix it with water from the spring at the end of the little wash. The women used it in the old dances, the ones the preachers made us forget because they were about women's blood power."

The little spring was dry, the sand splattered with human shit. Morning light shone like a pink lantern through the membrane over the rib cage of a decapitated bighorn lamb. Maggie crouched over the delicate spine. "Why would they kill a baby?"

Sarah wanted to reach up into the red vein and smear the powder below Maggie's eyes, so her tears would make salt-red paint. She wanted to see the paint dry in the wrinkles around Maggie's eyes, catch in all the sorrow lines. She would hold a mirror in front of her and make Maggie see how beautiful she was, but Sarah could not raise her arms.

"This is Sacred Blood Mountain. Or it was. We have to leave now. What's here could make us sick."

THEY OPENED THE CAR DOORS to let the heat out. "Sarah," Maggie said, "I have another name."

Sarah thought of Will Lucas who was Wildhair Boy who was Da Redman. And how she was Sarah Martin and Sarah Four, and once she had been Bladz. She remembered that some names are registered, some are not.

"I was Dissident Sister," Maggie said. "In the seventies. I sang, played a little guitar. It was a long time ago."

"*Was* a singer?" Sarah said.

"Was." Maggie shrugged. "Dead DC got jealous. I got older, which is the biggest mistake a chick rocker can make.

"But I don't think I'm going to be able to forget that dead lamb. It needs a lament."

{ 186 }

Maggie looked back toward the cliff. Only if you walked beyond the end of the road would you know what was there. For an instant, she remembered a line from a song she had never finished. *There's a signal coming in. From a dead star. There's a bad and beautiful light.* That had been the way the music had always come. A few words. A few notes. Then more, till she would feel a little crazy, make herself sit still, and the song would be there.

Sarah unfolded the shawl on her lap. She expected to see holes in it, maybe stains. Nothing. The shawl was a map of what had been. "We've got two places left," Sarah said. "A mountain and a spring south of Mica. I'm afraid of what we'll find."

"Why haven't I seen what was happening?" Maggie said. "I was a zombie."

"Besides, what if we had seen it?" Sarah said. "What could we have done?"

Plenty, Minnie whispered. *You just wait.*

ZACH aced an ollie to grind on the curb, tucked the board under his arm, and skidded down the steps to the boat ramp. Catclaw waited.

"Hey, wanker, I figgered I might find you 'ere," Catclaw said. He had his Cockney accent on, which was not actually a Cockney accent, but a morph he had taken from watching the old movie *Quadrophenia* about a hundred times.

"You figured right," Zach said.

Catclaw spit on the ramp. He looked like shit. He was skinnier than ever and his eyes were pink.

"Are you OK?" Zach said, and realized what a wiener thing that was to say. What he really wanted to say was, "Leave Spooky alone. If you fuck her up, I will personally kill your sorry tweaker ass, gringo."

Catclaw laughed.

It occurred to Zach that this drama was nowhere near as exciting as the movies said teenagers were.

"I," Catclaw said. "Oi mean Oi am a fuckload better than you're going to be, Beaner Boy."

Zach grinned. Catclaw narrowed his eyes. "This is boring," Zach said.

Catclaw twitched. "Huh?" He spit on the ramp.

"If you're going to fuck with me," Zach said, "just get it over with." He wondered what cool-sounding guy was saying those words.

"Well, actually," Catclaw said, "I been thinking we could just reach an agreement about Spooky until you leave." His gaze shifted from right to left, and back again. His right leg jittered so fast it was almost a blur.

"No," Zach said. "It's her call."

"I would, listen, I would fuck you up right this minute, but I don't feel so good. You got a cigarette?"

Zach picked up his skateboard and walked back up the ramp. When he turned to look down, Catclaw was looking in the water. Zach waved. Catclaw spit in the river. Zach wondered if the rest of his life was going to be like this— nothing changed, nothing different, not worse, not better, no big dramatic moment, just everything not quite right

JESSE AND RALPH TOO hotfooted it across the asphalt to the front door of the Crystal. Only as Jesse saw the cardboard sign duct-taped to the glass did he realize there were no cars in the parking lot. Ralph sidled into the shade of a fake palm.

The sign was scrawled in black marker: "The Crystal is under new management. Watch for our Grand Opening. Trespassers will be prosecuted."

Jesse led Ralph to the Riverstroll. His story would work better at one of the big casinos anyway. He'd never gambled in any of them, so they didn't know him. He pulled his bandana down over one eye and headed for the Tidewater. There was an abundant and cheap breakfast buffet. Later, Ralph Too could watch the feral cats that hustled behind the casino and feel superior.

JESSE smiled at the guy who once would have been the security guard. They didn't call them security guards anymore in the corpo-casinos. They called them "hospitality hosts," even if the hosts wore guns.

"This here dog," Jesse said, "is named Ralph Too. He is a fit dog. I got epilepsy."

He touched the bandana over his eye. "Nam. Shrapnel."

The guard gave him the old right-in-the-eye-I-was-there-bro look. "How's that work?"

"Ralph Too got trained up to know when I got a fit coming on. He barks three times and bumps me with his nose. And, I know to get my ass down on the floor."

"Ralph Too," the hospitality host said. "That's a good name for a good dog." Ralph wagged his tail, and they were in.

Jesse and Ralph Too dined. The young busgirl fell in love. With Ralph. She forgot Jesse's three Virgin Marys and slid a plate of fresh-sliced roast beef under the table. Ralph waited politely. "You go ahead, you big old puppy you," she said. Ralph dove in.

"Oh," she said to Jesse, "your beverages."

Jesse slammed down the first Virgin Mary. There was a queasy moment during which he was not sure whether that was smart. Than his stomach calmed down and he knew just how hungry he was. "Ralph," he said, "oh shit, I'm talking to a dog. Ralph, we're going to eat till our eyeballs spin, go home and get some sleep, and then we're going to see Old Ray for some advice."

The roast beef was gone. Jesse sipped the second Virgin Mary. "Stay put, boy," he said, and headed to the buffet for another plate of beef.

24 Sunbreak Crag rose out of the sage like a cobalt iceberg. If you were a greenhorn or a tourist zooming through, you wouldn't know the Crag was probably eight times taller than what you saw. Dunes, drifts, and atoms of Crag had filled the space to the ancient seabed below.

Maggie tucked the car out of sight in a little wash. She and Sarah rolled their sleeping bags out on a ledge on vertical miles of time. Maggie was asleep in minutes.

Sarah watched for a while. The sky was brilliantly clear, the moon an interrogation light. She pulled her hair over her eyes and went into its soft dark.

A dream drew her in. *She walked with a little girl on a street whose gutters ran with red mud. Sarah was afraid. There were stores on both sides of the street. Their doors were painted black. There was a snake in a jar in front of one of the stores. "There are names in the jar," the little girl said. "Yours is in there."*

The child pulled Sarah along more quickly than she believed she could move. The open doors began to glow. A black door vanished into smoke. An old woman's head appeared in a window, grinning, black eyes unblinking.

"Come in," the old woman's head whispered. "Come in."

"Where am I?"

"The Street of Going Through," the child and the old woman said. "Come in/ come in. Come in/come in. Alone/Alone."

NEXT AFTERNOON, as though she'd known the skill all her life, Sarah taught Maggie how to weave bird snares with their own hair. It was a craft both of them prayed never to have to use again, even though the snares were beautiful. You could not tell which strands were Sarah's and which were Maggie's, black and chestnut all the same in the desert glare. Sunbreak Crag breathed in night coming, exhaled day. The sun was a fat tangerine above low thunderheads.

Bushes rattled in the sunsetting wind. Sarah placed the snares as Hannah had once showed her.

"Listen," Maggie said. "Do we really have to stay awake all night?"

"You'll be OK."

"I'm not sure." Maggie hugged her knees. "I'm afraid of not being able to sleep. After DC left the third time, I'd drag my ass into our big empty bed and watch the clock. 1:00 a.m., warm milk and booze. 2:00 a.m., skip the milk. 3:00 a.m., skip the booze. 5:15, sleep. Sit up at 6:00 a.m., toast a Pop-Tart for Daniel, take him to school, go to some shit job. If it hadn't been for my kid— and one-night stands, I'd have killed myself."

Sarah tightened a knot on the snare. "This isn't like that."

MAGGIE fell asleep around midnight. It didn't matter. What they would do next Sarah could do for both of them. She remembered Minnie telling the children long ago the truth about sickness. "The word *b'ngi gsi'ki*, which white doctors call "being sick," is more like an accident, like the person went off the road and the gsi'ki forgot how to be."

She remembered the song Minnie sang.

The things I call their names,
The things I call their names

. . . .

I release them.
I release them.

JUST BEFORE FIRST LIGHT Sarah made coffee and built a tiny fire from a handful of sage. She woke Maggie, put a mug in her hand, her finger to Maggie's lips, and nodded toward the nearest creosote.

At first Maggie thought the snare was gone, then she saw a bright eye watching them. A tiny gray bird rested quietly in the snare. Sarah crouched next to it and whispered in Willow.

Light began to blossom above the saddle between Old Thunder Peak and Mascag. The sun threw long shadows to the north and south. Sarah pulled a knife from her pocket.

Light touched the bird. Its feathers glowed gunmetal blue. Sarah leaned forward. She cut the threads of the snare till the bird was free. It didn't move. She scattered corn chips at the base of the creosote. The bird chirped, scavenged a crumb, and was gone. Sarah gathered up the snare and dropped it in the fire.

> The things I call their names,
> The things I call their names
> I release them.
> I release them.

SARAH'S voice was harsh. She sang the old song four times four. Maggie was quiet. She thought of Creosote, of Jesse, of DC's letter. She wondered if she had called Jesse's name; she wondered if it was time to release him. Sarah's voice faded in. "Now," she said, "we wait."

"What are we waiting for?" Maggie said.

"I wish I knew."

The road below stretched empty most of the morning. Sarah climbed up through the sage. Maggie just watched and wondered why she had spent so much time doing anything but nothing. She knew she had $163 and a maxed-out credit card in her wallet—doing nothing might be the option for only as long as Sarah was climbing the mountain.

Maggie stretched out and watched what she could see at lizard level. Not much. Quartz flakes. Hyper ants. Then a car rattled onto the pull-off twenty feet below her. It was a sunstroke-gray late eighties Monte Carlo.

A skinny guy and a chunky woman in a purple mumu hauled themselves out of the car. The woman set two Maverick to-go cups on the roof. The coffee would be hot in ten minutes. Roadtrash solar power.

"Well, Terry," the guy said, "like you said, we're the only services for thirty miles in either direction. Let's get going."

The woman unfolded a red cloth and spread it over the hood. The guy put up a cardboard sign just off the road. The woman set a cactus salt and pepper set on the cloth; the man brought a box of car parts out of the backseat and began to arrange spark plugs in a neat line. "You want to make price tags?"

The woman shielded her eyes and looked west. "Why bother? Anybody stops will probably ask."

"*If*," the man said, "anybody comes along and stops." His voice was thin and gravelly, the sound of a man who loves disappointment.

"Dale," the woman said, "right now, we got no choice. We got no money and only enough gas to get us to ten miles this side of Carmen."

She draped a handful of cedar bead necklaces over the cloth. Dale picked up the fanciest necklace. A silver coin hung between two blue beads. He shook his head. "If only you'd of had . . ."

The woman smiled gently. "If only you'd of hadn't . . ."

"Terry," he said, "I'll be sorry the rest of my sorry life."

The woman laughed. "Or at least till the next deal goes down . . ." There was tenderness in her laughter.

Dale handed a mug to her and took one himself. They opened the doors on the highway side and sat, him in front, her in back.

"There's springs back up in there," Dale said. "My pap used to take us hunting up that little canyon."

"You told me. I think maybe Leon and I came down this road one time." She opened a box of donuts and offered it to the man. "No thanks, darlin'," he said. "My gut's on fire. Sugar don't help."

"One p.m.," the woman said. "We'll give it an hour. Worse comes to worse, we can thumb into Carmen."

"That fuckin' Jesus," the man said. "Two stinkin' nines. Clouset out-played his ass. For once in my life, I went with the safe money. Two stinkin' nines."

"That was a few months ago," the woman said quietly.

Maggie breathed slow. She was content to be still, suspended between the traveling flea market and an azure sky. There was a humming from who knew where so delicate that if she tried to listen, it disappeared in the pulse of her heart.

Dale checked his watch. "One thirty. I can't hardly stand to do nothing like this." He started to walk toward the sage brush.

"Oh no," Terry said, "you're not going for a little hike and leaving me out here alone. Not ever again."

He faced her. "Fuckin' nines, baby. If it weren't for those two fuckin' nines, we'd be laying up in the Villas, eating pink grapes, and thinking about nothing but how the next deal goes down."

"No," she said. "The nines are not what it's about."

Maggie heard Sarah's step behind her. She turned, put her finger to her lips. She had forgotten that Sarah was invisible. Sarah settled next to her without a sound.

"What are you tellin' me?" Dale said. "What do you know about what it's about?"

Terry looked up at the sky. "It's about the Big Guy," she said. "You know it. You just pretend you don't know it because if you admit you know it, then what?"

Dale flopped down on the sand. "Don't start. Please don't start with the Jesus Our Savior shit. I cannot take it. I cannot take one more piece of holy roller babble out of my wife's mouth. One fuckin' Jesus and his two nines is enough!"

"Fiddlesticks," Terry said. "You're the one thought an angel told you to bet Clouset instead of Jesus."

A blue-black King Cab half-ton Ford barreled toward them. Dale jumped to his feet. Terry moved the necklace with the silver coin so it would catch the light. The truck slowed for a second, then roared on. Dale yanked off his hat and threw it on the sand. "That's it," he yelled. "We're going. I've had it."

Terry checked her watch. "Let's give it a couple more minutes."

Dale picked up his hat and brushed off the sand. "Do you think," he said sadly, "we should try to get a couple regular jobs? It ain't no fun anymore. We're not kids."

Terry turned and looked up toward the summit of Sunbreak as though she was beseeching heaven. Maggie froze.

Terry's jaw dropped. "Who are you?" she said. "And, who's the Indian girl next to you?"

Dale looked up wildly. "Oh christ," he said. "There's no Indian chick there. There's just some white broad."

"Of course there's an Indian," Terry said. "Don't tell me you can't see her."

"What I see," he said, "is that my wife is nuts and I am through. I am through, Terry. Done. What you might call finished."

Dale climbed into the Monte Carlo and swerved out onto the highway. Beads and sprocket wrenches flew off the hood. "He'll be back," the woman said. "He just gets like that."

She crouched and picked something up from the sand. "It might be a good idea if you girls got out of here before he comes back. Take this," she tossed a string of cedar beads up to Maggie. "Don't worry, I made it. You know how it is out here. Everything's hitched up, and everything stands on its own."

"We can't leave you here," Maggie said.

Terry smoothed her red blanket out over the sand. "Oh yes you can," she said calmly. "You drive a little ways down the road, you're going to think me and Dale were nothing but a mirage."

Maggie and Sarah packed up their gear and hiked back to the Bird. They opened the windows and doors to let the car cool down. Sarah looked back toward the woman. She could see her facing the highway. The Monte Carlo pulled up. Terry climbed in, and the car sped north.

"What was that?" Maggie asked.

Sarah slid into the passenger seat. "The mirage?"

25   Maggie turned onto the dirt road that led to Cottonwood Springs and parked under a giant tree. The shade was a lover's touch. Sarah opened her window all the way. Maggie closed her eyes.

"I want to know more about Dissident Sister," Sarah said. She was surprised at her bossiness, but she wanted Maggie to have something for the next however long.

"Sure," Maggie nodded. She was used to a world where drunks and lonesome old ladies told you their life story, and wanted to know yours, in the time it took to serve a free watery rum and coke.

"Dissident Sister kept me alive," Maggie said, "and then she was eliminated."

"Not forever."

"I once thought so," Maggie said, "not sure now."

"She could come back for the next part," Sarah said. Her voice sounded like Minnie's. It pissed her off. It was more than weird to find yourself saying stuff you didn't know where it came from, besides being white-people bossy.

"Yeah," Maggie said. She opened her eyes. "Dissident Sister knew a lot, the essentials: tits, legs, hair, lots of eyeliner, and when you're singing about doing it, the average Bud Lite's gotta be able to look at you and want to do it." She grinned. "Unfortunately for the Sister, they did, and she thought *it* was love."

Sarah laughed. "Yep, you're a chick."

"My mother was a musician. She played jazz piano—in our living room." Maggie stopped. Sarah waited. Willow blood sang *patience, patience* in her veins. "And then this hippie chick taught me to iron my hair and pick out chords on an old twelve-string we bought at Goodwill. I was out of the house twelve hours after graduation."

"You're lucky to have something like that—making songs." Sarah thought about her cousin and silver, her aunt and everything she touched. She'd been waiting to see what her gift was going to be.

"I *was* lucky," Maggie said. "It's been a long long time."

Something older than Willow kept Sarah quiet. Something about what lies between a person and her gift. How private that is, how lonely. Then Sarah saw the bright dark pool in the heart of the cottonwood and she wanted to be there.

Maggie went up to the outhouse to change. Sarah walked down into the cottonwood light. Bees hummed around her. She sat on the edge of the little pool. Her hands began to shine like water. She wiggled her fingers. Mist drifted off them. She wrote *Sarah*. The words glimmered and faded. She wrote the old names of Willow Springs and Blood Mountain. She drew the shape of the smoke blue hills, the proud line of Will Lucas's shoulders.

Help us, she wrote. *Help Help Help.* Four times. The number Hannah and Minnie had told her was holy. The words faded away.

Sarah opened her eyes, saw tree shadows, saw slivers of light. Maggie stood next to her. "I was afraid you were gone," she said. "I am going to hate that."

Sarah was quiet. She patted the edge of the pool and Maggie sat.

Sarah slid in. "It's perfect." She lay on her back. Her long hair floated on the water. In that moment, she knew how sweet and sad freedom from life on earth might be.

MAGGIE AND SARAH drove on. Night moved up from the eastern mountains. They were at the turn that would take them to I-15 to Vegas when they saw the light. Molten. Awful. A flashback from the testing that once ate the Nevada sky.

"What is it?" Maggie said.

Sarah wasn't listening. Minnie was hovering outside her window, her black hair tangled, black paint trickling down her cheeks like charred tears. "Help me," she cried. "Please come home." And, was gone.

Help me. Please come home. The arc of a blood red moon cleared Virgin Peak. Sarah swallowed. "It's just the moon."

"Let's get out," Maggie said. She touched Sarah's hand. "Come on. The air is cooler. You'll feel better outside." She couldn't imagine why Sarah seemed paralyzed. They were safe. What she had thought was death was only the reflection that comes around and disappears and comes around again.

They took off their shoes and stepped carefully onto the warm sand. Sarah took Maggie's hand, and then they were howling like headbanger chicks into the rosy light. When there was no more breath, no more sound, they faced each other.

"Maggie," Sarah said, "you have to go on alone now."

Maggie stepped away from her. "No. Not yet."

Sarah wanted to climb back into the Bird. She wanted to forget everything she knew: how her gsi'ki had become like dead stars barely giving light, that Minnie's hair was matted and filthy, and that she, Sara, was going toward the unthinkable. She wanted to forget and she could not. *Help me. Please come home.*

"Now," Sarah said. "I have to go."

"Will we see each other again?"

"I don't know. I hope so. You know I hope so."

"Wait," Maggie said. "Just one more question." She knew, as she knew the moment DC stopped touching her, that there was no arguing with this good-bye. Maggie reached into the glove box. She held out her hand, palm up. Her willow deer lay there. "You never told me what these are for."

Sarah took her deer out of the tiny bag she wore over her heart. "They're for safe hunting. That's all I know. Minnie was going to tell me more when we got to Creosote. But, she's in trouble. I just saw her."

"Where is she?" Maggie said.

"I don't know. She asked me to come back. That's what scares me the most. Minnie never asks. She tells."

"Here," Maggie said. "Take this."

Sarah tucked Maggie's deer into her bag and gave Maggie hers. Maggie pressed her palms together. Sarah's willow deer seemed nothing more than a folded twig.

"Take the women's map," Sarah said. "For Lorinda."

"I'll go first," Maggie said. "I won't be left again." She turned and walked toward the car. She was a footstep away from Sarah when she knew something in her had changed—she was done with leaving. She turned around to tell Sarah and saw only sand and creosote. No shimmer. No T-shirt. No rhinestones. No black hair glinting in the red light.

Maggie tossed the willow deer from hand to hand. The light shifted, blood-orange to rose to silver. "I'm about over this," Maggie said to the moon. "You fucking rise and set, get skinny, get fat. You go away and come back. It's easy for you."

She knew she was talking to a big fat rock a zillion miles away. She was talking to reflection and dust. Dead DC's words hissed in her brain: *You can break anybody, Maggie. That's what I can't forget. That's what you'll never really know.*

He had taught her that, not while she was letting him break her, but before. Before he said to her again, the umpteenth time again, "No, it's not another woman. It's just me. I don't do close." Before all that, he had huddled in her arms on the shore of a desert river, babbling, "You can break anybody, Maggie. Doesn't matter if they're a true believer or tough as nails or love friggin' God—you, me, anybody can break anybody. It's easy. No sleep. Make 'em stand on one leg for a day. Shit, you don't even have to touch 'em." He had stared out at the water. "You don't even have to touch them."

{ 197 }

Which, three months later, was precisely what he did. This was worse. "ok," Maggie said to the moon. "I feel like shit. I'm scared. I don't want to be alone, which I was perfectly happy to be before Sarah arrived, with her god-damn cigarettes and her lousy death.

"ok, and before Jesse. Before him."

Of course, she wanted to drive into North Vegas and pick up some loser with a ready dick. When she thought about the fact that she was not going to kill herself, and she didn't want dawn to arrive with some dumb fuck beside her, and she wouldn't relegate Sarah to the hole in her heart labeled *Oh well*, Maggie decided a greasy buffet and the mindless ambiguity of nickel slots were the wisest choice.

She drove toward the ordinary moon, then headed north to Lazy River.

26 Ray's cast was off. He limped out to Jesse's truck. "Who's this?" he said. "Who's this good old dog riding in a *truck*?" Ralph's tail whacked violently against Jesse's arm.

"For chrissakes," Jesse said, "he's got you doing it."

"Doing what?" Ray tugged open the door. Ralph climbed carefully down.

"Talking to him."

Ray waved Jesse over to the lawn chairs. "Helen talks to that plastic Buddha," he said. "She says that talking to animals and inanimate objects is a sign of humility." He snorted. "She sure got humble last night talking to that Wild Cherry slot machine."

Jesse settled into what he had come to think of as *his* chair. Ralph sniffed one of Helen's fake yucca and decided it was not worth marking. Ray took hold of his collar and gently led him to the blue gravel lawn. Jesse felt tears prick his eyes and wondered what the hell had happened to Runner.

"What'd Clunker say?" Ray asked.

"He said he liked me because I was the only one didn't call him Clunker."

"Well, excuse me all to hell."

"He said they were cholla spines. He fixed Ralph up and said he's got arthritis. He didn't tell me what I got."

"What have you got?" Ray said.

"Ralph Too." Jesse heard himself. Fuckin' whiner.

"I'm working real hard here, pal," Ray said, "not to ask you anything about Vegas. Not because you'd run and I'd miss you, but because you'd leave Ralph, and I am flat out of T-bones."

BELTRAN'S answering machine picked up. No words. Just a beep. Bonnie thought about hanging up. She'd bet he had caller ID. She walked into the bathroom, looked in the mirror, saw wrinkles and longing, took a deep breath, and said, "It's me. I want to talk to you."

She gathered up her purse. Her stash of twenties in the hollowed-out Bible had gotten skinny. It was time to play blackjack; it was time to use her perfect memory, and count. She'd play at the Cachet upriver. They didn't know her, and what with their rich white clientele, they'd probably figure she was just a dumb old Negro grammaw.

The phone rang. Bonnie waited out three and a half rings. She knew Beltran would know that was what she was doing. She didn't care. She patted her heart.

"Hello," she said, her voice flat.

"Aunt Bonnie," Zach said, "it's me. I gotta talk with you. I'm going psycho here. Would you talk to me? And Spooky? Right now? Please? It's totally serious."

"Where are you?"

"At Spooky's mom's. She'll drive us down. Could we meet at the Blue Velvet? Me and Spooky are starving."

"What about your mom? You want her there?"

"It's her day off. This has gotta be private."

"Fifteen minutes," Bonnie said.

"We're gone," Zach said. "Wait. Aunt Bonnie, you know how you taught me not to judge people by how they look?"

"Don't worry, child."

MAGGIE woke in the Lazy River Casino Motel—to the knot in her gut that told her she had lost all but seventy bucks of what was going to get her by the first few days in Creosote. Still, there was a coffeepot on the sink and a buffet coupon in the plastic cup, so things could have been worse. A pale sliver of dawn glowed where the curtains didn't meet. She opened them, looked out on miles of pale blue desert, and counted her blessings.

She poured coffee and stepped out on the balcony. She had no idea what time it was, but from the lack of action in the parking lot, it must be early.

Maggie leaned on the railing. Purple shadows stretched west from the yucca, night spilled down behind the ragged mountains. A couple hundred bucks worth of caffeine washed hope into her bloodstream—hope that the buffet featured fresh-made crullers and corned-beef hash—because if it did, she and Lazy River would be even.

SARAH flew through the long night. Gsi'ki melted, shimmered, and were gone. She held her hand in front of her eyes. She had become a constellation.

"WHAT HAPPENED," Jesse said, "was reality. The village is gone. We killed everybody. Chuck killed everybody. Somebody killed everybody."

"How'd you find out?"

"A kid who could be my granddaughter showed me how to use the Internet. It was an out-of-body experience."

Ray nodded. "It's all that Mary Jane you punks smoked in Nam."

"I told the Anrahs you sent me," Jesse said. "They knew who you were."

"They got good memories," Ray said. "Jesus F. Christ. Some of these days, it seems like everything happened five hundred years ago."

Jesse went into the trailer for a glass of water. He looked out at the back of Old Ray's head. For a long minute, he was afraid to move. He was afraid that if he did, his friend would disappear. He thought how fast the future moved toward us, and he understood he was no longer young.

He grinned and went back to his chair. "Ray," he said, "you still got that HOF hat?"

"I do. Helen won't let me wear it. She says it's just the kind of thing makes people think dirty old men are dirty old men."

"Hopeless Old Fart? That's just natural. I was thinking maybe I could borrow the hat for a while, kind of meditate on it, get ready, more or less."

"That'd be a hell of a lot easier than growing up," Ray said.

THERE WAS A PACK of matches from Binion's on Maggie's breakfast table, with a nugget of Benny's wisdom: "Treat people right and the rest will take care of itself."

Maggie's waiter treated her right, topped her coffee off as soon as it dropped an inch, snuck her a plate of machaca from the employee kitchen. She treated him right and headed out to the Bird with five bucks less, two apple crullers, and a lucky token from the Nevada Landing in Jean.

She opened the Bird's windows. A premature whisper of fall was drifting through. It seemed to be the day when you knew that summer's back was broken, the day when the morning shadows held longer and twilight melted in before you'd decided to move to anywhere but Clark County.

She headed down 15, with the absolute intention to arrive in Creosote with sixty-five dollars intact. She got herself safely out of reach of the Strip. At nine in the morning the place seemed fly-specked and anemic. She was feeling darn good about her discipline when she saw billboards about thirty miles out of the city: "Our beds have mattresses! You get a fork with your meal! Free water! In the drinking fountain! Nevada Landing! Jean!"

She remembered the twenty-four-hour $4.99 prime rib dinner and the cheerful changewoman Lawanne, and how Joe, the Filipino slot manager always, always knew her name. Plus she was a sucker for irony.

The Bird pulled onto the exit ramp almost without her assistance. She found a shady parking spot, scattered apple cruller for the cowbirds, and pushed open the smoked-glass doors.

There was *nothing* like that first zap of cold smoky ozone—especially if you weren't going in as an employee. Maggie's heart raced. Her mouth went dry. And, when she realized it was Sunday, and Crazy Ray Swartz and Lee Marquette were on stage for the Brunch and Blues Special, she forgot she was recovering from a two-hundred-dollar spank not eighteen hours earlier. "Yes," she said. The toothless old gent at the first video poker machine gave her a thumbs up.

Five minutes later, Maggie converted her lucky token and ten bucks to 220 nickels and hunkered down in front of Cleopatra. She fully understood born-again x-ianity. She had played thirty-six nickels because maybe multiples of four *were* holy numbers for some white girls. Four gorgeous shimmering Sphinx appeared. "You've done it," Cleopatra said throatily. "You've won the bonus."

"Sarah, I believe," Maggie whispered, and sat back, hands in her lap, palms turned up. Her fifteen free spins began, Each Win Multiplied by Three. She was careful not to hope or say, "Oh fuck," when there was no hit. Hands open. Receiving. Not clutching. Letting go to the Big Whatevers. It occurred to her briefly that she was one lucky and deeply spiritual woman.

The aces and lotuses and scarabs fell into place, among them a perfect line of two Cleos in too much purple eye shadow and three Golden Chippendale-look-alike Pharaohs. Twelve thousand credits. Times three. One thousand, eight hundred bucks—and there was still an inch of strong coffee in her mug, The big fat winner music started to play.

Lawanne sailed up. She was a dreadlocked woman with impressive tits and no backside to speak of. "I heard the music," she said. They watched the credits climb. "Hand pay," she said. "Big one. Hey, it's you, that cocktail waitress at the Crystal."

"I was," Maggie said. "I'm not there now. I'm hoping my boss takes me back."

Lawanne shook her head. "The Crystal tanked. One of the big corporations bought it. They're going to make it all classy and exclusive. In Creosote, right!"

Joe showed up with Maggie's hand pay. "Maggie," he said, "too bad about the Crystal."

"It's been a month or so since I've been there," Maggie said. "I'm surprised I'm surprised, but I'll figure something out." Joe nodded. He knew they were all gypsies.

"You gotta stick around," Lawanne said. "Daemine and the boys are coming on right after Ray and Lee. He finally learned that Jackie Wilson "Lonely Teardrops." Makes me cry my eyes out every time he sings it—and I'm happily married."

"Lawanne," Maggie said. "Don't take it personally, but I'm gonna play, eat, and run. If I hang on to this hit, I've got my first two months' rent, groceries, and gas covered, and a tune-up and oil change for my car,."

"God bless, girl." Lawanne pulled her into a warm perfumed hug.

Maggie breathed deep. "Bless you too."

THE ECHO of Minnie's words called Sarah in like radar. *Help me. Come home. Help me. Come home.* There were no fixed coordinates being sent. There was only the long western slope of Beartrack Mountain and the wan glitter of downtown Bone Lake. The flat roof to the county extended care facility lay below her. She zeroed in on the dirty patio and landed just to the left of a row of plastic lawn chairs.

There was a silvery light in a first-floor window. The window was open. Minnie's voice was a vibrant rasp. "You are here, woman. I knew you would come."

JESSE closed his eyes. "Oh yeah," he said. "I can hardly take care of this geezer dog and you want me to grow up."

Ray was quiet. Jesse stayed in the soft dark behind his eyelids for a while. Nothing changed. He wanted some bud so bad he could taste it. Gray-green smoke burning down his throat, how it spread in his chest, somewhere around the vicinity of his faithless heart. How then everything made sense, even the senseless.

"Well yes," Jesse said. "Grow up." And then he opened his eyes and saw that Ray had put a piece of paper on the lawn table and was drawing the gallows for a game of Hangman.

"I go first," Ray says, "because I thought of it."

Jesse looked at the paper.

_ _ _, _ _ _ _ _ _ ' _ _ _ _ _ _ _ _ _ _ _!

"What's the category?"

"Happiness."

27 Maggie drove slow and easy down the long slope into Creosote. She felt like she was going home for the first time in maybe forever, and she wanted the feeling to last. She was surprised she was not afraid—not of the killer, or worse yet of running into Jesse and finding him gone cold. Instead she looked toward the casinos and the river as she had once looked toward any man who might have, but couldn't have, saved her life. Somehow, she knew that what lay at the bottom of the hill—cowbirds and backbusting job opportunities and maybe keeping her freakin' heart open—just might.

She turned into the Riverbelle parking lot. She wasn't ready for the Crystal's chained-up doors or the signs that would tell her something much better was coming. She locked the Firebird and walked past an old guy sitting on the pull-out steps of an eighties mini-RV. He smoked a cigarette, exhaling slow and watching the smoke drift. The sun had just dropped behind the upscale fifth-wheel parking lot across the road, and the light was exactly what you could see in a fire agate.

Maggie walked toward the pan-fried chicken and real mashed potatoes buffet—and playing till she got those squiggly eyes Wile E. Coyote would get after Roadrunner has lured him off the cliff. She wondered about Jesse, but with the prospect of a perfect evening of absolute unaccountability funded by the generous folks at Nevada Landing, she didn't much care. "Sometimes you're the nail," she whispered to the cooling light, "and sometimes you're the sweet fucking hammer."

The guy on the RV steps looked up. "Amen," he said, "and good luck." He raised his hand the way a driver coming toward you on one of those Bone Lake dirt roads would. Maggie waved back and kept going. When she reached the silver glass doors of the Riverbelle, she looked back. For an instant the tip of the guy's cigarette burned like a jewel.

She opened the Riverbelle door, sucked in a straight hit of "IT can happen for YOU!" smoky air, and remembered Minnie's words: *A good waitress can always get a job.*

BELTRAN. Cowbird. Bonnie Madrid wanted to kill both of them. Not really, but more like putting on those strappy five-inch spike-heel retro go-go boots Chelsea had showed her, and walking across a man's privates. Two men's. Specifically Beltran's. Specifically Cowbird's. Didn't matter. She couldn't believe she'd gotten herself into this mess. She was grateful the rest of the night was taken care of by Zach's call and her graveyard shift at the Sandbar.

She took the escalator up to the Blue Velvet and saw Zach inhaling a straw-berry waffle. It seemed like Zach had grown a couple inches in the month since they'd last talked. His black hair was spiky with mousse, and his legs were twisted around the chair rungs like a little boy's.

He looked up and gave her some complicated sign that she was supposed to automatically get because of her African-American heritage. Ricky guided her over to the table.

"I told you," she said. "I am from another generation. I don't know nothing about that Crips/Puff/J.Lo whatever baloney."

Zach shoved the last quarter of the waffle toward her. "He's not Puff Daddy anymore. Here, this is still warm."

Bonnie opened her napkin. "Thanks, l'il homey."

"See, you know that stuff. She's in the ladies' room. Her. She. You know. She got a little nervous."

"Of me?"

"I told her you were like my second mother."

Bonnie looked down at her plate. In that moment the lonesomeness of not having had kids, much less a manfriend who would have stuck around to be a dad, seemed like nothing.

"Yes," she said, "you are like my own son."

"Whoa," Zach said, "we better cut it out. Spooky's already nervous. If she sees me crying . . .

" . . . there she is. Oh my god. She's got a dress on."

Bonnie saw the look of a boy smacked by love. A girl walked toward them, a girlie girl in a flower-sprigged skirt and a powder-blue T-shirt that came well down over her belly, a girl wearing sparkly flip-flops and a flower in her pale blonde hair.

She held out her hand to Bonnie. "Hello," she said, "my name is Jen." She grinned at Zach. "Dude, it's me. Don't get weird."

"Hang on," Zach said. "I never saw you like this."

Bonnie took the girl's hand in hers. "I'm so glad to meet you," she said.

"Spooky," Zach said. "Don't. Don't change. I don't want anything else to change." His eyes were fierce. He put his hand over hers and Bonnie. "You've both got to understand."

He held tight to their hands. "I really like you, Spooky, Jen, whoever. I'm scared for you." He took a deep breath. "What it is," he said, his voice steady as his hand, "is I don't want to go back to Albuquerque. Ever."

"We know," Jen said. She looked into Bonnie's eyes. Bonnie nodded. She knew how it was when you didn't want to do what you had to do. "I'd like to meet who you really are," Bonnie said.

The girl nodded. "I'll be right back."

MINNIE sat in a metal chair at the window. Her black hair cascaded down her back. Her lips were drawn tight. "They want me to take pills," she said. "I pretend, but I keep them in my mouth and spit them out."

Sarah bent to kiss her cheek. "Who put you here?" Sarah knew what happened to old women in reservation towns. She and Yakima had been going to do something about that. They were going to make software to educate rez kids about their elders.

"Forget about him," Minnie said. "And it doesn't matter who put me here. My people meant well."

Sarah sat on the bed. The room was immaculate, what Minnie had been allowed to keep set out carefully on the dresser and bed table. A plastic hairbrush and comb. Hand lotion, white-people kind, too sweet, too thick. Shampoo, the same. There was no clock. No calendar. Much less sweetgrass or river pebbles.

Minnie nodded. "People steal things. That's what they told me. My apprentice took everything important from our place and hid it. They won't let him in to see me."

Sarah put her hands over her face. She saw through her flesh and bone. "Minnie," she said, "I don't have much longer. Tell me what to do. Please."

"There is nothing you can do for me," Minnie said. "That's like a TV show, that kind of fixing.

"Yesterday, the ones who brought me here believed they won. They gave me a shot to make me weak. They tied me down in the ambulance. That's why my hair was so ugly. I was twisting to get away. They were stronger.

"Today, I washed my hair. I combed it. I have stopped eating."

Sarah smiled.

"I'm going with you," Minnie said. "We will find the way."

MAGGIE never made it out of the Riverbelle's Blue Velvet Cafe for her night of guaranteed ruination. The Blue Velvet was fancier than Food for the Soul by one item—the Fresh-Made Strawberry Creme Waffle. Bitsy, the soft blonde waitress said she made the prettiest one, and she would take the time to fix one for Maggie, even though Razelle had flat walked out, leaving Bitsy to waitress the whole room on her own.

"That's the kind of shit that always happens to me," she said, "especially since I got canned from the buffet at that so-called upscale Cachet—for not busting my butt to take care of a high-roller snot from California when there were a dozen people ahead of the bitch.

"You're that cocktail chick from the Crystal," she said. "Don't worry, I'll fix your waffle up right."

Maggie sighed. "No waffle. Get me the steak and eggs. I'm going to need protein, because I'm about to take over Razelle's job."

Bitsy sank into a chair across from Maggie. "Honey," she said, "how do you want your steak, your eggs, and your toast? It's on me. When the manager shows up, which might take a few minutes, act like he's handsome."

Maggie sipped her water. Caroline's kid, Zach, sat down at a window table. There was girl with him. Maybe a boy. The kid had pale skin, its hair tucked up in a black skull cap. Maggie saw the kid was a girl and that she and Zach had the big gift. The girl stood up and walked toward the bathrooms.

Zach put his head down. Bonnie Madrid swooped in past the hostess and settled herself down across from him.

"You're that cocktail broad walked out on Sheree a few months ago?" The manager stood at her side.

"You could see it that way," Maggie said, "or you could see it that the Crystal walked out on everybody." It was going to be a stretch to act like he was handsome. She smiled up at him. "Besides, I just walked *in* on you, which means you get lucky, because you got exactly one waitress on the night before Labor Day. You," she checked his name tag, "you, Christopher, know the deal."

He nodded. "ok, we can do the paperwork later. You're gonna have to lose the sneakers after tonight. Get a pair of heels."

Maggie was allowed to eat her steak and eggs. She was sent downstairs to Uniforms and fitted out with a blue velvet miniskirt, satin bustier, and fake peacock feather headband that made her look not alluring, but faintly desperate.

Maggie learned fast, especially how to create the Fresh-Made Strawberry Creme Waffle. "The deal," Bitsy said, "is to get it to the customer before the whipped cream goes flat. You got about ten seconds."

Maggie hit her biggest waffle challenge about ten thirty. Four women in designer black, ranging from old, on-her-way-to-old, middle-aged, and barely legal waved her over. They each ordered a waffle and high-fived. They told her they were celebrating the fourth anniversary of the deaths of their pals, Shirley Marcone and Roselle Tucci, who loved Creosote above all places on earth.

"The ShirleySal bench," Maggie said.

The youngest gal smiled. "For sure. Later, we take four seats side-by-side on nickel Wheel of Fortune and play till dawn."

"And honey," the old woman said, "we don't care if the whipped cream goes flat."

JESSE figured he knew what Ray was up to, but he decided to draw it out. "How about an E," he said. _ _ _ , _ _ _ _ _ _ _ ' _ _ _ _ _ _ _ e _ e _!

"I bet you know already," Ray said.

"Not me. Let's try an L."

Ray drew the head of the hanging man.

"M." The neck.

"S." The oval torso.

"O." _ _ _ , _ o _ _ _ _ ' _ _ o _ _ o _ e _ e _!

"If you don't get it in the next four letters," Ray grinned, "you're dead. Or you might as well be. You know, like emotionally." He looked embarrassed. "Ah shit."

It occurred to Jesse that Helen might have been making Ray watch her beloved *Oprah*. Making him learn self-help stuff, Buddhism Lite, how to heal your heart with kids' games.

"Look," Jesse said. "Let's just get it over with."

"Shit," Ray said. "How the fuck are you gonna live, if you don't know how to play?"

"*Oprah!*" Jesse said. "Helen's making you watch *Oprah*." He looked around for the goddamn dog. "Come on, Ralph, we're out of here." He wanted to break the lawn chairs into shards. Cheap fucking chairs. Cheap fucking advice. How the fuck did anybody who hadn't been there know what the fuck it took to fucking forget it when you didn't want to forget it, you couldn't fucking forget it, because if you did then what the fuck had it all been about?

He remembered Ray *had been* there.

"OK." Jesse's surrender was made less impressive by the fact that Ralph Too had not budged from the shade under the lawn table.

ZACH shrugged. "I probably just blew it," he said. "I should have been more mysterious. I never am."

"Maybe not," Bonnie said. "They tell me there *are* women who like nice guys."

"What's my mom say about my staying here?" Zach said. He was careful to not say "going back," as though saying what he wanted could be a lucky charm.

"Not this fall," Bonnie said. She watched his face. He narrowed his eyes. She saw the man he would be. She wondered if a boy could be like an agave, could grow a year a minute in front of you.

"What then?" he said.

"You're almost fourteen. In this state, which is the state where the custody was resolved, at fourteen you can choose."

Zach nodded, and then he looked up past Bonnie. "Oh my god."

Bonnie turned. The girl skated toward the red velvet rope that held the starving hordes back, crouched, and scooted under the rope with an inch to spare. The girl stopped the board just next to Zach's chair, flipped it up into her hand, and sat. It was a tribute to the nature of the Blue Velvet clientele that not a customer looked up.

"So," the girl said, "this is the real me."

Her blonde hair curled out from under the black head rag. She'd lined her right eye in black; the left was plain. The left sleeve of the flower print dress was gone. There was a tattoo of a blue rose on her shoulder. She stuck one foot out.

"It's a Vans," Zach laughed. "The skate to annihilate shoe."

She held out her other foot. The pink sequins on the flip-flop sparkled.

"I am Spooky," the girl said. "I am Jen. We both did this." She held out a report card to Bonnie. All A's: history, math, English, modern dance, drama, and shop.

Bonnie held her hand next to the girl's scraped knuckles. "This," she said, "is Spooky's hand, and it is proof that there is hope for womankind." She checked her watch. "I gotta run," she said. "I'm on graveyard." She reached across the table and took Zach by the chin. "Your mom's coming on in a few minutes. You both sit tight till she gets here."

"Yes," Zach said. "We promise."

Spooky ducked her head. Bonnie laughed. "You've got nothing to worry about, girlfriend. Trust me."

MAGGIE finished the 3–11 shift, worked a few hours overtime, and walked over to the Crystal. The cool air was pungent with the scent of water and tamarisk, parking lot piss and exhaust. The Neon Way glowed above her. The parking lots were quiet, only the echo of Oldtimers' Rock 'n' Roll from the outdoor speakers at Traintown. Marianne Faithfull. "As Tears Go By." A flash of Jesse flickered under Maggie's skin.

All the purple bulbs were out in the big crystal. She read the signs on the door: "Coming soon. New. State of the art billiards and cigar boutique. Step into the West's Golden Gaming Past." "Not gaming, assholes," Maggie said quietly. "Gambling. That's what they did in the golden past. They played fucking cards."

Someone came up behind her. The eighteen hundred dollars, plus twenty-six bucks in tips, minus the tab for one employee-discounted Twilite Special Steak 'n' Eggs was tucked in her bra. Maggie spun around. The sign had pissed her off enough to smack somebody. But not the guy backing away from her.

"Oh my God," he said, "it's you. It's me. Cowbird. I thought you got killed too. Or lit out to somewhere." He grabbed her hand.

"I'm back," she said. "Where else would I go?"

"There's a letter for you," Cowbird said. "Ray's gave it to Sheree. It's from a lawyer."

Maggie laughed. She *was* back—in the town in which it was impossible to have a secret. Except she did have a secret. And that secret was far from here. Safe. Maybe.

"Hey," Cowbird said, "let's head back over to the Riv. Sheree's working the Sandbar. You can get your letter, and I'll buy you a beer. I got a job!"

"I'LL TAKE AN A," Jesse said.

_ _ _ , _ o _ a _ _ ' _ _ o _ _ o _ e _ e _ !

{ 210 }

"Big I."

_ i _, _ o _ a i _ ' _ _ o _ _ o _ e _ e _!

"It's Australian, right?" Jesse said.

Ray shook his head.

"J."

Ray drew a stubby arm.

"You saying I'm short?" Jesse said. *Short,* code for how long a grunt had in Vietnam before he was put on the Freedom Bird for home.

"You're so short . . . ," Ray said, and Jesse heard Darwin. "I'm so short they could fit me in a matchbox." *Yeah, Big D., now they can.*

"Come on," Ray said.

"D."

_ i d, _ o _ a i _ ' _ _ o _ _ o _ e _ e _!

"There was this guy," Jesse said. His throat went tight.

"Keep playing," Ray says.

"R."

_ i d, _ o _ a i _ ' _ _ o _ _ o r e _ e r!

Jesse knew Ray's recipe for survival, knew it was about a woman, knew he could get this dumbass game over. But, his stubborn heart took hold of him. "Q." Ray drew a leg. "X." Ray drew another leg. "W." A hand. "Z." A foot. "B." Another hand. "C." The second foot.

"I lose," Jesse said. "I'm dead."

Ray pointed the pencil at Jesse's heart. "Here's what I figure," he said. "There's twenty-six letters in the alphabet. You run through fifteen. The human body's got more than eleven parts. I'll draw the inside if I have to. Lungs. Guts. Dick."

"The dick's on the outside," Jesse said.

"Not so's you're going to notice if you don't got the balls to finish this game."

"OK," Jesse said. "T."

_ i d, _ o _ a i _ ' t _ o t _ o r e _ e r!

"And?"

"Y. U." _ i d, y o u a i _ ' t _ o t _ o r e _ e r!

"K. N." k i d, y o u a i n ' t _ o t _ o r e _ e r!

"Now, you're cookin.'" Ray did not smile.

"G," Jesse said. "F. V. OK OK."

Kid, you ain't got forever!

Jesse ran his finger over the almost hanged man. "ok."

"That's more like it," Ray said. "Now, tell me about that guy who was your friend in the war."

THE SANDBAR was quiet, unusual for a place in which you could get booze, bacon, and eggs any time of day or night. Sheree bustled up with the letter. Maggie put it in her purse unread. Cowbird and Sheree exchanged looks of deep disappointment. "It's personal," Maggie said.

Sheree laughed. "Nothing's personal here, except how I am not hiring you back no matter what."

"No problem," Maggie said, with the calm of one who was scoring a small jackpot. "I'm at the Blue Velvet. Come over for a Fresh-Made Strawberry Creme Waffle sometime. On me."

"How gracious of you." Sheree set down Cowbird's beer and nodded at Maggie. "You still not drinking?"

"More or less. Give me a Virgin Mary with three of those big green olives."

"You hear about Ray?" Sheree said.

"I did. What's the story now?"

"He's part-time dealing blackjack here." Sheree smacked Maggie on the arm. "Glad you're home. Gotta get back to the grindstone."

A black Amazon barely in her cocktail waitress outfit strode toward them, then veered away.

"That's Ms. Bonnie Madrid," Cowbird said. "She and I was an item. She used to work the Belle's Brews."

"I know her," Maggie said. "Damn, Cowbird, a job *and* a girlfriend."

"A usedtawas girlfriend."

Bonnie Madrid walked with ferocious dignity to the waitress's station, a triumph for a six-foot-tall near-naked woman in four-inch heels who was trying to be invisible.

"Listen, Maggie," Cowbird said. "That woman's heart is sweeter and colder than one of those frozen peanut koalas she's carrying."

"Hey," Maggie said, "love sucks." *Yep, that's me, except don't, please don't let Jesse walk in.*

Cowbird looked crestfallen. "Hang on," he said. "I *love* her."

"I'm sorry," Maggie said. "I've got a bad attitude." It didn't matter what she said. Cowbird was off and running.

"You know," he said, "it weren't really about us why we are no way an item anymore. It was about that pimp Beltran. Jesus Christ. You tell me how a fine woman like Bonnie Madrid could of got won back by a little fuzzy bear Velcroed around a plastic American flag hanging off a wilting rose?"

Maggie knew there was no real answer required. Cowbird slammed down his Bud. "We was fine up to then, Maggie. We wasn't living together. We're old enough to know better plus I get antsy indoors, but I can tell you that old Mojave moon burning down on the patio of her trailer while Bonnie and me swung in the hammock and didn't talk, *didn't have to talk,* was more like married than I'd ever hoped to know."

"Then something got funny," Cowbird said. "Beltran sniffin' out there in the creosote of Bonnie's desert heart." He pulled out a pencil stub and wrote on a napkin. "I do write poems," he said. "You probably didn't know it."

"Yeah," Maggie said. "I used to write songs. That's a real pretty line."

"You could do the music part? I got some stuff would make great songs."

"Another time," Maggie said. "What about you and Bonnie?"

"Well, I just *felt* we were a winning hand." He started in on Bud Two, which Maggie suspected was on the way to Bud Infinite. He caught her look. "Don't get mean," he said. "I gotta have something to hang on to."

Maggie dangled her slot player's card in front of him. "10,486 points in two months and *I'm* gonna tell *you* how to live?"

"Well, you know what the doc said about my liver. Plus what with the stress of Bonnie—shit, you want to know about how I found out? The whole story?"

With her privacy gone, a Virgin Mary and three olive pits in front of her, Jesse who knew where, Sarah even farther gone, and a letter from yet another ghost in her backpack, Maggie couldn't imagine anything better than getting lost in Cowbird's deathless prose.

"July 4," he said. "July 4 eve, actually. Just before midnight. I was down eighty bucks. The table was stony cold. So, I decided to fuel up and see Bonnie. Had me that $1.99 Midnight Special, you know, three eggs, three pieces of bacon, three sausages, home fries, and sourdough toast—plus you can get biscuits and gravy for a couple bits more."

Maggie realized she'd drifted off into a movie in her head in which Jesse and Sarah came into the Sandbar, Maggie woke, and the whole fucking however long since before Sarah's death was revealed to be a dream. Cowbird clanked the Bud Three can softly on the table. "I could sure go for one of those specials right now," he said. "But it ain't midnight, so maybe another Bud?"

"Beer and bacon on me," Maggie said. "I got lucky in Jean."

He patted her hand. "You are a real lady, gal. Next one's on me." He leaned forward and waved to Sheree. She held up two fingers. He nodded.

"So here we go. Bonnie had brought me my food, gave me a kiss on the cheek, and said something about me getting my present in the morning, if you know what I mean. A delivery kid came through the door and set a friggin' rose on the counter. Bonnie picked up the flag. There was a little bear wrapped around the stem of the rose. She read the card and closed her eyes. Shit, Maggie, she kinda wobbled and put her hand over her heart. I flat fuckin' out knew it was Eddie Besame Mucho Beltran had sent that cheap piece of shit."

"Kinda pissed you off, huh?"

Cowbird nodded. "I kept my mouth shut, drank three more cups of coffee, paid my check, kissed Miss Bonnie Madrid's cheek, and headed out at 12:23 July 4 morning to the Crystal for one of the finest nights of my life, with no idea that where I was really headed was for the Heartbreak Hotel.

"We had a nice businesslike table. Mostly dealers and keno chicks from the other houses. Rikki was dealing. Everybody bet. From that minute on, I was King of the River. Full House. Flush. Straight. Straight flush king high. And, the last fuckin' hand before I got smart and got out? A pair of nines, which I bluffed and the other guys were jack high and folded."

"Exactly like Jesus," Maggie said.

"Exactly! I cashed out and hotfooted over to the coffee shop, where to my everlasting heartbreak, Miss Bonnie Madrid was gone. Haven't seen her since except with a tray in her hands."

Cowbird struck a match and held it up. "See that? That's me. A little bitty candle burning so she can find her way home." He set the match in the ashtray. As it flickered out, he looked up. "And, I'll tell you what, gal, I'm about to do more."

"I wish you luck," Maggie said. "But I don't really know shit about what goes on between men and women, not shit." She patted his shoulder and left him staring wistfully toward the bar.

COWBIRD walked along the highway carrying a spraypaint can. Cars whizzed by. It was easy to disappear into the dried grasses at the base of the little cliff, easy to find a foothold, another, and go up. He was glad the moon had set. Headlights coming down the long slope into Creosote flashed on him and were gone. Any predawn driver was hell-bent for leather. He climbed with the same sureness that had carried him up Asian basalt when he was eighteen.

Cowbird stepped onto a narrow ledge. He ran his palm over the cliff, found the smooth patch of rock face, and began to write. He made the letters big and a little fancy so she wouldn't miss them. He downclimbed to the sand and looked up. A big rig flashed its lights. The driver honked. The white letters glowed like neon against the rock: "Bonnie Madrid, I love you still."

28   Maggie totaled up her slot card points, found she had a week's free rooms, and checked into the Riverbelle. Her room was papered in red brocade. There was a queen-size bed, with two riverboat steering wheels for a headboard. There was an abundance of hypothetically free shampoo. Maggie filled the tub, lit a candle, and, as she settled into the warm water, remembered the waterfall trickling down into the warm pool above Willow Springs, and wished she knew how to pray.

She wondered if wishing you could pray counted. If you were wishing, then you were maybe believing something was listening, and if you maybe believed something else was listening, then you might as well talk to it.

"OK," she said. "What do I do now? I do whatever dumbass opening up my heart to love I'm supposed to, could you work on Jesse a little, no, make that a lot because I am not spending even a second with the mean motherfucker he can be."

She climbed out, wrapped up in the shawl, and opened Dead DC's letter.

There were three envelopes, one from a lawyer, most of the words a mystery, until the last paragraph: "And to my beloved, whether she believes it or not, ex-wife Maggie Foltz, and my son David Deacon Campbell, I bequeath a nine-day Colorado River oar trip to be taken at their convenience."

The second envelope held two gift certificates for a weeklong oar trip from Lee's Ferry to Phantom Ranch, shuttle included. The third envelope held an elegant river knife. She remembered that his last beloved had been a river-runner chick.

"Dead DC," she said, "when did you ever leave the living room, much less run a river? The last thing I want to do is float in a boat and the even more last thing I want is to do it with Deacon."

MINNIE drifted up out of her shriveled body. She laughed. "I'm going to miss that Black Lake boy, but this is better."

Sarah watched Minnie gently close the eyelids on her former body. "Look," the old ghost said. "See how the color of my body is changing. Soon, you will think it was a bundle of cottonwood roots." She sighed. "Not a bad-looking bunch of roots. I had a good time in that body."

Sarah remembered how she had looked down on her broken body after the killer was gone, how she had seen what the body was, and wasn't. How beautiful she had been, and how all those times she had thought she was fat and ugly, she had been wrong. She wished she had touched the eyes tenderly, had covered her bruised and naked flesh with something soft.

"There is no going back," Minnie said. "But, your wish will circle round."

"I don't know what you mean," Sarah said. "But then, I almost always didn't know what you meant."

Minnie laughed. "Maybe if you had listened."

HELEN pulled up to the trailer just as dawn began to get pretty on the tops of the Peacock Mountains. It was her favorite time and one of her favorite situations: four hundred bucks of the Cachet's money in her purse, the air still cool, her two favorite men asleep in their lawn chairs. She saw the empty bottle of Old Popocat and what appeared to be a game of Hangman.

She snooped. *Kid, you ain't got forever.* She let the sleepers be and invited Ralph Too in for breakfast. "Thanks again," she said to the Buddha and tucked her winnings under its butt. "I especially love taking money from rich folks."

She put coffee on and started frying bacon. "That'll wake the boys up."

Ralph bumped her ankle with his nose. "Excuse me," she said, "first things first." She was dishing last night's stew onto Ralph's plate when Jesse came through the door.

"Child," Helen said, "you look like shit."

MAGGIE lasted exactly one week at the Blue Velvet. Some busybody in Human Resources discovered Maggie had once been a peer drug counselor. CORPSE, as the Corporate Scum Eaters were known by the grunts, decided that they better comply with a federal regulation requiring a "Crisis Specialist" on call. They offered Maggie eleven bucks an hour *plus* benefits, and they gave her an office just off the buffet pantry in the first-level basement, *and* a five hundred dollar bonus for signing on. Maggie knew they could not have made a better choice. Crisis Specialist. She had the Ph-phuckin'-D.

Her first shift was 3–11, so she had time to find a studio apartment, take a shower, kick back with a few hours of slots, and report back to work. Her first case came to her not in her office but as she was at her favorite machine. She heard a moan. Ella, the old cleaning woman, stopped reaching for the ashtray to Maggie's right and fell backward.

Maggie crouched over the old woman. Security rushed toward them. The woman grabbed her around the neck and said, "I don't have health insurance. I'm a temp. God help me."

Maggie held her hand while they loaded her on the emergency gurney. The whole time, her words getting more blurred, the woman kept saying, "No health insurance. Tell them no health insurance." Maggie rode with her to the emergency department. The first thing the intake clerk said to her was, "And the name of your health insurance company?"

Maggie used her crisis specialist skills on the intake guy. They wheeled Ella into the maze of cubicles. Maggie considered returning to the mysteries of nickel ancient Egypt, which were becoming increasingly predictable, and decided to make a social call, and then a fact-finding mission to Helen and Ray's.

SUE was watering Leola's garden. She dropped the hose and grabbed Maggie around the waist. "You're alive!" She stepped back and wiped her eyes.

"Just four months ago, Lee got these strawberry plants over in Bullhead.

She was gonna plant 'em in that beer keg her grandson sawed out for her." Sue waved at the drooping strawberries and a pot of straggling geraniums. "She said this garden was the only church she needed. She said growing plants in a hellhole was miraculous enough for her."

Sue sprayed water over the limp plants. "I'll keep at these even when they're toast. Besides, I put her in those geraniums."

"Geraniums hate direct sun," Maggie said.

Sue picked up a pot. "Grab the other one. Let's get her inside."

The house was cool and scented with cinnamon. They set the geraniums on the kitchen windowsill.

"You got time for coffee and a pecan roll? I just baked them."

Maggie sat at the little table. "I do." The table was just right for two people and set with one placemat, napkin, and plate.

Sue put down another placemat, coffee, and a warm roll. "There's butter in that little crock."

Maggie broke the roll apart. "Sue, what happened to the investigation? What happened to Sarah's ashes?"

"We haven't heard a thing. That girl cop Lucy came around a few times. She told Sheree she couldn't get the higher-ups to actually give a hoot. She told us she was keeping on it when she could.

"I think she's still got Sarah's ashes. Go talk to her. She's a sweet kid."

"I'll check it out," Maggie said, "and I'll let you know what I find."

BLUE SHADOWS flowed into Secret Pass Canyon. Maggie remembered Jesse telling her they were rivers of time. "I want us to follow them wherever they go. We'll lie down where the shadows stop. We'll watch night come in to cover us." It wasn't night and he wasn't at her side, but maybe down the road she'd catch a song from the shadows.

She was happy to pull up and see Ray and Helen at the kitchenette table. She was even happier to smell that Helen had roasted a turkey. Helen threw the door open.

"Maggie," she yelled, "get in here." She fixed her a plate of dark meat, mashed potatoes, and brussels sprouts with cashews. Ray was busy picking the brussels sprouts out of the cashews, but he looked up long enough to say, "Welcome home kid. Jesse's OK."

"As though she cares," Helen said. "You put those brussels sprouts right back."

"As if I care," Maggie said. "Where is he?"

Helen and Ray continued to chew happily. "I've got icebox cake for dessert," Helen said. "It's a good thing you're here because it won't keep."

"It never gets a chance to keep," Ray said. He patted her hip. "It's all right here."

"Listen," Helen said. "Oprah says our partners have nothing to say about our personal bodies."

"So," Ray said, "were you asking about Jesse?"

"More or less." Maggie looked at Helen. "Is there a note for me? From him, I mean. From Jesse, I mean. Shit, Ray, what do you know?" She had to put down her fork and fucking cry. Helen grabbed a dish towel. Maggie buried her face in it. The smell of sun-dried cotton was so dear to her, she cried even harder. Not about Jesse. She could see brilliant green cottonwoods and maybe the best friend she'd ever had floating in a shining pool. There was no way that woman could be crammed into some little box in the Creosote substation of the Las Vegas Police Department.

Maggie knew she couldn't tell Helen and Ray the entire truth, not because they wouldn't understand, not because they would think she was crazy. The entire truth was between Sarah and her, so she told a sliver of the truth, which made her cry even harder. "It's not just Jesse. It's Sarah. I miss her so much."

"Jeez, Helen," Ray said. "Do something."

"Men," Helen said. "They don't know when to leave well enough alone."

"What do you know, old woman?" Ray snapped. "You weren't here that night me and Jesse played Hangman." He caught himself. "Oh shit, now I'm in for it."

Helen and Maggie looked at him. There would be no mercy.

"You better tell us," Helen said.

Maggie grinned. She had that gorgeous hollow feeling that follows a good cry. She had exactly enough room in her for whatever came next. Icebox cake. Truth.

"Women," Ray said. "The eternal mystery."

"Tell us," Helen said, "or that cake stays put."

He opened the fridge, took out the icebox cake, and cut fat pieces for them. Chocolate cookies layered with real whipped cream. Helen had made it the day before, which was the secret alchemy, the magic Maggie's mother had known. "You're a genius," Maggie said.

"That's why I keep her," Ray said. "Plus the Buddha." He settled back in his chair. "Here goes. Jesse's been humping a 180-pound pack since he was in the war. Dead weight, Injun weight."

"GRANDMOTHER, I'm sorry I didn't listen," Sarah said. "I'm listening now." She hoped they were not going to have to stay one minute longer in the county extended care facility. "But, can we go someplace else?"

Minnie smiled. "We can go anywhere we want."

They drifted through the walls and up to the top of Beartrack Mountain. They sat on cool rock that Sarah now understood breathed beneath them. They watched light flow over the dirt roads and old trailers into the dark streets of Bone Lake. Sarah saw that she was no longer fading. She and Minnie were the same, gsi'ki shining bright.

"Am I all the way dead?" she asked.

"Not quite," Minnie said. "You have a few more things to remember." She looked west. Clouds gathered over Diamond Peak, which was not possible in early August. They raced in toward Minnie and Sarah from the wrong direction, rose, gold, then cobalt and green. Sarah saw the clouds were ocean. The cloud tsunami rolled over them.

A voice called from the wave. "Look," Minnie said. "And listen like you never did."

A dark face moved out from the heart of the clouds.

"I am Yiang Cuteq.

"I have never died, never dreamed of dying. You have given me ten thousand names and I am beyond words. I am the murmur of cells dividing, song of fluids swelling, pulse of membranes stretching, splitting, drying, and falling away.

"Spirit of the Earth, your people named me. Yiang Cuteq. They fed me rain-swollen rice, buffalo blood, songs and poems, sandalwood smoke, and the pain that throbbed in their skulls after days and nights of drinking maize beer from the eight-straw ceremonial jar.

"They lured me in from the forest, from the places where the soil was brown or black. They gave me new earth, or earth that had rested a long while. 'We do not like to cut young forest,' they said.

"Sometimes when a woman ran her fingers through the dirt around the rice, or a man stopped at end of day and watched light fade on the pale sprouts gleaming like silver in the dark earth, I sang in their bodies.

"Where we lived, where I murmured in every root and stalk and leaf, in every bud and blossom, where they sang to me and prayed, now there is nothing. The fields are gone, the bananas and plantain and manioc. The jungles are gone, the teak trees, the tiny orchids, the moss and giant vines. The old villages are gone.

"And yet I am still adored. A woman sings to me in a Louisiana rice field. A dark-eyed Minnesota schoolgirl waters a sprouting avocado seed. In a three-by-five-foot patch of soil in a North Carolina city backyard, a grandma picks jade green tomato worms from a young plant. They raise their ogre heads and hiss. She laughs and hisses back. 'Yiang Cuteq,' she sings, 'watch over these baby plants. Yiang To-may-to, thank you for your gifts.'"

The voice faded. A second voice emerged, sibilant and insistent. *Hãy nghe tôi.* There was no face, no mouth speaking. The voice told an ancient story, begun with possession and jealousy, carried on waves of vengeance for centuries, from generation to generation, from murdered to murderer, to a lost boy with knife and fire in his hands, to Sarah's body. It was a story told in code. There were secrets and lies. The old need for vengeance could not be hidden.

Sarah looked into the story as though she looked into eyes filled with emptiness. "No more," she said. "There will be no more vengeance."

The clouds and ocean shifted into miles of dark sage stretching away from the base of Beartrack. Sarah's heart side yearned toward Hannah's trailer, toward fry bread and red pop, toward the possibility of taking Lorinda under her wing. Her other side skidded back in time, howled under her mother's limp body, shuddered as strange food was pushed between her lips, settled into a restless sleep as the plane carrying her little self flew through the night; woke wide-eyed as a young Hannah took her into her arms.

"I know what killed me," Sarah said quietly. "I know why I was cut and burned. My soul was to never go home.

"Now I know what I am. I am Willow. And I am Mountain Vietnamese.

"I am Little Bird. I am Sarah Four. I am Sarah Martin. And I am going home."

Minnie smiled. "Yes. There were four Sarahs in the group of children the missionaries brought to America. The Jesusway people could not say your last names. So they named you the best they could. And, they found your father."

"My father."

"Your uncle," Minnie said. "He loved your mother very much. He would not have left Vietnam except he loved Hannah more."

"I PROMISED JESSE, more or less, I wouldn't tell this to anybody," Ray said. "Maggie, I knew you were gonna be the more or less."

Maggie waited.

"It wasn't nothing no soldier hasn't done before," Ray said. "Or it was more like hasn't *hasn't* done."

"He didn't save somebody's life," Maggie said.

"He didn't. He couldn't—but he won't see it. His best friend. A Navajo guy named Darwin Yazzie."

"Ah shit," Maggie said gently.

Ray told most of Jesse's story. He figured the part about the lost lover and the kid might be for later . . . or never. By the end Maggie knew she hoped with all her heart to hear it a second time, from Jesse, and that if she did she'd pretend she had never heard it before.

"So," she said, "*is* he around?"

Helen was in the kitchen wrapping up turkey and stuffing. "You can take this out to him," she said. "I suspect he'll be glad to have it. You know how single men are."

"I'm not ready to go out there," Maggie said.

"Sure you are," Ray said. "You haven't got for-fucking-ever."

"He told you everything," Maggie snapped.

"We're family," Ray said gently.

"Then you're going to understand I have something I have to do before I talk to him again. And, you're going to give me your blessing."

They all looked startled. "You know what I mean," Maggie said. "Who I mean."

Helen handed her the sack of food. "Take this for yourself," she said, "and this guy." She put Buddha in the plastic bag. "He can help with the lost."

29

Jesse woke to the stink of rot. He reached for his glasses and knocked the ashtray to the floor. He picked it up, identified a quarter inch of joint by touch, and swallowed it. He'd been smoking for three days straight, stopping long enough to cram food in his mouth and feed Ralph. None of it, the smoke, the food, the dog care, had slowed down the 3-D movie in his mind.

Again and again, Darwin looked surprised. Again and again, he went absolutely still. Again and again, Jesse set his hand on Darwin's throat and felt nothing.

Jesse wanted to kill Ray. Ray and his dumb fucking game, Ray and his touchy-feely bullshit right off the TV screen. All that Fourth of July, Coming Home, welcome-a-vet-and-thank-him cheap pop psychology. There were things better left buried in the red muck of Vietnam, in the smoking mountains of Afghanistan. There were things better left unsaid.

Jesse found his glasses and staggered toward the front door. His foot slid on something. He aimed his headlamp at the floor. Ralph Too had made a mess just inside the kitchen. It was dog-disgusting. Ralph was curled next to the fridge. By the time Jesse got to him, he was ready to forget everything he had said to Ray, and everything he had promised himself in Picture Canyon. He was ready to beat the shit out of the mutt. Ralph looked up and blinked.

Jesse froze.

The dog's eyes were yellow. He dropped his big head onto his paws. Jesse could hear Ralph's labored breathing. "No," he said. "No more hurting." He headed out the door to the buried knife. Better to put the dog out of misery fast and clean.

Ralph staggered down the trailer steps. He shit again. Jesse looked at the puddle of blood-dark feces. He stepped toward Ralph. The dog couldn't lift his head. Jesse reached down and scratched him behind the ears. Ralph tried to get up. No luck. His tail wagged.

"OK," Jesse said. "We are going in the truck."

It was a long drive to Cocker's place, about a year longer than you might think a twenty-mile drive would take. Jesse had hefted Ralph into the passenger seat. Ralph had not moved. His eyes were closed. Jesse drove with one hand on the dog's side. He felt Ralph's breath barely moving his big ribs. As long as he could feel that, Jesse told himself, everything was going to be OK.

Cocker's garage was locked. Jesse went around the back and pounded on the trailer door. There was a sharp hiss, then a groan. Cocker opened the door. ZZ crouched at his feet, doing "Go ahead and make my day" lizard push-ups. Cocker rubbed his eyes. "What the fuck?"

"Ralph Too," Jesse said, and witnessed the miracle of a sodden drunk sobering in as long as it took him to pull on a pair of shorts.

"Leave him in the truck for now," Cocker said. "I don't want to move him till I seen what's going on."

Jesse didn't want to open the truck door, didn't want to find Ralph still in the way death is still. Cocker went ahead of him and opened the door. "He's alive, bro."

Cocker moved his fingers gently over Ralph's back and sides. "He's got some swelling in his lymph nodes, but it's the bleeding I'm most worried about. That yellow in his eyes is because his liver is working too hard, which is good news, because I think he ate a poisonous plant, don't know which one, but that gives us an easy choice."

Jesse hunkered next to Ralph. "Such as?"

"We get him to puke," Cocker handed Jesse a gallon jug. "Open the garage door. Then get me some water. We'll mix up a dose of pukeweed."

"What's pukeweed?"

"Beats me, but that's what that Quartzite chick calls it. I tried it once. Worked for me."

Cocker lifted Ralph gently off the seat and carried him into the garage. They dosed Ralph. He swallowed, looked at them abjectly, and threw up in the oil change pan Cocker had stuck under his nose. Cocker gave him plain water and waited. Ralph threw up clear fluid.

"Kind of funny," Cocker said, "what with him being named Ralph and all."

Jesse didn't laugh.

"Whoa," Cocker said. "I'm sorry. You got no way of knowing what I know: what don't kill this dog is gonna make him one strong son of a bitch. So to speak."

He opened a little vial, poured clear fluid into the water pan. "This here's a blood strengthener, what you call homeopathic remedy. It shouldn't work, but it does. You help him get it down. Then, I'm gonna work on his lymph nodes."

Jesse guided Ralph's nose to the water dish. The dog hesitated, then lapped up the solution. Cocker set his big beat-up hands on Ralph's side and began to massage him.

MAGGIE stashed the turkey and stuffing in her freezer. She knew she was not ready to see Jesse—not because she was afraid of what she'd find, but because she had a job to do; more like a half dozen jobs she didn't know how to do, jobs that had begun to seem like weight she had humped in *her* pack for a long, long time.

The first seemed easier than the rest. She was sure the cop would be eager to be rid of Sarah's ashes. She remembered the real kindness in the woman's eyes and bet it had something to do with what had once been called sisterhood.

MAGGIE walked through the door of the Creosote Police Department. Mojave Kate was working the front desk. She waved Maggie over. "I didn't tell anybody I was moving on. My cousin up in the Vegas Division knew this 'Skin dispatcher who said she could use her juice. And, here I am. No cigarette smoke. No whiny assholes. No horny whiteboy asking me if I've got Injun love medicine for his broken heart."

"My people," Maggie said, "are simple but spiritual."

"Oh god," Kate said. "You sound just like Sarah. *Where* have *you* been?"

"I had to take a break," Maggie said. "Sarah and I were tight, then she and Leola get killed. Somebody sent Sheree a Polaroid of me with the eyes burned out. Call me a titty baby—it seemed smart to get out of town."

Kate nodded. "Did you hear about the Crystal?"

"I did. You won't believe this. Human Resources at the Boat made me a low-rent "crisis specialist." You can't tell me self-destruction doesn't pay off in the long run."

Kate snorted and fielded a phone call. Maggie used the time to make herself ready to ask for Sarah. Kate hung up.

"Sue told me you guys might have Sarah's ashes."

"Let me see if Lucy's here," Kate said. "I think she kept them. That chick will not give up. She says if you don't crack a 'Skin case in the first thirty days, there's nobody gives a shit." She picked up the phone. "How's Sue?"

"Staunchly in place. She's got Leola's ashes in her geraniums, which I persuaded her to bring in out of the sun. I . . ."

Kate held her fingers to her lips. "Lucy. Sarah's friend is here. She's come after the ashes. She's the woman you talked to right after Sarah was killed." She gave Maggie a thumbs-up. "She's on her way. I think she'll be kind of relieved to have them gone."

Maggie's rich history with petty crime had never taken her into a cop's cubicle. Lucy pretended to open a door. "Come in," she said. "You taxpayers provide nothing but the best for Creosote's finest."

Lucy waved Maggie to a chair and moved her chair from behind the desk. A huge poster of snow-capped mountains covered one wall, a headshot of Ani DiFranco was on the second. There was nothing on the third but a small map of Creosote with two red pins in it, and a quote from one of Van Morrison's lesser known songs, a quote that suggested Lucy was a woman familiar with both persistence, the carnal ground, and great rock 'n' roll.

Low shelves ran along the base of the fourth wall. They held worn climbing gear, a dried sunflower, and a gray cardboard box.

"That's Sarah, right?" Maggie said.

"It is."

Maggie ran her finger over the top of the box. She wasn't ready to pick it up, to feel the weight of all she didn't know.

"I'm hoping you can fill me in a little," Lucy said. "We can't find anything out about Sarah Martin, or Sarah Four, or whoever she was. Our leads dead-end in Seattle at some Native American rights group that went bust.

"As far as Leola—she didn't have an enemy on the planet, though she was the most prejudiced human being I ever met."

Maggie wanted to tell her everything about Sarah. A cop who listened to Van Morrison was a woman who might believe in ghosts; better yet, she was a woman who might believe that not only were there veils, there was something underneath.

Maggie checked the location of the red pins. They marked Sarah's trailer, and Leola and Sue's house. "That's all I've really got," Lucy said. "Two little red pins. But, I can give you Sarah's ashes no questions asked. You'll have to sign a release form." She looked Maggie hard in the eyes. "But, I want you to know this. I'm not about to give up on her murder. Or Leola's."

"I made a vow on *these*." Lucy took a pair of earrings out of her pocket. One was a tiny silver lightning bolt, the other a fake gold gun.

"I know those," Maggie said. She remembered the afternoon she and Sarah had watched the rain come in over the swimming pool. The earrings had shone softly in the stormlight. Sarah had touched the lightning bolt. *Will put this in. Yakima gave me the gun. It was to remind me a smart Red sister is always on guard. He left out the part about him!*

Lucy handed Maggie the earrings. "These are yours. We'll avenge her. Somehow."

"I don't know if there is any vengeance for how she was killed," Maggie said, "but you've got *my* promise I'll see this through." She picked up the box. "I never held someone's ashes before. They're so heavy."

"Don't leave quite yet," Lucy said. "I want you to know something. Maybe it'll help us help each other with this."

Maggie held the box in her lap. Memories drifted across the surface of her mind: Sarah, a fierce shadow in a rhinestone-studded T-shirt. Sarah, a tiny girl crouched over twig dolls. Sarah, a radiant woman laughing, saying, "That boy is so much mess around."

"The Van Morrison quote on the map?" Lucy said.

Maggie nodded.

"I put it up there after I started having nightmares. There was fire in them, not flames, more like accident flares. Silver. Pink. The light glared on a wo-man's face.

"Sarah's face. You remember that employee ID?"

"How she wasn't there, and she was. Underneath," Maggie said.

"I have this method for finding killers," Lucy said. "You pay attention. You gather details. You cook them. What isn't essential boils off. What's left are answers—or threads to answers.

"One of the guys here played me that song. I knew what Van knew. And, as much as I hated the nightmares—the other part of my method is that I dream."

Maggie stood. "Thank you for what you're willing to know."

Lucy nodded. "More like being willing to not know." The phone rang. She grinned. "I'd see you out, but I bet that call's the next pile of happy horseshit."

BONNIE knew fall was on its way. Shadows drifted across the ramada earlier in the day and they were a softer blue. When she took a deep breath, the air moving through smelled like rain coming. It amazed her that she had learned to read this hard country and to love it—and still, whenever she remembered how night slammed down on Manhattan, how her blood had once seemed to run neon, she longed to be not where she was, but *there*. Three thousand miles away. Thirty years ago.

Not here, but there. Not there, but here. Always her theme. *Here* was Cowbird, whom she had frozen out. *There* was Beltran, who might always be an irresistible deadly fire. She was old enough to know that a woman can't be both here and there. She knew the choice she was about to make. And how it would be imperfect. She hoped it would be more than *her* choice. And even if it wasn't, she hoped she would be able to pass what little she knew about choices on to Zach.

Caroline was bringing Zach out for supper and a sleepover. There was a plot—and a pan of fried chicken staying warm in the oven, molasses-spiked sweet potato pie, and, though he'd piss and moan about having to eat them, collard greens and fatback. She figured what with his bus ticket back to Albuquerque already in Caroline's purse, he was going to need his strength.

There were two surprises. She knew he'd love the first one—and maybe hate part of it, but that was the long shot. It was the second surprise that might have been bringing on her hot flashes. She picked up a postcard from the Riv and fanned herself. If she closed her eyes, she could pretend her mama was there.

ZACH hunched down in his seat. First off, the duct tape holding the Monte Carlo's passenger sun visor had finally cooked off so the visor drooped and the sun was shining right in his eyes. Second, he wanted his mom to see how miserable he was. She was humming "We've Come This Far by Faith," which told him her sense of humor was either gone or Satanic.

"Is Aunt Bonnie going to give me some kind of pep talk?" he said.

"I don't know what she's up to. All she said was she had a couple good-bye surprises for you. And, could I use for you to stay over because the evil boss Maureen booked me back-to-back. *The* day before you leave."

"It won't do any good," Zach said. "If there's a pep talk I mean. I hate Albuquerque."

They pulled off the highway onto Scratch Creek Road. "Me, too." Her jaw was set. "And your dad, and that woman." She shook her head. "I swear, Thanksgiving seems a million years away."

Zach patted her knee. He wondered what it would be like to have a mom who had time to be a mom, a dad who knew how to be a dad. "Hey," he said, "we could be on Jerry Springer."

"Don't you be woofin' me!"

"Really. Born-again Christian completely funny casino waitress moms. Highly intelligent college professor completely boring dads. Pinche gringo beaner greaseball kid. It would be unique."

"Look," she said. "I'm working on something. I don't even want to think about it because if it doesn't happen my heart will break, so trust me. OK?"

Zach sighed.

"No," she said, "not what you think. This is not about Jesus. Well, no more than anything is. Zach, don't you look at me like that!"

Zach kind of knew. The Creosote grapevine was awesome. Katie, who was the kid of Rico, the head maintenance guy, heard about the plan from the feral cat lady when she had come through to trap the calico mom and her six babies. Plus Pat, the sometime graveyard kung pao poker dealer, who thought pigeons were the most beautiful birds on earth, told Zach's best Creosote guy friend Nicky, whose dad was the pit boss at Cachet, a job he hated, a job he did because he thought he was going to put Nicky through college, which Nicky hadn't had the heart to tell him was not in the works at all. "I skate," Nicky said. "Simply put, dude, I am going to be this century's Jay Adams. Before you are."

And then, of course, there was Spooky, who could see things before they happened.

Zach's mom pulled into Bonnie's driveway. Zach smelled fried chicken and sighed. Good news, bad news. With Aunt Bonnie and her life-in-balance philosophy, fried chicken meant collards. "I'll be back at seven thirty sharp," his mom said. Zach grabbed his backpack and climbed out of the car.

30 Maggie set her bag down next to her seat at the blackjack table. It continued to amaze her that the ashes of a small woman could be this heavy. She remembered Lucy's smile. "People are always surprised at the weight," she had said. "You consider we're mostly water. You would think the ashes would be nothing."

Maggie thought of Sarah's words about giving the corpse to the hungry birds. She had almost told Lucy that the Willow people believed ashes *were* nothing. And then she had remembered the road ahead and how she needed to travel it with only a ghost for company.

"Do you know what you're going to do with them?" Lucy had asked.

"I do," Maggie had said. "She won't be alone."

MAGGIE pushed a twenty across the table. The old woman next to her nodded. "You're in the right spot," she said. "Me and the grandkid here are doing A-OK." The grandkid was a young brunette whose plump beauty ought to have been illegal.

"I'm ready," Maggie said. "I got a little project I need to finance." She didn't add that she knew how to count, so the few grand she needed were practically sitting right there in her pocket.

Maggie made a two-dollar bet. She tapped the box of ashes with her foot. "Help me out here, girlfriend," she whispered. "We need to finance another road trip."

BONNIE slid the videotape into the VCR. Zach was slamming down his second piece of sweet potato pie. "Is this the surprise?" he said. The tape began. A man looked directly into the camera. There was a locked metal door behind him. He wore a leather jacket over an old skate T-shirt. His blond hair was buzz cut, his voice a hesitant whisper. Zach stopped chewing and put the plate carefully on the couch next to him.

"Who is that?" he said. "I almost know him."

"It's Jay Adams now," Bonnie said. "In jail. Watch." Zach slid off the couch and sat at the foot of the television. The face seemed flat, as though it was nothing but skin and bruises over a skull. The eyes were dead. Jay Adams tried to smile, flinched, and shrugged his shoulders. "I made some mistakes," he said.

His face melted into a boy crouched on a skateboard, his blonde hair fanning out like a wild halo. The board was not some modern laminated honed-to-perfection mega-bucks job, but homemade. One hand hovered over asphalt, the other was stretched out in front of him, as though he was a skinny Moses parting the Southern California air.

"Where did you get this?" Zach whispered. "Can we rewind it?"

Bonnie hit the remote. The tape rewound. Jay Adams threw a perfect Berk in reverse. Waves morphed into the battered face. "A friend of mine in LA knows an old Thrasher photographer," Bonnie said. "They're trying to put together enough money to make a movie."

"Fuck," Zach said. "I'm sorry, Aunt Bonnie, there is no other word for it. This is flat fucking amazing."

"I love this part the best," Bonnie said. Jay Adams was maybe seven. He was laughing into the camera, and you could tell that there was no one he would rather have been than his bright-eyed, mouse-faced little self.

They reran the tape a dozen times. Bonnie saw more and more: how Jay Adams and his board *were* a wave, how he was crazy, how he had been whole.

"I want to show you something else," Bonnie said. "It's about what *I* loved."

Zach nodded. "What I hate, Aunt Bonnie, is how dead it is now. Like you can't say you *love* something. Or somebody. Plus everything is *you can get busted for this.* Like if you tried to sneak under a fence into somebody's backyard, it would be some totally heinous felony. Plus if you tried to say it was better back then, everybody'd be like 'You're so gay.' "

"Bite your tongue," Bonnie said. She replaced the tape with another. "This is a movie about back then. It was better. And, it was definitely gay."

Zach stared at her. "Hang on," he said. "Gay doesn't mean a homo or anything. When we say 'gay,' we just mean duh, or whatever you said when you were young."

"We used to say 'jive,' " Bonnie said.

By the time they had watched *Paris Is Burning* for an hour, Zach was absolutely still.

"You OK?" Bonnie said.

"I didn't know," he said. "My mom's going to kill you for showing me this."

"I don't think so," Bonnie said. "She and I go blood deep." They watched two gorgeous queens, one black, the other Puerto Rican, slinging insults at each other. "Once upon a time, colored people used to call this signifying," Bonnie said. "These girls called it 'throwin' down.'"

The camera panned to the circle of girls watching the queens throw down. Zach leaned farther forward. "Can you rewind it, just back half a minute?"

Bonnie smiled. "I can."

The camera moved in on a stunning young black woman. Her makeup was more subtle than that of the others, except for the rouge on her cheeks and forehead. She was laughing, but what her face contained was much more than amusement. It was pure joy.

"That's you," Zach said. "Aunt Bonnie, that is you."

"It is."

"Dude. I mean Aunt Bonnie. I mean holy shit."

Bonnie turned off the tape.

"You didn't want to be what you really were," Zach said.

"It's more like I wanted to be what I really *was*," Bonnie said.

Zach looked at her and saw a nice middle-aged lady, almost like the women who played bingo at the Riverbelle. He saw her wrinkles and the loose skin under her throat. The veins in her big hands ran dark and twisty as tree roots. He felt sad for her. But maybe proud.

"Aunt Bonnie," he said. He looked at the blank television screen as though it held the words for his next question. "When you were a kid, did you know you didn't want to be a guy?"

Bonnie turned to him, her smile that of the beautiful young girl in the movie. Her gold tooth flashed. "Baby," she said, "I knew the second I popped out my mama. And I'll tell you this: I hated being a guy as much as you hate Albuquerque."

MAGGIE had been on her blackjack seat for six hours. She'd put nothing in her body but damn near a gallon of bad coffee. She wondered if she was imagining the dozen plus stacks of chips in front of her. Green chips. Black chips. She suspected there was at least four thousand dollars there.

The dealer was a skinny chick with that honed ex-dancer look. Her eyes were outer-space emerald, which Maggie figures was due to contact lenses. The dealer's nails matched. "Hey. Dealer to the lucky. You in?"

Maggie looked to her right. There was a sharper smoking a vicious cigar—a sure sign to get the fuck out.

"No," she said. "I know when to quit," and slid a few hundred bucks across the felt. "For you."

The dealer tucked the tip away. She flashed a smile. "Come back anytime."

"I think I'm going to need something for these chips," Maggie said. She stood and felt her knees buckle. "Whoa." She sat back down and bumped Sarah's ashes. "Thanks," she said.

"You talking to the floor?" the dealer said. "Lady, you better get something to eat. I'll get Security over here to help you with the chips."

Security carried the chips. Maggie carried the box. "Got a bomb there?" Security said.

"Just a friend."

"How'd you get him in there?"

"It's not a he," she said.

By the time the chips had been tallied, Maggie understood just how good a pal Sarah had been. The cashier counted out four thousand, three hundred, seventy-five dollars. Maggie eschewed the tax deduction, tipped the cashier and the security guard, and headed for the buffet.

She was inhaling a plate of beef ribs and fried chicken when she remembered the two red pins on the map of Creosote. She knew she had to tell Lucy about Sarah. She had told no one in Creosote. Only she and a few Bone Lake people knew.

She stopped eating. Whom *would* she have told—not Jesse, not as the Mean Motherfucker. She began to think about how alone she was. She wondered what Minnie Siyala would tell her. And, she wondered if Minnie Siyala was still alive. Ghosts had become her closest family.

Maggie opened her pack and took out the envelope from Dead DC. She read the gift certificate and knew again how much she did not want to float in a boat with her furious kid. And she knew that was exactly what she was going to do. Sarah's words echoed in her mind. *And the river is one of the places our souls go when they are free.*

She patted the wad of bills in her pocket. It was remarkable how having six months' rent covered could give a woman room to remember.

JAY ADAMS spun slowly through Zach's dreams. Jay skated an empty swimming pool in which there seemed to be no bottom. Palm trees rose like jungle. Jay's skinny arms were lifted to the sky, his left hand palm up, his right hand palm down. Some Alice Cooper golden oldie blared in the background. Jay circled and circled as though he skated the edge of a giant sea shell.

The pool began to fill with dark green water. Jay Adams slid through the tube of a giant wave. Gulls screamed. Zach wanted to be on that board. He wanted it so bad he thought he would almost die to be there.

"Wake up." His aunt stood next to the couch. "You were making funny noises." She held out a cup of cocoa.

Zach sat up. "Thank you," he said. "That part you said about a kid can choose which parent when the kid is fourteen?" Zach was careful to not say "how I could." If he thought of the kid as "the kid," then he didn't have to imagine the choice the kid would make, and the look on the father's face when he found out.

"It seems like a hard call for a kid to make," Bonnie said.

"I'm choosing my mom," Zach said. "She told about some plan she maybe has. You remember the last plan."

Bonnie laughed. "We should have known that anything that involved the intervention of poor old Jesus wasn't going to be airtight."

Zach sipped the cocoa. It was Bonnie's finest. She grated Mexican chocolate and used Mexican sugar, so the cocoa looked almost black and smelled of cinnamon. "I guess I better tell my mom what I'm going to do."

"I never told my mama my plan," Bonnie said. "I just went away and did what was necessary. I wrote her every week. I sent her money. I knew if I told her it would kill her. She was old-timey. She would have reckoned I was going to burn forever in hell."

"Didn't she wonder why you didn't come home? Didn't she feel hurt?"

"She couldn't write very well, but we talked on my brother's phone a few times. She never asked me anything. All she ever said was, 'Bless you, baby. And, you take care.'

"When my brother told me she was dying, I cut my hair, put on an afro wig and sharp suit, went back and sat by her bed for three days. She was drifting in and out. She kept calling me by my long-gone daddy's name. I wanted to put my head down on her bosom and tell her the truth. I wanted to say, 'Your baby girl is home.' I didn't."

"That is so sad," Zach said. "It wasn't fair."

Bonnie understood she was talking to a child. And felt blessed. She had never told anyone about that vigil, about the way her mother clung to her hand just before the end, and whispered, "I missed you so much, child," without so much as a hint of blame in her words.

"I wonder what it would be like," Zach said, "to never see my mom again." He remembered Jay Adams gliding through the giant wave. He wished that was life. You just found your balance, spread your arms like wings, and whatever you were riding carried you through.

"Aunt Bonnie," he said. "I think I want to be a philosopher when I grow up. Or maybe like those guys in Wu Tang Clan."

Bonnie had no idea what Wu Tang Clan was. She had always been a girl for show tunes. But, she bet it was a rap group, and she bet the lyrics were about things not being fair. "Oh lord," Bonnie said, "we do have us a crusader here." She stood. "Your mom is pulling into the driveway. Let's go get some breakfast started."

JESSE squeezed three drops of medicine in Ralph's bowl. He had not left his place for a week. He had watched Ralph every waking minute, and held him close through the night. He knew every bone in the dog's rib cage as though it were his own. He had, at times, found himself breathing the same rhythm that was at times the only sign Ralph was alive.

There were no blackout curtains on the windows. Light poured in, late summer glare softening to rose agate in the evenings. Cocker had told him heat would be good. "Ralph needs to cook it out. I couldn't say about you for sure, but you got that fog in your eyes Marcella would tell you a sweat could fix. What the fuck, Corbeaux. You got nothing to lose."

Jesse dug his fingers gently into the places along Ralph's knobby spine. Cocker had showed him where, showed him exactly how much pressure to apply, told him to be sure Ralph drank a lot of water. Ralph could have cared less. All he knew is the man he loved—who could, at any instant, be replaced by Cocker or someone equally adoring—was touching him just fine, and later there would be chopped-up steak.

"Seems like it's pretty basic," Jesse said to Ralph. "Hands-on. And hanging in there." His gut knotted. "You look this good tomorrow, Ralph, we're going to get in the *truck* and go see Ray and Helen."

Ralph was asleep. Jesse finished kneading his tail and stood. His knees ached. The scars on his back were tight. He couldn't remember feeling his body as much as he had during Ralph's convalescence. Not even when he was fucking. Not even when he was stoned brainless.

"Man," he said, "this better be worth something." He heard himself and put his hands over his face. What it was worth lay on the floor. Alive. Asleep. And, maybe someone who could be loved standing over Ralph, sucking in hot desert air and a few dog hairs.

LUCY looked up and grinned. Her eyes were tired. "You caught me unawares."

Maggie sat. "Everything is catching me unawares these days."

"Maybe that's reality."

Maggie nodded. "I want to tell you something that could get me locked up." Lucy eyes went flat.

"Not like that," Maggie said. "More like in the nuthouse."

"Let's go somewhere else to talk," Lucy said. "Your call. Give me an hour."

Maggie smiled. "There's a bench down on the Stroll."

"The ShirleySal," Lucy said.

"That's the one."

"I was working that night," Lucy said. "Took an hour with the Jaws to get them out. But, what was really strange was that their faces were peaceful."

Maggie nodded.

"You know," Lucy said, "weird shit happens on the river."

MAGGIE was glad to walk back to the Riverstroll alone. She needed time to remember, time to let what she could say come to the surface. She didn't have much hope she could tell Lucy anything that would help in the real world, or even in the not-quite-real neon world that jangled in front of her.

The light was already cooling behind the casinos. The neon signs were that first sexy kiss. You didn't have to think about how predictable the seduction would be, or how you'd wake up later wondering how you'd forgotten the truth about vampires.

You didn't have to think about what was already going on inside. Since it was Tuesday, just a little after 6:00, Joanne was at work in the Belle, humping bags of nickels on her refill job. The CORPSE had sent down what they called a side promotion for Joanne—from a comfortable stool in the cashier cage to refill. Joanne was sixty-four. Her hair looked like a rusting Brillo pad. The joints of her hands were so swollen from arthritis that she was stuck with the wedding ring from the marriage that had ended four years ago when her husband had walked out.

Maggie imagined Joanne hefting the heavy nickel bag into the machine and talking out of the side of her mouth to the lucky winner, just in case Betty Lou, the slot manager, was in range. "Listen," Joanne would be saying, "it's simple. There's no promotion in side promotion. Any promotion that isn't up, is down."

You could bet the customer didn't say anything. You could bet the customer was watching the shimmer of nickels, was sticking an ashtray under the payout chute, and barely heard what Joanne said next: "Honey, I don't *like* hefting twenty-five-pound bags of nickels, but let me tell you about my last job. Proofreading vegetable can labels. Big old sheets, maybe four foot by four foot. You'd give 'em a quick check, count down fifteen sheets, flip the bundle over, then check the next sheet. Eight to five, two fifteen-minute breaks, half hour for lunch, minimum wage.

"I lasted five months. The gal with the most seniority had been there thirty-five years. She lived on Doritos, coffee, and as many cigarettes as she could smoke during breaks and lunch. See that gull poop on the deck outside. Her skin was that color."

And it was a hundred to one the customer wouldn't tip.

It was an even safer bet the pale blonde with the Coach bag was shoving credit card after credit card into the ATM, looking up after each flash of No Funds Available on the video display, smiling brightly at the video keno players around her while she slid in another card and tapped the ATM with one long fingernail painted the exact mineral red of cinnabar; and there were two boys in the arcade, their hair in dreadlocks, their hip-hop shorts hanging off their skinny butts, and they couldn't be much older than seven, their older sister hunched over a plastic Uzi, blowing away dark figures on the screen. There was the old couple from Redlands, who had just missed the Seniors Fulla Fun bus home, who were broke, who had nowhere to stay, who were wandering the Riverstroll, the man saying to the woman, over and over, so quietly you could barely hear him, "You stupid old woman. You stupid fool."

And the river was shining silver, and sundown glowed molten on the thousands of hotel windows.

"Sarah," Maggie said, grateful that in a casino town people talked to themselves all the time, "I hope you understand what I'm about to do."

BONNIE settled into the hammock and watched the empty sky as if there might be a hint for the choice she had to make. She knew there wasn't going to be some big wave carrying *her* through. No way.

As the shadows began to move across the ramada, she picked up the phone and dialed Beltran's cell. Beltran answered on the fourth ring. She wondered where he was and if he was alone. Was there a woman next to him, a woman he held tight, with one hand gently over her laughing mouth? Was he driving the Strip, watching for the kids he would meet later, the kids he called his rats, because they could appear and disappear in an instant. Had he made her wait just because he could always make her wait?

Beltran was silent.

"You know it's me," Bonnie said.

"I do. I like to make the moment last."

She waited for the blossom of heat in her breast. There was nothing. And still she wanted to see his face, his smile, his hands. "I was hoping," Bonnie said, "that we could get together sometime soon."

He laughed. "What have you got in mind?"

"Talk."

"You sound like a gringa. They always want to talk."

She walked out toward the edge of the patio. The sun burned straight across the tops of the Shadow Mountains. "This won't take long."

Beltran laughed. "Then do it now. I got a few minutes left on this cell."

Bonnie moved farther out under the sun. The top of her head seemed on fire. She closed her eyes and felt the sear across her cheekbones, her lips.

"Chica," Beltran said, "you better speak up. You ain't getting any younger."

Bonnie saw herself reflected in the trailer window, her face, her throat, her shoulders lit from behind. "I'm out," she said. "It's over."

She heard the click of a lighter. "If that's how you want it," Beltran said. "I would never force a lady." He waited a beat. "Besides, you'll be back."

Bonnie pressed the phone against her heart. As though he could hear the steady beat. She knew that was not the real reason. She was taking what was left of Beltran straight into her heart—she was taking in signals bouncing into icy space and back. She felt dizzy with the speed of that minute she had been moving toward for so many years.

"Good-bye," she said. By the time she brought the phone to her ear, there was silence on the other end.

THE SHIRLEYSAL bench was empty. Maggie leaned on the Stroll railing and looked down at the silver-green water. The Jet Skis were gone. Only the Riverbelle ferry moved slowly south. She could hear the voice of the tour guide. "And there, waving his famous arm, is the famous neon cowboy. Whaddya think he's saying, folks? I can tell you. He's saying, *Get on over here and get rich!!!*"

Lucy came up next to her. She had a bag of takeout from the chain Chinese place in the Tidewater. "I got us some dinner," she said.

"Thanks," Maggie said. "I met the gals who put up this plaque.

They were here for the death anniversary a few weeks back, dressed head to toe in black, eating strawberry waffles in the Blue Velvet. Casey reserved four Wheel of Fortune machines for them, right where Shirley and Sal used to play. They were still there at 7:00 a.m. when I came by on my way to work."

"I love it here," Lucy said. "Where else are you going to find loyalty like that."

"Anywhere you got suckers," Maggie said. "That's where."

Lucy bit into an egg roll. "I apologize," she said, "for this meal."

Maggie closed the container. "I'm not sure I can eat anyhow," she said. "This is what I know about Sarah."

31 Every morning he woke up alive, Ray Cooper muttered, "Thank you." It came as close to praying as he ever would. He hauled his lawn chair back of the trailer, lowered himself slowly into the seat, and watched light move up from the Music Mountains. He raised his coffee mug in salute to dawn. Jesse's truck moved slowly up Estrellas Road. A guy driving slow was usually a sign of something dicey, maybe a terminal hangover, or worse. When Ray saw the big white head just above the passenger seat, he let out his breath.

"Helen," Ray yelled. "Jesse and Ralph are on their way."

He heard the TV go off, then the sound of pots and pans in the kitchen. "I hope he's OK," Helen hollered.

"He is. I told you, he's got Ralph with him."

Jesse pulled up to the trailer. Ralph tilted his head out the passenger window and sniffed the air. Jesse leaned over and opened Ralph's door. The dog stepped carefully down, limped over to Ray, licked his hand, and headed up the trailer steps.

"You dog," Helen said. "You silly old dog."

"You talking to me?" Ray yelled.

Jesse sat across from Ray. "When are you going to divorce that woman?"

Ray nodded. "When you going to get one?"

"I'm heading out for a few days," Jesse said. "Over to Flagstaff, then up to the rez."

Ray understood Jesse had answered his question. "You got time for a decent meal before you hit the road?"

"How could I not?"

MAGGIE woke slowly. For the first time since she and Sarah had parted, she was truly happy to come up out of sleep. She looked around the little studio. Since the rent was low, the hits in Jean and the Riv had granted her a few months to work part-time; and to take off the week for Dead DC's gift. The CORPSE were thrilled, since that meant they didn't have to pay vacation benefits.

She thought of Lucy's face as she listened to Sarah's story. When Maggie was done, Lucy had said, "This is beyond logic. There isn't a computer program or an analysis that is going to tell us anything we both don't know now."

"Are you going to take out Sarah's pin?" Maggie had asked.

"No way. I keep thinking about this old card player we had to haul in every now and then because he'd stop taking his meds and decide he was Doc Holliday. Last time, he grabbed my hand. My first reaction was to call for backup. Before I could, he whispered "Pal, you always get dealt the same old hand. Sometimes, you got to play the cards a new way."

JESSE cleaned his plate. Ralph was disappointed, but Helen had rules about no animals eating off human plates. Besides, Ralph had his own dish, a beat-up tin pie plate which he was now carrying proudly around the patio. The humans look at him fondly.

"I never thought I'd give a shit about a dog," Ray said.

Jesse nodded. "Me neither."

Helen laughed. "I never thought I'd give a shit about a man, much less two of them." She picked up their plates and went into the trailer.

Jesse leaned back in his chair. Ray waited. Jesse stalled. Ray drummed his fingers on the lawn-chair arm. "I was going to suggest we play a game or two of Hangman to ease into things," Ray said. "But, seeing as you're in such a hurry to spill the beans, go ahead."

"Ah shit," Jesse said. "Here goes.

"After I got back from the war, I buried a couple copper bracelets up by an old buffalo statue near the San Francisco Peaks in Flagstaff. One was mine. One was Darwin's. This old Bru mama-san had given them to us. A woman didn't usually do that, but she told me Darwin was the ghost of an ancestor of hers. She didn't tell *him* because she guessed he would have been scared shitless to hear that."

"You going to dig up those bracelets."

"You bet. And, I'm going to take his up to the rez. Maybe I'll bury it somewhere. It won't change anything."

"Maybe," Ray said. "Maybe not."

"Jesus, Ray," Jesse said, "since you retired you got positively profound."

Ray glared. "I'm supposed to say stuff like that. I'm old." He heard himself, looked down at his bony hands and closed his eyes. "I got one question."

"Yeah?"

"What was the name of Darwin's favorite dog when he was a kid."

Jesse picked up the pencil next to the newspaper crossword. He drew a gallows in the margin, and _ _ _ _ _.

"R," Ray said. "Of course."

"OK," MAGGIE WHISPERED to the quiet. "Deacon, here comes your mom."

She called and told him what she wanted. There was a long pause. "I will be there," he said. "If Dad wanted it, I will absolutely be there."

Maggie closed her mouth around the words that could kill the moment: *Yeah, and what if I wanted it?*

He would meet her at Lee's Ferry even though Jeannie had her hands full with the kid and his boss was going to kill him. Deacon's kid voice was gone.

"Listen," he said. "We don't have to talk about anything deep while we're down there, OK? I mean what happened has happened. It's time to get on with our lives."

"You bet," Maggie said.

"There's one thing," he said.

"Go for it."

"Don't call me Deacon anymore. I'm Daniel. Plus, I *love* being a husband and a dad. OK?"

"That's three things," Maggie said.

Long pause. And then, Deacon/Daniel laughed, and she felt the knot in her chest loosen.

BONNIE sat in the ramada, her back straight as a young ballerina's. She twisted the gold screw in her left ear. Cowbird leaned against the trailer wall. He wanted to hunker down next to her, but he was so afraid to make a move he'd gone bone-cold. The trailer wall was still warm from the sun. He pressed against it.

"You OK?" she said.

Cowbird didn't move. "Maybe." He shook his head. "OK, lady, I'm gonna ask you a question. But, I want you to know that no matter what you answer, I'm ready for it.

"I swear, Bonnie, I have *never* met a woman I liked better. I mean, just plain liked. When we talk, I feel like I'm a truly smart man instead of a toasted bozo who just keeps walking back into the fire." He took a deep breath. "See what I mean. I don't say stuff like that to anybody else. Well, except once to Maggie when my heart was broke."

"You go ahead," Bonnie said. "You go ahead and ask me, baby. I am ready."

Cowbird dropped on one knee so their eyes were level. "See, I noticed some stuff. I heard some rumors. Are you a man?" he said.

"I once was." Bonnie took a deep breath. "I am now a woman."

"So," Cowbird sighed. There was a pause of at least a light year. "Is Beltran out of your heart? And will you drive us out by Ransom Dam so I can show you something?"

Bonnie put her long fingers over Cowbird's cold hand. "No," she said. "And, yes."

ZACH MARTINEZ climbed onto the bus and sat down. It was midnight. His mom waited by the Moonglow entrance, pink neon washing over her. She looked just like that dumb song, "Honky Tonk Angel," that she had played about a million times after his dad had left. He wanted to tell her that, but he couldn't seem to move. The bus was filled with LA homeys, scary tweakers, and girls who were much too beautiful to be riding alone. If he yelled out to his mom, he'd look so immature. He told himself to be a man.

Then, the driver climbed on and Zach found himself walking to the front of the bus. "Hey, Zach," the driver said, "you heading back to your Dad's?"

Zach swallowed hard. "I am, and I wonder if I could take half a minute to say good-bye once more to my mom. I gotta tell her something I forgot."

"*Sixty* seconds," the driver said. "If you're not back in sixty seconds, the bus goes without you."

I wish, Zach thought. He skidded down the steps and ran across the parking lot. His mom had not moved. She never left until he was gone. Zach wrapped his arms around her and realized the two of them were the same height. "I'll be back," he said. "I promise."

She bumped his shoulder with her forehead. "I know that, honey. It's going to take a little bit to pull together, but after October 10, you're your own man."

Zach stepped back. "I just wanted you to know," he said. "I was looking out the bus window and you look just like a honky-tonk angel."

She smiled.

"Like in the song, you know. Like Dad used to call you. You are one. You'll always be one." He wished he could just shut up.

Caroline looked at her son. "God bless," she said. "God hold you safe, honey."

The driver honked the horn. Zach felt himself suspended. He remembered the dark green water in his dream, and how Jay Adams hadn't had to do a thing but step up on the board.

"You too, Mom," he said. "I mean about God. I love you." And, Zach Martinez moved out onto the warm black asphalt in front of the Moonglow Casino Greyhound station as though it were a perfect wave.

SARAH couldn't believe how easy it was being all-the-way-dead. And how endlessly interesting. She thought of something Maggie had told her, how Maggie's dying mom had looked around the hospital room and said, "This. None of this. None of *this* matters."

Sarah and Minnie watched the living. They had been told they were only to watch, and it had been made clear that they were not to intervene in anything.

"Sometimes," their teachers had told them, "we might drop something down in front of a human. We see which way they go. There is something else you can give them; we'll show you when you've learned to watch."

Sarah watched Hannah put on a pot of coffee. She saw Lorinda carefully outline her dark eyes in black. She saw Maggie packing a bag with shorts, sunscreen, and the badger skull candleholder. She watched Will Lucas walk out to the highway. His old pack was slung from one shoulder, a green scarf tied around his long hair, and his right thumb was up.

Minnie watched her young apprentice break into the cold room at the funeral home. She sighed. He was particularly beautiful in black. He had smeared charcoal over his face and hands, tied a black bandana over his hair. His dark glasses shone like other-world eyes. She remembered his dark skin, the fire-rock shine of his hair, how his eyes would go flat, go bright. She saw him gently lift her body. He left a raven feather on the gurney, and she remembered how wonderfully young and dramatic he was.

When he set her body down on a boulder high on Beartrack Mountain, she remembered his strength. He fanned her long hair out over the stone and waited. Dawn moved up. First light glowed on the face of her body. The

Black Lake boy raised his arms, his gaze, and saw the vultures moving in. He stumbled.

Minnie wanted to return, not to save him, because that was not necessary. He caught his balance and began his descent. Minnie wanted to stand before him, and, for less than a second, take off his dark glasses. She would look into his bright eyes. Drop her love in front of him. Only that. And, with that longing, she knew what else the watchers were allowed to send the living.

"That Black Lake boy," she said to Sarah. "It is sad that he lost his way for such a long time."

32 Ralph rode next to Jesse, the look on the dog's face the quiet joy of a creature who knew he was finally being rewarded in the manner he so richly deserved. They had stopped briefly at the Pilot in Kingman, where Jesse bought Maggie a blue harmonica and a mood ring. They'd cruised past the BIA offices in Valentine and the Orlando Motel in Truxton, where there was No Vacancy and a dozen busted-down muscle cars parked outside.

Jesse was truly hungry for the first time in weeks. Ralph was hungry for the first time in minutes. Jesse drove into Seligman and pulled into the Sno Cap Diner. The air was filled with the divine smoke of charbroiling burgers and hots.

"You stay in the truck," Jesse said. He climbed out and stretched. He was achy again, all the more so because his usual rest stop under the cottonwoods along the little creek has been fenced off. The common declarations of development hung on the posts. He wondered, as usual, where the hustlers were going to get the water; and he thought, as usual: fuck 'em.

The old Delgado guy was at the counter. "Half a straw," he said in some vague eastern European accent and offered Jesse a box of straws cut in half. He offered to put mustard on Ralph's hot dogs, and before Jesse could say, "No, they're for the dog," aimed a mustard bottle at Jesse and squirted him with yellow plastic string.

"For chrissakes," Jesse said. "I hope you're planning on being here forever."

"Why not?" Old Man Delgado said, and tried to sell him half a rubber chicken.

MAGGIE took the turn to Crazy Creek. She figured she'd stay the night for old times' sake and take the Utah shuttle out of St. George to the river put-in at Lee's Ferry. She checked into her comped room at the casino motel, ate barbecue, and then suffered a minor failure of substance abuse.

She lost a hundred bucks in an hour, betting nine nickels at a time, having to talk herself into being anticipatory, then mildly interested about each bet. A two-hundred-buck bonus later, there was no buzz. Something was seriously awry. She figured it was time to quit.

She went to bed early and lay awake for hours having brain chats with Deacon. When she stopped alternating between the scenario in which he flat didn't show and the one in which he fell into her arms crying and they were pals again, she remembered the night she'd spent in the Crazy Creek motel only a few weeks ago.

She felt completely removed from that woman, a woman who had imagined her next weeks would be spent scuffling for rent, keeping her secrets, moving ahead alone, with only the little willow deer to remind her that Sarah was real. A woman who had seriously considered finding a stranger to fuck.

She felt the past blown away, the present just the quiet room and her breath moving in her throat. And then she lost even that. Her body seemed alien to her. It was an effort to move her fingers, to feel her skin. She spiraled in and out of panic.

Nothing had prepared her for this. Nothing seemed to carry her through it. Nothing. She was nothing. She tried to think of Jesse. The letters that formed his name scrambled and were gone. The same with S A R A H, the same with her own name.

Maggie wondered if someone had slipped something in her coffee or if her fool's life had caught up to her, blocked an artery and withered her brain. The thought of throwing on her T-shirt and shorts and finding her way back to the casino felt like death. "Oh fuck," she whispered, "I'm fucked," and was briefly comforted to know she still had a foul mouth, whatever a *mouth* was.

She dissolved and reformed. If she opened her eyes, all she saw was what she hadn't done. If she closed them, there was only the relentless cycle of unmaking and making.

Finally—she couldn't gauge when because the glowing numbers on the clock made no sense—she told her body to sit on the edge of the bed and stand. All the while, her brain nattered, *You don't know what words mean. You've forgotten how to move. You are lost. Lost. Lost.*

Another voice whispered, *I'm watching this. I'm listening. I see it all. The coming apart. The re-forming. The woman who tells herself with words that she doesn't understand words.*

The woman who finally understands gsi'ki.

Maggie opened the blinds on the front window. Pure white light streamed up from the roof of the casino. Two white birds flew into it and disappeared. They curved back into the pale dark and shone like abalone. They vanished again in the light. They arced in and out, in and out. Beyond them, dawn was a thin green line.

Maggie didn't know how long she watched. When the birds were gone and the sky soft gray, she saw the numbers on the clock. 4:47. Dawn, she thought. I'm OK. I can think. Coffee.

She clicked on the pot and sat at the window. "Sarah," she said and felt her blood warm. "Jesse. Lucy. Helen and Ray. Deacon. Daniel. Whatever." She wiggled her fingers. She remembered when her thumb and forefinger were calloused, her hands those of a woman who knew how to bring the music through. A mother who shared a joint with her son, played guitar with him, watched with him the miracle of moths disappearing and appearing in the glow of a streetlight.

Maggie rummaged through the nightstand for stationery and a pen. She dragged a chair out to the balcony and began to write:

Dear Lucy,

I hope this finds you. I haven't said this to anyone: I keep thinking that what killed Sarah isn't human.

Last night, I went a little crazy. Not like I drank myself stupid and picked up some jerk I didn't know. It was as though somebody had slipped acid in my coffee.

I couldn't sleep and I couldn't stop worrying about being with my kid tomorrow, and then I started disappearing, and then it would come to me that I was thinking that I couldn't understand my thoughts, and then there was nothing but pure fear. Finally I had to just lie there with it. I don't think I've ever been so happy to see morning.

How do people like Sarah and me, you and me, find each other? What kind of people are we? How come I can write this to you as easily as I could tell Sarah?

I'll call when I get back. Maggie

p.s. I don't think anybody, Indian or whatever, has a franchise on mystery.

Dear Jesse,

I hope this finds you. I have been traveling with Sarah's ghost for a few months and now I am alone. I'm meeting my kid at Lee's Ferry so we can float in a fucking boat for a week. I keep wanting to turn around and forget the whole thing. You probably have no idea what I'm talking about, but I just need to say it to you. Sarah, that is, her ghost, you don't know about her ghost, isn't here anymore, and she was the only person I could talk to, really talk to. Except for a lady cop. I have to find someone else. You win.

That isn't all. I wish you hadn't left. That's the plain truth. If that freaks you out, so be it. I'm sick of being alone. If that freaks you out too, so be it too. I don't know what happened out there near the bird refuge, but if you've got an idea, I'm willing to hear it.

I lost my sanity last night for a while. I'm telling you all of this as though you were here and life was ordinary. We were just having a fine loser morning together.

I'm working at the Riv. You can find me. I'll be back in a couple weeks. You can always leave a message with Helen and Ray.

love, Maggie

p.s. I know about Ralph Too.

She began to fold the letter, stopped, and tore off the last line.

Dear Helen and Ray,

Be home in a couple weeks. I'll bring the turkey. A medium one. In case there is company.

love, Maggie

Minnie and Sarah watched Maggie pull out of the casino parking lot. She dropped letters in the mailbox, took a hit off her coffee, and reached for a Van Morrison tape to slide in the deck. A semi loaded with doomed pigs, driven by a guy who had been grinding his teeth since Denver, swung off the highway in front of her.

Maggie swerved neatly around him without spilling the coffee. The guy hit his brakes and flipped her the bird. She waved cheerfully and headed for the on-ramp.

"I thought I was going to have to drop something down there in front of her," Minnie said.

"I did," Sarah said. "That's why she didn't spill the coffee."

They fell silent. Below them, a line of cars crawled up the Virgin River Gorge. They watched the canyon bighorn ewe pick her way delicately down the rocks to the river. Somebody tossed a pop can out of a truck. It glinted in the sun, arced, and fell harmlessly a few feet from the sheep. She kept grazing.

"It is nearly time for us to leave," Minnie said.

Sarah looked away. "I'm afraid," she said. "I'm going to miss you."

"I wonder if we will miss *anything*," Minnie said quietly. "Oh yes, I will. My little old yellow dog, you never knew her. And, the Black Lake boy. And you."

Sarah touched the velvet bag at her throat. "We don't know anything, do we? What the priest said about heaven, what you told me about the river, what that professor taught us about nirvana, none of it makes a difference now."

"That's right." Minnie lifted a strand of Sarah's hair away from her face. "I'm afraid, too."

They watched the Bird cruising up toward the Utah border. Sarah laughed. "Did you ever hear Meatloaf?" she said.

Minnie looked at her hard. "Meatloaf don't talk."

"No," Sarah said. "He's a white rock musician. I can't remember the exact line, but it was something about life being a road and our souls being cars."

"Girl," Minnie said, "those white people have gone all the way crazy."

JESSE couldn't find his old route to the buffalo. He followed the old road till it disappeared near a block of condos and reemerged as a blocked-off dirt track headed nowhere. There was a huge medical complex across the street on what used to be one of the last untouched chunks of forest in the area. He pulled in and parked. They'd retained the biggest trees, but the little limestone draw was gone.

There was a Navajo kid at the reception desk. "Do you know how I get to Buffalo Park?" Jesse asked.

The kid fielded a call, then pursed his lips at the door behind Jesse. "You just keep going up this street. You'll see a sign for USGS on the left. Turn."

Jesse almost asked him if the buffalo was still there, but the kid had put on his headphones and was staring at his computer screen. "Thanks," Jesse said. He wrote the word on the Post-it pad next to the kid. The kid nodded.

Jesse drove up the hill. He could feel the mountains' beautiful weight to the west. He wouldn't look till he turned left. Ralph shoved his nose into the crack between the window and the frame. He was trembling.

"Me too," Jesse said. He turned onto the road that seemed to flow straight toward the mountains. He loved the shock of seeing them, blue-gray, aspen shining on their flanks. It was a day on which the mountains were huge. Other days they could seem a tiny Japanese painting.

Jesse took in the mountains with every cell. He felt the long southern slope under his boots, breathed the clouds that haloed blue-black Agassiz. He remembered Darwin saying, "What you call Mount Humphreys, we call Old Glittering Top. She is a goddess. She watches over us Navajo guys." They'd been sixteen and stoned out of their gourds that night, and Jesse would have sworn he'd seen moonlight on the mountaintop shatter into diamonds.

Ralph Too bumped Jesse's shoulder with his nose. "We're going," Jesse told him and parked.

The buffalo stood in front of the basalt archway. He was tarnished. Someone had planted a garden of flowers around him. Jesse remembered an old alligator juniper beyond the water tower. Ralph tugged him forward. The tree was still there. Jesse pressed his face against the corrugated bark and smelled the wild nights of his young manhood.

The civic improvers had set up an aluminum bench. Ralph finished marking his territory. Jesse sat. Ralph lay at his feet. The mountain aspen were turning gold. A cluster of thick green mullein caught the late afternoon light, their tiny yellow flowers fireworks. Jesse knew the one good thing he had taken away from Vietnam: A guy on long-range patrol in alien country paid attention. A guy on long-range patrol studied what he saw, because the green stalk waving up the trail could have been food. It could have been medicine. It could have been death.

"Let's head on out, boy." Ralph creaked to his feet. They walked across the red cinders and pale wild grass. Ralph was suddenly young. He pranced ahead, sidestepping prickly pear, trotting between the chunks of black basalt.

The light seemed to shift with every step they took: quartz to pale blue to salmon rose. Jesse's breath caught in the thin air. I'm home, he thought. Where the fuck have I been? Where am I?

Maggie. Would she come here with him? Would he ask her? Who the fuck knew?

Ralph stopped. Ten feet ahead a red-tailed hawk danced on the back of a dead jackrabbit. A woman jogged toward them. She wore headphones. Jesse raised his hand for her to stop. She kept coming. The red-tailed startled, shuddered, and took off with the rabbit's limp body hanging from its talons.

Ralph shook his head. "Face it, pal," Jesse said. "It just wasn't yours."

JESSE AND RALPH came off the trail in last light. Moms with jogging strollers, a wiry old Hopi guy, and a stocky man with the black handlebar mustache of an old-time gambler walked to the parking area. Jesse put Ralph in the truck, grabbed the entrenching tool, and studied the base of the buffalo.

The buffalo stood on three layers of cement. Jesse was going to have to go in diagonally. He figured if anybody asked him why he was digging in the cinders, he'd tell them he had lost his harmonica. When he checked himself in the truck's side-view mirror, a scrawny unshaved guy with dust-devil hair and a weird light in his eyes, he knew nobody would bother him.

He jammed the tip of the entrenching tool into the cinders. Nothing much gave. He remembered the drinking fountain just beyond the archway and went to the truck for Ralph's water dish.

It took a while for the water to loosen things up, long enough for the crowd in the parking area to thin. Jesse snuck the flask of Old Popocat out of his jacket and took a sip. The sun dropped red gold below the tops of the dark pines. The tequila was the same burn down his throat.

The cinders finally gave. By the time the moon was bright on his work, two slender arcs appeared. The smaller one was near eroded through. Jesse picked it up and held it on his palm.

"You're going home, bro," he said. He felt like a cliché, some sappy-eyed cammie-hound pouring a beer at the foot of the Wall. "Partner," he said, "that wasn't us." He shoveled the cinders back. "What the fuck, I might as well go for broke."

He walked through the dark archway into full view of the mountains. Moonlight caught the tip of Humphreys. Jesse raised the bracelets in the air. "Old Glittering Top, I'm Jesse." He was careful not to say the name of the dead. "Please take care of my friend."

JESSE AND RALPH slept in the truck just off a forest service road and made Cameron by breakfast. There were huevos rancheros for Jesse, a paper plate of machaca for Ralph. Jesse looked at the Navajo silver in the jewelry case and decided to wait. Who knew where She was, who knew where She would be? He wished he had a pebble of hash to blur the edges. He had begun to think of Maggie as She. He was in trouble.

LATE RAINS had flooded the rez around Chinle. The wet sand was the color of old blood. Jesse introduced Ralph to the incomparable pleasure of a Navajo taco without the vegetables. They sat on the edge of Canyon de Chelly and watched night fall over Spider Rock. Ralph farted. Jesse moved downwind.

"Have some manners, pal," Jesse said. A truck roared into the parking lot. Somebody smashed a bottle. Ralph growled. His big ears swiveled. There was the raw and tedious thump of pop hip-hop. Ralph strained at the leash. A kid howled. Somebody racked a shotgun. Ralph's growl seemed to fill the air.

"Uh uh," a soft male voice said. "We're outta here." The truck roared and squealed out onto the highway. Jesse watched the red taillights jitter and shrink, stoner eyes, embers in a dying fire.

Jesse and Ralph were alone. "You can fart anytime you want," Jesse said. Ralph settled his head into Jesse's lap.

"I love you, old dog," Jesse said. There it was. He had said the L-word. "Yeah," he said, "I love love love you."

The top of Spider Rock glowed silver. Jesse heard Darwin's voice. They had been hunkered in the triple canopy black under what was left of a temple. "We went up that Spider Rock," Darwin had said. "It was like the moonlight was leading us. Well, okeydokey, there was the beer. And this skinny chick in Teec Nos Pos dared me to do it. I was sixteen!

"Me and Baxter had his climbing rope and gear. He went ahead. We was crammin' and jammin.' Eight hundred fifty feet. Five what you call pitches. Ever now and then, I'd lean back and let that moonlight hit my face. I was scared. My people wouldn't dare to climb that rock.

"See, when I was little, they told us kids there was bones up there. Navajos hate bones. I can't tell you why we do, it's gotten be a broken story for a white person. Even though I love ya, bro.

"I wanted to see those bones. See if they looked like white fire like the old folks said.

"There wasn't no bones. Just rock and moon. That was all. And, Baxter sayin,' 'Ah fuck, now we gotta get down.'"

Darwin had passed him the last millimeter of their joint. "I'm sorry, bro. I kinda had to tell you the broken story, but you remember what that old mama-san told us, how when you don't know how to talk the language, it's too dangerous to hear certain parts."

Jesse studied Spider Rock. He started to take out his binoculars and remembered Darwin's words. Let it be, he thought, and he understood there couldn't have been a better place to toss Darwin's bracelet out into the dark. The bracelet flashed moonlight and was gone.

"Come on, Ralph," Jesse said. "We're going home." He helped Ralph to his feet and realized he'd forgotten something. He took the other bracelet from his back pocket and clasped it next to the Anrahs' bracelet on his left wrist.

33   The river at Lee's Ferry was not the road-kill snake it would become south of Vegas. The water was jade, its scent the same, something Maggie couldn't name that slowed her heart and breath. She was grateful to be alone. Katz, a wiry guide in a faded Grateful Dead bandana, had taken the rest of the group to their campground.

The huge dam loomed upriver. She could feel it. Katz had told them it was temporary, the reservoir already silting up. Maggie thought of the crumbling walls of the old Gold Road mine. She slipped off her sandals and walked into the shallow water. She wanted to feel the pebbles under her feet. They were the consequence of fault lines, of current, of the power of water; they were evidence of what continues.

Later Maggie set up her tent. She remembered the last time she had rolled her sleeping bag out, below Sunbreak Crag with Sarah. She put Sarah's tiny willow deer on her pillow and traced its twig bones. Only then did she wonder where Deacon was.

NEXT MORNING they waited a half hour for Deacon. Karen, their boat-woman, said, "I'm sorry, Maggie. We're on a tight schedule." She laughed rue-fully. "So, you guys can relax."

Maggie clipped in the river knife. "It's OK. He's got a really busy life." *Get over it, Deacon. Thank you, Deacon, I'd rather be alone. Plus, I won't have to call you Daniel.*

They climbed into the raft. Karen turned to her passengers. "You've got a smooth stretch to learn the signals. When I give them, don't think. Get them in your bloodstream.

"If we flip, or I yell FLIP, hang on tight, take three big deep breaths, and hold 'em. If you go in, trust your jacket. Once you're up, point your feet down-stream. There's a boat behind us. You'll get picked up."

They learned to high-side. They learned to get down. "Get down," a male voice said from the back. "Wid yo' bad self." Maggie knew exactly what she'd see when she turned around: a flabby guy in his late forties with a Hard Rock Cafe T-shirt. Maggie trailed her hand in the icy water. "Take my brain," she whispered to the river. "So I won't spend the rest of the trip rehearsing the moment I clarify *wannabe* for him."

Karen pulled for shore. "Maggie," she said, "that's your kid, right?"

A lanky man stood at shoreline. Maggie's heart opened all the way. Her boy's gear was a gym bag and a daypack. He wore homey-in-the-hood shorts, black sneakers, and a brand-new Mighty Ducks cap. "That's him," Maggie said.

Karen beached the raft. "Hi," Deacon said, "I'm Daniel. Sorry for the mix-up. We got lost." Deacon stepped into the raft.

"OK, people," Karen said, "here we go." The joy in her voice was palpable. "Next services: seven days away."

DINNER FIRST NIGHT WAS RUMAKI. Turkey chili. Eggplant parmesan. Garlic bread. Caesar salad. Marionberry/rhubarb cobbler. There was wine. Beer. And for the metabolically and spiritually challenged, water.

Maggie watched her son move toward her like a great blue heron. Slow steps. His long neck. He took a full minute to fold himself down next to her.

"Pretty nice," he said. "Pretty cool of Dad to do this."

Maggie nodded. Anything she thought to say was wrong: *Well, your dad finally got something right. How's you boring wife? Your whining kid?*

"I really appreciate," he said, "that you've been calling me Daniel."

Oh swell. Who ARE you? Do you remember how we watched the moth become a candle? And how your hands moved over your guitar?

"Well, you're your own man now."

He smiled. "Not really."

Maggie waited.

"I'm Kelly and Shiloh's man, Maggie."

"I'm Mom, Daniel."

"Whoa."

"You're Daniel; I'm still Mom."

They were silent. Not quiet, but silent.

"Maggie," he said. "Let's just let it go. OK?" He stood up faster than a great blue heron ought to be able to.

"Hey," Maggie said, but before she could say she was sorry, he was a shadow against the river.

JESSE drove an old road become new, the long wearisome hump from Kayenta to Tuba quietly beautiful. He was in love with the fleshy sandstone pouring back into dark canyons at Tsegi; in love with the guy pissing on the Black Mesa Mine slurry line supports; with every sign that said, "Warning. Do not enter if flooded." And, while he and Ralph wouldn't be able to sleep in the Flamingo Motel in Flagstaff, due to its having been annihilated to provide room for what was easily the ugliest big box bookstore in America, there would be El Charro mariachi and Mexican chicken-fried steak.

He scratched Ralph's ears and thought about Flagstaff midnights. How the sky was shiny as obsidian, how the stars brushed the top of your head, how a skinny young guy with what seemed like a constant hard-on could hardly wait to get away from all of it, sky, stars, cops, and boredom. How that kid had listened to Cream and thought about what the "white room" held and how the line about not being secured with strings was the truest thing he knew.

"Ralph," he said, "I'm still skinny, the hard-ons eased off a little, but I might be ready to tie it up with somebody besides you."

The sun headed down toward the North Rim of the canyon. A plume of smoke towered between the truck and the dying light. When Jesse looked east, he saw the shadow of his truck racing across the red sand.

"Holy fuck, Ralph," he said, "we're a couple lucky old dogs."

MAGGIE tossed the remains of her meal into the willows. She guessed she was probably not supposed to do that, but she figured they could tell it to the ravens and ringtails. She carried the empty plate to the kitchen. Karen looked up. "Anything I can do," Maggie said. "I need to get busy."

"You can wash dishes," Karen said. "Katz is setting up the system."

Maggie followed him. "You OK?" Katz said.

"What are you?" Maggie laughed. "A shrink?"

"Yeah," Katz said quietly. "When I want to be."

"Well then," she said. "I'm about as good as a mom with the maternal instincts and expertise of an amoeba can be with her pissed-off grown kid about four boulders away."

Katz nodded. "Let it be," he said, and pointed to the washtub of dishes. "Get your hands in that warm water and forget everything you can't forget."

Maggie crouched at the washtub. She looked out over the black river. The light above the canyon wall was thin blue. She closed her eyes and plunged her hands into the suds.

MINNIE walked away, back straight, black hair rippling over her shoulders. She was barefoot, her toes splayed wide. She stepped out across the packed red sand, arms swinging.

Sarah watched. She wanted to cry out one last good-bye, but she saw Minnie stoop for a basket in the sand and set it on her head. A scrawny yellow dog appeared at her side. Minnie snapped her fingers. The dog followed.

They moved up onto a sandstone ridge, past a few scraggly Joshua trees, up the long slope of a dark mountain. Vultures circled above them. The wind carried Minnie's laugh back to her. Then Minnie and the little dog were gone.

Sarah watched the empty sky. She waited. She knew this country. If you waited, something would tell you when to go. Thunder would move you toward shelter. Sun would move you toward shade. Where she stood was perfect, a circle of sweet gloom in a greater brightness.

The shadows shuddered as though she stood under a great cottonwood. At a curve in the trail ahead, a great boulder offered the next shade. Sarah moved out into the sunlight and was surprised to find she did not feel heat. A few steps away from the boulder, she saw it was a crouching ape, stone supple as muscle, stone solid with life. She stepped into its shadow. She pressed her hands against its cold surface, pressed until her hands ached. "I'm ready," she said. "I'm ready to go."

Imagine a woman falling into a boulder. Imagine a woman falling into night. Imagine a woman finding herself flying above a great river. Imagine Sarah on her way home.

JESSE picked up fried chicken at the Bellemont Truck Stop, listened to the waitress bitch to the busboy about the walled development going in just off 40. He wondered who would want to live less than a quarter mile from a highway, and then he remembered there was a rich boys' biker bar on the other side of the road and figured if you build it, god help you, they will come.

It was dark by the time he turned off the highway toward his place. Ralph was asleep. Two fried chicken breasts would do that to an old guy.

Jesse pulled up to the buried knife. He turned off the headlights. He could find the knife blind. The sand was still a little warm. He looked up and saw Orion slipping up from behind the eastern mountains. The Mojave was moving into the Season of Bliss. Soft days, sweet cool nights.

Jesse felt the dull blade under his fingers. Later, he would bring it into the trailer and hold it in the yellow light of the kerosene lantern. He'd study the animals carved into the handle, the figures that could be dogs or apes. Neither Xi nor Yuan had been able to tell him what they were—not because it was secret, but because only the carver who had dreamed the animals knew their names.

The moon followed Orion. Jesse woke Ralph, and they walked slowly along the road. He circled his wrist with his right hand. The new bracelet was already familiar. He thought he might give it to Maggie. He wondered where she was.

MAGGIE woke to the sound of the river, the rise and fall of a dark whisper, the clatter of pebbles at shoreline. She said good-bye to her fantasy of Deacon falling into her arms crying with gratitude over their reunion. She felt fortunate that she desperately needed to take a piss. Otherwise, it would have been too easy for her to hide in the tent till somebody rolled her up and carried her to the raft.

She was the third human awake. Karen made coffee. Her husband, Fish, set out donuts and all the healthy stuff everybody would eat after they'd obliterated the donuts. Maggie found her way to the groover, pulled down her shorts, and peed. The river ran directly in front of her, an eddy like a swirl of malachite just beyond the broken shoreline.

Maggie patted herself dry. She couldn't remember ever enjoying a piss quite as much, unless it was the time she had just made it into the filthy Vegas john.

Karen greeted her with a mug of coffee, waved her toward the breakfast table. "Whatever you want. The donuts are from a little bakery in Flagstaff. Fish is 100 percent buy local." She waved toward Fish. "Look at that puppy," she said. "He is such a fine little pain in the ass."

DEACON waited till the rafts were nearly loaded to ask Fish if he could ride with him. "Dead DC," Maggie said to the brilliant sky, "your plan isn't working."

Karen rowed perfectly through House Rock Rapid and Redneck. Joe Cool made an obligatory joke about rednecks. Karen let Maggie take the oars through a smooth stretch. "Follow the bubble line. The current does the work."

Maggie laughed. "Not quite my style."

They zinged through Indian Dick Rapid. Joe Cool was silent. Maggie was grateful. "We're going to ace these next two rapids," Karen said. "They're sixes, tops. But we're going to scout Twenty-four and a Half. We probably don't have to, but there's a nasty hole there and you need to learn the basics of a scout."

The scout at Twenty-four and a Half seemed to take forever. The sun burned logic out of Maggie's brain, so that Karen's perfectly reasonable explanations of current and bubble line and flow sounded like Sanskrit. Deacon stayed behind on the beach. Maggie looked down on him from the scout trail. "I'm sorry, Deac," she whispered.

Maggie looked down into the hole and saw what seemed the cold eye of malice. She remembered Karen's words the night before: "If you go into a hole, swim into it. It'll spit you out—if you're lucky."

A waist-high chunk of purple volcanic rock lay between Maggie and the river. She touched it. The stone was hot, its broken edges sharp as glass. She ran her finger lightly over the boulder. There was no cautery for fear. She looked back into the hole. There was nowhere left to go but downriver.

Karen gathered them on the beach. "Remember what I told you. Three deep breaths. And, if you go in, look for an old guy. Bert Loper flipped here and died in 1940. He was seventy-nine, and rumor is he'd checked himself out of an old people's home for his last run. I can't think of a better way to go."

Karen's entry into the rapid was smooth. "Check out that hole," she yelled back. The whirlpool looked bottomless.

"Hang on," Karen yelled. The world spun. Maggie was in the water under the raft. There was nowhere to take three breaths. She remembered the cargo netting, reached up, felt her fingers hook in the web. She had no idea which way to go, went anyway, and felt herself free and rising.

She surfaced, tried to take three breaths, and found herself sucking foam. She sank. Into vast blue-green light.

Something dark moved toward her. Sarah drifted in front of her. "You're wearing my earrings," Sarah said. "Good. I won't need them. I'm free. They are yours."

Maggie touched the lightning bolt. "You're here."

Sarah smiled. "Thank you for everything."

"What did I do?"

"You got me a job making fry bread," Sarah said.

"God damn it, Sarah, I already miss you so much."

"That's how it is when you love somebody," Sarah said. "I'm not going to give you any blather about the hereafter. Love is what you got now girlfriend. And, missing the people you love when they're gone."

"Swell," Maggie said. "What do we do now?"

"We say good-bye."

Maggie suddenly remembered the two red pins in Lucy's map. "Wait. Who killed you? Who killed Leola? You must know by now."

"I know who killed me," Sarah said. "He is a boy with an ancient heart. He is, as I was, part Vietnamese and part American. He was born here, but he carried an old old story. He had no choice. He was burned raw by crack. He couldn't have known why he had to kill me the way he did, but he knew he had too."

"But where is he? What if he kills again?"

"They'll find him. That's part of the story. And, it doesn't really matter *who* he was. *What* he was has always been and always will be. *It* is everywhere."

"Yes," Maggie said. The blue-green light grew colder. She could go into it. She would be sublimated as snow goes to vapor.

Sarah grabbed Maggie's life jacket. "*It* can come into any of us. Fight it."

Maggie was silent.

"Girlfriend," Sarah said, "I don't have much longer. I want you to know that my part of that old old story is over. I have finished it. Now it's your turn." She touched Maggie's hand.

Maggie took hold of Sarah's fingertips. "I'll take my chance."

Sarah was gone.

Maggie's cells yowled for air. The blue-green glittered white.

"Maggie. We've got you. Help us, damn it."

Maggie hated it when guys snapped at her, but these guys were saving her life. Fish grabbed her wrist. She grabbed his. He pulled, and she was in. Sarah's earrings were still in Maggie's ears. Somebody yelled, "Twenty-five on us. Heads up."

Maggie saw Karen sailing by on the bottom of the upturned raft. They watched her perfect unaided run, saw her eddy out, wave and wait.

They glided out of Twenty-five and moved toward shore. Joe Cool sat blank-eyed in the back of their raft. Deacon had his arm around the guy.

"Hey," Deacon said, "that was cool."

"It was, Daniel," Maggie said. "But, only because I'm alive." She wished he'd called her Mom. And then, as she saw how relieved he looked, she understood "Mom" wasn't granted by giving birth, or a spectacular near-death experience. "Mom" was a gift on the bubble line.

34 Jesse bedded down in the ramada, Ralph stretched out at his feet. The stars shimmered beyond the juniper boughs. Plane lights webbed the soft dark. He wondered why he had wanted to leave the desert. Ralph frog-crawled to Jesse's hand. "I think us being bachelors is short." Jesse scratched Ralph's head. "I think our time alone together is so short you could fit both of us in a matchbox."

Orion strode in perfect silence across the beautiful and compromised dark. "We're going to Sacaton Canyon tomorrow," Jesse said. "We'll go slow, stop when you need to. I want to see what's up there again."

JESSE AND RALPH were perched on a ledge at the end of Sacaton. Skull Rock stared out over Creosote. Jesse had never known if *Skull Rock* was written on any map, but when he'd seen the huge sockets in the boulder's face and the curve of a giant's bony cheekbone, he had known. He and Ralph were having a snack in the hanging garden that looked down on the skull. Peanuts, one warm beer, and a cold burger.

"It's too easy," he said. Ralph paused mid-gulp. Jesse nodded. "Yeah, I'm talking to you." He tilted out the last of the beer. "It's too easy to think that's Death looking down, making some kind of judgment about Creosote."

He thought of Ray and Helen and all the other grunts busting their asses to earn a living down there, and the even more people handing their livings over to the suits in Vegas. "I'm one of all of them," he said. "I sell three dollars worth of obsidian and bone for thousands of bucks to guys who never go far from their eight-thousand-square-foot mansions or their corner offices. And, I tithe a fifth of my earnings to the suits who own the blackjack tables. Same same, dog-san."

He took Maggie's letter from his pack and opened it for the tenth time.

Dear Jesse,

    I hope this finds you. I have been traveling with Sarah's ghost for a few months and now I am alone. I'm meeting my kid at Lee's Ferry so we can float in a fucking boat for a week. I keep wanting to turn around and forget the whole thing. You probably have no idea what I'm talking about, but I just need to say it to you. Sarah, that is, her ghost, you don't know about her ghost, isn't here anymore, and she was the only person I could talk to . . .

    That isn't all . . .

Jesse looked up. The skull still looked out over Creosote. Ralph still licked his chops. But Jesse could hear the Freedom Bird coming in for the landing. He patted Ralph's bony back. "Get ready, my man," he said. "Our big lonelies are so short, they're almost gone."

IT WAS SUDDENLY the last night of the trip. "River time is like that," Karen said. "Long long days and then, bam, it's over." They camped just above Hance Rapid. Maggie helped unload, set up her tent, and walked down to the shoreline. She stood in the cold green water hidden by gold coyote willow for what seemed hours. She heard the voice of her tripmates. It worried her that she felt muzzily affectionate. It worried her that she had been having thoughts of a commune. Acres of land with separate dwellings, being alone, being near neighbors. She was saved by the knowledge that it was precisely that fantasy that was driving the subdividing of the best of the west, a fact she had not known prior to Fish's "Gated Ghetto Blues."

> There's coots in the duck pond;
> the elk ate my lupine;
> my wife's drunk at the clubhouse,
> under the security guard who's supine.

She and Deacon had maintained careful kindness. She figured she had twenty-four hours left to make her move, whatever that was. She had a little chat with Dead DC, pointed out to him that for once he better follow up on a grand gesture. There was, as there had nearly always been, no response.

"Hey," Deacon called, "Maggie, where are you?"

"I'm down here."

"Come up to your camp," Deacon said. "You'll love this."

Her dry bag lay empty on the sand. Clothes, books, and her last bag of Basha's superlative potato chips were scattered everywhere. A tube of toothpaste lay at the periphery. One hole had been poked in it. The chip bag was empty.

Deacon pointed to the ground. Raven prints covered the sand. "Oh my god," he said. "They even checked out the toothpaste. And went, 'No way!'"

"My chips," Maggie said. "Those fuckers got my potato chips."

"Hang on," Deacon said. "Are you really mad?"

She sat down next to him. "Daniel, they got my favorite chips."

He looked at her sidewise, his eyes slitted. "Mom . . . I mean, Maggie . . . I mean Mom. You're fooling."

"Hey," she said. "It's me. It's us. You don't have to call me Mom. I haven't earned it." Maggie traced a raven track with her finger. She wished she knew how to pray. "Besides, your wife calls me mom."

Deacon sighed, "Seems like she calls everybody mom."

Maggie sensed a crack in the wall. "I want to see you and Jeannie and the kid more often," was the best she can do.

Deacon glared at her. "The *kid's* name is Shiloh."

Maggie bit her tongue.

There was an eternal silence. Finally Deacon shrugged. "OK, Shiloh's middle name is Margaret."

"Why?"

"Because of the moth," Deacon said. "You know that candle? It couldn't possibly have burned as long as it did. But, it did. I guess, even with all that mental health stuff about letting go, some kids never give up."

"In that event," Maggie said, "how about if we sneak down to the kitchen and see if we can find the Pringles." *I love you. Daniel Deacon Duncan, I love you and I am sorry.*

"You know," Deacon said, "I normally hate those jive-ass things, but down here they taste like kettle chips from Heaven."

IT RAINED a little in the night. Rare for Jesse's chunk of the Mojave, but not unheard of. Jesse woke in the ramada to the scent of wet juniper. Ralph lay on his back, his big paws in the air, his tongue hanging out of his mouth. The first time he did it, Jesse's heart had jumped. Now he knew Ralph was simply a master of canine yoga.

Jesse started breakfast. While he waited for the water to boil, he opened the trunk at the foot of his bed and found the blackout curtains. It would be a good day for a bonfire.

Ralph scratched at the screen door. "What do you think, old guy?" Jesse said. "How about we burn these old blackout curtains and then grab a few steaks and take them over to Helen and Ray?" The coffee boiled up. Jesse turned off the stove. Darwin had taught him to brew coffee that way. "Injun coffee," he had said. "It'll rip your heart out."

Jesse draped the blackout curtains over his arm, grabbed the gas can from the back of the truck, and carried everything to the rusted oil drum at the edge of his property. He watched the clouds scud in. He remembered monsoons slamming down from the sacred mountains into Flagstaff—and monsoons boiling in the red dirt of Lang Bu. One hundred and seventy miles away. Ten thousand and farther.

The air was fat with rain coming. He threw the curtains in the barrel and splashed in gas. The fumes yanked him back to the charred coyote pups. He bowed his head. "Thank you, whatever you are, for making me run from what might have locked up my heart forever."

He lit his old Zippo and tossed it in.

The curtains flared; a thread of black smoke rose. Jesse hoped the fire patrol boys weren't up early. The smoke thinned and was gone.

THEY PULLED ONTO THE BEACH at Phantom Ranch. Maggie walked up to the store. There were brownies, fresh-made lemonade, and an abundance of half-naked gorgeous young men. She bought a brownie, lemonade, five postcards, put on her shades for boy watching, and walked to the beach to begin the rest of her life.

She was amazed how easy it was. You inhaled the brownie, chugged the lemonade, and in the flash of carbo-bliss you realized all the boys looked alike. So you wrote to the people you loved—most of whom had wrinkles.

The postcards would be stamped: *Carried by pack-mule from the bottom of the Grand Canyon.* When the lucky recipients read the cards, they would know that Maggie Foltz sat in the heart of her life and thought of them.

Dear Daniel, Jeannie, and Shiloh,

What are you doing for Thanksgiving?

love, Maggie

Dear Helen and Ray,

Two nights ago, we had Dutch oven ham and beans. I thought of you. No offense, Ray.

love, Maggie

Dear Jesse,

See you soon.

itsa Maggie

Dear Sarah,

I am taking what is left of you home. I will miss you till we meet again.

love, Maggie

35 Maggie wondered if she would live long enough to keep the promises she had made on the postcards. The last mile of switchbacks up the Bright Angel Trail had so far lasted twelve centuries. Maggie talked to the Big Whatevers under her breath. "If you let me live through this with an intact back so I can fool around again, I swear I will never, ever tell one of my clients they need professional mental health help. I will do nothing but nod and murmur soothing things."

The beauty of the canyon was lost on her. She was bloated by heat and lingering PMS. All the beauty she wanted to see was the elegant hulk of the El Tovar Lodge and the words Iced Coffee on the menu.

JESSE was driving down the long slope to the bridge when he saw a slash of white glowing on the rock to his left. He slowed. A jack-off in a Hummer cut in front of him. Jesse wished for the thousandth time that he had an antiaircraft gun mounted on the hood of his truck. And then he forgot about jack-offs and Hummers and revenge because he could read the graffiti: "Bonnie Madrid, I love you still."

"Cowbird," Jesse said to Ralph. "I wish I'd thought of that."

He suddenly knew what his note to Maggie would say. He pulled a U-turn, parked in the sand below the graffiti, pulled out a pad and pencil, and began to write. Two copies. He'd drop Ralph and the note at Ray and Helen's, promise steaks all around, and head into Creosote. He figured to play it safe, he'd drop the second copy of the note at the Riverbelle Human Resources office.

MAGGIE slept through the long Greyhound ride to Kingman, woke long enough to buy Helen a string of fuchsia lucky beads and eat a burger and fries. She had one last promise to keep before she could settle into "chop wood, carry water," and obsessing about Jesse calling.

"Phone Time," she muttered to herself. Phone Time, as in waiting for aeons, as in not yanking the receiver from the cradle and smashing it on the floor, as in not making yourself go out on an errand, because then at least you would have the pleasure of thinking the message light might be blinking when you got home.

She told herself at least she didn't have e-mail or a fucking cell phone, and she knew one thing: It was Jesse's move. She had done everything she could.

HELEN wanted to read Jesse's note.

"For cryin' out loud," Ray said. "It's none of your beeswax."

"In a way it is," she said. "Those two are like the kids we *should* have had."

"Then what you're conniving them into is incest."

"Oh that's nice," she said. "That's a real nice mouth you got on you."

She folded her arms over her bosom. Ray stared out the window. They had been known to stay in these positions at least an ice age. Ray decided he'd rather have the thaw. He took the note out of his pocket.

Helen set her jaw. "Come on," Ray said. "You know you hate being mad at me." He handed her the note.

"That man," she said. "You know those femlib women are right. Men have a learning disability in sweet talk."

"What's it say?"

Maggie. Drive out by that stretch of cliff just past the Ransom Dam turnoff. There's graffiti on the eastern cliff. Use your imagination. And, think about maybe going on a date with me. Jesse p.s. I'll have to bring Ralph Too.

"That's gonna get her heart going pitty-pat," Helen said. "Besides, what the hell does it mean?"

Ray pulled himself up. "We'll just drive out there and find out."

"I am so glad neither of us is nosy."

Ralph looked up. "You bet, buddy," Ray said. "We're going in the Malibu." Ray's tail thumped on the floor. Ray hadn't had the heart to tell Jesse about Ralph's vehicular infidelity.

MAGGIE couldn't wait to get off the bus. She wanted to run home to her apartment. Get busy. Start unpacking. But Road Time was melding into Phone Time, so she decided to pick up the Bird, drive out to Helen and Ray's, not out of any particular hope that Jesse had left her a note, but because she needed to return Helen's Buddha. She found herself humming the opening to Alvin Bishop's "Fooled Around and Fell in Love," and knew she was kidding herself. You could fool a fan but you couldn't fool a player.

The bus was almost to the bridge. Just opposite the Ransom Dam turnout, a flicker of white caught her eye: "Bonnie Madrid, I love you still." Cowbird had sure enough tended the little candle glowing in the creosote of his heart.

RAY AND HELEN'S beater Malibu was gone from the driveway. Maggie tried the trailer door. She was in, and astonished to see four hundred dollar bills in the center of the coffee table. She could hear Helen, "Hey, easy come, easy go." She set the Buddha down on top of the bills and draped the lucky beads around his neck.

There was no note for Maggie anywhere. *No note. For Maggie.*

All she had to do was drive out to Jesse's trailer; if she'd been the Maggie she'd once been, she would. But, she was neither the Maggie to whom a note would not have been written, nor the Maggie who had plenty of ways to not care whether or not a note had been written.

She sat at the dinette table and considered tucking her hands under her butt. If she—the new Maggie who was worth a guy crawling on his belly over Mojave August noon desert to get to—sat on her hands, she could not put them on the Bird's steering wheel and drive out into the same old, same old.

Maggie sat at the dinette table a long time. She loved the silence and the rose-blue twilight. She understood she was hugely tired. She had a sitting-up dream. In it, Sarah was not alone. Sarah and a black-haired man floated around the peak of a mountain whose long southern slope was a twin of Fuji-yama's. The two clouds drifted. They did not settle. They circled for seasons, years, centuries, and floated away to the west.

Maggie drove home in light the grimy sheen of the breast feathers of the Riverstroll pigeons. Smoke billowed up from the generating station. The volcanic hills went black. She saw the silhouette of an old mine shack and an ocean of what newcomers always called *Nothing*. She remembered the years when she believed that the only place she would ever live was in the guts of a hard and crowded city.

No more.

JESSE had no trouble persuading the head of Human Resources to let him leave a note on Maggie's desk because the head of Human Resources was not there. There was a preprinted card with a little clock set at 3:00: "Be back soon. Ready to make your employee experience at the Riverbelle a happy one." It was 4:45.

Jesse sat in Maggie's chair. It tilted to the side. The desk was an old Formica table. Red boomerangs on black. You'd almost not know it was Maggie's desk, except for the strings of Crazy Creek Mardi Gras beads wound around the pen holder. He taped his note to the scarlet beads. No one showed up. He decided to go up to the Blue Velvet room and have a happy experience with an enchilada special.

Bitsy was on. She wore the brave and weary smile of the perpetual victim. He considered leaving and grabbing a beer and late breakfast at the Sandbar, but she had spotted him.

"Jesse," she said wanly. "How *are* you?"

"Great," he said. "Hungry." She looked crestfallen.

Jesse sighed. He was trapped. "I mean, I just got off the road and I'm starving. I figure you were on and I knew you'd make me the best waffle in Creosote." He didn't want to say the next words, but it was as though good kind Ralph Two was running his mouth. "How you doing?"

"Well," Bitsy said, "now you heard what happened to me over at that snooty Cachet?" Before Jesse could answer, "Yeah, about four thousand times," she steam-rollered on. "About that rich woman and all. Well you won't believe it, there's more."

By the time she finished her story, a four-top of natty golfsters had given up waving feebly and Jesse had eaten six packages of crackers. He ordered, and as Bitsy wandered away, he wondered if he should suggest she go down and talk to the new crisis specialist in Human Resources.

MAGGIE set Sarah's ashes on the sill of the west window before she unpacked. She would next be gone for two days and one night. When she returned, she must return to *home*. She set the moth candleholder on the dresser and lit it. She threw out all the suspect food in the fridge. She unpacked the Ka'gsi'ki shawl from the cardboard box and unfolded it on her bed.

It was past midnight when she finished her work. Maggie slipped naked under the shawl. She ran her fingers over the woven creatures that were also places. *Black Peak, Beartrack, Willow Springs, Star Giant, Sacred Blood Mountain, Sunbreak Crag, Cottonwood Springs.*

She did not dream, and when she woke before dawn she was afraid and sad about every part of her life. After her first three sips of coffee, she wondered why there was no religion that held coffee to be a sacrament. She was no longer afraid, and the only sadness in her heart was that she would not see Sarah suddenly appear in the passenger seat of the Bird. She tucked the willow deer in her jacket pocket. "Always," she said. "What we are."

MAGGIE drove straight through Vegas. It was just before midnight when she pulled up to Hannah's trailer. The place was dark. Maggie crawled into the backseat of the Bird, curled up, pulled the Ka'gsi'ki shawl over her, and settled in. There was a gentle tap on the window. "Maggie," Hannah said. "Come in. You must be starving."

Maggie threw the shawl over the box of Sarah's ashes and locked the Bird. "You don't have to do that," Hannah said. "We're not like some people."

"Sarah," Maggie said, "is in the box."

"So," Hannah said, "bring her in."

She went up the steps into the trailer. Maggie wrapped the box in the women's shawl and followed Hannah in.

"Sit down," Hannah said. "I'll nuke what's left from supper." She slid four dishes into the microwave and put salad and home-baked rolls on the table. "There's mutton stew and mac and cheese, some of my mom's hominy and her apple cobbler."

Maggie still held Sarah's ashes. "Where should we put these?"

Hannah pursed her lips toward the top of the TV. "Up there is good. Sahmi can't reach it."

Maggie carried the box over and set it next to a new picture of Lorinda. Her hair had been styled in a power cut. She wore a wine-red suit, little gold earrings, low-heeled teal pumps. She smiled directly into the camera. "That's from when we visited the business college down in Phoenix, Arizona," Hannah said. "She was so proud of herself."

"When did you go?"

"Back in early August."

"Damn," Maggie said.

"Really," Hannah said, "I liked to died. Ladies our age need to stay out of that kind of heat."

Maggie was only a little surprised that they were having a conversation ladies their age could be having anywhere, while the ashes of one lady's beloved niece who was the other lady's best friend rested on top of the TV. She'd learned enough about death in the last few months to regard the ashes, the perfect mutton stew, and the words moving out easily from her lips as spokes on some big wheel rolling.

"I brought the women's shawl for Lorinda."

"She's doing her next Ka'gsi'ki ceremony when she comes home from school in December," Hannah said. "I just hope she doesn't get so citified she forgets who she is."

"Not likely," Maggie said. "Not with Sarah watching her back."

Hannah pushed the cobbler toward her. "You better eat this," she said. "You need to keep your strength up so you can tell me everything."

"SARAH'S gone on."

"I guessed that. When Minnie passed over, I knew. Her body disappeared from that nursing home. Her people were carrying on fit to kill. Hypocrites. Next thing you know, they go out to her trailer to fight over her stuff. There was nothing there. Not a piece of furniture, not a bag of sugar, not one of her special things."

"Huh," Maggie said. "What a shame."

Maggie spooned the cobbler into her mouth. There was syrup and cinnamon and butter easy on her tongue. The apples were tart. "This is wonderful," she said.

"My mom has a few apple trees up near a little spring," Hannah said. "The County man told her she wouldn't be able to grow them because the soil is too acid. But, she read everything she could about apples and figured out ashes would sweeten the dirt. Good thing we've got some."

Maggie put down her spoon. "Sarah told me she was so sad they had cremated her, because she wanted her body to be food."

"Apples," Hannah said. "They're prettier than old turkey buzzards."

36 Maggie drove home in peace. She had a bag of home-dried berries and a peck of Violet's apples. She and Hannah had planned to meet in Vegas in November. There was going to be a Native American entrepreneurs' convention at the Plaza. Hannah had one of Minnie's Rainbow Casino hats for good luck.

Maggie camped at Cottonwood Springs. She curled up in the backseat of the Bird. She could hear water trickling into the little sandy basin. There was a nightwind in the cottonwoods. Still, she couldn't sleep. She wished she had thoughts of Jesse-for-sure to lull herself to sleep with. And, she knew Jesse-for-sure was no way near as intriguing as Jesse-for-maybe.

A car cruised in. She heard two people walk down to the pool. There were whispers, giggles, the sound of boots thudding to the ground. There were sounds that did anything but lull her to sleep.

She remembered nights lying next to DC's rigid body, listening to the sounds of the couple next door, and how she had believed that not just her heart but every cell in her body would shatter from loneliness. *This time,* she ran her fingers over her face, touched her lips, and laughed softly. *This time.* Jesse or no Jesse, she would never be that lonely again.

JESSE cleaned. He'd always been a tidy guy, but he scrubbed the sink and heated water in the old tub so he could wash his two sheets. "We're going to dry 'em on the creosote," he told Ralph Too. "No woman can resist sun-dried sheets—if I can get that woman here, that is."

He started pacing while the water was heating up. "For chrissakes," he said, "she's just a woman. At least half the people in Nevada are broads. Women. Broads. Jesse, calm the fuck down."

It was noon by the time he had the sheets clean and ready to hang. He wrung them out by hand. He thought of whoever once batched it in this place. He'd found the old sardine cans, sun-lavendered whiskey bottles, and mouse-eaten long johns of what he'd always assumed was a spectacularly unlucky prospector. Did the guy sit in the door of his shack, with a bundle of soapy long johns in his banged-up hands, and wonder: is this as good as it's going to be? Was the guy a woman, some fierce, withered, and blazing green-eyed old broad who'd once, just once, had her heart broken?

Jesse unfurled the faded green sheet into the air onto the spiky branches of the old creosote. The old *Lion King* sheet he'd picked up at the Searchlight Goodwill was a bright banner against the sky. He tossed the pillowcases over a couple more bushes and stopped.

Now what. There were two forks, knives, spoons, and steak knives to polish—if he were crazy, if he weren't a man with a hundred bucks in his pocket and a good dog who knew how to behave under a blackjack table—a smart dog who had been trained to sense his master's nonexistent fits.

"Ralph," Jesse yelled, "we're going in the truck."

MAGGIE drove home before she did anything. She wanted to race out to Helen and Ray's so bad her bones ached, but she remembered her thought at Cottonwood Springs. *Jesse or no Jesse, I will never be that lonely again.*

A woman with a home, not just a studio, but a home with soft yellow light glowing from the eastern window, did not need to be lonely. Maggie carried her road gear and food up the stairs. She started to check the answering machine and remembered she had yet to replace the one she had smashed.

She took a deep breath. *I'll just take my time here. I'm going to make a pot of coffee, put a new candle in the moth holder, and see if my vibrator still works, and if it doesn't, I'll have a short nervous breakdown.* She started the coffee. There were no candles. The vibrator was somewhere in an unlabeled box.

She poured coffee and sat on the balcony with the phone. Before she settled into her nervous breakdown, she would call Lucy. She wouldn't call Helen and Ray to see if there was The Message for Maggie. She was now a warrior woman, a woman who had lived through rapid Twenty-four and a Half of the raging Colorado. She was chicken.

Lucy told Maggie she had information, but she wanted to talk face to face. The ShirleySal, a little after five.

It was noon. Five fucking hours to go. Warrior woman took a shower. She ate a handful of Hannah's dried berries, opened the first packing box, looked into pure chaos, and closed it. 12:30. Four and a half fucking hours to go.

Maggie studied herself in the foyer mirror. She saw the new silver strands weaving through her red hair. Sarah's earrings caught light. "Big chicken Maggie," she said. "Big chicken chick."

"OK, when the going gets tough, the tough go gambling."

THERE WERE THE SMOKED-GLASS DOORS. There was her hand pushing them open. There was fifty thousand square feet of Christmas morning. The Riverbelle dealers looking a hell of a lot like Santa's helpers.

Maggie decided to check her desk in Human Resources before she hit the Cleopatra twenty-line slot near the doors to the river. The office was empty, and there was a note taped to her Crazy Creek Mardi Gras beads. She opened it.

Maggie. Drive out by that stretch of rock just past the Ransom Dam turnoff. There's graffiti on the eastern cliff. Use your imagination. And, think about maybe going on a date with me. Jesse p.s. I'll have to bring Ralph Too.

A date? A fucking date? The graffiti against the dark rock: "Bonnie Madrid, I love you still." Maggie used her imagination, and then she was sobbing all over the words she hadn't imagined she would ever read. She cried until it felt like the only thing left to do was hydrate and win some nickels. Jesse was a smart fellow. He'd figure out how to find her.

She tucked the note in her breast pocket, draped the beads around her neck, and headed upstairs. The elevator doors opened. She was home.

"Hey," a chubby brunette in slot manager maroon yelled, "welcome back." Maggie waved. The chubby blonde headed for the bank of Double Diamond machines, where another chubette in a platinum wig high-fived her. "Hey, Betty Lou." The slot manager put her hands on her hips. "Hey, Peggy Sue."

Maggie hotfooted it for Cleo. She skidded into the seat just as a grim-faced woman in tasteful beige linen came around the corner. "Oh," the woman said, "I was planning to play that machine." Maggie had heard the words before, she had said the words herself, but she had no mercy. "Possession is nine-tenths of the law," she said crisply and slid in a five.

The woman sat next to her and slid a Jackson into Silver Moon. "Oh," she said, "you only play twenty at a time."

"I work for a living," Maggie said.

The woman smiled foggily. "I understand how you feel. I'm a licensed psychologist."

Maggie nodded. The woman played out her hundred, kicked the machine, and was gone. Something continued to be lacking in Maggie's relationship with Cleo. She wasn't exactly losing, but the credits steadily hovered around a hundred. Five bucks. There was something familiar about this stasis, something akin to her former lifetime of loser love.

Maggie decided to mosey over to the Tidewater, see how the feral cats were doing and maybe give blackjack a shot. She took off the Mardi Gras beads that marked her as a slot weenie and put on her shades. She checked her watch. 2:30. *I am warrior woman. I am not going to race home and wait for the phone to ring.*

JESSE couldn't believe his luck. Rather his lack of it. Ralph was asleep with his head on Jesse's foot. Otherwise Jesse would have been long gone. The cold-hearted Tidewater dealer, who a few weeks ago had been Jesse's best friend, dealt himself a king and hauled in everybody's chips.

"It ain't personal," he said.

Jesse shoved his last two chips forward. He had one more twenty in his back pocket, enough gas for the round-trip to the trailer, and a couple thousand in a coffee can under his bed.

Ralph jolted up, slammed his head on the rung of Jesse's stool, and whimpered. "Jesse," the dealer said, "you got one of those fits, which I have never seen you have, coming on?"

Maggie sat calmly down next to Jesse. He turned. "Oh yes, I sure do have one of those fits coming on, I surely do."

Maggie looked puzzled. "You don't have fits."

The dealer grinned. "I knew it."

"What fits?" Maggie said. Jesse nudged her ankle.

"Ohhh." she said. "*Those* fits."

"You in?" the dealer said.

"Oh yes," Maggie said, "I surely am." She bought twenty bucks' worth of chips.

"So," Jesse said, "did you get my note?"

MAGGIE AND JESSE were both broke by the time they left the table. "I'll see you at the ShirleySal after Lucy and I finish up, probably about six," Maggie said.

"I'm going home for money," Jesse said. "A guy can't take a woman on a date without money."

Maggie started to tell him about her abundant comps and realized she would never, ever, not *ever* foot the bill again. "You got that right."

The Riverstroll was the heart of a jeweled dream reeking of fast food. Maggie ran her fingers over the ShirleySal plaque, put her feet up on the railing, and watched the lights of high-roller private planes drop down into the Arizona airport. The Tidewater renegade DJ broadcast the sound track to *Boogie Nights*. Maggie had a cup of truly tragic coffee, a vastly overrated Crunchy Creme donut and a grown-up date ahead of her; so life could not have gotten much better.

Lucy sat down next to her. "You look different, girlfriend," she said.

"How?"

"My acute highly trained law enforcement officer observational skills tell me there is something going on in your love life."

"Mmmm," Maggie said. "Want this last donut?"

Lucy took the donut and broke it into chunks for the kamikaze pigeons. "You want to hear the news first, or tell me juicy stuff about your personal life?"

"News."

"Vegas has a suspect in Sarah's killing. I can't tell you too much, but he's a kid, a tweaker, half Vietnamese, half American, born here. He was part of a rat's-ass gang, what you might call the people on the periphery, dealing tweak, snatching purses, pathetic shit. One of his bros narced him out."

"Why'd he kill her? That way?"

"Hard to say. You know what tweak does."

"Why'd he kill Leola?"

"He didn't," Lucy said. "It turns out Leola was dishing out sweet grand-motherly advice on unions to the grunts here. Maybe somebody high up in the corporations decided to take her out, make it look like a pattern of mutilations. Some nut case, not nice respectable businessmen.

"It's going to take longer to untangle Leola's murder. But, I've got hope— and a staff of hundreds. Lots of the grunts are pissed off by Leola's murder; and they'll keep their ears open and their mouths shut till it's time to talk to us. Somebody will hear something. Some working girl. Some valet. You can bet I'm not turning loose of this."

"What about the picture of me?" Maggie paused. "The burned eyes."

Lucy looked out over the copper river. "It could have been the kid; it could have been CORPSE. It was definitely somebody who believed in the power of fear. My hunch is that it was done to keep up the pretense of a pattern. I think you're safe, but we're going to keep an eye on you now and then."

"Thanks," Maggie said. "But I find myself longing for the good old days of a clean baseball bat and cement wing tips."

"Yeah, this is nastier. What we're working with is going to go much bigger than two women's murders. Maybe we can prevent more."

Maggie remembered Pella, the hooker, talking about the Life: *It's easy to misplace a chick, 'specially if she ain't white. You realize you ain't seen Jasmon for a week, a month. You ask yourself when was the last time the sweet thing was sittin' right there, drinkin' her iced tea and waitin' to go on? Or Darnell's sister, D'Andree, the one who was so fussy about her nails and how she absolutely was goin' to the community college in the fall and get out of the life! Gone overnight.*

"There's one more thing," Lucy said. "We had a jumper a few days ago. Indian kid. He left a backpack. The only thing in it was a green head rag."

"He's a warrior," Maggie said. "Sarah won't be alone. His name was Will Lucas. He was from Bone Lake and he loved, he loves her."

Maggie untied Lorinda's bracelet from her wrist. "Have you got kids?"

"A daughter," Lucy said. "She's in the godhelpus times. She wears an armful of those bracelets, almost no clothes, and I get to play mom all alone."

Maggie handed Lucy the bracelet. "Sarah's half-sister gave me this. If your daughter wants it, it's hers."

"Thanks. I'll leave it somewhere so she can find it. If it comes from me, it's soooooooooo lame." Lucy tucked the bracelet in her shirt pocket. "I better get. We still try to eat supper together. It's my night to cook."

"I haven't had many women friends," Maggie said. "No time, not much interest. Maybe we could hang out?"

Lucy grinned. "We are. Besides, you still gotta tell me all the juicy boy stuff. It might give me hope."

MAGGIE walked down to the beach. Blue shadows raked the sand. A full moon crested the Black Mountains, burning big as the end of the world. Maggie slipped off her sandals and walked into the cold water. She scooped river into her hands and tossed it back. The spray glittered neon. She took the willow deer from her pocket and set it on the water. "Will Lucas, you go find Sarah," Maggie said. "You bring her so much mess around." A Jet Ski wave rocked the deer. And then, the river took the deer.

JESSE AND RALPH waited on the bench. Ralph wore a bright red bandana. Jesse held a white corsage box. He looked down at the beach. All he could see of Maggie was the back of her head and outstretched arms. She walked out of his sight.

He watched the steps up from the beach. She seemed to be taking her time. Maybe a year or so. When she first appeared, her eyes looked sad. And then she saw him, and he was looking at a barely legal girl on her first date. She walked slowly to the bench and stopped in front of him.

"You actually showed up," she said.

"Well, yeah. For fucksake, Maggie, why wouldn't I?"

She scooted Ralph over with her hips and sat next to him. "You are sooooo romantic."

Jesse held out the box. "I am."

"A corsage?" she said. "I hate dead flowers."

Jesse saw that the wish he once made in Helen's kitchen for ludicrously real love was coming true. "Just open the box."

She lifted the cover. "Oh no," she said. "This is not fair."

"You bet," Jesse said.

Maggie lifted out the mood ring. "Don't put it on yet," Jesse said. "Let me keep it for now." She handed the ring to him and took the blue harmonica from its nest of shredded newspaper.

"You owe it," Jesse said, "to Paul Butterfield."

"I was a guitarist," Maggie said. "I never played harp."

"I couldn't fit a guitar in a corsage box, woman. Jesus, now I sound like Ray." He handed her the instruction pamphlet he snagged from a local music store.

She laughed. "It says here, that if you can use your lips and fingers, you can play the blues."

"Yeah?"

"I have a much better idea."

AN HOUR OR SO LATER, after they had kissed and talked till their throats were dry, Maggie dropped her hand to Ralph's head. She knew she needed to ask Jesse to tell her the story she almost knew by heart.

"How," she said, "did Ralph Too get his name?"

Jesse wanted to bolt. He wanted to ask her if she wanted to hear for the hundredth time about Bitsy's awful luck at the Cachet or if she knew whether Bonnie had finally dumped Beltran. Any gossip, any happy horseshit.

He took Maggie's hand. "Me and Darwin were up in the hills above Lang Bu. We were about as weed-whacked as you could get and still be upright. The locals laced their shit with opium. Darwin finally gave up and lay down with his head on his pack. He kept sliding off. Each time he got the giggles worse, which in a plump Tuba City boy isn't a pretty sight.

"Every now and then he'd say, " 'Raaaaaalf. Raaaaalf. Ya A Tey. Raaaaalf.'

"I was so fucked up his words sounded like they were coming through

{ 278 }

jello. 'Raaaaalf. Raaaaalf.' I thought he was talking Navajo. Praying maybe. Chuck was everywhere that night and we were both scared silly.

" 'What's that mean?' I said. 'Raaaaaalf. Is it Navajo for Oh Jesus fucking Christ, get us out of this alive?' "

"My dog," Darwin said.

"It means 'my dog'?"

"Nooooooooo. Oh no," Darwin said. "I wet my pants."

"He grabbed the tree he was under and pulled himself up. I did the only thing that made sense, which was to roll another joint. Darwin pulled off his pants and sat down bare-assed on his poncho. 'Ralph,' he said, 'is the name of my dog.'

" 'Well, fuck,' I said, 'why didn't you just say that?' "

"I just did."

"Why Ralph?"

"Because, you dumb bilagáana, that's what dogs say. *Ralph. Ralph. Ralph.*"

Maggie knew the next part. She gave them both a little break. "What did Ralph One look like? Was he as devilishly handsome as this guy here?"

"I asked Darwin once. He said, 'He's a rez puppy. Whaddya think?' "

"Yellow," Maggie said. "Wormy. Ribs sticking out."

There was a long silence.

"And then," Jesse said, "you can guess. About Darwin."

Maggie waited. Jesse studied the river. "Listen," he said. "I was thinking about leaving Creosote."

Maggie smiled nicely. She wondered if the rich bitch had taken over the twenty-line Cleo machine and if the cocktail waitresses would serve you Tanqueray for free if you promised them a real King Kong Georgette tip. She figured she'd listen for two minutes more, then politely, with no bad feelings, none at all, snatch the mood ring from Jesse's hand and throw it in the river, then knock the motherfucker off the bench onto his chickenshit tragic vet-with-a-story ass.

Jesse looked at Maggie. The last time he'd seen a thousand-yard stare as bad as hers had been twenty-five years ago. "Hey," he said. "You don't have to listen. I know it gets boring listening to all those my-buddy's-brains-were-on-my-sleeve stories."

"What?"

"No, *you* what."

Maggie jammed the harmonica into his hand. "I don't really need to learn to play the blues, thank you very much."

"Wait," Jesse said. "Wait. Wait. Wait. That is the most times I ever said *Wait* to a woman."

"You've got one minute to change that part about leaving."

"I said I *thought* about leaving." He imagined Ray looking at him as though that look could pull Jesse through.

"I went back to Flagstaff to take care of some things, and it was cool and green and I got homesick, that's all. I came back here and knew this rat's-ass beautiful country is my home."

"Sure," Maggie said.

"Look," Jesse said. "Look at this pathetic river. Look at this insane light. Look at that guy over there."

A cadaverous fellow in an impeccable beige trench coat leaned on the railing and looked down at the beach. "Where else are you going to see Raincoat Carl? You know that guy. Carl "If you ain't playing the ponies, you ain't playing" Raincoat Carl. Watch."

A black long-haired cat with white feet and a Fu Manchu mustache hobbled up the beach stairs. Raincoat Carl pulled a can of cat food out of his pocket and snapped it open. "Come on Bad Cat," he said. His voice sounded like gravel running over gravel. "Come on pal, come get your supper."

Carl turned to Jesse and Maggie. "Look at this little old guy," he said. "See his feet. See how they look like stahs. Some jagoff declawed him. And, Bad Cat's still the toughest son of a bitch on the rivah."

"Stahs?" Maggie asked.

"Stahs. You know, like up in the heavens."

"Where else?" Jesse said. "Where else could we live?"

He took Maggie's hand and tried to slip the mood ring on her finger. It didn't fit. "It's OK," she said. "I'm in."

She held the ring tight, then opened her hand. "It's pink," Jesse said, "and green. It's not just one color."

Maggie touched his face. "It never will be."

They snapped the lead on Ralph's collar and climbed the steps to the Riverbelle's restaurant deck. Jesse's arm was around Maggie's shoulders, her arm around his waist. "There's just one thing," he said. "I really hope Bitsy's our waitress."

"Are you nuts?" Maggie said. "Why?"

"You know," Jesse said, "there's just a couple details about that awful unfair business at the Cachet I'd like her to go over again. You think we could persuade her to?"